THE BAREFOOT BRIDE

OUTLAW'S BRIDE

JOAN JOHNSTON

THE BAREFOOT BRIDE

OUTLAW'S BRIDE

Rhapsody

Garden City, New York

This edition was especially created in 2004 for Rhapsody by arrangement with Dell Publishing, a division of Random House, Inc.

Published by Rhapsody, 401 Franklin Avenue, Garden City, New York 11530

ISBN: 1-58288-102-2

Book design by Christos Peterson

Printed in the United States of America

❈ CONTENTS ❈

THE BAREFOOT BRIDE

This book is dedicated to my children
Heather and Blake,
whom I love very much.

Love has no reason.
Love just is.

❊ 1 ❊

Montana Territory
1868

"FIGHT! FIGHT! IT'S THE doc's brat, Patch! She's whompin' the tar outta the preacher's middle boy!"

Fort Benton's rowdiest saloon cleared like a bedroll with a rattler in it. Miners, bullwhackers, and freightmen raced onto the muddy street to surround the two fighting children.

A ragamuffin twelve-year-old girl had a knee braced on the nape of a ruddy-faced boy. She held his arm twisted high behind his back. Her elfin features contorted as she raged, "You take that back, you varmint! Dang you for a durned pig-faced—"

"I won't take it back, 'cause it's true!" the boy bellowed. "Your pa's a yellow-bellied, lily-livered—"

That was as far as he got before Patch put the full weight of her knee on his neck, shoving his mouth down and filling it with mud.

A pair of large hands caught Patch by her frayed collar and the seat of her britches, lifting her into the air. "That'll be enough of that, you runty little scapegrace."

The crowd laughed as Patch flailed ineffectually against the rough hands that had separated her from her victim. The preacher's middle boy quickly made his escape between a pair of legs at the edge of the circle of men.

Patch sputtered with fury at her helplessness. "I'll get you, Ferdie Adams! You better watch out you—you—"

"What's this all about?"

Patch looked over her shoulder to see who had hold of her. It was Red Dupree, the bartender at the Medicine Bow Saloon. Red must have had hair that color once upon a time, but now Patch winced at the sun's glare off his bald head. He was a huge, intimidating man, and Patch stopped struggling and hung limp in his grasp.

Nevertheless, she wasn't going to admit in front of all these leering, spite-faced men that she had been defending her pa's honor, because he couldn't—wouldn't—do it for himself. Her lips clamped tight, and her chin took on a mulish tilt.

Red sighed in disgust. "Let's go find your pa."

"Doc Kendrick's takin' care of some men got shot by Injuns," someone shouted from the crowd. "Down to the stage depot."

"Don't be too hard on her, Red," a bearded man said. "Kid's got guts—more'n her pa, anyway," he added with a snicker.

Patch stiffened in Red's arms.

Contemplating another attack from the feisty minx, Red tightened his hold. "Hold fast, young'n," he said in a quiet voice. "Don't take it so personal, what they say."

"But my pa ain't what they say," Patch gritted out through a throat swollen with hurt. "He ain't!"

Out west a man was judged by whether he stood up to those who challenged him or backed off. Doc Kendrick would as soon step aside as fight. Patch knew her father wasn't afraid, but she had no explanation for why he wouldn't raise his fists to another man or even carry a gun. So she had taken to fighting his battles for him.

People in Fort Benton knew better than to say a thing against Doc Kendrick. If they did, it was likely their horse might find its tail-hairs cropped, or their zinnias might start looking stark naked, or they might just find themselves locked in the outhouse. Patch had determined to be as ruthless as her father was mild-mannered. No one was going to say a word against her pa without answering to her.

She tried once again to tear herself from Red's hold. "There's no need to bother my pa."

"Sorry, kid, but this is the third time this week I've had to rescue some poor—"

"Dang it, Red! Didn't hit no one that didn't deserve it!" Patch argued.

Red surveyed the bruised swelling around Patch's right eye. "What was it this time?"

"He had no right to say what he did. My pa's the bravest, strongest—just 'cause he don't carry a gun don't mean he's a . . . a . . ." Patch couldn't say the word aloud, but it echoed in her head.

Coward.

Red snorted. "Can't fight the whole damn town, Patch."

"The whole dang town, the whole durned country if I have to. I—"

Patch shut her mouth as they entered the open-sided tent where her father was hard at work removing a bullet from the fleshy part of a man's calf. The wounded man was lying on a makeshift table created from two sawhorses and a few planks of raw lumber. A second man stood nearby, his arm already resting in a sling. A crowd of freight-men had gathered around to observe the doctor's ministrations.

"Took my whole poke of gold, them Injuns did," the man on the table said to the crowd that surrounded him. "Weren't more'n twenty mile south o' here when the stage was surrounded by shriekin' redskins."

"We'da been stone cold dead right now, if it hadna been for that masked fella," the man with the sling said.

Patch couldn't keep still. "Garn! Was it the Masked Marauder?" she asked in an awed voice. "Was it?"

" 'Spect so. Bravest thing I ever saw, how he rode up on that big black horse of his'n and started shooting from them twin pistols. Never missed a shot, that Marauder fella," the miner with the sling said.

"Was he wearing a black mask?" Patch asked. "Was he?"

"Sure 'nuff was, kid," the miner said. "With his black hat pulled down low, couldn't tell who it was for beans."

"But he must live around here somewhere," Patch guessed. " 'Cause he always arrives in the nick of time. Garn! I wonder who it is?"

The men looked around at each other. The identity of the Masked Marauder had become a burning question in Fort Benton. The man seemed to know whenever some golddust miner on the stage was about to be robbed and rode to the rescue with guns blazing. For some reason he had decided to remain anonymous. Over the past six months he must have rescued at least a dozen miners from Blackfoot renegades intent on relieving the men of their gold, which the Indians then traded for rotgut whiskey.

Patch looked at her father, his tall, broad-shouldered form stooped over the injured man. She wished he could be more like the Masked Marauder, brave and dashing and admired. She imagined he *was* the Masked Marauder. But her delightful imaginary bubble didn't last long before it burst.

"Say, Doc," one of the freightmen said. "These fellas here have offered a reward to anybody who can get their gold back. We're formin' up a posse to hunt down them Blackfeet. You wanta come along?"

Seth Kendrick's lips curved in a smile of self-mockery as he said, "I wouldn't be much use to you men. I'm not a good hand with firearms. Besides, I've got to be around to check on Mrs. Gulliver. Her bowels are acting up again."

There were several guffaws and a chuckle or two. While the laughter might have been directed at Mrs. Gulliver's uneasy bowels, Patch couldn't help feeling it was aimed at her father's feeble excuse for avoiding the danger of riding out with the other men. Why, oh why, couldn't he go with them just this once? Why couldn't he prove to them once and for all that he wasn't a—

Coward.

Patch mentally backed away from the word and in so doing inadvertently jerked in Red Dupree's grasp.

"Whoa, there, kid," Red admonished. "Your pa's about done. Once he's free—"

"I'm free right now, Red," Seth said. "You can let her go. Thanks. I'll handle things from here."

"You better, Doc," Red warned with a growl that was more bark than bite. "The kid cleans out the saloon every time she starts one of them fracases."

"It won't happen again, Red. I appreciate you taking care of my girl."

Seth laid a hand on Patch's shoulder and felt her flinch beneath his touch. He didn't want to start an argument with so many interested ears listening, so he let her go on the pretext of needing to pack up his medical supplies. He avoided his daughter's eyes as he closed up his black bag and left the tent. Patch followed him, feet dragging, as he returned to where he'd left his buggy.

"Get in," he said. "We'll talk later."

Patch climbed up to sit beside him on the cracked leather seat. Seth whipped the big buckskin gelding into a trot, then headed south toward the ranch he and Patch had called home for the past two years.

In the distance they could see the Highwood Mountains, an isolated range about thirty miles long. There, in the foothills about twelve miles from town, his ranch was nestled in a stand of cottonwoods along the river.

Seth spent the better part of the trip home staring at his hands. They weren't the hands of a doctor. They were big and callused and scarred from the calamitous events of long ago that had molded him into the man he was today.

Seth knew what was said about him in town. He had his suspicions about why Patch got into so many fights. He wanted to explain everything to her, to make her understand why he chose to walk away rather than to face down another man. But he couldn't. All the same, her fighting had to stop.

Seth wasn't sure how to confront his daughter. It seemed lately he couldn't talk to her without setting up her neckhairs. She was growing up. Soon Patricia Wallis Kendrick would be a woman. Only, at the rate she was going, Patch Kendrick—hoyden, tomboy, pugnacious brat—would be no lady.

The frustration Seth felt made his voice harsh when he spoke. "I thought we agreed you weren't going to fight anymore. What was it this time?"

Patch's lower lip stuck out in a stubborn pout. With the black eye rapidly forcing her right eye shut, it would have been difficult to argue that she hadn't been fighting. Nor could she admit to her father the real reasons she had attacked the preacher's middle boy. So she improvised. "That Ferdie Adams called me a flibbertigibbet, Pa. I couldn't let him get away with that."

"You know, Patch," he began, "the things people say—the words they use—can't hurt you."

"But, Pa! How can you stand it when somebody calls you a—a— bad name?"

There was a long pause before he said, "Words aren't worth fighting over, Patch." He took another, even longer pause before he added, "When you're older, when you've seen a little more of life, you'll understand why—"

"I don't understand!" Patch cried in an anguished voice. "And I won't stand for it!"

Seth stopped the buggy abruptly and turned to grab his daughter by the shoulders. He shook her until her blond hair tumbled over her brow and hid her eyes. "Listen to me," he said in a hard voice. "This fighting has got to stop. You're getting too old to be wrestling with boys in the mud, coming home with black eyes and torn clothes."

He felt a band tighten around his chest at the sight of his daughter's quivering chin. Patch was blinking furiously to stem tears. As abruptly as he had grabbed her, he released her. With a shaking hand he reached out to straighten the bunched material at her shoulder.

Patch shoved his hand aside and straightened the shirt herself, clamping down on her teeth to still her chin. "Garn, Pa—"

"And that's another thing," he interrupted, both frustrated by and furious at her refusal to allow him to express the tenderness he felt for her. "I've heard about all the *garns* and *dangs* and *durns* I want to hear from you. You have to start acting like a lady, Patch. You have to—"

"I ain't never gonna be a lady, Pa!"

Seth opened his mouth to contradict his daughter but snapped it shut again. No, not at the rate she was going. Didn't she want to be a lady? Another look revealed that it was despair rather than defiance he saw in his daughter's wretched blue eyes.

He wanted to pull her into his arms and hug her tight and tell her they would work things out. But he didn't think he could stand it if she pushed him away, as he was certain she would. So he sat without touching her and saw her back stiffen with resolve. No coward, his Patch. She had enough courage for both of them.

"You need a mother, Patch," he murmured. "A woman to show you how to be a lady. To comb this mop of hair"—he ruffled her tangled blond hair, which was as close to a caress as she was likely to allow, and tucked it behind a dirty ear—"to sew dresses for you, to teach you to cook and how to act."

"Dang it! We don't need anyone, Pa," Patch protested. "We manage fine by ourselves."

Seth didn't argue, just picked up the reins and started the buggy homeward again. He pictured the disorder that reigned at the ranch house they called home. The barren windows and walls, the dirty dishes stacked in the sink, the laundry that grew in piles until Patch finally gathered it all up and boiled it for an hour with homemade lye soap. She was too young to have the kind of responsibility that had necessarily fallen on her shoulders in a bachelor household.

But Seth had never been able to bring himself to marry again. He had loved Patch's mother in a way he could never love another woman.

Nine years after Annarose's death, his memories of her were as vivid as ever. He was yanked from his reverie by an outburst from Patch.

"Garn!" she exclaimed. "Why on earth do you need a wife, Pa? Haven't I done a good job of taking care of things? Maybe I ain't such a good cook, but we haven't starved, have we? The ranch house is a little messy, but so what? We're hardly ever there. And maybe I do dress in trousers, but with the mud in town, a dress wouldn't be the least bit practical. And I know ding-dang well you see Dora at the Medicine Bow Saloon to satisfy your manly lusts.

"See, Pa, you don't need a wife. And I don't need a mother," she added in case he had missed the point she really wanted to make.

Seth was appalled at Patch's knowledge of his visits to Dora Deveraux. He hadn't imagined she understood enough about what happened between men and women to even suspect what he was doing when he disappeared into town on Saturday nights. Which only served to convince him that something had to be done, and soon, or Patch would be lost beyond redemption.

Only, finding a wife wasn't as simple as it sounded. Not many respectable unmarried women traveled up the Missouri River on their own. Whenever one showed her face in Fort Benton, she was as popular as licorice at the mercantile store. Seth ought to know. He had advertised in the St. Louis paper three times in the past two years for a nurse to work with him. Each time, the woman had come up the river by steamboat and ended up being courted and married within a week of her arrival.

So why don't you advertise for another nurse, and when she arrives here, court her and marry her yourself?

Seth had no time to examine that astounding idea because they had arrived at the ranch. Patch bolted out of the buggy and raced toward the man who stood beside the corral.

"Ethan!" she yelled at the top of her lungs. "We're home!"

As if Ethan hadn't seen them driving up the road, Seth thought. He felt that constriction in his chest again as Patch allowed Ethan a quick hug of welcome. Seth quickly repressed the unwanted jab of jealousy. Ethan Hawk was his best friend and for the past six months had been his partner. Still, it hurt to see the way Patch smiled at the younger man as though he hung the moon. That sort of smile ought to be reserved for a girl's father—at least until she found a husband.

As Seth stepped down from the buggy, Ethan started toward him with Patch tucked under his arm and her arm firmly around his waist. They made slow progress because of Ethan's limp, and Seth met them more than halfway. Ethan's walk—long step, halting step, long step, halting step—was ungainly. But put him on a horse, and the man had all the grace of a centaur. Seth couldn't be sorry for Ethan's limp, tragic as it was, because it had been the cause of their meeting each other and the beginning of their friendship.

"The Masked Marauder has been at work again," Seth said. "He saved the bacon for a couple of miners on the stage from Virginia City."

"Oh, Ethan, can you just imagine it?" Patch asked in the reverent voice she reserved for anything having to do with the Masked Marauder. "Imagine him dressed all in black, mounted on his black stallion and riding to the rescue. Oh, how I wish I could meet him just once!"

"I trust you won't need rescuing anytime soon, little one," Ethan replied with a grin.

"Well, of course not," Patch retorted, pulling herself from his side. "You know I can take care of myself."

"Of course you can," Ethan agreed. "But there are some chickens out behind the house that can't. So how about spreading some feed for them?"

Patch grimaced. "Dang, I forgot. Sorry, Ethan. I'll do it right away."

Seth stared after his daughter, marveling at how quickly she had obeyed Ethan, and he fought another stab of jealousy.

"Anybody seriously hurt in the raid?" Ethan asked.

"A bullet in one miner's arm and in another's leg."

"You'd think the stage line would have heard enough about the renegade Indians around here to put another shotgun rider or two on board," Ethan said.

"There's an easier solution to the problem," Seth said.

"Which is?"

"Put Drake Bassett out of the illegal whiskey-selling business. If there's none of that coffin varnish available to buy, the Indians won't have any use for the gold they're stealing. And the raids on the stage will stop."

Drake Bassett owned the Medicine Bow Saloon, but he spent most of his time at his office in one of the several warehouses he owned along the levee. To all appearances, he was an honest business-man. It was through Dora Deveraux that Seth had learned about Drake's connection to the illegal whiskey—selling operation that was causing so much trouble.

"Unfortunately, to get to Bassett, you have to go through Pike Hardesty," Ethan pointed out.

There was a moment when neither man said anything. They were both thinking of the man Ethan had named. A gunfighter and a bully, Pike Hardesty was mean as a rattlesnake on a hot skillet. Thanks to Pike, there was no longer any law in Fort Benton to speak of. He had shot the sheriff in a supposedly fair fight eight months ago. Now the only restraint on Pike's viciousness was Drake Bassett, a man without morals himself.

"I could take care of Pike," Ethan said.

"No."

"It would solve a lot of problems."

"No," Seth repeated. "The Masked Marauder seems to have everything well in hand. If the Blackfeet are unsuccessful in their raids, they won't have any gold. And without gold they won't be able to buy that tarantula juice Bassett is pawning off as whiskey."

They had wandered back over to the corral that held the few mus-tangs that remained to be gentled and delivered to the army at Fort Shaw.

Ethan braced his boot on the bottom rail of the corral and said, "I notice Patch is sporting another black eye."

Seth's gray eyes turned bleak. "I'm at my wit's end, Ethan. I've tried everything I can think of to keep her from fighting. I don't know what else to do."

"You could tell her the truth," Ethan said in a quiet voice.

Seth faced the younger man. Ethan had sandy brown hair that had bleached in the sun, green eyes above a straight nose, and a wide, full mouth. He should have looked as young as his twenty-five years. But there were hard edges to Ethan's face; lines bracketed his mouth, and those piercing green eyes had seen sorrow and disillusion and disap-pointment. Ethan was nearly as tall as Seth, but Ethan's shoulders weren't quite so broad, and he was lean and wiry, where Seth was all muscle and sinew.

Seth stuck his hands in his pockets. "You know I can't tell her anything," he said. "She wouldn't understand."

"I think you underestimate Patch," Ethan countered. "She's got a good head on her shoulders. She could handle it."

"No," Seth said. "She's got enough worries as it is, without adding any more. In fact, she's got way too heavy a burden for any kid to carry. She needs a mother, Ethan," Seth admitted with a sigh.

"That would mean you'd have to take a wife," Ethan said. "After Annarose . . . I didn't think you wanted to marry again."

"I don't," Seth said flatly. When Annarose died, he had felt grief so strong it had made him want to die too. For a while he had tried very hard to get himself killed. Then Ethan had come along and convinced him he had to live for his daughter's sake. Seth had been forced to build a stone wall around his heart to protect himself from the pain of living without Annarose. Over the years, his vivid memories of her had forced him to keep the wall strong. There was no way feelings of love for anyone besides his daughter could breach that barrier.

Nonetheless, Seth told Ethan, "I may not want to marry, but I think I need a wife—for Patch's sake."

"All right. Let's say Patch needs a mother. Let's say you need a wife. Where do you propose to find a woman to fill that role?" Ethan asked.

"I've decided to advertise for a mail-order bride in the St. Louis papers," Seth answered.

Ethan turned to stare at his friend. "You're joking."

"I'm perfectly serious. Patch needs the influence of a woman who can turn her into a young lady."

"Is that really fair to a woman, to marry her just so she can be a mother to your daughter?"

"I'd be giving her a home, feeding her, and clothing her. That sounds like a pretty fair trade to me," Seth argued. "My face wouldn't be so bad to stare at across the breakfast table." He cocked a brow and said, "A woman could do a lot worse."

Ethan smiled crookedly. "Yeah, I suppose so. What about . . . the personal side of things."

There was a pause before Seth answered, "I've got Dora. I don't need a wife for that." He took off his hat and thrust a hand through his hair in a gesture that betrayed his uncertain feelings about what he was contemplating.

"If you're bound and determined on this course, I have a suggestion," Ethan said. He waited for Seth to nod before he continued, "Put your advertisement in the papers back east."

Ethan didn't allow Seth to voice an objection, just kept right on talking. "Think about it," he urged. "You're a lot more likely to get a 'lady' if you advertise where there are a lot of them. By the time a woman's spent any time at all in St. Louis, the 'lady' gets ironed right out of her. You ought to put an ad in the Boston and New York and Philadelphia papers."

Seth pursed his lips in thought, then stroked his chin, feeling the two days' growth of whiskers. Having a "lady" for a wife was going to mean a lot of changes for him too. He wouldn't be marrying at all if it weren't for Patch. But for his daughter, he would make any sacrifice.

"All right," Seth agreed gruffly. "I'll take your advice. But just in case no one wants to travel that far, I'm going to put an ad in the St. Louis paper as well."

He was distracted by the sound of chickens squawking noisily. "What the devil?"

"Pa! Ethan!" Patch shouted. "Come quick!"

The two men raced toward the frantic cry that had come from behind the house. Ethan was slowed by his gait. Seth rounded the corner ahead of him, all his senses alert, ready to protect and defend his daughter. He stumbled to a halt when he saw her. Patch stood before him covered with a dusting of chicken feathers and grinning from ear to ear. Dangling by the neck in her outstretched hands was the obvious reason for the ruckus in the henhouse.

"I caught him, Pa!" she crowed with glee. "The raccoon that's been stealing our eggs! You can see he's still just a baby. Can I keep him, Pa? Can I?"

Seth didn't know whether to laugh or cry. Would anyone be able to turn his darling, adorable hoyden into a young lady? He opened his mouth to say yes to keeping the raccoon and snapped it shut again. Whoever heard of a young lady with a pet raccoon? But he didn't have a wife yet, and he didn't have the heart to disappoint his daughter. "Sure," he agreed with a grin. "If you keep him fed, maybe I'll be able to have eggs for breakfast again."

"Oh, thank you, Pa!" Patch cried. "I'll just take him inside now and make him a bed."

Seth lifted a hand to say a raccoon didn't belong in the house, but she was gone before he could speak. He grimaced. Besides, the inside of the house, unfortunately, was eminently fit for raccoons. In that instant, whatever reservations he'd had about marrying simply to have a mother for Patch were put to rest.

At the same moment Seth reached that resolve, Ethan rounded the corner of the house and joined him.

"I saw the raccoon," Ethan said with a grin. "Looks like Patch has a new pet to add to her collection."

"At least for a while," Seth said.

"Surely you aren't going to make her get rid of it," Ethan protested. "Did you see her face? She's already in love with the poor thing."

"I'm not going to do anything," Seth said. "But I can't speak for the woman who'll be my wife." Seth's eyes turned flinty. But as he began mentally composing the advertisement for a mail-order bride, he added the words: *"Must like animals."*

❧2❧

"What are you doing, Mama?"

"I'm writing a letter."

"To Da?"

"No, sweetheart. Da is in heaven. This is a letter to a man in Montana named Seth Kendrick." Molly Gallagher set down her pen and pulled her four-year-old daughter into her lap. Nessie had lost the plump limbs and cherubic face common to all babies and was showing signs of the person she would become. Her brown eyes were still huge, but her nose had lengthened and straightened. Round cheeks had thinned to reveal the same strong Irish bones Molly possessed and a pair of charming dimples. Her chin was already a bit pointed, like her da's had been.

The little girl reached for the half-finished letter on the desk. She held it out in front of her with both hands, as though she could read the slanted script. "What does it say, Mama?"

"I'm telling Mr. Kendrick a little bit about myself."

"Why?"

"Because he wants to marry me."

"Why?"

Molly thought for a moment. What could compel a man to be willing to marry a woman sight unseen? He had given reasons; these she gave to Nessie. "He says he needs a lady to keep house for him and a nurse to help him do his work. He's a doctor, you see."

"You nursed Aunt Hattie."

"Yes, I did."

"But Aunt Hattie went to heaven. Like Da."

Molly sighed. "Yes, darling. Just like Da." It was the death of James's aunt that had caused the crisis in which she now found herself.

Molly had come to live with Aunt Hattie when she'd received word that her husband's whaling ship had been crushed in the northern ice and been sunk with all hands. James had already been gone to sea for nearly two years, and Molly had been living on the expectation of his share of the whaling catch. When word came that her husband had drowned, the mortgage holder had given her a week to vacate the home in which she lived with Nessie and her ten-year-old son, Whit.

Aunt Hattie's grand old New Bedford cottage, with its ladder leading through a trap door in the roof to the widow's walk, had been a refuge in a very bad storm. Molly had spent hours pacing the rectangular railed platform, coming to terms with her grief. She had looked out over the lonely sea and wondered . . . and wished . . . and worried.

Now, barely a year later, Aunt Hattie was dead, and James's cousin Rupert had inherited everything. Just as the crocuses were blooming, Rupert had written to say he had sold Aunt Hattie's house. Molly and her children now had to vacate the cottage by the first of June.

Cousin Rupert hadn't left her totally without recourse. He had offered her the opportunity to move in and be a companion to his mother in a small house on the outskirts of New Bedford. Living as Sadie Gallagher's companion would be a step up from the poorhouse, but it was not a choice Molly would have made for herself.

Molly hadn't minded nursing Aunt Hattie because she had truly loved the old woman. But Rupert's mother was another matter altogether. Sadie Gallagher was the worst sort of harridan, and the old woman didn't much care for children.

Thus, Rupert's ultimatum had left Molly feeling panic-stricken. James had been a good whaler, and a wonderful husband and father. But two of his three whaling ships had been sunk by the rebel cruiser *Alabama* during the war. That financial loss had been compounded by the increasing use of fuel substitutes for whale oil, causing a drop in the price of each hard-won barrel. They had continued to live well, but it had taken a toll on their savings. When Aunt Hattie died, Molly had finally realized how very little she had been left with at James's death.

Alone, she would have managed somehow. But Whit was ten, and already growing tall like James. His wrists and ankles seemed to sprout from his clothes. As for Nessie, Molly dreaded the thought of her four-year-old being regularly hushed to accommodate a crotchety old woman.

So on the day Molly got Rupert's letter, the words BRIDE WANTED had fairly leaped at her from the month-old Boston newspaper. She had carefully unwrapped the dampened paper from around the codfish she had bought for supper and read the rest. The ad was short and to the point.

BRIDE WANTED. Thirty-five-year-old doctor seeks educated woman to work as nurse and manage household. Must be lady of good character. Also must like animals. Reply to S.K. General Delivery Fort Benton, Montana.

It had taken her a while to find Fort Benton on the atlas she had used to track James's whaling adventures. It seemed like the other side of the world. Because she'd had nothing to lose, Molly had immediately sat down to compose a letter to the mysterious S.K. And because she didn't think it would ever come to anything, she hadn't mentioned the existence of Whit and Nessie.

Molly had been sure the doctor would have so many replies that hers would be lost in the confusion. She had been surprised, if not pleased, when he responded.

Dear Miss Gallagher,

I'm a country doctor and live a very simple life. It's good to hear you have nursing experience. That will be important here, where a real nurse is desperately needed. My home is a sturdy pine structure suited to the harsh elements. It is set along a creek bordered by cottonwoods.

Out here, the sky is endless and the prairies roll on until they meet the mountains to the south. No one who sees this part of Montana can deny its beauty.

However, it's frigid in winter, scorching in summer, and the wind almost always blows.

It can be a lonely place.

You asked me to say a bit about myself. I try to be patient and understand the other fellow's point of view. Mostly, I succeed.

I can offer you my name and my protection. That may not sound like much. But out here, where there isn't much law and order, it's a lot.

Your servant,
Seth Kendrick

Molly had been disappointed that there wasn't a single word in the letter describing his appearance. She tried to imagine any man being as handsome as James and failed. But then, she wouldn't be marrying the mysterious S.K. for his good looks.

She felt a little guilty that her "nursing experience" amounted to no more than putting a cool cloth on Aunt Hattie's brow until she died of old age. But she didn't correct Seth Kendrick's mistaken impression when she wrote to him a second time. Instead, she explained that she was a widow, that she had loved James with her whole heart and soul, and that she didn't expect to find love in a second marriage. Molly also wrote that Montana sounded beautiful and that someday she would love to see it. For reasons she didn't wish to examine too closely, Molly still made no mention of Whit or Nessie.

Seth Kendrick's second letter intrigued her.

Dear Mrs. Gallagher,

I must say I was relieved to read from your most recent letter that you do not expect love as part of the bargain. I, too, am a widower, so I can very much understand your feelings. My heart isn't free either.

Will you marry me?

Your servant,
Seth Kendrick

P. S. Directions to Fort Benton are enclosed.

Molly had been composing her response to the Montana doctor's proposal when Nessie interrupted her. She still hadn't made up her mind what her answer would be. Over the months they had corresponded, the spring sun had done its work, turning New Bedford into a warm place full of color. Yellow lilies and orange poppies. Buttercups and violets. Always, everywhere, defiant clumps of dandelions. The wind-tossed sea provided brilliant blues and greens or stormy grays, depending on the weather. How could she even think of leaving it all behind? But the June day when she would be forced to leave Aunt Hattie's cottage was inexorably coming. She must move somewhere—and soon.

Molly wished she were daring enough to accept Doctor Kendrick's offer and go all the way to Montana to become his wife. But she had never been beyond the boundaries of Massachusetts in her life. She hadn't the courage to go haring off halfway across the country on a whim.

Maybe that was why she had fallen in love with a rough-and-tumble whaling man like James. Molly had seen the world through her husband's eyes as he sailed the seas. She had vicariously lived his adventures in the marvelous ports where his whaling vessel called. It had always been enough for her. But now James was dead. Any adventures she had in the future would have to be her own.

"Are we going to Montana?"

Nessie's question snapped Molly from her reverie and forced her to focus on the decision she knew must be made. She wanted to throw caution to the winds and say yes. But the words just wouldn't come. "I don't think so, Nessie."

"Good," Nessie said. "I don't want to go away. If we go away, Da won't know where we are. He won't be able to find us when he comes home."

Molly hugged her daughter tight. If she said nothing, Nessie would eventually realize that her father wasn't ever coming back. But that seemed more cruel than forcing Nessie, even as young as she was, to face the truth. So Molly said, "Do you remember how I explained that Da died and went to heaven?"

"Yes."

"Heaven is a wonderful place, Nessie, but when you go there, you can't ever come back. But Da can see us, and no matter where we go, he'll know where we are. And he'll watch over us from above."

Nessie's tiny brow furrowed. "Are you sure?"

Molly brushed the soft bangs away from Nessie's troubled brown eyes. "I'm very sure."

Nessie's face crumpled. "I want my da!" she cried. "Why doesn't he come home?"

Molly held Nessie and comforted her as best she could. But the little girl was inconsolable. Her tiny fists tightened in a death grip on Molly's dress as sobs wracked her body. Molly fought the welling emotion in her throat. She wasn't going to cry. She had done all her crying months ago, and tears hadn't changed anything. But still, one slid past her guard and fell in a hot stream down her cheek. And then another. Molly squeezed her eyes shut and buried her face in Nessie's silky black hair.

Molly sat in the growing darkness holding Nessie until the little girl finally cried herself to sleep. Molly was startled when she finally lifted her head to find her son standing by the parlor door staring at her.

"I was looking for you earlier," Molly said. "Where were you?"

"Down to the wharf," Whit answered. "The *Mary Lee* is taking on provisions for another whaling voyage."

A shiver raced down Molly's spine. The *Mary Lee* was the whaling vessel that had seen James's ship go down. Roger Sturgis, the captain of the *Mary Lee*, had been James's best friend. Molly felt queasy at the thought that someday Whit would want to go to sea and be a whaler like his father. She leaned back in the captain's chair in which she sat and arranged Nessie more comfortably in her lap, tucking the little girl's head under her chin.

"Did you say hello to Captain Sturgis?" Molly asked.

Whit's gray-green eyes sought out the seams in the planked wooden floor. "I did."

"What did he have to say?"

Whit's whole attention focused on the toe of his shoe, which he was trying to fit into a knothole one-tenth its size. "Not much. Only that the *Mary Lee* is ready to sail on the morrow."

Molly shook her head and smiled faintly. "He never was a talkative man, as I remember. Well, dinner will be ready soon. Go wash up."

Whit seemed reluctant to go. He stood there a moment longer, opened his mouth, shut it, then backed his way out of the room.

Molly had never understood the attraction of any man for the sea. The sea was so unforgiving, and it took as often as it gave. She had already tried to interest Whit in some other occupation than whaling, but so far, without much luck. She took comfort in the fact that Whit was an obedient child; she only hoped she could lead him away from a life on the sea.

Dinner was a quiet affair. Whit said few words. Nessie said nothing. Molly was too absorbed in her own thoughts to notice. She put Nessie down to bed right after they had finished eating and soon after came to help Whit get settled for the night.

When James was alive—and at home—he had helped Whit at bedtime while she took care of Nessie. Then they had changed places for a last good-night kiss. Now Whit depended on her to follow James's ritual. Molly wasn't James, and she couldn't ever take his place. But because she understood Whit's loss, she did as her son asked and ignored her own feelings of awkwardness.

She sat down beside Whit, gave him a quick hug, then helped him scoot down under the covers. She began firmly tucking the wool blanket around him, following the shape of his lanky frame down one side, as he had told her James used to do.

Molly was tucking her way up the other side when Whit stopped her. "Wait," he said. "You forgot to do my toes."

"What?"

"Da always used to go around my toes."

Molly took a deep breath and bit down on the cry that sought voice. *I am not your father. Your father is dead!* Instead, she forced a smile and tucked down Whit's side again and around his toes and back up the other side.

"Thanks, Mother," Whit said. "That was almost as good as Da."

Almost as good. Molly leaned over and kissed her son on the forehead. The ceremony was done. Not as good as Da. Not perfect. But all either of them had. And a constant painful reminder to both of them of all they had lost.

"Good night, Whit. I love you."

"I love you, too, Mother. Remember that. Whatever happens."

Molly frowned. She opened her mouth to ask what Whit meant, but he turned and tugged the covers up over his shoulder—in complete disregard of all those careful tucks—and said, "Good night, Mother."

She blew out the lantern and left the room to seek out her own bed. She could finish the letter to Seth Kendrick in the morning.

—————•—•———

But in the morning, her son was gone. All Molly found was a note on Whit's pillow.

Dearest Mother,
I'm to be cabin boy for the *Mary Lee*. Please understand that I have to go. Da would expect it of me. I'm the man of the house now. I shall bring home my share of the whaler's catch to provide for you and Nessie. You don't have to cry anymore.

Your loving son,
Whit

Molly raced for the wharf that cloudy spring morning with her heart in her throat. She couldn't seem to catch her breath and held a fisted hand against the agonizing stitch in her side nearly the whole way. She half-laughed, half-cried in relief when she reached the wharf and saw the *Mary Lee* had not set sail. From the activity on deck, it appeared she didn't have much time to find her son.

"Hold! Please, hold!" she cried as she stumbled up the gangplank.

"Hey! You, there! No women on board ship!" a sailor cried, reaching out to stop her. "It's bad luck!"

She eluded him, shouting at the top of her lungs, "Whit! Whit! Where are you? Please, don't do this!"

A superstitious lot, the sailors turned ugly. The intruding woman might prove an ill omen for their entire whaling voyage. The men on deck formed a menacing circle to keep her from stepping farther into their domain.

Molly perched her fists on her hips and tipped her chin in the air. Her long black hair whipped in the brisk wind. "I'm not leaving without my son. Now please find him and bring him to me."

"Here, now. What's the trouble?" Captain Sturgis wasn't happy about being called on deck by the first mate to settle a disturbance. He couldn't believe his eyes when he sighted Molly Gallagher.

"Why, what's this, Molly? What are you doing here?"

Molly let out a heartfelt sigh of relief when she saw the friendly face before her. "It's Whit," she explained. "He's signed on as your cabin boy."

"Yes, I know," he said.

She waited for him to say more, but with dawning horror realized that James's friend approved of having her son on board his ship. "You can't take him," she said, her voice sharpened by anxiety. "I won't let you."

"The boy wants to go, Molly," the captain said. "You can't keep him a child forever."

"I don't intend to!" Molly retorted. "But I'll not lose another of mine to the sea. So bring him here, and I'll take him home."

"He wants to go," the captain said.

"I don't care what he wants," she snapped back. "I'm his mother. He'll do as I say."

Captain Sturgis turned to a nearby sailor. "Tell Whit Gallagher I want to see him on deck."

Molly's heart lifted when her son appeared. But from the defiant look in Whit's eyes, it was clear he wouldn't come of his own accord. She turned to the captain, her feelings bared for him to see. She said only, "Please, Roger."

"Come here, Whit," the captain said.

The tall, reed-thin boy obeyed immediately. The brisk sea wind ruffled the boy's collar-length black hair as he stepped forward. His fisted hands were hidden deep in his pockets.

"Your mother does not wish you to go, lad."

"I am the man now, sir," Whit replied. "I must earn a living for my family."

"No!" Molly said. When they looked at her she added, "It's not necessary. I've found a way to take care of us."

"Oh?" The captain arched a questioning brow.

Molly swallowed hard and said, "I'm going to be married again. To a man in Montana. That is why Whit must come with me *now*. There'll be no one for him to come home to when you return in three or four years." Her throat had tightened so much in fear that the last few words came out in a raspy whisper.

"I see," the captain said. "Well then, lad, I think you had best go with your mother."

"But, sir—"

"I am the captain, lad. You will obey my order."

A flush began at Whit's neck and worked its way up to pinken his fair-skinned face. It was the only visible sign of his distress as he answered, "Yes, sir."

Molly reached out to put a hand on her son's shoulder, but he jerked away and started down the gangplank without a word to her.

"Thank you, Roger," she said to the captain. "Thank you for my son." She rushed after Whit.

The sun had come out, but the narrow streets of New Bedford did not feel it. The warmth was held at bay by giant oaks and hickory, bushy elms and pointy-leafed maples.

They had traveled more than halfway home before Molly finally caught up to her son. When she touched Whit's shoulder, he whirled on her. In his face was all the agony of humiliation and embarrassment a ten-year-old boy can feel when he is trying to act as a man before men, and his mother treats him as a child.

"I'll just find another ship," he said, his face flushed, his sea-green eyes bright with unshed tears. "Next time I won't leave you a note. Next time I won't give you a chance to stop me."

"Whit, I—"

"How could you lie like that?" he demanded. "Captain Sturgis would never have put me off the ship if you hadn't told that made-up story! There is no man to marry in Montana, is there? I mean, there couldn't be. You would never force us all to go so far from New Bedford—so far from the sea. Would you?"

Molly didn't know which accusation to answer first. But the thought of Whit running away again—and he could easily manage it with the number of whaling ships that would be leaving New Bedford over the next few weeks—made it clear what she must do. She struggled for the words to explain her decision to her son.

"It's true, Whit. I am to be married again. For the past several months I've been corresponding with a man in Montana who advertised in the paper for a mail-order bride."

"How could you do such a thing?"

"I don't know why I answered the ad. Yes, I do. I wanted something better for us. And Whit, he wrote me back, and he sounds like a very nice man. He's a country doctor and . . . in his most recent letter he asked me to come to Montana. He asked me to be his wife."

Whit was aghast. "You can't marry another man. Da is—Da is—"

"Dead." Molly spoke softly, but the word had a finality that was unassailable. She yearned to reach out and fold her son into her arms. But it was clear that even though he was a boy in years, he had a man's pride.

Whit scrubbed at his pooling eyes with the back of his hand. "You don't have to do it," he said. "I can earn a living for us."

"By going to sea? No, Whit, I shan't allow it. I've made up my mind. I'm going to marry him."

"You can't do it! You can't! Da is barely cold in his grave!" Whit whirled and fled toward home.

Whit's threat made it imperative that Molly act, and with all possible speed. Once her mind was made up, she didn't waste any time. A letter was posted that same day to Seth Kendrick, agreeing to marry him and promising that she would be heading west within the next several days.

Molly also wrote to Cousin Rupert saying she was "sorry not to be able to take him up on his kind offer."

Then she began packing. Among those items she couldn't bear to leave behind were her mother's rose-patterned china, a walrus tusk carved by the Esquimaux that James had brought home from a whaling trip to Point Barrow, and a ship in a bottle that James and Whit had made together the year James had been laid up at home with a broken leg—the year Nessie had been born. Last, but not least, was a painting of a sailor harpooning a bowhead whale amidst the icebergs of the Arctic. In the distance, a whaling ship—James's ship—was pictured in all its splendor.

All their warmest woolen clothes got packed, of course, since Doctor Kendrick had warned that Montana winters were harsh. She added a box of books—including an autographed volume by Massachusetts-born poet Emily Dickinson—because he had said the winters were lonely. Only they wouldn't be quite so lonely now, she supposed. Even less lonely than Doctor Kendrick expected, actually. Because he would be getting a little more family than he was counting on. An additional son and daughter, to be precise.

The three of them left New Bedford a mere two days later, during which time Whit was never out of her sight. The trip across country by train as far as St. Louis, and by steamboat from St. Louis up the Missouri River to Fort Benton, was as fascinating as it was frightening.

It wasn't so much the change in terrain that made Molly realize the momentousness of what she had done. Although the terrain did change tremendously. The lush, tree-laden hills in the east flattened out into grassy rolling prairies. More telling was the size and number of the towns they encountered. As they traveled farther west, the settlements became fewer and farther between and grew smaller. Finally, they were no more than mere whistle-stops for wood and water tended by a single man. That was when it dawned on Molly that she had left the civilized world behind and was heading into the wilderness.

They were in bustling St. Louis only a single day before the *Viola Belle* left on its journey up the Missouri. In contrast to the tiny Pullman sleeping car on the train, their accommodations on the steamboat more closely resembled those in a sumptuous hotel.

Molly had reserved one of the two staterooms aft, a spacious cabin with a four-poster bed, washstand, and built-in closet. A door with a curtained window in the upper half of it opened onto the deck, which ran completely around the boat.

They made about fifty miles the first day, at the end of which Molly saw her first Indian. He rode along the bank following the steamboat, practically naked on his pony. His posture was proud, erect—graceful and threatening at the same time. He was a Sioux, the captain told her, part of a tribe that expected them to be carrying flour and tobacco for tribute—tribute that wasn't on board. That night they anchored in midstream, and the captain left guards posted to keep a sharp lookout for attack.

Molly didn't close her eyes all night, terrified of being killed in her sleep. The next morning, the sun dawned bright and hot, and it was as though the threat had never existed. That day she saw her first herd of huge, shaggy buffalo, so vast they seemed to cover the entire prairie.

The places along the river had strange names—Rattlesnake Springs, Wolf Point, Alert Bend, Painted Woods, Devil's Race Ground, Mule's Head Landing, Osage Chute, Brickhouse Bend, Hole in the Wall, Elk Horn Prairie—all of which sounded as untamed as the land through which they traveled.

In the towns where they tied up at night, she met army wives who told of their loneliness. She saw it for herself when they steamed past log cabins where solitary women sat barefoot in rockers with children on their laps. Molly began to have an inkling of the immense difference in the life she and her children could expect to have on the frontier. As the unknown became known, her trepidation increased. In all-too-short a time, their journey was at an end.

Molly laid a hand across her brow to shield her eyes so she could better see the landing at Fort Benton. The town was easily visible from the upper deck of the steamboat *Viola Belle*.

It was situated on a flat piece of land right at the edge of the river. There were no docks, just a muddy bank leading down to the water, stacked high in places with machinery and other freight. A row of one- and two-story wooden buildings that appeared to be warehouses fronted the levee. Signs labeled some of the other buildings—Wells Fargo, Schmidt's Hotel, Carroll & Steell, North Western Fur, I. G. Baker & Co., and the Medicine Bow Saloon. At one end of town stood the crumbled adobe brick buildings that had been the original Fort Benton. Along the horizon, a butte rose about a hundred and fifty feet above the town and ran for several miles into the distance.

There were no bricked roads in the town, nor any sidewalks, nor even any grass that she could see. Just dirt. There was not a single tree, not one. The word that came to mind was *desolate*. But Molly shut out the stark picture before her. She denied the evidence of all those lonely miles she had traveled to arrive at this barren place. In her heart, she felt hope; in her mind, she saw a shiny new beginning.

"We're here, Mother! I can see the faces of the people waiting on the levee," Whit said.

Molly smiled at the excitement in her son's voice. It was the first emotion besides resentment or anger that she had heard him express during the entire trip from Massachusetts to Montana. She felt a tug on her skirt and reached down to lift her daughter into her arms. "We're here, Nessie," she said, playfully tugging one of the little girl's braids. "We've arrived at our new home. We'll start a new life here and put the past behind us."

The solemn-faced child said nothing. Ever since the night she had fallen asleep sobbing in Molly's arms, Nessie had been unnaturally silent. Molly had to believe that time and patience and love would restore the light to her daughter's once-laughing brown eyes.

"Be careful, Whit," Molly said. "Stand back from the rail. There's bound to be some jouncing when we tie up at the levee."

"Not nearly so much as on a real ship," her son responded with the disdain of a true sailor's son for a boat run by steam. Then, wistfully: "I should be cabin boy on a whaling vessel right now, Mother, if only . . ." His eyes narrowed as he turned back to gaze at the levee. "Do you think *he* is down there somewhere, waiting for us?"

Molly did not mistake the resentment in Whit's voice now, or the nervous pounding of her heart. Whit had made it clear he had no intention of liking, or even tolerating, the man she had come all this way to marry.

When the steamboat whistle blew their arrival, Whit headed on the run for the stairs. "Wait for me on the main deck, Whit," Molly called after him. "Nessie and I will come down and join you as quickly as we can."

It wasn't that she thought Whit would purposely provoke a scene if he greeted Doctor Kendrick on his own. But it couldn't hurt if she was there by her son's side the first time the two males stood face to face.

Molly pulled Nessie close as the *Viola Belle* bumped against the levee at Fort Benton. Within moments she would be meeting the man with whom she had determined to spend the rest of her life. What would the kindly country doctor do when he realized she had not been entirely honest with him?

If he gave her a chance, she would explain everything. Molly thought of what her children had endured over the past year and vowed she would *make* him listen. Besides, the last of her savings had been spent getting here. She had no money to make the return trip.

There was little time to ponder her transgressions as the gang-plank was lowered and people and cargo began moving from the main deck of the steamboat onto dry land.

Molly took her daughter's hand and led her downstairs to the main deck to join Whit.

"Can we go ashore now?" Whit asked.

"I wrote Doctor Kendrick that we would wait for him here."

Whit glowered and turned away to stare at the bustle of activity along the levee.

Molly set Nessie down, and the little girl grabbed hold of the narrow railing beside Whit and held on. "Be careful!" Molly cautioned. "Hang on tight so you don't fall in."

"I don't know why we had to come here," Whit complained. "It's dirty. And ugly. And there aren't even any trees. I hate it! And I hate him!"

"That will be enough of that, young man," Molly snapped. "Now stand there and be quiet. When Doctor Kendrick comes, I expect you to greet him politely. Do you understand me?"

Whit's sullen voice was barely respectful when he answered, "Yes, Mother."

Molly fought the nerves that had her hands trembling. Whit had clearly made up his mind that he was going to hate Seth Kendrick. Maybe she had been wrong. Maybe this wasn't the best choice after all. But it was too late now. In a matter of moments Doctor Seth Kendrick would be here to claim his mail-order bride—and her two children—from the main deck of the *Viola Belle*.

❦3❧

"STAY CLOSE, PATCH," SETH admonished his daughter as they stepped onto the deck of the *Viola Belle*. "I want to introduce you to Mrs. Gallagher when I find her."

"I don't want to meet her, Pa."

Seth ushered Patch into a quiet corner where they could stand without being buffeted by the crowd. He put a forefinger under his daughter's chin and raised her eyes to meet his. "I want you to be on your best behavior today. We don't want to scare Mrs. Gallagher off before she even gets her feet on solid ground," he said with a smile. "I'm expecting you to make her feel welcome."

Patch's eyes flared with rebellion before her lids lowered, hiding her enmity for the dreaded Mrs. Gallagher.

But Seth didn't see. He was already searching the foredeck of the *Viola Belle* for the woman who had agreed to become his wife.

Snatches of Molly Gallagher's last letter came back to him as he examined each of the women standing there. She had given him just enough information to identify her, without actually saying what color dress she would be wearing when she arrived.

I have long black hair. James said it was my crowning glory. However, I usually cover it with a hat to keep the sun off my nose. Otherwise I get freckles.

He eliminated every female who wasn't wearing a hat. That took care of a goodly number. Unfortunately, it was difficult to tell the hair color of those whose heads were covered. He wished he knew whether she wore her hair up or down.

I've become a mite too thin, but somehow food lost its taste after James died.

That left him only four women to choose from.

I hope you're not too tall, because I'm barely shoulder high to a

31

grasshopper. Well, perhaps that is a slight exaggeration. But not much! James called me his "little darling."

He narrowed it down to two women.

Oh, yes. I have a small mole near my mouth. James said it was becoming. I hope you'll think so too.

Neither woman was looking at him at the moment. He marched up to the closest one and tapped her on the shoulder. She turned, and he exhaled the expectant breath he hadn't realized he'd been holding. It wasn't her.

As he approached the other woman, she turned toward him. Seth stopped in his tracks, stunned by her elegant beauty. Why hadn't she warned him? Her face was framed by a black straw bonnet trimmed with a fringe of black crystal beads that caught and reflected the sunlight.

He had an impression of anxious doe-brown eyes and alabaster skin—freckled across the nose—that flushed when she met his gaze. Even white teeth worried her full lower lip, but she held her chin in a defiant tilt. The mole was there near her mouth, just as she had described it. But it was more than merely becoming. It tempted. It tantalized. It invited.

His body tautened, hardening with desire that he had no wish to feel. This wasn't what he had wanted from a mail-order bride. Not a woman who made him long to possess her. Not a woman to make feelings he had thought long dead spring to demanding life. Especially since they had both agreed this was to be very much a marriage of convenience.

Seth took two steps toward her. As he reached out, she laid a delicate hand in his.

"Mrs. Gallagher?" he managed in a raw voice. When she nodded, he felt his gut tighten.

"Yes. Doctor Kendrick?"

"Yes."

He wasn't at all what Molly had been expecting. A doctor shouldn't have such disturbing gray eyes or such shaggy black hair. A doctor shouldn't be so fierce-looking or have such a powerful frame. A doctor shouldn't remind her of the savage on horseback she had seen along the river, or cause her whole body to shiver at the touch of his surprisingly callused hand.

Molly thought the crow's-feet at the edges of his eyes and the deep creases that bracketed his mouth gave his face character. She approved of his straight nose, his cleft chin, and his wide, sharp cheekbones. He was wearing a kind of hat she hadn't seen much in the east. It mostly covered his wavy black hair, except where it curled down over his collar in back. But it was his eyes—enigmatic, smoky-gray eyes—that drew her to him and held her in thrall.

One second they were standing on the main deck of the *Viola Belle* staring into each other's eyes. The next, Molly's hand was torn from Seth's as someone stumbled hard against her, forcing her over the short rail into the icy waters of the Missouri. She caught a fleeting glimpse of an impish face peering down at her before the breath was knocked out of her and her mouth was filled with muddy water.

Seth had a split second to register that *Patch* had knocked Molly Gallagher overboard before he too was shoved from behind and felt himself falling into space. He gave fleeting thought to wringing his daughter's neck before he hit the water with a resounding splash. He came up sputtering and quickly blinked his eyes, trying to clear them enough to spy the culprit who had shoved him over the rail.

Before he could get a good look, Molly broke the surface choking and cried, "Help! I can't swim!" and promptly sank again.

Molly's lungs felt as if they might burst, but she daren't take a breath. Was this what James had felt? This awful burning pain in the chest? The frigid cold of the water? Had he thought of her and Whit and Nessie in his last moments, as she was doing now? Molly struggled against her fate, her splayed fingers moving desperately through the murky water for the light at the surface. But the immense weight of her many layers of fashionable clothing forced her inexorably down. She felt dizzy. She couldn't last much longer. Soon she would have to breathe. Then her lungs would fill with water, and she would drown.

She couldn't give up. Her children needed her. She must live! She fought against the pull on her clothing, refusing to give up her life to the river.

Something tugged on her skirt and just as quickly let go. Someone had jumped in after her! *Save me! Don't leave me here.* She reached out blindly to grab hold of her rescuer's neck and promptly had her hands torn away. Which made her even more desperate.

A muscular arm snaked around her from behind, grasping her firmly across her breasts. She was so shocked at the intimacy of such a hold that she froze for an instant—which was time enough for her to realize that they had begun moving upward. She forced herself to remain calm, which was the only way she could aid her own rescue.

Molly gasped as she broke the surface of the water and immediately began coughing.

"You're safe now, Mrs. Gallagher," Seth said in her ear. "Just relax, and I'll swim you to shore."

By now, those on board the *Viola Belle* had been alerted to the fact that two passengers had fallen overboard. There were hands ready to take Molly from Seth as he lifted her up onto the levee, and to drag him out of the water as well.

Seth spied Ethan in the crowd that had gathered and said, "Take care of her while I get my medical bag from the buggy."

Molly lay on the ground with her eyes closed, grateful to be alive. The sun felt so warm, and she was so tired. She had no desire to move from this spot anytime soon.

"Step aside. Get out of the way. Give her some room to breathe," Ethan said.

When Molly opened her eyes, she saw a handsome man with sandy brown hair and bright green eyes kneeling beside her. He untied the soggy ribbons from under her chin and removed what was left of her best Sunday bonnet.

"Are you all right?" he asked.

Molly's mouth formed the words, "I'm fine," but nothing came out. She closed her eyes again. She felt the heat of a second body beside her just before she heard Seth's deep, rumbling voice.

"How is she, Ethan?"

"I can't tell, Seth. You better check her over."

Molly felt the buttons of her dress being undone and managed to drag a hand up to try and stop whoever it was.

"It's all right, Mrs. Gallagher," Seth said, moving her hand back down to her side. "It's me. Seth Kendrick. I'm a doctor, remember?"

"No." She didn't care if he was a doctor. He was a stranger. But his practiced hands made short work of the buttons on her bodice. Molly gasped as smooth, cool metal touched the skin above her left breast. The gasp set off a fit of coughing. Seth turned her over and patted her back. When she quieted, he laid her back down flat and once again placed the stethoscope so he could hear her heart.

Molly shivered at the slight touch of his fingers on her skin around the edges of the instrument. He moved the metal disc around as he checked her lungs. His fingertips left a spot of heat everywhere they touched. This had to stop. She didn't want to feel so—so—much.

"Doctor Kendrick," she managed to whisper, "please stop."

"I'm almost finished," he said, and continued what he was doing. "I don't think any permanent damage has been done," he announced at last. "Can you open your eyes, Mrs. Gallagher?"

Molly squinted her eyes open and quickly closed them to shut out the bright sun.

"Let me help you up."

Seth's arm surrounded her shoulders, and in short order she was nestled in the cleft created between his thighs as he knelt on the levee. As soon as she was upright, the bodice of her dress, which was still unbuttoned, fell open. She grabbed awkwardly to save her modesty, only to have Seth reach over her shoulders and matter-of-factly begin to button her back up again.

Molly closed her eyes, but she could do nothing about the flush that pinkened her skin and raced his buttoning fingers to her neck. There was no respite even when he removed his hands, for the heat kept on rising right up her neck to her cheeks.

"I . . . I think I can get up now," she said, anxious to remove herself from the embarrassing position between his legs.

Once again that muscular arm slipped around her. At the same time Seth rose, he lifted her effortlessly to her feet. Once they were standing, she saw that his sodden clothes—black broadcloth suit, white shirt, and string tie—conformed revealingly to the shape of his body. And she realized her wet bodice must be clinging to her like a second skin.

"Are you all right?" she asked, crossing her arms protectively to cover herself.

"Fine," he said with a brief, reassuring smile.

The smile softened his face but was too quickly gone. "It was courageous of you to jump in after me," she said. "You saved my life. I can't thank you—"

"I didn't jump in after you."

"You didn't?"

"I was pushed."

"Are you sure? Whoever would do such a thing?" But Molly had an awful, sinking feeling who it might have been. Suddenly she realized her children must be worried about her. She searched the spot on the main deck where she had been standing with the doctor. Sure enough, Whit was leaning over the rail with a smug look on his face. Well, he wasn't going to be looking quite so pleased with himself when he had to apologize to the doctor. She cringed at the thought of introducing them to each other. But of course it must be done. And the sooner the better.

Molly had already opened her mouth to speak when it dawned on her that she hadn't seen Nessie standing anywhere near Whit. She whirled around to look again. The little girl was gone. Her heart began to pound when another look did not reveal her daughter. Where was Nessie? Had she wandered off the *Viola Belle* alone? Was she now lost in the crowd?

Immediately, all thoughts of conciliating the man beside her fled. Molly didn't bother to explain where she was going, just lifted her soggy skirts in both hands and shoved her way through the gathered crowd toward where she had left her children.

"Wait!" Seth called. When Molly didn't even slow down, he hurried after her.

Molly hadn't a thought to spare for the towheaded waif in baggy trousers standing on the foredeck glaring daggers at her. She headed straight for the boy neatly dressed in knee-length trousers and a jacket, standing nearby.

"Where's Nessie?" she demanded of her son.

Surprised at his mother's question, Whit looked around in genuine consternation. "She was right here a minute ago."

"Was that before or after you pushed Doctor Kendrick into the river?" Molly demanded angrily.

"Before." Whit grimaced as he realized what he had just admitted. "I don't know where Nessie—" The boy snapped his mouth shut, scowling at something over his mother's shoulder.

Molly turned to discover that her husband-to-be had joined her. Had he heard Whit's confession? Her face paled when she saw the white lines of fury around his mouth. A quick look revealed bunched fists. For a moment she thought he was going to lay violent hands on her son. Every muscle in her body tensed to stop him.

But when his powerful hand closed around cloth, it was the small towheaded child dressed in a wrinkled cotton shirt and baggy corduroy pants that he held in his grasp.

"Would you like to explain what happened here?" he demanded of the child.

"It was an accident!" the urchin said. "I tripped."

"And just happened to fall against this particular woman?" the doctor asked in a sarcastic voice.

Molly suddenly recognized the impish face as the one she had seen leaning over the rail when she landed in the river. In the same moment she realized that the child was not a boy, as she had first thought, but a girl with her hair tied back with a string at her nape. She put a calming hand on Seth's sleeve. "I'm sure it must have been an accident, as she claims."

"You are, are you?" he snarled.

Molly drew back, astounded by the violence in his eyes and the harshness of his voice. She opened her mouth to tell him it was only a little water and that she would dry, but sneezed instead.

She watched through watery eyes as Seth turned his fierce look back on the rumpled girl and demanded, "Apologize to the lady."

The girl's chin came up pugnaciously. "No."

Seth's face was both furious and incredulous. "No?"

"I won't apologize." The girl's voice rose in distress as she cried, "I'm not sorry I did it. I hope she catches pneumonia and dies. She should go back where she came from. I don't need a mother!"

Confused, Molly turned to Seth for an explanation.

"This devil's helpmate is my daughter, Patricia," Seth admitted through clenched teeth.

"My name is Patch," the girl muttered.

"You have a *daughter*?" Molly asked in amazement. "But you never said a word about having children."

"It's why I need a wife," he admitted in a gruff voice. "You can see she needs a woman's influence."

"It appears so," Molly agreed with alacrity. "Even so—"

Whit interrupted with, "She's the one who gave me the idea to push *him* into the water, Mother."

Molly felt her heart miss a beat as Seth turned his steely gray eyes on her.

"Did I hear the boy right?" he demanded.

"That depends," she hedged, lowering her lashes so she wouldn't have to deal with those piercing eyes of his. "What did you hear?"

"Are you the boy's mother?" Seth demanded with asperity.

Molly's chin came up, and her eyes met his. "And what if I am?" She shot a quick glance at his daughter. "Surely what's sauce for the goose is sauce for the gander."

"Look, lady—"

"Watch how you talk to my mother," Whit warned.

"Yeah, well you watch how you talk to my pa!" Patch retorted, putting herself toe to toe with Whit.

"Whit!"

"Patch!"

Both parents grabbed hold of their respective children.

"I'm sorry Whit pushed you in," Molly said.

"Out here a man speaks for himself," Seth said, his eyes meeting Whit's. "What have you got to say for yourself, son?"

"I'm not your son," Whit retorted. "And I'm not sorry. I'd do it again! I wish you'd drowned. I wish we'd never come here. You'll never be my father!"

Seth's steely gaze never left Whit's face.

Molly's dark brown eyes flashed at Seth.

Patch focused glaring blue eyes on Molly.

Whit's sea-green eyes shot daggers at Patch.

Any second, fireworks were bound to explode.

Molly nearly jumped out of her skin when she felt a hard tug on her sodden skirt. She looked down to see Nessie standing with her thumb in her mouth. Molly had completely forgotten about her daughter in the confusion. She reached down to lift the child into her arms. At the same time, she realized that if she held Nessie close to her, the child would get wet. She ended up holding the little girl the outstretched length of her arms.

Seeing her difficulty, Seth took the child from Molly and seated her in the crook of his arm. "And who might this be?"

Molly swallowed. "My daughter, Agnes. We call her Nessie."

"You have a son *and* a daughter?" Seth asked in a carefully controlled voice.

Molly's spine stiffened. She arched a brow as she stared him down. "Yes. It appears we have three children between us."

"Don't marry her, Pa!" Patch cried. "That boy of hers is a danged rowdy one, for sure. And that one you're holding—why, she's still a baby! She'll drive you crazy in a week with her whining and crying."

Patch's argument left something to be desired, since Nessie hadn't made a sound since she'd arrived on the scene. But Molly took one look at Seth's daughter and saw the genuine distress in Patch's blue eyes at the sight of her father holding the other little girl.

"Perhaps this isn't going to work out after all," Molly said.

"Why not?" Seth demanded.

Molly's eyes slid away from his steady gaze. "I should have told you about the children."

"Dang right you should've," Patch was quick to agree.

"I was no more honest than you were," Seth conceded. "And the fact that you have children doesn't change things. I still need a wife. And my daughter needs a mother."

"Dang it, Pa! I don't—"

"That'll be enough, Patch," Seth said in a warning voice.

"Send her home, Pa," Patch begged. "Send 'em all home."

Molly could see that Seth was torn. It was clear he would have walked over fire for his daughter. And Patricia—Patch—wanted them gone. But Molly needed a home for her children. If she had to fight Patch, she would do it.

Seth saw Molly's shoulders square for battle even as her black lashes lowered onto pale cheeks in exhaustion. A strong, inexplicable need to protect rose within him. He thought of a line in her second letter. After explaining that her parents and husband were all dead, she had written, *I am alone in the world now.* Now he knew she had meant that she alone was responsible for the welfare of her two children. Where would she go if he decided not to marry her? And after all, he had been no more honest than she had been.

He put a finger under her chin to lift her face up toward him. "Molly?"

At the sound of Seth's voice, Molly's lids lifted, and she saw that his hard gray eyes had softened. She let herself hope.

"Molly," he repeated, as though the name were foreign and not a perfectly ordinary Irish name. "I have a preacher waiting. If you'll still have me."

Molly refused to look at Patch. The child wouldn't have changed her mind, and Molly felt her pain too strongly to ignore it. "Seth, I think—"

She was interrupted by a cry from shore.

"Hey, Doc! Pike Hardesty gunned down a man in Bassett's saloon. Better come quick!"

Seth cursed under his breath. "I've got to go," he said, quickly handing Nessie over. "Hardesty doesn't often miss. It'll be a near thing at best, and if I don't hurry, I'll be no help at all. I'll meet you at the hotel in town when I'm finished."

"Say, Pa," Patch said. "Maybe she should go along." When her father frowned, Patch added, "I mean, maybe you oughta find out if she's any good at nursing before you agree to marry her. After all, you don't want a wife who faints at the sight of a little blood."

Molly swallowed hard. "Blood?"

Seth slanted a look at Molly, who had turned a little green at the gills. "I could use the help." He looked at Nessie in her arms. "But I understand if you can't leave your daughter."

"Whit can look after her," Molly said. Seeing the mutinous look in her son's eyes, she added, "I'll just walk them to our stateroom. I'll be back in a minute."

Seth watched her walk away, graceful despite the weight of the water-soaked skirt. He had taught himself to ignore women's bodies when he was doctoring them. But he hadn't been able to ignore Molly Gallagher's. He had seen the shape of her breasts through the wet cloth. Worse, the chill had made her nipples peak. He had been very much aware of her as a woman every moment he was unbuttoning her dress. Nothing with Molly Gallagher was turning out as he'd planned. How in the world had things gone so awry?

"You better be careful, Pa," Patch said.

"What?" Seth replied absently, unwilling to give up watching the widow Gallagher.

"She looks like more trouble than she's worth," Patch said earnestly. "And think about that whiny baby, Pa. It'll be a misery for sure having her around the house. And lord knows what mischief that boy'll start. I—"

"She's going to be my wife, Patch," Seth said. "And she'll be your mother. Her children will become part of our family. You'd best get used to the idea."

Patch shook her head no. "I won't stand for it, Pa."

Seth hardened his voice against the pain he saw in his daughter's eyes. "You don't have any choice."

"Durned if I don't!" she cried. "Marry her if you gotta, Pa. But she ain't gonna be my ma. And they ain't gonna be my kin!"

Seth clenched his fists as he watched Patch thrust her way through the crowd on deck and scramble down the gangplank. He was doing this for her own good. Someday she would thank him for it. He shoved a hand through his damp hair in frustration.

"Shall we go?"

The sound of Molly's husky voice sent a shiver down Seth's spine. She hadn't taken the time to comb her hair, but she had grabbed a shawl to wrap around the bodice of her dress. He forced himself not to remember the way the wet material had clung to her figure. There would be time later to think about the hell on earth he had created for himself with this marriage of convenience.

"Let's go," he said tersely. "I have a bullet to dig out of a man's hide."

Molly extended her step to match Seth's stride. All in all, things hadn't gone as badly as she had feared they might. At least he wasn't sending them right back to New Bedford on the next steamboat. Now all she had to do was prove she could be a competent nurse. That shouldn't be so hard. Why, she had gutted fish all the time back in New Bedford. Could the sight of a little blood from a gunshot wound be so very different?

❋4❋

MOLLY HAD NEVER SEEN so much blood in her life. It soaked the checkered shirt of the man lying on the floor of the Medicine Bow Saloon and stained the sawdust beneath him. She swallowed down the bile that rose in her throat and stayed as close as she could to Seth's side.

"Put him up on the bar," Seth said, setting his travel-worn medical bag down on the polished surface.

"Aw, come on, Doc. I'm trying to sell whiskey here," Red complained.

"I need a place where I can see to work."

Red grimaced. "You boys heard Doc Kendrick. Haul him up here."

Several bystanders hoisted the man from the floor onto the mahogany bar. Seth carefully pulled the fabric away from the gaping hole in the man's chest. Bloody bubbles of air surrounded the wound.

"Am I gonna make it, Doc?" the wounded man gasped.

"What's your name?" Seth asked.

"Wally Flanders."

"Just take it easy, Wally. I'll do my best."

Molly wasn't sure what she was supposed to do. So at first she did nothing, just stood and watched as Seth cut away the cloth from the wound. At Seth's command she supported the wounded man's head while the bartender held a whiskey bottle to his lips, then watched him pour whiskey from the same bottle over Seth's hands.

Seth motioned for several men to hold the wounded man down while he probed for the bullet.

Molly's hands gripped the smooth mahogany bar and held on as the man screamed and fainted.

"Thank God for that," Seth muttered. "Mrs. Gallagher," he said, "come over here and hand me my instruments when I ask for them."

"I don't know—"

"Come over here," Seth ordered. "I'll teach you what you need to know."

Molly sighed inwardly with relief. She could follow simple instructions. Seth need never find out she wasn't a real nurse.

Molly retained only impressions of the operation that took place over the next several minutes: Seth's large hands, strong and sure, yet gentle. An economy of movement and efficiency of action. The sickly sweet smell of blood. An urgency that hovered in the air around them as the country doctor fought death. And lost.

Molly knew it was over when she saw the slump of Seth's shoulders. He seemed to curl in around himself. His hands stopped their deft movements. And she heard the soughing death rattle as the man gave up breath and life.

"Shouldn't have wasted my time," Seth said in disgust. "Must have nicked the lung. Thought so when I first saw him, but I hoped . . ."

"You did the best you could," Molly offered.

"What I did wasn't worth spit."

Molly recoiled at the anger in his voice, the rigid tension in his body. "Was it something I did—or didn't do?"

Seth shook his head abruptly. "No. You did fine. A doctor couldn't ask for a more competent nurse."

Molly breathed an inward sigh of relief. Her deception had done nothing to contribute to a man's death. But she couldn't take the chance that next time she wouldn't be so lucky. She took a deep breath and confessed, "Doctor Kendrick, I haven't ever assisted in an operation before."

"I know."

"You do? What made you suspect—"

"You didn't stop shaking the whole time," he said with a wry twist of his mouth. He took her hand and held it up between them. It was still shaking. "But you did everything I asked, when I asked. If you can follow instructions that well from now on, you'll do just fine."

Molly pulled her hand from his and clasped it with the other in an attempt to still the tremors. She was appalled and amazed when she realized everything she had just done. Now she stood beside a dead body. She had been exposed to nothing so grim in New Bedford; it was going to be a very different life in Montana.

Seth turned to the men who had already resumed their various occupations in the saloon and asked, "Anybody see what happened here?" There was a restless shifting, but no one spoke. "Red?"

Red shrugged. "Didn't see a thing."

Seth's eyes found Pike Hardesty, who had never left his seat at the poker table in the corner. He sat with his back to the wall, his thumbs tapping a rhythmic tattoo on the table. The hand of cards the dead man had played still lay scattered on the green felt. A chair stood awry some distance from the table as though it had been shoved there. A trail of blood led from the chair to the spot where the unarmed man had fallen in the sawdust.

Molly read the truth of the matter, just as she was sure Seth had. For a terrified moment she thought Seth might say something to provoke the man at the table, whose left cheek was sunken and scarred as though skin and bone had once been crushed. He had a thick moustache that flowed beyond the edges of a narrow mouth. His shaggy brown hair hung over his brows, half-masking snakelike eyes that were simply black, with no distinction of pupil or iris.

Abruptly, the scarred man stood. Molly saw he was both taller and heavier than Seth and wore a gun tied down low on his right hip. His fringed buckskin shirt and leggings were stained and slick from wear.

Casually, as though he hadn't noticed the scarred man's actions, Seth turned his back and began wiping his medical instruments clean and repacking them in his bag.

Molly stared at Seth, a frown growing between her brows. What sort of man was this? James would have stood toe to toe with the scarred man and welcomed the fight. Many was the time she had nursed James's bruised and swollen face and bathed his bleeding knuckles after a barroom brawl. She wasn't averse to Seth not fighting, just surprised by it.

However, in the west it seemed a man didn't have to go looking for trouble. It found him wherever he was.

To Molly's horror, the scarred man sauntered over, leaned back against the bar, and hooked his bootheel on the footrail. "You got something you want to say to me, Doc?"

"Nope."

"He was cheating," Hardesty said. "Got what was coming to him." He surveyed the room, daring anyone to contradict him. No one did. He turned his attention to Molly. "Haven't seen range calico like you around here in a long while. Name's Pike Hardesty. Who would you be, purty lady?"

Molly shrank back until she came up against a solid wall of muscle. Startled, she glanced over her shoulder and saw the rigid line of Seth's jaw.

"She's no business of yours," Seth said in a quiet voice. "Come on, Mrs. Gallagher. I shouldn't have brought you in here."

"Hold on just a minute," Hardesty said, stepping in front of Molly. "I asked this here lady a question. I expect an answer."

"You got the only answer you're going to get," Seth said.

For a "patient man who tried to understand the other fellow's point of view," Seth's voice held a decided edge to it. Molly quickly said, "My name is Molly Gallagher. I came here to marry Doctor Kendrick."

There was a stunned silence in the saloon, and all eyes turned to stare at them.

"Well, now, Molly Gallagher," Hardesty said with a lurid grin. "You don't want Doc Kendrick. Why, he's got guts slack as old fiddle strings. Don't even wear a gun. Probably scared he'll shoot himself in the foot." Hardesty laughed at his own joke. "Why not try a real man instead?"

Molly had thought nothing of the fact that Seth Kendrick wasn't wearing a gun. No one in New Bedford carried a gun. In fact, anyone carrying a gun would have been highly suspect. But apparently things were different in Montana.

She wasn't sure afterward exactly how it happened. But Pike Hardesty took a step toward her, and the next thing she knew, he was lying flat on his back in sawdust.

"Sorry," Seth apologized, reaching down a hand to help Hardesty up. "Thought you saw my foot there. Didn't mean to trip you."

Hardesty knocked Seth's hand away and scrambled to his feet. Red-faced, he began brushing himself off. "If I didn't know you better, Kendrick, I'd say you did that on purpose." His voice was vicious as he finished, "But you being yellow-bellied clear through to your backbone makes that purely unlikely."

Molly watched as Seth's face paled. A muscle in his jaw jerked. Yet he made no move to strike the scarred man. He said nothing to defend himself. She was appalled and confused. Surely no man could tolerate such an insult and hold his head up high. But if anything, Seth's shoulders had squared more firmly. What manner of man was this who did not regard another's slander? Was he the coward Pike Hardesty had named him? She looked at Seth, and there was nothing in his face that told her one way or another.

"Let's go, Mrs. Gallagher," Seth said at last.

When Hardesty moved to intercept her, Red's shotgun barred his way. "Leave them be, Pike. You can be replaced. We only got one doctor hereabouts."

That explained their tolerance for a man with no backbone, Molly thought. In a land as violent as this was turning out to be, a doctor seemed a dire necessity.

Seth's hand at her elbow urged Molly out of the saloon. She walked beside him, her head held high, looking neither right nor left as they headed back to the levee. She felt the speculative stares of the townsfolk. What did they really think of Seth Kendrick? she wondered. Did everyone believe him a coward? How would they treat the wife of such a man? He had promised her his protection. But what was to keep someone like that awful scarred man from accosting her in the street if no one feared her husband's retribution?

Neither spoke until they reached the door to her stateroom on the *Viola Belle*. Then Seth turned to her and said, "Pike Hardesty is a bully and a braggart. I should never have taken you where you'd meet up with a man like that."

"Why did you let him get away with saying those things about you?"

"Maybe because they're true."

Molly frowned. "Are they?"

A bitter smile tilted his lips. "That's for you to decide."

"Were you afraid to fight him because you aren't wearing a gun?" she asked, the crease between her brows deepening as she sought to understand him.

"Let's just say that fighting wouldn't have proved me right, or him wrong."

"So you stepped aside."

His lips curled cynically. "That's certainly a kind way of describing what I did."

"You're an unusual man, Doctor Kendrick. I don't know what to make of you."

"Does that mean you've changed your mind about becoming my wife? Say so now, and I'll make arrangements to get you back to New Bedford."

Watching him closely, Molly saw him tense as if for a blow. She was tempted to take him up on his offer. She was frightened of what lay ahead of her. Seth Kendrick was so different from James, such a mass of contradictions. Strength and gentleness. Decisiveness and restraint. And though she didn't want to think him a coward, he had admitted he wouldn't willingly choose to fight. Would he be able to keep her and her children safe in this wilderness to which they had come?

She had to pray he could, because going back offered no solution to her problems. She must keep Whit away from the sea. And Nessie needed the security of a home.

It dawned on her that perhaps Seth hadn't made the offer of release out of consideration for her feelings. Perhaps he wanted out himself. That shocking thought gave her pause. "I haven't changed my mind," she said. "But now that you know you'll have two extra mouths to feed and care for, perhaps you've changed yours."

"Your boy looks like he'll make a fine man. And I won't mind having the little one around," Seth said. "Are you willing to be a mother to my daughter?"

She met his serious gaze and promised, "I'll treat her as though she were my own."

"And make her a lady," he added.

Molly tried to picture Patch as a lady and failed. "I'll do my best," she murmured.

"Then we have a deal. Shall we shake on it?"

Molly shivered with mixed fear and excitement at the touch of Seth's callused palm. She had just agreed to put her well-being, and that of her children, into the hands of this stranger. Only time would tell whether she had made a good bargain—or the worst mistake of her life.

"Change into whatever you want to wear to the wedding," Seth said. "There's a parlor in the hotel. I thought we could be married there. We'll have to hightail it out of town afterward if we hope to get to my ranch before dark."

"You don't have a house in town?"

His eyes slid away to the horizon. "No, I don't. I catch and break horses for the army. My ranch is south of town about twelve miles."

"But you're a doctor," she blurted.

"Yes. But I can't make a living that way."

At her quizzical look he explained, "This is a hard land. It's not just smallpox and typhoid that plague you. It's rattlesnake bites, broken bones when your horse steps in a gopher hole and throws you, and amputated joints when the woodsman's ax slips. Many a man gets shot by renegade Indians or outlaws like Pike Hardesty. A lot of my patients die, Mrs. Gallagher. And dead men don't pay. So you see, I need another way to make sure I can feed myself and my daughter."

Molly flushed. "I had no idea Montana would be so—so violent. Even what you do when you're not doctoring—breaking horses—isn't that kind of dangerous?"

He flashed a quick grin. "It can be. But I have a man who helps me, Ethan Hawk. You'll meet him at the wedding. Anything else you want to know?"

"Do we have neighbors?"

"Sure. Iris and Henry Marsh live about five miles west of my place."

Molly's jaw dropped. "Five miles!"

Seth grinned. "That's a stone's throw here in Montana. You can ride that distance in no time."

"On what?" Molly asked with asperity.

"A horse."

"I don't know how to ride."

"Don't worry. I'll teach you."

They heard voices inside the stateroom, and sounds like furniture being moved.

"We'll talk more after the wedding," Seth said. "I'll be back to pick you up as soon as I find Patch."

He bowed slightly before he turned and walked away. For a moment Molly was too stunned to do anything but stand there and watch him. No wonder he had said Montana was lonely. Imagine, neighbors no closer than five miles away! And to be twelve miles from the closest town was unthinkable. What had she gotten herself into? Why hadn't she asked more questions before she jumped into this with both feet?

To Molly's surprise, when she opened the door to her stateroom, Patch Kendrick was sitting cross-legged in the middle of the four-poster bed. The girl started guiltily and slanted a warning look at

Whit, who wore an equally guilty expression. Molly stepped back outside to tell Seth she had found his daughter, but he had already disappeared into the crowd on the levee. When she came back in, both children looked as innocent as angels.

"Your father's looking for you," she told Patch.

"I told Red Dupree where I'd be, so Pa can find me. I was just getting to know Whit," Patch replied. "After all, we're going to be family."

Molly's eyes narrowed suspiciously. This reasonable speech didn't sound at all like it came from the same person who had mercilessly shoved a perfect stranger into the muddy Missouri. What was the girl planning now? Molly shook her head. What an imagination she had, to think that this freckle-faced child was hatching some plot against her. After all, there wasn't much one little girl could do to interfere with her plans. Most probably, Patch had simply accepted the inevitable.

Molly gave the girl the benefit of the doubt. "I have to get dressed now. You're welcome to stay and visit if you like. Your father will undoubtedly be back here in a little while to escort us all to the wedding."

Patch exchanged another quick look with Whit. "Uh, well, okay. If you don't mind, I think I will."

"Why don't I take Nessie for a walk?" Whit offered.

"That sounds like a wonderful idea," Molly agreed. "Just stay where you can hear me when I call you." She turned her back on them to sort through her trunks for the dress she planned to wear.

Molly carefully unfolded the dress of violet silk that she had packed as her wedding gown. It had been a gift from Aunt Hattie on her twenty-eighth birthday. The color was appropriate for the mourning she was still observing, but the hem was embroidered with a decorative design of grape leaves. It had a simple bodice that buttoned up the front with a foulard at the neck and a lilac mantilla scarf to be worn around the shoulders.

Molly stepped behind the screen in the corner of the room. Once she heard the door close, she began stripping off the still-damp gray silk dress that had been ruined when she fell into the river.

"Do you mind if I watch?" Patch asked.

Molly nearly jumped out of her skin. She had naturally assumed that Patch had left the room along with Whit and Nessie. Obviously she had not. Patch sat on the corner of a trunk staring at Molly with wide, innocent blue eyes.

Molly's first instinct was to shoo the girl out. But she had promised Seth Kendrick she would treat the child as her own, and Nessie had often sat and watched her at her toilette. After all, that was how a child learned, by example. What better way to begin to make a lady of Patch than to show her the proper attire she must soon begin to wear?

"Of course I don't mind," Molly said. She finished unbuttoning her dress, which was trimmed with black corded fringe and small pewter buckles. Perhaps she could salvage some of those for another garment, she thought as she set the dress aside.

"What's that thing?" Patch asked.

Molly followed Patch's pointing finger. "It's called a tournure. It's made of crinoline and supports the bustle of my dress, along with several petticoats."

"I know what a petticoat is," Patch said with disgust.

Molly arched a brow. "Then you usually wear one?"

"I didn't say that."

Molly gave an unladylike grunt of relief as she untied the white satin corset and let it fall. "I must say, I never did much appreciate the restrictions of a corset. But every lady wears one."

"I ain't gonna," Patch muttered.

Molly was left wearing a low-necked pointed basque-waist, lace-trimmed drawers and white stockings, all of which were a great deal the worse for their dip in the Missouri.

Patch appeared fascinated. "I had no idea you were wearing so much rig."

"There are certain rules of fashion that every lady must follow."

Patch snorted. "You won't catch me in none of that stuff. Couldn't hardly move wearing that durned getup."

"You'll learn," Molly said.

Patch grimaced but didn't argue.

"You'll have to get up a minute," Molly said. "I need some things from that trunk you're sitting on."

Patch stood beside the trunk fidgeting while Molly sorted through it for fresh underthings.

"Uh . . . those shoes of yours would dry quicker if I put them out where they could catch the breeze," Patch offered.

Molly was touched by the girl's thoughtfulness. Why, Patch could be sweet when she wanted to be. Molly quickly closed the trunk and sat down on it to remove her black kid boots. "I appreciate you doing this for me," she said, handing the boots to Patch.

"It's my pleasure." She beat a hasty retreat before Molly had a chance to consider the reason for the brief appearance of that familiar impish grin.

Molly took advantage of Patch's absence to skin out of her under-things and put on new ones, blessing the foresight that had caused her to bring extras of the items she had thought might be harder to find in the west.

Once she was dressed except for her shoes and stockings, Molly came out from behind the screen and sat down at the dressing table to fix her hair. She parted it down the center and created two thick braids. The end of each braid was fastened under the beginning of the other and secured with hairpins. Small wisps of hair escaped around her face, softening what would otherwise have been a severe look. Last, but not least, Molly added a fetching crape bonnet the same lilac color as the mantilla scarf.

Molly was just adjusting the angle of her bonnet when someone knocked and the door was thrust open.

Seth Kendrick stood there. "Red Dupree said Patch was here." He looked around the room, but when he didn't see his daughter, said, "I should have known she'd send me on a wild-goose chase."

Molly hurried toward him. "She was here. She's just—" Molly looked past Seth out the door of her cabin and spied Patch standing at the rail of the steamboat. The girl held Molly's boots in her out-stretched hand. While Molly watched in disbelief, Patch stared her straight in the eye and let go. Molly's precious kid boots dropped into the river like two big black stones.

There was not a speck of remorse on Patch's face. The little girl marched back to the door and stood beside her father, clearly daring Molly to say anything.

Molly was amazed at the sheer gall of the child. And devious! Patch Kendrick could teach a corkscrew to curl. She opened her mouth to vent her spleen and snapped it shut again when she realized she would be doing exactly what Patch wanted her to do.

Molly gritted her teeth and fought to control her Irish temper. Several words that James had brought home from the docks came to mind—but found no voice. Molly Gallagher wasn't going to let a mere child provoke her into making an unladylike scene in front of Seth. Neither was she going to let the fact that she and Patch could look forward to *years* of such confrontations change her mind about marrying the girl's father.

"Are you ready to go?" Seth asked, completely unaware of the war of wills going on between his daughter and his future wife.

"I'll just be a moment." Molly headed for the trunk where she had packed a second, older pair of boots. She had to take nearly everything out to get to the bottom of the trunk. When she did, the boots weren't there.

Molly's spine straightened with a snap. She whirled to confront a grinning Patch. The girl was positively *gloating*.

At that moment, Whit arrived in the doorway with Nessie and shared a conspiratorial glance with Patch. Then he turned and stared at Molly. One look at her son's outthrust jaw told Molly the whole story. Whit must have told Patch about the second pair of boots. He might even have helped Patch find them. How could he do such a thing?

Molly's throat tightened until it hurt to swallow. What chance did this marriage have if their children were so set against it? How angry they must be, how frightened and confused, to connive so desperately to prevent it! She looked around the room but had no idea what she was looking for.

She sought out Seth's gray eyes but found no answers there—only more questions. There was admiration in his gaze and, more disturbing, desire. His eyes were haunted, hungry.

Molly had no idea it was her breathlessness, her pinkened cheeks and the spark of fury in her brown eyes that had excited Seth. She felt a stirring deep within her, a response to his magnetism that was raw and primitive. It was unsettling to want a man—a perfect stranger—this way. She balled her fingers into fists to hide the fact they were trembling. The constriction in her throat eased, replaced by the thrumming of her pulse. She couldn't drag her eyes away from the man standing before her.

Seth gave her an encouraging smile and said, "You look beautiful, Mrs. Galla—Molly. I can't imagine what more you could need to do. Shall we go?"

Molly curled her naked toes against the varnished deck. She couldn't very well admit she hadn't any shoes to wear without explaining what had happened to them. She couldn't do that without causing the confrontation Patch so clearly desired. For better or worse—and both despite and because of the children—she made her choice. She cleared her throat and said, "I guess I'm as ready as I'll ever be."

Molly felt the first stirring of satisfaction when she saw the astonished look on Patch's face. If Patch Kendrick thought being barefoot was going to slow Molly Gallagher down, she had another think coming!

———— ·•· ————

Patch followed glumly behind her father and his mail-order bride as they headed down Front Street toward Schmidt's Hotel. Whit had been shooting dark looks at her ever since they left the *Viola Belle*. Dang it all! It wasn't her fault Whit's mother was still going to marry her father. Patch had done her level best to give Molly Gallagher a disgust of her, but the ding-dang woman had been too dumb to take a hint. She had thought pushing her father's mail-order bride into the Missouri would be enough to send her packing. That had backfired when Whit shoved her father in after the woman.

She had hoped Molly Gallagher might be one of those women who fainted at the sight of blood. But she hadn't been that lucky. From what Patch had been able to see through the plate-glass window of the Medicine Bow Saloon, Molly Gallagher had passed her nursing test with flying colors.

That was when Patch had devised the plan to leave the consarn woman barefoot, certain that no *lady* would ever think of crossing a portal unless she was completely dressed. Durned if that plan hadn't failed as well!

Patch was good at using her wits to get what she wanted. She had hoped to provoke the detested Mrs. Gallagher into making a scene about being barefoot. Her father would be disgusted by the woman's ranting and raving and change his mind about marrying her. But that Mrs. Gallagher was danged smart. She hadn't fallen for the trap.

Instead, at this very moment Molly Gallagher was walking barefoot up the main street of Fort Benton on Seth Kendrick's arm. And Patch couldn't say a word about it without getting herself into trouble!

Patch wasn't about to admit she had met her match. Molly Gallagher might marry her pa, but that didn't mean they had to stay that way. And they wouldn't. Not if she had anything to say about it. She would find a way to make Molly Gallagher call it quits. Before the brief Montana summer was through, those Gallaghers would be long gone.

❈5❈

MOLLY STARED AT THE simple gold band on her finger in awe. She had worn James's ruby and diamond family ring for eleven years. Now it was gone, replaced by a circlet as elemental as the wilderness to which she had come. She looked up into the face of the man who had just become her husband. His gray eyes were somber.

"You can kiss the bride, Doc," Reverend Adams said with a wide grin.

Seth's hands framed her face, and she felt his breath on her cheek an instant before his lips brushed hers. Oh, the softness, the sleek dampness of his mouth! She stared, stunned, as Seth let her go and stepped back.

"Congratulations, Doc," the reverend said. "That's a mighty fine-looking woman you got for yourself."

"You're a beautiful bride, my dear," Mrs. Adams concurred.

Molly blushed as Seth murmured his agreement. An instant later, she was gathered up in a bear hug by the man Seth had introduced as his partner and best friend, Ethan Hawk. She recognized him as the man who had removed her hat after her dousing in the river.

"Seth deserves a little happiness," Ethan whispered in her ear. He chuckled and added, "I'm sure you're just what the doctor ordered."

Molly found the young man so approachable that she led him aside to ask, "Do you think you could arrange to buy a pair of shoes for me?"

Ethan immediately looked down. From his startled expression, Molly knew he had detected her bare toes peeking out from beneath her skirt.

"What happened to your—"

"Shhh! I don't want Seth to find out."

Ethan raised a brow in speculation, then grinned and said one word: "Patch."

Molly couldn't help laughing. "How did you know?"

"I know Patch. How'd she manage it?"

"With great aplomb," Molly said. "I promise to tell you the whole of it later. Would you—could you buy me a pair of shoes so that when we leave here I don't have to do it barefoot? I have some money—"

"Keep your money. It'll be my wedding gift to you, Mrs. Kendrick. Just let me have another quick look so I can figure out a size."

Molly felt self-conscious as Ethan took her hands, stood back at arm's length, and looked her up and down.

"Don't worry," he said. "I'm a pretty good judge where these things are concerned. I'll be back in a heartbeat." He winked mischievously before he turned and slipped out of the hotel parlor.

Seth scowled at the sight of Ethan leaning close to his wife. His eyes narrowed when Ethan took Molly's hands in his. He knew Ethan with women. The man could charm the feathers off a duck. Well, Ethan could just find somebody else to charm. Molly belonged to him!

Seth snorted in disgust at his idiotic musings. The feelings of possessiveness that rose in his breast were unfamiliar and left him feeling foolish.

He had married Molly Gallagher to have a mother for his daughter, not to have a wife to warm his bed. And yet whenever he looked at her—at the curve of her bosom, the flare of her hips, the velvety brown of her eyes, and the soft, pink lushness of her lips—he found himself painfully aroused. He had visions of his body mantling hers, of holding her in his arms and feeling her soft breasts nestled against his chest, of his hips thrust in the cradle of her thighs.

He deeply regretted the inference in his letters to her that this was to be merely a marriage of convenience.

So why not renegotiate the terms of your agreement?

The thought hadn't been far from his mind since the moment he had laid eyes on Molly Gallagher. And why not? They were married. It wasn't wrong for him to desire her. Or for her to desire him.

He licked the small drops of sweat from his upper lip, conscious of the flare of excitement he felt at the thought of making love with his wife. He let his eyes find her again. She was beautiful in the violet dress, but he would rather have seen her in a brighter color. It had been nearly a year since her husband's death. Surely by now she was ready to set aside the memories of another man.

Only now that he thought of it, in her last letter to him, nearly every sentence had been written to reflect her relationship to her late husband: "James thought." "James believed." "James said." He had to admit that didn't sound like a woman who had permanently laid her first husband to rest.

But she would. He wasn't asking her to love him; he didn't expect to love her. His late wife held his heart in a grip that was as strong as it had been the day she died. No one could ever touch him that way again. Of that he was very sure. The stone wall around his heart was firmly in place.

But that didn't mean he couldn't *want* another woman. He very much wanted the woman he had made his wife. She might have memories of James Gallagher, but he would be the man sleeping in her bed tonight.

The tug on his pants leg surprised him. When he looked down, he met a miniature pair of brown eyes like Molly's. "Hello, Nessie," he said. "Is there something I can do for you?"

"Are you going to be my new da?" the little girl asked.

Seth cleared his throat to give himself time to think. "I suppose so," he said at last.

"Will you pick me up?"

When she reached up, he grasped her at the waist and lifted her into the air. A burble of surprised laughter escaped her lips. Seth marveled at how light and fragile a four-year-old could be.

And felt a small crack in the stone around his heart as he settled her in his arms so they were eye to eye.

"Whit doesn't like you," Nessie promptly announced.

"He doesn't?"

"No. He didn't want you to marry Mama."

"Oh?"

"So he helped Patch find Mama's boots."

"Why would he do that?"

"So Patch could throw them in the river, of course."

"Of course," Seth said. His eyes sought out his daughter, and he found her sulking in a corner of the parlor. "Why would Patch want to do a thing like that?" he asked, afraid he already knew the answer.

"Patch said no lady would ever go barefoot to her own wedding."

Seth thought about that for a second and asked, "Are you saying that your mother is barefoot?"

"Well, of course she is," Nessie replied as though he were a particularly slow student, to whom things had to be explained twice. "Patch threw her boots into the river."

"Of course," Seth repeated in a slightly stunned voice. He searched for Molly and perused the hem of her skirt. He hadn't really thought much before about the fact that it dragged on the floor. Then Molly took a step, and he distinctly saw several toes beneath the violet fabric.

As he watched, Ethan returned to the room with a small brown-paper-wrapped package, which he handed to Molly with a grin.

Shoes, Seth realized.

A series of feelings assaulted Seth, leaving him shaken. First, there was embarrassment that his daughter would do such an awful thing, in defiance of all propriety. Second, there was disappointment that Molly would go to Ethan for help instead of coming to him. Third, there was certainty that he had chosen the right woman for his wife. Raising Patch to be a lady was going to be a considerable challenge. It appeared that Molly Gallagher would be equal to the task.

When Patch saw her father pick up Nessie Gallagher, she felt sick to her stomach. Nessie had attached herself like a leech, and her pa seemed more than willing to hold the little intruder. Patch couldn't remember the last time her father had held her in his arms like that. Not that she wanted him to, mind you. Or would let him if he tried. But he was *her* father. And she didn't intend to share him!

Patch glanced over to where Molly Gallagher Kendrick stood *barefoot* drinking punch and laughing with Ethan. For the first time, Patch admitted a grudging respect for the formidable adversary who was now her stepmother. Molly Gallagher Kendrick had gumption all right. But that didn't mean Patch had to like her—or obey her.

"I thought you said Mother wouldn't come to the wedding barefoot," Whit muttered into Patch's ear.

Patch turned wrathful eyes on him. "A *real* lady wouldn't have come."

"What are you saying?"

"Figure it out for yourself!"

"You take that back," Whit hissed.

"Make me!"

Patch was spoiling for a fight, and it appeared Whit was willing to give her one. She was two years older and wiser, but he was a good three inches taller. As far as she was concerned, that made them about evenly matched. Only, when she put up her fists, Whit just laughed.

"I can't fight a girl," he protested.

Her knuckles rapped him in the nose and rocked his head backward.

He yelped in surprise as blood spurted down his face. "Hey! Stop that!"

Patch walloped him in the stomach with a fist, bending him over double.

Whit forgot chivalry and fell on Patch like a tomcat in an alley fight. Only, when he swung, she stepped out of his path and his fist floated through thin air. He sagged as she belted him again in the stomach. He grabbed for her and used his greater weight to force her down. He heard her cry out in pain when her head hit the wooden floor.

Abruptly, the two combatants were yanked apart. Ethan held Whit by the shoulders, while Seth pulled Patch to her feet. Reverend Adams and his wife stood staring in disapproval. Molly was stuck holding Nessie, who'd been thrust into her arms by Seth as he ran to stop the fight.

"Oh, Whit! How could you?" Molly cried.

"What's going on here?" Seth demanded in a harsh voice.

"See, Pa!" Patch said. "I warned you he'd be trouble."

"She started it!" Whit shouted.

"I did not. I was minding my own business—"

"Liar!" Whit said.

"I am not! I—" Patch suddenly crumpled. If Seth hadn't been holding onto her, she would have fallen.

He lifted her limp body into his arms, thinking that she was pretending. But she couldn't be faking the total lack of response he now felt in her body. "She's unconscious," he said with astonishment. "What did you do to her?" he demanded of Whit.

"I didn't do anything," Whit said in a tremulous voice. "She hit her head when she fell."

"A concussion?" Ethan speculated.

Molly saw that Seth was rattled. He hadn't moved, and he hadn't taken his eyes off Patch's motionless, pale face. He was acting more like a parent than a doctor. Molly found that the most encouraging sign she'd yet seen that he would make a good father for her children.

"Seth," she said in a calming voice, "take Patch over to the settee and lay her down." Once she got him started in the right direction, he was fine.

Molly turned to the preacher and asked, "Reverend Adams, could you and your wife please have the hotel manager arrange for me to get a bowl of cool water and a cloth?"

As the preacher and his wife left the room, she turned to Whit and said, "Go sit down on that chair beside the settee. Tilt your head back and pinch your nose until it stops bleeding. Ethan"—Molly tucked a stray wisp of hair behind her ear while she thought what else needed done—"can you find Seth's medical bag?"

"It's in the buggy. I'll go get it," he volunteered.

"What about me?" Nessie asked. "What can I do?"

"You can give me a hug," Molly said. Nessie was more than willing to comply. Molly found the feel of Nessie's tiny arms around her neck a comfort. She could imagine the horror Seth must be experiencing as he watched over his unconscious daughter.

"Nessie, it would be a big help now if you would go and stand by Whit and make sure he keeps his head tilted back. Could you do that for me?"

"All right," Nessie said as Molly set her down.

Within moments, the hotel parlor was bustling with people. The manager appeared with the items Molly had requested, and Ethan delivered Seth's medical bag. Once Seth saw the bag, he seemed to wake from his shocked stupor. He checked Patch's eyes and realized that although she might have a slight concussion, it wasn't serious. Ethan knelt beside the settee, his hand gently brushing Patch's tousled hair away from her forehead in concern.

Meanwhile, Molly put the damp cloth to work cleaning the worst of the blood off Whit's face and fingers.

Seth waved some hartshorn under his daughter's nose, and the ammonia smell brought her coughing and sputtering to life. Patch's first words, once she was fully conscious, were "I want to go home, Pa."

"That sounds like a good idea," Ethan said to Seth. "Unless you get started soon, it's going to be dark before you get there. I'll ride ahead and make sure there's a fire in the stove and some hot coffee waiting for you," he offered.

Molly met Seth's eyes across the room, and she nodded her agreement.

"I appreciate your offer, Ethan," Seth said. "We'll be leaving as soon as I can get the Gallaghers' trunks loaded on the buggy."

"I'll give you a hand," Ethan said.

Once the two men had left the room, a pall descended. Molly had no intention of stirring up dust that had barely settled. She took advantage of the peace and quiet to rinse her muddy feet in what was left of the bowl of water.

Mrs. Adams stared bemused for a moment before asking, "My dear, is there some reason you came barefoot to your own wedding?"

Molly wasn't about to tell her the truth, so she made up a tale. "Oh, it's an old Irish custom, Mrs. Adams."

"It is?"

"We always start our marriages the way we intend to go on."

"I don't understand," the preacher's wife said.

Molly leaned over and gestured Mrs. Adams closer so she could whisper in her ear, "Barefoot and pregnant."

Mrs. Adams gasped and drew back from Molly as though she were contagious.

"Of course, I'm not in the family way," Molly explained, finding it hard to keep a straight face. "But with Seth being such a virile man, I'm sure it won't be long before I am."

Flustered beyond words, Mrs. Adams excused herself and left the room.

Molly looked up at Him and asked for forgiveness. Then she used the peace and quiet to open the package Ethan had given her. She smiled with delight when she discovered that besides shoes—a delicate pair of kid boots with patent leather tops—he had also purchased white stockings. And he hadn't lied. Both shoes and stockings were a perfect fit.

Ethan Hawk was obviously a man who knew a lot about women. He had made her feel perfectly at ease from the first moment she had met him. She wasn't a tenth so comfortable with the man she had just married. Whenever she got near Seth, she felt a strange tension, a feeling of expectation, of excitation, that she couldn't explain. Molly hoped that as she and Seth got to know each other, these inexplicable feelings of agitation would ease.

Molly ushered the three children outside, where Seth and Ethan were just finishing.

"There's plenty of room for everyone in the buggy," Seth said. "You might have to sit close."

Patch scowled at Whit, and he frowned back.

Seth didn't miss the exchange and said, "I don't want to see any more fighting between the two of you. If you've got differences, find a way to settle them peaceably, or I'll settle them for you. Do you both understand me?"

"Yes, Pa," Patch muttered.

"You're not my father," Whit said. "And I don't have to do what you say!"

Rather than say anything, Seth simply walked away to make sure the buggy was hitched up properly. Seth knew he couldn't win that kind of argument. So he refused to engage in it. He fiddled with the harness until he was ready once again to face his new family.

But he found it hard to believe the situation in which he now found himself.

When Seth had first imagined the drive home from Fort Benton with his mail-order bride, he had thought it might be an awkward trip. After all, he'd be sitting in the front seat with his new wife, and his daughter would end up being a twelve-year-old chaperone in the buggy's back seat. As it turned out, the drive was every bit as awkward as he had expected, but for a very different reason.

In order to ensure peace on the trip, he put Patch beside him in the front seat. Whit, Nessie, and his new bride sat in back. At first Seth tried to carry on a conversation with Molly, but he was forced to turn around to hear her reply or let her talk to the back of his head. Neither alternative was comfortable, so he soon fell silent.

Every time Seth turned to check on them, Molly gave him what she hoped was a bright smile but knew must look more like a grimace. So many feelings were struggling for dominance within her that she only felt anxious and wished the trip were over. The grassy prairies were endless, and the mountains seemed very far in the distance.

Molly thought she heard Seth sigh with relief when a peak-roofed log cabin came into sight. A thin stream of white smoke drifted from a stone chimney at one end of the house.

"We're almost home," Seth announced. "It won't be long now."

The time went more quickly when they could see their destination, and very soon Seth was helping Molly down in front of her new home. As his letter had promised, it was nestled in a copse of cottonwood along a creek. There was also a pond not far from the house.

"I know it isn't much," Seth found himself saying.

"It's fine," Molly replied as she took the three steps up onto a shaded front porch that ran the length of the cabin in front.

Seth opened the door, but before she could walk through it, he scooped her up into his arms.

"Every bride should be carried over the threshold," he whispered to her.

Molly lowered her eyes, moved by his gesture. Then he set her down, and it was a good thing she was feeling in charity with him. Because what she saw was enough to make any woman turn tail and run the other way.

The house was split in half. A log wall to the left had two doors built into it that were closed. The righthand side of the house, the one onto which the front door opened, was all one room. It apparently served as parlor, dining room, office, and kitchen combined.

In the center of the room stood a scarred maple table and four mismatched chairs. The sideboard on the righthand wall was filled with an odd assortment of half-empty medicine bottles. A rolltop desk had been shoved half-open to reveal a clutter of papers and medical books. It was situated on the front wall and looked out a window that provided a vista of the mountains.

Along the back wall was a sink with an indoor pump—a real luxury, Seth assured her. There was also a new four-hole stove he'd had shipped up from St. Louis when he'd found out she was coming. To the right of the stove was a window with a view of the cottonwoods that lined the creek. To the left of the sink was a back door leading to what she could see through the window was another shaded porch.

There was no decoration in the room, nothing on the walls, nothing to ameliorate the bleakness of the place and label it a home. The crackling fire Ethan had lit in the stone fireplace was the only spot of cheer in the room.

"Pa and I neatened up the house for you," Patch said.

"I can see that." Dirty dishes were stacked neatly in the sink. A heap of dirty clothes were layered neatly over a dining-room chair. A pile of dirt had been swept into the corner of the wooden-planked floor and hidden neatly behind the broom. "You did a fine job of neatening things up," she said with a perfectly straight face.

"We sure don't need you," Patch pointed out belligerently.

"But two hands make the load lighter, don't you agree?" Molly asked.

As she focused on the two closed doors on the opposite side of the room, it dawned on Molly that the house had only two bedrooms. Where were they all going to sleep? As Seth opened the door to what he described as "his" bedroom, the same thought seemed to occur to him.

As he stepped to the other door he said, "This is Patch's room." He looked at the three children who stood huddled before him, then back at the room. Daylight was fading fast. A decision had to be made. So he said, "Nessie can share with Patch."

"Durned if she will!" Patch retorted. She ran to stand protectively in her doorway. "I don't want that baby in here breaking my things, Pa."

"Look, Patch—" Seth cajoled.

"What about Whit?" Molly asked, trying to keep her growing apprehension out of her voice. "Where is he supposed to sleep?"

Seth was silent a moment. "I guess he can sleep in the barn until—"

"The barn!" Whit and Molly shouted together.

"Just until I get another room built."

"Absolutely not!" Molly said. "My son sleeps in the house."

"Where?" Seth asked pointedly, his eyes going first to one bedroom door, then to the next.

Molly folded her arms across her chest. "You and Whit can share one room. "Patch, Nessie, and I will share the other."

"The hell you will!" Seth retorted.

"That's telling her, Pa!" Patch chimed in.

Seth marched over to stand in front of Molly. "You're my wife. You'll sleep with me."

"And Whit will sleep where?" Molly asked.

"He can go stay with Ethan," Seth suggested, trying to rein his temper.

"And where, exactly, is that?"

Patch piped up, "Ethan has a cabin just beyond the trees. It's about a five-minute walk from here."

Molly met Seth's gaze and said flatly, "No. That's too far away. My son stays in the same house with me."

Seth shook his head in disgust. "Hellfire."

Molly put her hands on Nessie's ears. "Remember you are in the presence of children of tender years," she admonished.

"Hellfire and damnation!" he roared, at the end of his patience.

"That's telling her, Pa!" Patch chortled with glee.

Molly opened her mouth to give Seth a piece of her mind and let out a scream instead. Something furry had just rubbed against her leg! She jumped straight up in the air and threw her arms around Seth's neck. "There's something"—she gasped—"something's in here! Let me go! I have to save Nessie. Run, Whit!"

Nessie began to cry, and Whit backed toward the front door, eyes wide for the demon that had frightened his mother.

"Hellfire and damnation," Seth repeated. "Patch, get that raccoon out of here."

Molly gasped. "Raccoon?"

"Come on, Bandit. It's about time I put you to bed." Patch scooped the perfectly tame animal up into her arms. Its bushy, black-ringed tail promptly curled around her neck.

Molly watched in amazement as Patch disappeared into her room with the small, black-masked creature. She turned stunned brown eyes to Seth. "She keeps a raccoon in her bedroom?"

"It was sucking eggs in the henhouse," Seth explained.

"So she made a pet of it?" Molly asked incredulously.

"Can I see the raccoon?" Whit asked. "Do you think Patch will show it to me?"

"I want to see the raccoon," Nessie said.

Molly shook her head in disbelief.

Seth took command of the situation, ushering her two children into Patch's room. "The Gallaghers want to meet Bandit. Why don't you introduce him while I talk to their mother?"

Seth didn't really give his daughter any choice, leaving the room and shutting the door behind himself. He marched over to Molly and took her by the elbow, then walked her over and sat her down in the chair behind his desk. Then he went around the room lighting lanterns to stave off the dark.

"I think we better have a talk," he said. He took a spread-legged stance in front of the stone fireplace.

Molly sat stiffly on the swivel chair, her hands folded tightly in her lap.

"I hadn't counted on you having any children," Seth admitted. "If I'd known about them, I might have made some arrangements." He raised an accusing brow. "However, since I didn't, it appears we'll have to manage as best we can until Ethan and I can get another bedroom built."

Molly took a deep breath and let it out. "I won't be able to sleep unless I know my children are under the same roof as I am."

"So what do you suggest?"

"You and Whit can share your room. Patch, Nessie, and I will manage in Patch's room."

Seth shook his head no. "I don't think Patch will go for it."

"Patch is a child. She'll do as she's told," Molly said, exasperated.

"That's what you think," Seth muttered.

Molly folded her arms across her chest. "That's my final offer."

That was her *only* offer, Seth thought ruefully. He was more frustrated than he could remember being in a long time. He wanted Molly in *his* bedroom *alone*. It wasn't that he'd been that long without a woman. He'd seen Dora Deveraux not more than a week ago. But he wanted Molly. And his best estimate on building another bedroom onto the house was a good two to three weeks. He had no intention of waiting that long to bed the woman he had just made his wife.

So be it. There were other places they could use for a marriage bed. A stack of hay in the barn or a grassy spot beneath the cottonwoods would do just as well. He would find the time and choose the place. And make her his.

"Shall we go tell the children our decision?" he said.

"All right."

When Seth opened Patch's door, he wasn't sure what to expect. To his surprise, Nessie was sitting cross-legged on the foot of Patch's four-poster bed. Whit and Patch were hunkered down in the corner beside the raccoon's box.

"Patch. Whit."

The two of them stood and faced Seth. "Molly and I have talked it over, and we've come to a decision. Whit and I will share my room, while Molly and you girls will sleep in here."

"This is my bedroom!" Patch protested.

"Don't argue," Seth said in a no-nonsense voice.

"I won't stay here with them," Patch said. Before Seth realized what she was going to do, she slipped out the open bedroom window and was gone.

"Aren't you going after her?" Molly asked.

Seth shrugged. "She's just going to Ethan's place. She'll come home when she gets over being mad."

Molly put a hand on his arm and felt his muscles tense beneath her fingers. "I'm sorry for all the trouble. I'll make it up to you. I promise."

Seth sighed. "I'll go get the trunks." A few minutes later he was back. Molly marveled at his immense strength as he set two huge trunks down lightly on Patch's floor. Seth crossed to the door, then turned and said, "You come when you like, Whit. But once I'm in bed, the lanterns go out, and it'll be dark finding your way."

A second later Whit followed Seth out the door.

Molly was in awe of the way Seth had manipulated her son without forcing a confrontation. But then, as she was quickly learning, that was his way.

"I'm tired, Mama," Nessie said, yawning hugely.

"I'm not surprised, darling. It's time we all went to bed. If I'm not mistaken, morning comes very early in Montana."

Molly found a nightgown for Nessie and tucked her in, all the time wondering how Whit was getting along. She knew he would be mortified if she came and tucked him in, but all the same she missed the traditional bedtime ritual. How quickly their lives had changed!

Once Nessie was settled, Molly undressed and put on a warm flannel nightgown. She honestly tried to sleep, but the foreign night sounds she heard through the open window kept her awake. After shifting and tossing for an hour, she decided enough was enough. The house was quiet, and as stealthily as a thief, she stole from her bedroom out the front door to the porch. She had just sat down on the steps when a hand clamped down on her shoulder. Another hand quickly clamped over her mouth, cutting off her scream.

❋6❋

MOLLY FOUGHT LIKE A wildcat, writhing and clawing and kicking against the hands that held her. At last she began to tire, and the hissing sounds she had been hearing through a haze of terror took form as words.

"I'm not going to hurt you. Settle down before you wake up the whole house."

Molly shuddered. It was Seth. Good lord. She'd been fighting her own husband. Her knees felt like jelly. He helped her to sit as her legs collapsed under her, then joined her on the steps.

She covered her face with her hands and fought to hold back a sob of relief. "I thought you were—I don't know what I thought."

"I didn't want you to scream and wake everyone up," he said. "I'm sorry I frightened you. What are you doing out here?"

"I couldn't sleep." She met his concerned gaze and raised a sardonic brow. "I thought it might be relaxing to sit on the porch for a while, maybe take a walk."

"It's not safe for you out here alone."

"So I found out."

His smile flashed white in the moonlight. "Come on. I'll walk with you."

"That's not necessary. I—"

He took her hand and pulled her up and without looking back started off toward the pond. He stopped abruptly when he heard her yelp in pain. "What's wrong?"

Molly stood on one foot and lifted the other to expose a huge sticker.

"Don't you ever wear shoes?" he asked with amused exasperation.

"Believe me, I will from now on," she responded tartly.

"Here, let me help."

Before she could object, Seth lifted her into his arms and headed back to the porch. He set her down on the top step and sat down near her, but on the lowest of the three steps. Gently, he lifted her foot into his lap and turned it so he could see the burr in the moonlight. A moment later, he had it out.

"That wasn't so bad, was it?"

"Not nearly so bad as the beesting I got running in a field of clover when I was seven," she agreed.

He smiled again. "So going barefoot is an old habit with you?"

She laughed. "When I was little, my family had a farm in Ireland. I can still remember the feel of grass between my toes and the cool softness of new-plowed earth. Funny, I haven't thought about that in years."

His hand surrounded her foot. His thumbs pressed into her arch, causing a disturbingly erotic response.

Molly tried pulling her foot away, but he not only held on, he reached for the other one and rested them both on his thigh. "Your feet are like ice. Let me warm them up."

"No, really, I—" She gasped as he pulled up his long-john shirt and set her feet against his bare flesh. She instinctively curled her toes into the wiry black hair that covered his chest.

He chuckled and grabbed her toes to hold them still. "You're liable to tickle me to death if you aren't careful."

Instantly Molly stilled, abashed. In all the years she had been married to James, they had never done anything quite like this.

"So how does an Irish farmer's daughter become a Massachusetts lady?" he asked as he began to caress her feet again under the pretense of warming them.

Molly was slightly breathless as she answered, "Like so many others, my father brought his family to America, looking for the pot of gold at the end of the rainbow." She shivered from the touch of his hands and hid it with a shrug. "He found it—selling whiskey on the waterfront in Boston."

With her feet situated where they were, Molly felt Seth stiffen. She didn't know what she had said to offend him, but guessed, "Is it spirits in general you're against? Or those who sell them?"

He stopped what he was doing and searched her face a moment. "For married folks I guess we really don't know much about each other," he admitted ruefully. "As a doctor, I've seen too many hurt by bad whiskey—and good whiskey, for that matter. In Fort Benton there's a man named Drake Bassett who's selling the bad kind. He's hired Pike Hardesty to back him. I guess my neckhairs just naturally came up when you mentioned the subject."

He began stroking her feet again, his thumbs pressing into the tender flesh of her arches, his fingers caressing her toes. It was the most exquisite, the most sensual experience Molly had ever had. But it wasn't only the soft soles and arches of her feet that caught fire. With every titillating brush of his fingers there was a corresponding flare deep within her. She knew it had to be wrong to let him do this to her. They'd only just met, for heaven's sake! But he made it seem a mere kindness. And after all, it was only her *feet*.

"About this man selling bad whiskey," Molly said. "Why doesn't the law stop him?"

"There isn't any law to speak of in Fort Benton right now. Pike Hardesty shot the sheriff eight months ago—in a fair fight—and no one else has been willing to take his place. Pike has everyone too scared to make a move." He paused and added, "Except the Masked Marauder."

"Who?"

Seth grinned. "The Masked Marauder. Nobody knows for sure who he is or where he comes from. But he's on the side of the law, which makes him Bassett's enemy. Whenever someone is in trouble, the Marauder rides to the rescue, guns blazing."

"He sounds like a very brave man. Why do you suppose he keeps his identity a secret?"

"He has his reasons, I'm sure."

"I'll bet he's well known in town," Molly guessed. "And if people saw him, they'd recognize him."

"Maybe," Seth said. "And maybe he's nobody and wants to stay that way."

Molly angled her head so she could see Seth's face. His features had hardened, along with his voice. She caught her breath and said, "You know who he is."

Seth abruptly stopped rubbing her feet. "Nobody knows who he is." And to make sure she knew the conversation was at an end, he said, "Are you about ready for bed?"

With Molly sitting on the top step and Seth on the bottom, they were almost eye to eye. She reached up a hand in an unconscious action to smooth the hair from his brow, as she might have done with one of her children. He grabbed her wrist to stop her, then changed his mind. His hand dropped to his side.

Self-conscious now, Molly met his piercing gaze as she finished what she had started. His black hair was thick and surprisingly silky. She felt him shiver as her thumb brushed his temple. Then her hand fell away, and they sat there staring, totally aware of each other.

"I don't love you," Seth said in a quiet voice. "I'm not sure I can ever love another woman. But I want you—desire you—with every breath I take."

"Seth, I—"

He began murmuring words he might have used to soothe a frightened colt, because he could tell she was skittish. He had never suspected that simply caressing a woman's feet could arouse her. It had started innocently enough. But as her lids had lowered over her eyes, as her mouth fell open to draw shorter, panting breaths, and as her toes curled sensuously against his flesh, he had realized she desired him. His hands circled her ankles, and slowly, languidly, he began to draw her legs around his waist.

As she slid down onto his lap, his hands traveled up the velvety length of her legs, pushing her flannel nightgown up and out of his way so that her bare legs could surround him.

Moments later, she was sitting on his lap facing him, the heart of her snug against the heat of him. Her hands rested tentatively on his shoulders. Wide-eyed, she stared at him as his hands slowly curved around her naked buttocks and lifted her up and more fully onto him.

Molly couldn't breathe, the feelings were so exquisite. She could feel him. He was hard. And there was a throbbing heat. Molly laid her head on his shoulder but could not bring herself to do anything to further his seduction of her.

Seth framed her face with his hands. He forced her head back and looked deep into her eyes to see what she was feeling. And then his mouth closed over hers. It was a kiss of possession.

His voice when next he spoke was hoarse with need. "Come to bed with me, Molly."

Molly blushed scarlet. "But Whit—"

"We can go to the barn or—"

"I can't! I never intended—"

"I want you, Molly Gallagher Kendrick."

"I can't! James—"

"You're my wife now!" he said fiercely.

Seth's mouth was hard, and his embrace nearly crushed the breath out of her. His need, raw and honest, spurred her response. She thrust her fingers into his hair and opened her mouth under his. His tongue plundered, his hands ravished. He grasped her hips and pulled her hard against him. The cloth of his jeans abraded her tender skin, sending small tremors of pleasure rolling through her. Molly couldn't catch her breath; she felt out of control and couldn't catch up with the turbulent sensations roiling through her body.

"Mama?"

Seth and Molly broke apart like two teenagers caught spooning when the preacher comes to call. There was a mad scramble as Molly tried to scoot out of Seth's lap. He just grabbed her at the waist and stood. Her bare feet dropped to the ground, and the flannel nightgown surrounded her once more. He held her tight against him for an instant. Then with a monumental effort of will and a gusty sigh of resignation, he let her go.

A moment later, Nessie shoved open the front door.

"I couldn't find you, Mama," the little girl said. "I got scared."

Molly scooped the child up in her arms as she tried desperately to regain her equilibrium. Her breathing was still ragged, her pulse thrumming. "I couldn't sleep, Nessie. I just came out to sit for a while on the porch with Seth. Come on. Let's go back to bed."

As she stepped inside the house, she threw a quick look over her shoulder. Seth stood in the shadows, tall and forbidding. It had been a narrow escape. She might even now be lying beneath him on a bed of straw, had Nessie not interrupted them. And how would she have felt tomorrow morning if she had?

Wonderful! It would have been wonderful! a voice cried.

But the grieving widow was appalled at what she had nearly done. It was nearly dawn before Molly closed her eyes at last.

Seth didn't have much more success getting to sleep. He hadn't stayed on the porch much past Molly's departure, just long enough for his blood to slow and his body to settle down. When he finally returned to his bedroom, he found Molly's son sitting up in bed waiting for him.

The whites of the boy's eyes showed his fright. "Who's there?" Whit asked in a small voice.

"It's me, Seth."

He watched the boy visibly relax.

"I woke up," Whit said, "and no one was here."

Whit didn't admit he was scared. With what Seth had seen of the kid's pride, he knew the boy probably would have been appalled to know Seth even suspected such a thing.

"I just stepped out for some fresh air," Seth said. "You'd better get to sleep. We've got a hard day ahead of us tomorrow."

Whit lay back down, but his body was stiff. Seth pulled off his boots and socks, then skinned out of his jeans, leaving him in his long john underwear. Normally he would have removed that as well, but in deference to the boy, he left it on. He slipped under the covers and lay as stiff as the youth on the other side of the bed.

He closed his eyes, which made his other senses more acute. He heard Whit's indrawn breath and the muffled sound of what might have been a sob. And felt the small jerky movements of the body beside him. Seth wasn't sure what he could, or should, do. To notice at all would be to humiliate the boy.

Suddenly, Whit rolled over and pulled the pillow hard against his mouth. His legs drew up into his stomach. Seth felt Whit's desolation; he couldn't ignore it.

"I lost my father when I was only a little older than you," he began. "I was fifteen. My mother died when I was born. Pa always told me if I wanted to see her, I could look in the mirror, because I had her eyes."

The sobbing stopped abruptly, and the small form on the other side of the bed was still. Seth kept on talking.

"Pa and me, we had a small place southwest of San Antonio with a few head of cattle. Texas had been annexed by the States, and Mexico decided to make an issue of it. I wanted to join the army and fight Mexicans. Pa absolutely forbade it."

Seth paused, remembering the ferocious argument they'd had, the harsh words that had been spoken.

A small voice from the other side of the bed said, "I wanted to go to sea, to be a whaler, like my pa. I left a note when I ran away, but Mother came and made me get off the ship. She brought me here to keep me away from the sea."

Seth smiled in the darkness. That explained why Molly Gallagher had accepted his offer of marriage so promptly. "That story sounds a lot like mine," he said.

"One night, I took my hunting rifle and a bag of food and set out to enlist in the army. I didn't get far before I ran into a band of cut-throat Mexican outlaws. Those bandidos had my rifle and my horse, and I was saying my final prayers when my father showed up to fetch me home.

"I'd never been so glad to see anyone in my life. He'd been a Texas Ranger, my pa, and he knew how to fight bandidos. When the shooting stopped, what Mexicans weren't dead had turned tail and run. But my pa had been mortally wounded. He died on the trip back home."

Seth didn't say that he'd always blamed himself for his father's death. Or that remorse over that one incident had shaped a great deal of his life. "My pa was one brave hombre," he murmured.

"I saw my da fight once on the waterfront," Whit said in a wistful voice. "He was a brave man too. I want to grow up to be just like him."

"That's a good goal, Whit. A man can't wish for more than to have his son grow up following in his footsteps."

Only Whit's father was dead. And the only footsteps for Whit to follow would be Seth's. Suddenly, the immensity of what he had done, the responsibility he had accepted, struck Seth. Would the boy see who he really was? Or would he only see the man Seth must pretend to be?

"I miss Da," Whit admitted in a choked voice.

"You always will," Seth said. It wasn't much, as comfort went, but it was all he could offer. "It'll get easier as time goes on. You'll always have your memories of him, of the good times you had together. They'll stay with you the rest of your life."

"Da used to tuck me in at night."

Seth held his breath. Was Whit asking him to do that? Would he let him? Not if Seth asked. The boy had too much pride for that. Seth didn't say what he was going to do, didn't ask permission that the boy couldn't, or wouldn't, give. He just sat up and leaned over and tucked the covers firmly around the boy, up one side, and down the other.

"You forgot my toes."

Without a word, Seth leaned down and tucked the blankets firmly under Whit's long, narrow feet. Then he lay back down and turned on his side away from the boy. "Better get to sleep. Dawn comes early."

Whit closed his eyes, unaware of how he had found solace, only knowing he had. *Almost as good as Da,* he thought as he drifted off to sleep.

When Seth walked into the kitchen the next morning, Molly greeted him with a smile that took his breath away. He remembered the night past, the taste of her, the feel of her lips. He wanted to kiss her good morning, to start the day with the feminine softness of her in his arms. But she had turned back to the stove the instant she saw him, sending a message loud and clear without saying a word.

She was wearing simple clothes this morning—a white shirtwaist and dark brown broadcloth skirt, covered by a faded red apron that he recognized as one from the sideboard—that made her seem more approachable. But though she was apparently not angry over what had happened last night, she was keeping her distance.

When he started to sit down at the kitchen table, she asked, "Aren't you going to shave?"

Seth felt the day's growth of whiskers. It was a small sacrifice. "Sure. I'll be out back."

But as he started out the door, she handed him a bowl of warm water. "For shaving," she said.

Seth stared down at the bowl and then back up at Molly. "Thanks," he said as he took it from her. He would never have heated water for himself, but as he held a warm-water-soaked cloth to his face to soften his beard, he realized there were a lot of things about having a woman in the house that he'd forgotten about.

When he came back inside, Molly smiled at him and waved him to the table. "Have a seat. The coffee's nearly ready. I had to scrub the pot before I could start. There must have been three days' worth of grounds in it."

Seth opened his mouth to say it took three days' worth of grounds to make a decent cup of coffee but snapped it shut again. It was another of the changes he'd have to accept.

But there were compensations, he thought as he watched his wife busy herself at the stove. Her absent-minded humming made a nice accompaniment to the sounds of coffee perking and the sizzle of frying bacon. He loved to watch her move, enjoying the feminine grace of each gesture.

"What's that I smell?" Seth asked, sniffing the air. "Are you baking something?"

"You must mean the biscuits," Molly replied. "I found some flour and I thought—you don't mind, do you?" She lifted the lid on the Dutch oven on top of the stove. Seth got a glimpse of the most beautiful, fluffy golden-brown biscuits he'd ever seen in his life.

At that moment, Patch appeared in the kitchen doorway and announced, "I always make Pa's breakfast. And he hates biscuits."

Seth couldn't deny that he hated Patch's biscuits. They were hard as shoe leather and half as tasty. His mouth watered as Molly served up a dozen aromatic biscuits into a straw basket and set them on the table in front of him. He wanted one of those biscuits so bad, he could already taste it, loaded down with butter and blackberry jam. But eating one of those biscuits was going to be a diplomatic nightmare, after the way he'd disdained Patch's efforts.

"I . . . uh . . . think I ought to have one just to be polite," he said to Patch, grabbing one from the basket.

"That's not necessary," Molly said, lifting it right out of his hands and setting it back in the pile. "I'll toast some bread for you instead."

Seth swore under his breath. "No, really," he said, picking up another biscuit. "I don't want to put you to any extra trouble. Biscuits'll be just fine."

This time Patch took the biscuit out of his hands. "You know you can't abide these things, Pa."

Patch sat down to the right of her father and began to slather the biscuit with butter.

"What can I get for you to drink with that?" Molly asked Patch.

"A cup of coffee."

Seeing Molly's surprise, Seth explained, "We don't have a milk cow." He found himself adding, "But there's no reason why we couldn't get one."

"Good. Then I could make some buttermilk," Molly said.

Seth shuddered at the thought. He couldn't think of a worse-tasting thing to swallow, but he kept his mouth shut and counted his blessings—her biscuits—instead.

"Look what I found out back." Ethan stood in the kitchen doorway holding Nessie. The little girl was still dressed in her nightgown and curled up like a teddy bear in his arms.

"Can't that baby even walk by herself?" Patch snapped. Her chin jutted in response to Ethan's frown of disapproval. "Durned Gallaghers," she muttered. "Troublemakers. All of them."

"Patch," Seth warned. "Watch what you say."

Ignoring the hostile undercurrents in the room, Ethan asked, "Is breakfast ready? Something sure smells good." He looked around the table and saw that there were only five chairs—the swivel desk chair had been pulled up to the table. Clearly, Molly had made accommodations for her children but hadn't been expecting him.

Seth tensed, unsure whether Ethan's presence at the table would result in another confrontation with Molly, like the one they'd had the previous day over sleeping arrangements.

"Ethan always has breakfast and supper with us," Seth said cautiously. "We're usually out working at noon, so we take something along to eat while we're gone."

"That's fine," Molly replied, equally cautiously. "I'll be sure to set an extra plate from now on."

Ethan set Nessie down in one of the three empty chairs at the table. But the child was too small for the chair. Her chin barely reached the edge of the table.

Seth reacted first. He simply leaned over and lifted Nessie into his lap. As though it were the most normal thing in the world, the little girl settled back against his chest and accepted the biscuit he handed to her. "Go ahead and sit down, Ethan," Seth said. "There's room now for you at the table."

Patch stared at Nessie in disbelief.

So did Molly.

Within moments, Molly turned back to the stove; Patch turned purple. She jumped up and said, "Pa, I told you that baby would be a bother."

"She's no bother," Seth replied as he met Patch's troubled blue eyes. "She hardly weighs a thing."

Patch struggled for words, but nothing came. Her lips thinned as she watched her father dandling the Gallagher girl on his knee. "I've got to go feed my animals," she said at last.

Seth looked at the nearly untouched plate of food sitting before his daughter. "You didn't finish your breakfast."

"I'm not hungry." Patch turned and shoved her way past Whit, headed for her bedroom.

Seth wondered how long Whit had been standing in the doorway like that. "Come in and sit down, Whit."

"I'd rather not," he retorted.

Apparently, in the bright light of day, their bedtime talk was forgotten.

"It's a long time betwixt breakfast and supper," Seth said. "We'll be working hard. You'll need some vittles to make it through the day."

"I'm not hungry," he insisted, eyeing his mother's biscuits with the look of a starving coyote.

"Suit yourself," Seth said with an apparently careless shrug. But a muscle in his jaw worked as he gritted his teeth against saying something provoking that he would regret later.

The tension eased some when Molly suggested, "I'll pack a few biscuits for you, Whit. You can eat them later when you're feeling hungry."

"That's not a bad idea," Ethan said as he slathered blackberry jam on a second biscuit. "I wouldn't mind having a few extra of these myself for a midmorning snack."

Seth sighed heavily. Not only was he being denied Molly's biscuits at breakfast, he was going to have to watch Whit and Ethan enjoy them later in the day. He threw down his fork and said, "I've got work to do. The sooner I get started cutting down logs to build that extra bedroom, the sooner it'll be finished."

Seth handed Nessie to Molly on his way past. At the kitchen door he turned and said, "Meet me out in the barn when you're done, Ethan. Bring Whit with you. And tell Patch I expect her to work inside today with Molly."

Molly took one look at her son's rebellious face, handed Nessie to Ethan, wrapped several biscuits in a cloth napkin, and started out the door after Seth. She was breathless by the time she caught up to him in the barn. He was leaning back against a stall, his spread legs braced out in front of him, the heels of his hands pressed hard against his eyes.

"Seth?"

His hands came down immediately and rested in balled fists on his thighs; his gray eyes looked bleak. Molly walked up to him and stood between his outspread legs. "I'm sure things will get easier as we go along."

Seth snorted. "They couldn't get much worse."

"Perhaps not," Molly agreed with the beginning of a smile. She laid a hand on one of his fists, and it unfolded and his fingers entwined with hers. She brought his hand up and drew his knuckles across her cheek. "Thank you for being so patient with Whit."

"He doesn't make it easy," he grumbled.

"I know." She brought his hand down from her face and opened his fingers, setting the napkin in his palm.

"What's this?"

She grinned. "Biscuits. For someone who doesn't like them, you seemed awfully anxious to have one."

"I was. I am." He grinned wryly. "Thanks." He leaned over and quickly kissed her on the mouth.

Startled, Molly's hand came up to caress the dampness on her lips. She looked up into his eyes and saw the hunger there—and not for biscuits, either.

Slowly, carefully, Seth curled his hand around her nape and drew her face up to his. Slowly, gently, he laid his mouth on hers, feeling the softness of her lips under his.

Molly felt her body tensing, felt the slow curl of desire wind its way upward. She parted her lips slightly and felt him do the same. She opened her mouth wider, and—

"Pa! Where are you?"

Seth snapped upright as though a bullet had hit him. He looked down at himself, and then up at Molly. There wasn't any hiding how his body had reacted to her. And his daughter would be here any second.

Molly hid her trembling hands in the apron. She turned her back to him, letting the width of her skirt over several petticoats conceal Seth's problem. Moments later, Patch came hurtling around the corner and into the stall.

"I don't want to stay in the house," she said to her father. "I want to work with you."

Seth put a hand on Molly's shoulder. "I want you to help Molly in the house."

"But you need me," Patch protested.

"Ethan and I will manage. And I've got Whit to help."

"Whit Gallagher doesn't know a blamed thing about anything."

"He will by the end of the day," Seth said, cutting her off. He turned his back on her to take down two axes and several wood saws that hung on the barn wall.

Patch was just getting warmed up. "Why, that boy couldn't tell skunks from housecats! He's grass-green and brain-shy. He'll be no good to you at all, Pa. Why, he's a scatter-brained lumpkin, a want-wit who—"

Seth took one look at Molly's shocked face and realized maybe he'd been too tolerant of Patch's tirades in the past. "Go back to the house, Patch," he said firmly.

"But, Pa—"

He ignored the desperation in her blue eyes and said, "I want you to spend the day with Molly and watch what she does. It's time you stopped acting like some tomboy and started acting like a lady. I'll see you at supper, and you can tell me what you've learned."

Molly thought for sure Patch was going to argue. Instead, the girl hung her head and said, "All right, Pa. I'll see you at supper." She ran out of the barn as abruptly as she had entered it.

Molly turned to Seth and said, "She's very attached to you. Maybe it isn't a good idea to change everything all at once."

"I want her to be a lady. A lady doesn't spend her day chopping down trees." He hesitated, then gave Molly a quick, hard kiss on the mouth. A moment later, he stepped into the sunshine carrying an assortment of lumbering tools.

Molly stood in the barn, which smelled of hay and horses, and stared at her husband's retreating figure. She didn't understand her strong attraction to him. And she couldn't help feeling guilty for it. James had been everything to her. She could never love a man the way she had loved him. So what, exactly, was it that she felt for Seth Kendrick? Molly was very afraid it was something much less honorable, much more visceral. What kind of woman did that make her? A woman very much alive, who must learn how to survive in new and very different circumstances.

One of the most difficult of those was being a stepmother to Patch Kendrick. The most Molly realistically hoped for was some sort of truce between herself and Seth's daughter. Seth seemed to think Patch would accept her banishment to the house. Molly wasn't so sure. Patch's head had been bowed when she accepted her father's will, but her lips had been pressed flat and her arms had been rigid at her sides.

Was it any wonder Molly had the feeling Patch wasn't going to be anywhere near as agreeable as her father thought?

As Molly crossed to the house, she passed Ethan and Whit on their way to join Seth. Ethan had a hand on Whit's shoulder and was speaking in a voice too soft for Molly to hear. Whit was listening so intently, he didn't even see her as they passed each other. Molly felt suddenly bereft. James had been gone to sea so much that she had often had Whit to herself. It appeared those days were gone. Molly knew she could not cling to the past. She must allow Whit to change and grow, and she must change and grow as well.

But that brief, wrenching moment when it felt as if she were losing Whit gave her tremendous insight into what Patch must be feeling. And made her much more tolerant than she might have been of the situation she found when she arrived in the kitchen.

7

Molly's daughter was sitting cross-legged on the kitchen table with the raccoon in her lap, while Patch fed it scrambled eggs from her fingertips. Molly's immediate fear was that the wild animal would bite Nessie. But as she watched, her heart in her throat, she realized the raccoon was not the only threat. Sitting beside Patch was a huge wolflike creature. It turned its head to stare at her. Though it made no sound, it bared ferocious teeth at her, freezing her where she stood.

"Bandit here never bites unless he gets scared," Patch said as she fed the raccoon a bit of egg. "Now Maverick, my dog—he used to be real mean." She absently patted the wolflike creature on the head. "That's because he belonged to this man in town who was real mean to him. I talked to Maverick and asked him if he wanted to come home with me. He said he did, and he's lived here ever since."

"Dogs can't talk," Nessie said.

"You just have to know how to listen," Patch explained. "Like Bandit here. He just said he's had enough and he's ready for a nap."

Molly noticed the raccoon had curled up into a ball in Nessie's lap.

Patch stood and scooped the furry animal into her arms. "It's time to put Bandit to bed." As she rose, she saw Molly, who was still frozen in the doorway. "Don't move," Patch warned, "or she'll attack."

Molly's eyes were riveted on the dog Maverick, so she was aware when the hackles of fur rose on its neck. It growled low in its throat.

Patch quickly dropped the raccoon back into a delighted Nessie's lap and turned to face Molly. "She's right behind you in the window, and her tail is twitching, so it isn't going to be long now. I'll to try to get to her before she leaps, so stay perfectly still."

Molly's mind raced to assimilate what Patch had told her. In the window? *Behind her?* The eerie scream Molly heard was almost human and made the hairs stand straight up all over her body.

Patch shoved Molly aside as she intercepted the yellow blur that launched itself from the window. Molly screamed as Patch fell, entwined with the animal that had attacked her. The two of them—Patch and a golden brown beast with teeth and claws—went tumbling over and over on the floor. Horrified, Molly screamed at the top of her lungs, "Seth!"

It was over as quickly as it had begun. Patch was sitting on the floor with what looked like a lion stretched out on its back in front of her, its paws dangling in the air. Patch grinned up at Molly while she scratched the great cat's stomach. "Her name is Rebel. Somebody shot her mother. I raised her myself. She likes to sneak up behind you and try to surprise you."

Molly was still gasping for air, her jaw gaping, her eyes wide with fright that had not yet turned to relief, when Seth arrived at the door on the run. He was followed closely by Whit, who was trailed by Ethan. Molly flew into Seth's arms and buried her face against his chest.

"What happened?" Seth demanded of Patch as his arms tightened around his terrified, trembling wife.

"I think Rebel scared her," Patch said innocently.

Molly tore herself from Seth's arms, her fear rapidly evolving into fury. "You could have warned me!" she hissed at Patch. "You could have simply told me that . . . that . . . clawed monster is as tame as a tabby cat. Instead, you scared the wits out of me!"

"Now, Molly," Seth said. "I don't think Patch intended—"

"Oh, she intended it, all right," Molly retorted.

"Is that true, Patch?" Seth asked.

A crocodile tear appeared in Patch's left eye and rolled down her cheek. Her lower lip stuck out like a buggy seat. "I swear I didn't do it on purpose, Pa. Don't you believe me?"

"Of course I do," he said.

Patch shot Molly a sideways look of triumph beneath lowered lashes.

The girl was a formidable foe, Molly realized. "Nevertheless," Molly said through tight jaws, "that cat—"

"Mountain lion," Seth corrected.

"That *cat*," Molly repeated, "has no business being in my kitchen." By now, Molly's fists were perched on her hips, and her legs were spread wide in an unmistakably militant pose.

Discretion was the better part of valor, Seth decided. "Maybe you'd better take Rebel outside, Patch." He realized the dog-wolf was also in the room. "And Maverick too."

"And keep them out," Molly said.

"Now, Molly," Seth cajoled. "Patch's animals—"

"Belong outside," Molly said firmly. "Not in the house."

"But—"

"Do you want her to be a lady or not?" Molly demanded.

The expression on Seth's face was ludicrous. He had been well and truly hoisted by his own petard. Molly wanted to laugh but forced down the impulse, afraid it would come out sounding as hysterical as she felt. She refused to look at Patch, taking no chances that the girl's wiles would work on her as well.

Patch rose from the floor with a grace and dignity that Molly thought many a lady might yearn to emulate. She put one hand on Rebel's yellow fur and another on the silver gray hackles that rimmed Maverick's back. Ethan held the kitchen door wide as Patch made an exit worthy of a queen.

Molly shook her head in disbelieving admiration.

"I guess I should have warned you about Patch's pets," Seth said.

"Are there any more surprises I should know about?"

"If by surprises you mean animals, there are a few more— Outlaw, Tramp, and Hermit come to mind."

"Don't keep me in suspense. What are we talking about here?"

Seth looked sheepish. "A bear cub, a crow, and a snake."

"Maybe you should have been a vet."

Seth smiled, relieved to see that Molly had a sense of humor. "I have been known to treat the occasional four-footed patient. In fact, most of Patch's animals have come to her through some kind of tragedy. In most cases they would have died if she hadn't adopted them. Except for the raccoon, Bandit. He was eating my eggs."

Molly turned to where Nessie still sat on the table with the satiated raccoon in her lap. "I hate to be the one to tell you this, but he's still at it."

Seth grinned. "Yeah, but I get first crack at them."

Molly laughed and shooed Seth toward the door. "Go back to work. Now that I know what to expect, I'll be fine."

He hesitated. "Patch—"

"Don't worry about Patch. We'll be fine."

When the ragtag girl made a reluctant reappearance at the kitchen door, Molly said, "I want to do some unpacking today, and a little cleaning. I could use your help."

"Do I have any choice?" Patch asked, glancing up at her father.

"No," he said.

She shrugged. "Fine. Tell me what to do."

Seth glanced quickly from Molly to Patch. "Guess I'd better get back to work." He beat a hasty retreat with Ethan and Whit.

All afternoon, Patch was a model of cooperation. But Molly didn't underestimate Seth's daughter. She knew the clever child hadn't pulled the last rabbit—or should she say wolf, raccoon, or mountain lion—from her hat. But Molly was determined to make a lady of Patch Kendrick if it was the last thing she ever did. With the array of wild animals at Patch's disposal, she realized it very well might be.

She and Patch worked side by side through the afternoon. Molly cleaned and straightened, and it was helpful to be able to ask Patch whether something belonged to Seth or to her, or had somehow found its way into the house through one of its animal inhabitants.

Molly removed the medicines from the sideboard and carefully restacked them in a box beside Seth's desk in the corner, where Nessie would not be able to get to them. Then she placed her mother's rose-patterned china on the upper shelves of the sideboard. The painting of James's ship in the Arctic sea she hung above the fireplace. With just those small changes, the room looked more like a home.

However, it was the two very personal items she had brought to Montana that fascinated Patch.

"What is that?" Patch asked, pointing to an ivory-colored object.

"It's a walrus tusk, carved by the Esquimaux to look like a whale," Molly said. A spout of water shot from the whale's blow-hole, and the impressive width of its tail flukes curled up behind it. It didn't surprise Molly that Patch didn't ask, simply reached out and caressed the carving.

"It's so smooth! And it feels cool, like maybe there's ice inside or something."

"You know, I've always thought the same thing. But I felt a little silly saying it."

Patch looked suspiciously at Molly. It was clear that she didn't want to be on the same side as her stepmother regarding anything.

Molly put the whale on the chest in her bedroom, where she could see it each morning when she awoke. She would transfer it into Seth's room when she moved there. She didn't want to think about how soon that might be.

But it was the ship in the bottle that sent Patch into raptures. Molly placed the bottle on one side of the pine mantel above the fireplace.

"Garn!" Patch said. "Just look at that! Garn! How did that ship get inside there?"

"You'll have to ask Whit," Molly said with a smile. "He made this with his father."

That option obviously didn't appeal to Patch. "Don't you know?"

Molly shook her head. "James wouldn't let me watch. He said it's a sailor's secret. He taught Whit because he expected him to become a sailor."

"Durn. I sure would like to see how that's done."

"You'll have to ask Whit," Molly repeated.

Although Molly had definite plans for what she could do to the house to make it more of a home, she was less certain what steps she ought to take to make Patch more of a lady. Two obvious things came to mind. First, the girl needed a bath. Second, she needed to be dressed in some feminine clothing.

But when Molly suggested the idea of a bath to Patch, she got the quick response, "Don't need one." And when she asked where Patch's dresses were, so she might iron one for her, Patch said, "Don't have any."

Molly considered trying to manhandle Patch into a tub or getting her to stand still while she was measured for a dress. *I'd probably come off better tangling with the mountain lion*, she thought.

But throughout the afternoon, Molly put her mind to ways she could accomplish those first two goals. She felt like a general, planning a major campaign. It took the better part of the afternoon to devise her strategy. She put her plan into action that evening after supper.

While everyone was eating dessert, she put several kettles of water on the stove to heat.

"What are you cooking now?" Seth asked, imagining something as wonderful as the dried-apple pie he was finishing.

"Nothing. I'm heating water for Patch's bath."

"Don't need a bath," Patch said, looking warily at Molly.

"When was the last time you had one? A bath, I mean."

Patch frowned. "Don't remember."

"Then it's time for another one," Molly said firmly. She had found a large wooden tub outside the back door that looked like it doubled as a bathtub and had cleaned it earlier in the day. It was situated now in the corner by the stove. She began to fill it with warm water.

"I ain't taking a bath. You can't make me," Patch said to Molly.

"I don't plan to try," Molly replied. "I expect your father to do the honors."

Patch and Seth spoke at the same time. "What?"

"Your father can do for you whatever needs done. All I'm concerned about is that you get clean. Later, I need to take your measurements so I can make a dress for you. Come on, Whit, Nessie—let's go for a walk."

Ethan grinned at Seth and said, "Much as I'd love to stick around and see the fireworks, I think I'll join them."

A moment later, the house was empty except for Patch and Seth.

"Are you going to let her get away with this, Pa?" she demanded.

Seth tugged one of Patch's ears forward, revealing the grime there. Then he took her chin in his hand and angled her face one way and then the other. With his thumb he brushed at a stubborn smudge on her cheek. He took her hands and held them out in his. Molly had insisted Patch wash her hands before supper, but dirt was still crusted under her broken fingernails.

"She's got a point, Patch," he said at last. "You do need a bath."

"I ain't gonna do it, Pa."

Seth's eyes narrowed. "I say you are. Now take off your clothes and get into that tub without any more of this nonsense."

The blood bleached from Patch's face as it became clear her father had no intention of leaving the room. "I won't," she rasped. "And you can't make me."

If it had only been the two of them, Seth might have let it slide. But he shuddered at the thought of Molly's reaction if he couldn't get his daughter to bathe. He remained unyielding. "Get in the tub, Patch."

She glared at him, defiant. He rose from his chair and started toward her. She jumped up and took several steps backward until her legs came up against the tub. Staring at him the whole time, she pulled off her boots and socks and then stepped, fully clothed, into the tub. Before he could get to her, she sat down.

"There. I'm in the tub."

Seth was furious—not only at the fact that she'd thwarted him but at the way she'd chosen to do it. He didn't think, just reacted. An instant later he was beside the tub and had pulled Patch to her feet. One jerk downward in front sent buttons pinging across the wooden floor. A second jerk at the collar in back, and he had the shirt off her. Her arms immediately curled around her chest.

The only sounds were Seth's grunt as he wrapped an arm around her waist and hauled her into the air, and Patch's yelp of dismay as he yanked both trousers and drawers down and off over her kicking feet. Her pants landed on the floor at the same time he dumped her back into the tub with a resounding splash.

Patch moaned and immediately curled in on herself. Her head bowed as she drew her knees up to her chest and surrounded them with her arms.

"Now wash yourself," he commanded.

"Go away," she mumbled against her knees.

Seth didn't hear the plea in her tone, only the words of defiance. "By God, if you won't bathe yourself, I'll do it for you!"

Patch's head snapped up, and her panicked eyes sought his. "No! Pa! Please!"

He had already gone down on one knee and grabbed the wash-cloth Molly had left on the side of the tub. Grasping Patch by the wrist, he pulled her arm up over her head so he could wash under it. And stared, stunned at what he found.

Hair.

Because he was holding her arm up out of the way, he could see what else she had been hiding in that protective fetal position.

Budding breasts.

Patch's face flushed an agonized red, and she moaned again.

Seth let go of Patch's hand, which she immediately used to hug her knees tight against her breasts. He sat back on his haunches and exhaled a deep breath. "I had no idea, Patch," he said. "I knew you were becoming a woman. I just—I didn't realize you had . . . It's nothing to be ashamed of," he said.

"Please don't talk about it," she said, mortified.

"Look, Patch, I'm a doctor. I see bodies all the time. I—"

"Pa!" she wailed. "Go awaaaaay!"

Seth didn't know what to do. He wanted to stay and talk to her, but he was all too aware that her father was the last person she wanted there. "Be sure to wash your hair," he said, and rose and left the room.

Seth didn't know he was looking for Molly until he saw her with the children and Ethan coming toward him. When he met up with them, he said to Ethan, "Why don't you take Whit and Nessie and show them that spot down by the pond where the frogs congregate and sing?"

Ethan raised a brow in speculation. One look at the taut lines around Seth's eyes and mouth told him there was trouble. "Sure, Seth." He headed Molly's children toward the pond and said, "You kids have a real treat in store for you."

Seth started walking beside Molly back in the direction of the house.

Sensing his distress, she asked, "What's wrong?"

Seth stopped under a cottonwood and stared out toward the mountains. He looked for words to explain what had happened that wouldn't make him sound as bad as he felt. "It's Patch," he said at last. "She wouldn't take her clothes off and get in the tub. That is, she got in the tub with her clothes on. I lost my temper and stripped her down and—"

"And what?"

"She's got breasts!" he blurted.

Molly put her hand before her mouth and coughed so Seth wouldn't see her smile. "That explains her resistance to a bath. She's probably been hiding the fact that she's growing up from you for some time. A bath would have given her away."

"I acted like a fool and an idiot."

"None of us is perfect," Molly said with a teasing smile.

Seth groaned. "What can I do now?"

"Just keep doing the best you can." She thought for a moment and asked, "Do you think she'll take the bath?"

"She'd better."

"Then I think the best thing is to leave her alone long enough for her to finish in private. Then you act as though this never happened."

Seth looked relieved. "I can do that?"

Molly grinned. "I don't see why not. Next time she takes a bath, we can arrange for her to have the privacy a young lady needs. I'll have plenty of time when I take the measurements for her dress to find out if there are other questions Patch needs to ask or have answered."

Seth felt better, but he couldn't have said why. Nothing had changed. He had still embarrassed his daughter. She still had those budding breasts. Only somehow, Molly had made everything all right.

But over the next several days, it was clear the battle lines had been drawn. Molly was determined to introduce Patch to the womanly arts; Patch was equally determined to thwart her; Seth was caught in the middle.

To Molly's chagrin, Whit was being equally troublesome to Seth. Seth held his ground; she was caught in the middle.

Molly wasn't sure what she could do to make them a family, but she was determined not to give up or give in.

About a week after their arrival, Molly decided that things were enough under control in the house that she could surprise Seth, Ethan, and Whit with a picnic lunch. She made fried chicken and mashed potatoes and packed it up in a basket. Just before noon, she and Nessie and Patch set out for the stand of pines where the men were working.

When she arrived, Ethan was cutting limbs off a downed tree, but Seth and Whit were nowhere to be seen.

"Where's Seth?"

"He's farther up the mountain, chopping down another tree."

"Is Whit with him?"

"I suppose so."

That sounded too uncertain for Molly's peace of mind. She left Nessie and Patch in Ethan's care and went searching for Seth and her son.

When she saw Seth, she just stopped and stared. He had taken off his shirt, and dappled sunlight danced on the muscle and sinew in his shoulders and back. A trickle of sweat started down the crease in his back and eventually dampened the cloth at his waist. The sculpted beauty was marred by two large scars, one on his right shoulder and one on his lower back, just above the waist of his pants. She watched in awe as he lifted the heavy ax gracefully over his head. The echoing sound of the ax hitting wood brought her to her senses. She realized Whit wasn't with him.

There were reasons why her son might have left here momentarily. There was no reason to panic, so she didn't.

"Hello," she called.

When Seth turned, she caught her breath. He was truly a magnificent man. A smile flashed white in his tanned face. She smiled back and asked, "Where's Whit?"

Seth leaned against his ax and mopped his forehead with a red kerchief that had been hanging out of his back pocket. "Don't know," he admitted. "He decided he was tired, so he quit. He left here a while ago."

"Where was he going?"

"He didn't say."

Molly's heart began to pound. "You just let him leave?" She looked out at the dark expanse of jack pine and juniper, evergreens and leafy birch trees. "Why aren't you out looking for him?"

"He knows where I am," Seth said.

"But he may be lost. There are Indians out there, and wild animals and—"

Seth drew an arm-waving Molly into his embrace and held her there. "Molly," he said, trying to cut her off.

"—and buffalo and mountain lions and—"

"Molly."

"—and desperados and—"

Seth shut her up with his mouth. She had kept her distance from him ever since that night a week ago on the front porch. He had watched her, and wanted her, every moment of every day. But there had never been a time when their children were not around. Now that he had her in his arms, he took full advantage of whatever moments of privacy they might have.

He pulled her up snug against him, fitting himself in the cradle of her thighs. He could feel her breasts against his chest through the thin cotton material of her dress. He grunted his disapproval when he discovered her waist was corseted. One hand held her head so she couldn't escape his kisses, and he plundered her mouth, taking what he needed.

Molly was overwhelmed by the astonishing heat of his passion. Hands that had come up to push him away, roamed his sweat-slick shoulders instead, feeling the muscle beneath smooth skin. When his tongue slid along the edge of her lips and she opened her mouth to protest, he thrust inside. He compelled a response from her, and her body gave what her heart would have withheld.

His mouth left hers to seek the flesh of her neck. She gasped at the curl of desire she felt as he sucked on tender skin. She hid her face against the muscle at his shoulder and accidentally tasted the salt on his skin. As his ardor increased, so did hers, and when he nipped her shoulder, she bit him back. And discovered it was pleasure, not pain she had caused.

With some sixth sense necessary to the frontier, Seth realized they were being watched. He abruptly pushed Molly behind him to protect her.

Molly gasped when she saw the look on her son's face.

Whit turned and ran. She started to go after him, but Seth stopped her.

"Let him go."

"I have to talk to him!"

"What can you say that he doesn't already know?" Seth asked.

Molly stood apart from Seth, refusing to let him draw her back into his arms. "I don't know," she said. "But for him to see us . . ."

Seth's lips flattened. "What he saw was a husband kissing his wife. There's nothing wrong with that."

But they both knew there had been more to it than that. It had not been a matter of simple kisses. There had been raw, explosive passion between them. And James Gallagher had been dead for less than a year.

"I brought a picnic," Molly said. "I'll leave it for you and Ethan . . . and Whit. I'm feeling tired all of a sudden. I don't think I'll stay to eat with you."

She turned and ran. Molly was breathless when she got back to the spot where Ethan was working. She grabbed Nessie and, with a quick excuse about the little girl's nap time approaching, headed back to the house.

Molly lay down on Patch's bed with Nessie and read her daughter a fairy tale—one with a happy ending. As the little girl drifted off to sleep, Molly tried to make some sense of her confused emotions.

She couldn't deny her attraction to Seth. It would be foolish to try. Molly simply didn't understand how it was possible to feel so passionate in another man's arms when she was still grieving for James. Only, when she was in Seth's arms, she didn't think about James. Something magic happened. And the only face she saw, the only man she wanted, was Seth. She needed time to understand her feelings. But she was very much afraid Seth wasn't going to give it to her.

When Molly woke up, Nessie was gone. Something else had taken her place.

Molly stared wide-eyed at the snake on the pillow beside her and forced herself not to scream. She wouldn't give Patch the satisfaction. The rest of Patch's menagerie, once she had become acquainted with them, had all turned out to be harmless. Surely her snake—what was its name?—wasn't poisonous. Molly looked at the head to see whether it formed the triangle Seth had warned her meant a snake was venomous. It didn't look deadly. But better safe than sorry. She would just lie still. Patch would soon tire of waiting for her terrified reaction and come and collect her pet.

Only Seth showed up first.

"Don't move," he said.

His caution surprised Molly. Was he afraid of snakes in general? Or just this particular snake? He crossed slowly to the window and pushed it all the way open. She lay perfectly still as he reached for the broom standing in the corner. He slipped the wooden handle under the dark brown snake, which opened its mouth, revealing sharp fangs in a huge white expanse. In one continuous movement, Seth flipped the snake off the pillow and out the window, where it slithered away.

Seth pulled Molly up into a hard embrace. "Are you all right? You weren't bitten?"

"No. I—I thought it belonged to Patch."

Seth laughed shakily and hugged her tighter. "Oh no, my little tenderfoot. That was a cottonmouth."

"Venomous?"

"Very."

"How did it get in here?"

Seth nodded his head toward the open window. "Most likely through the window. Mostly the cottonmouths stay down by the water, but we're close enough that they sometimes wind their way up to the house looking for frogs. You have to be careful."

Molly began to shiver, a delayed reaction to the danger she'd been in.

Seth felt her reaction and rubbed her back to calm her. "You're all right. There's nothing to be afraid of now."

Molly shuddered. At one point, she had actually considered picking up the snake and confronting Patch with it. Imagine the child's reaction if she had! Molly laughed. It was her first genuine laugh for a long, long time. But really, enough was enough.

Misunderstanding Molly's hysterical laugh, Seth murmured soothing words of comfort. "Take it easy, sweetheart. You're fine. I won't let anyone, or anything hurt you. Relax, Molly. Relax, little darling, I—"

"What did you call me?"

Seth's stream of words was halted by the touch of her fingertips on his lips.

"Sweetheart? Darling?"

"Little darling," Molly said. "You called me little darling. James used to call me that."

Seth stiffened and started to release her.

"Please don't let go," Molly said. "I—I'm still feeling a little scared, if you want to know the truth."

Seth's arms closed around her again. He put one hand under her hair to rub her nape. Her head eased forward to give him greater access, and her cheek rested against the chambray shirt he had donned.

"What are we going to do about our children?" she murmured.

"I don't know," Seth said. "I'm doing everything I can think of to make it easier for Whit, but he doesn't seem to want to cooperate."

Molly stiffened at his criticism of her son. "He's only ten. You can't expect him to be able to do such hard work."

"Out here, a boy learns to do a man's job in a hurry, or he doesn't survive."

Molly's head came up. "Well, he's not a man, he's a boy," she protested.

"You expect a lot from Patch, and she's just a little girl," Seth said.

"She's twelve!"

"She's a kid."

"She's a—" Molly cut herself off.

Seth grimaced and stood. Neither of them felt very loverlike at the moment. "I only came by to say I have to make a trip into town to get some window glass tomorrow, and to invite you to come along. I thought maybe you'd like to get some curtain material or something."

Molly opened her mouth to continue the discussion—all right, argument—they'd been having about their children, then shut it again. It was a long ride into Fort Benton. She would have plenty of time, and privacy, to talk with Seth about his daughter—and her son. "I would very much like to go," she said.

"Fine. You might want to ask Ethan to keep an eye on Nessie."

That evening at supper, Seth announced that he and Molly would be driving in to Fort Benton the following day.

"Can I come, too, Pa?" Patch asked.

Molly's heart sank. If Patch came, they wouldn't have a chance to have that heart to heart talk. To her surprise, Seth said, "I'm taking the buckboard so I can get supplies. There won't be room for you."

"I can sit up front with you," Patch said.

"Molly's sitting up front."

"Oh."

Molly waited for further complaint from Patch. When it didn't come, she eyed the girl suspiciously. Patch never gave up when she wanted something, she just went about it another way. Molly decided that it wouldn't hurt to keep watch over her shoulder when they left, to see if they were being followed.

❊8❊

ETHAN'S NOSE TWITCHED AT the heavy smell of perfume in the darkened room. "Dora?"

"Over here, Ethan. I'm at the window."

He lit a lantern before trying to cross the room and then was glad he had. Dora collected dolls. They were all over the room, on shelves, on the dressing table, on the bed, and even in boxes on the floor. Ethan wove his way around the clutter and sat down on the windowsill. Dora was sitting in the rocker facing out, caressing the yarn hair of a Raggedy Ann.

"Drake was here tonight," she said. "He had me try everything, but nothing worked. Poor man."

Ethan was sure from the way she said it that Dora wasn't the least bit sorry. "Any news?" he said.

"He's setting up another operation on the butte west of town, where his whiskey-seller can see for two miles around who's coming. Do you think the Masked Marauder can manage to get the drop on him?"

Ethan smiled. "He usually does."

"Cal gave me this doll," she said, holding the Raggedy Ann like a child against her breast. "Said he was gonna give me a Raggedy Andy to go with it. That was the day before Drake had Pike Hardesty shoot him." She leaned forward and grasped Ethan's thigh. Her nails bit into his skin clear through the denim. "Drake has to die. He had Cal killed, and he has to die."

Ethan put a hand on hers, forcing her to release him. "I owe you, Dora. I'd've lost my leg if it hadn't been for you. Whatever I can do, I will."

Dora's voice was barely audible when she said, "Cal wanted to marry me, Ethan. I would have been the sheriff's wife. I would have been an honest woman. Drake Bassett took that away from me. He has to pay."

For the tenth day since those Gallaghers had shown up, Patch made a bed for herself on the buffalo skin in front of Ethan's hearth. He slept in the bedroom, which was divided from the main room by a red-striped gray blanket across the doorway. Thanks to the upheaval in her life caused by the appearance of the Gallagher family, she had recently spent many a sleepless night reliving distressing incidents from the day just past.

Even now she cringed at the memory of the humiliation she had felt three days ago when her father had stripped her naked and dumped her willy-nilly into that tub of water. He had seen *everything*. She wasn't his little girl anymore. She didn't want to grow up; but her body was doing it despite her wishes.

Her stepmother had come into the house after that disastrous business with her pa and insisted on measuring her for a dress. Not that Patch would ever wear it. Not willingly, anyway. It was bad enough that her body was conspiring to make her a woman; now Molly Gallagher seemed intent on finishing the job. If that woman had her way, Patch could say good-bye to trousers forever.

She had barely gotten her long johns on after her bath when that woman had confronted her with a measuring tape in one hand and a silk dress in the other. It had certainly been a pretty dress, a kind of mossy green. And it had looked a good deal softer than the chambray and corduroy Patch usually wore. But she wasn't about to let herself be bribed into doing anything Molly Gallagher wanted. She had watched warily as the woman approached her.

"I want to see if I can cut this down to fit you," she had said as she laid the dress over the back of a chair.

Patch hadn't been able to resist reaching out and caressing the fabric. It was as soft as it looked, as sleek and silky as Rebel's underbelly.

"Hold your arms out, please," Molly said.

Patch had thought seriously about refusing, but the possibility of her father being called to enforce Molly's request convinced her to obey.

Molly measured her shoulders, the length of her arms, and then beneath them, around her budding bosom. "I'll have to take in the bodice slightly."

Patch flushed a deep red, but Molly had already gone on to measure the distance to her waist from under her arm.

"When I was a child growing up," Molly said, "my father used to spend time with me each evening, talking to me while I took my bath. He told me funny stories about the customers in his saloon. We laughed a lot, and we both enjoyed it immensely. Then a day came when I felt uncomfortable about having him there. I had changed. Things had changed."

If Molly hadn't had the measuring tape around Patch's waist, she would have bolted right then and there. But there was no escape, so she was forced to listen as Molly continued, "I didn't quite know how to tell him that I was growing up. I felt sad that I wasn't his little girl anymore."

Patch stood frozen as Molly measured the length for the hem.

"Fortunately, I had a mother to turn to. I told her how I felt, and she explained my feelings to my father. I knew everything was all right when he came to me the next night at bedtime instead of bathtime to tell all the funny stories about his customers. We hadn't lost any of the closeness we had shared before. He had simply acknowledged that I was a young woman entitled to my privacy."

Molly had finished measuring and began winding up her tape. "There. That wasn't so bad, was it?"

"Bad enough," Patch muttered. She stared with narrowed eyes at her stepmother. Her pa must have said something about what had happened here tonight. Was Molly offering to speak to her pa on her behalf? Had she already done so? Patch wanted no repeat of the embarrassment of this evening. Better to be safe than sorry. She cleared her throat and said, "I'm—uh . . . I need some privacy myself."

"Of course you do," Molly agreed. "I was just telling your father tonight that we need to make some arrangements to curtain off a portion of this room for baths."

"Uh . . . sure."

"I'll just get started on this dress." She had eyed Patch's long underwear, tapped her chin with a finger, and added, "I think some dainty underthings are needed as well."

Molly had left her standing there feeling both confused and relieved. In the past, Patch hadn't needed anybody helping her get along with her pa. Why had she been willing to let that Gallagher woman intervene now? Maybe there were just some things a girl shouldn't have to explain to her father. Patch consoled herself with the thought that she hadn't *asked* for help, she had just been smart enough to take it when it was offered.

Last night, Patch had taken a bath in absolute privacy. To her relief, her pa hadn't said a thing to her. When she found herself feeling grateful to her stepmother for the way things had turned out, she reminded herself that if Molly Gallagher hadn't married her pa, the issue of baths and privacy would never have arisen in the first place.

Anyway, the sooner that woman was gone, the sooner things could get back to normal. Patch closed her eyes, tightened her fingers in the thick fur of the buffalo robe, and imagined that everything was back just the way it had been before the Gallaghers had arrived. But even that thought didn't bring the comfort she had hoped for. Because things hadn't been perfect even then. She fingered the slightly chipped tooth she'd gotten in the fight with the preacher's middle boy. At least with the Gallaghers here, forcing her to stay around the house, she hadn't been in a fight lately.

When the front door rattled, Patch sat bolt upright. Not that she was afraid, with Ethan asleep right in the next room. But she had lived long enough in Montana to see the results of an Indian raid. And she had overheard tales of the cruelty of the small bands of Blackfoot renegades that roamed the plains. Patch rose on her haunches when the door opened just a crack, as though someone were sneaking in. She searched the room for a weapon she could use and settled on a medium-size log from the woodpile near the fireplace.

Tiptoeing, she edged her way over to a spot behind the door. As the intruder stepped inside, she raised the log over her head. It was at the top of its downward arc when she heard Whit whisper, "Patch? Are you in there?"

It took every bit of muscle she had to swerve the log so it didn't crush Whit's skull. "Durn it, Whit! I nearly smashed you flat!" she hissed.

Whit had a hand at his throat, and his eyes were wide as he confronted the raging girl. "I need to talk to you," he said, keeping his voice low. "It's important. A matter of life and death."

Phrased like that, Patch couldn't very well turn him away. She looked down at the baggy red long johns that were all she was wearing, shrugged, and said, "Come on over by the fire where there's more light. And be quiet so you don't disturb Ethan. He's sleeping behind that blanket over there."

Whit followed her, Pied-Piper style, across the room. "Golly!" he said in a hushed voice as they settled on the buffalo robe. "Is this real?"

Patch snorted disdainfully. "What do you think?"

"Golly!" Whit repeated. "This is great. Look at those antlers over the fireplace. I've never seen the like. That must have been a huge deer!"

"It was an elk," Patch corrected impatiently. "Did you come here to talk or to admire the furnishings?"

Whit sat cross-legged, and he pounded a fist against his knee. "I came because I have to get out of here. I have to get back to New Bedford—to the sea."

"Why are you telling me? If you want to leave, just go. And good riddance!"

"I wish I could. But I need your help to get to Fort Benton. I figure that from there I can stow away on a steamboat downriver, then hide on a train heading back east."

Patch was a little in awe of Whit's resolve. "Aren't you scared to go all that way alone?"

Whit sat up a little straighter. "Naw. It'll be easy," he said with bravado.

Patch's eyes narrowed speculatively. Get rid of the boy, and the mother and that baby were sure to follow. "All right," she said. "You heard my pa say he's going to be taking a buckboard into Fort Benton tomorrow. I'll help you hide in the wagon. How does that sound?"

"Fine. Except, how will I find my way to the levee once I get there?"

Patch rolled her eyes. "Someone who's planning to cross the whole country by himself ought to be able to find his way across one little town."

"Well, I don't think I can! So are you going to come along and help me or not?" Whit demanded.

Patch shrugged. "Sure. Why not?" Then she had a sudden thought. "For a price."

Whit frowned. "I don't have any money."

"I don't want money. I want to know the secret of how you and your pa got that ship into that bottle."

"I can't tell you that."

"Then I can't help you."

"Aw, come on."

Patch crossed her arms resolutely. "If you want my help, tell me how it's done."

Whit grimaced, then leaned over and cupped his hand beside Patch's ear and whispered to her.

"Why, even *I* could do that!" she exclaimed when he was finished. Suddenly the front door creaked open.

Patch's eyes rounded at the sight of the tall, dark figure in the doorway. "I thought you were in bed asleep!"

Ethan grinned ruefully. "I could say the same thing about you." As he stepped into the room, he removed his hat and hooked it on an antler on the wall beside the door. "What are you doing up? And what is Whit doing here?"

"Uh . . ." Patch couldn't think of a logical reason why Whit would have come to visit her. After all, they had barely spoken to each other since she'd given him a bloody nose.

"I wanted to see where you lived," Whit volunteered.

Ethan cocked a disbelieving brow. "In the middle of the night?"

"*He* keeps me too busy working in the daytime to do much of anything else," Whit retorted bitterly.

"It's late," Ethan said. "You'd better get on home before your ma comes looking for you."

"That's not my home!" Whit said. "But I'll be going." He gave Patch one last surreptitious look before crossing the room and letting himself out the door.

Ethan sat down in the wooden rocker beside the fireplace. He leaned back and hooked the ankle of one leg across the knee of the other. "What was that all about?"

"Oh, nothing." Patch knew that Ethan wasn't going to stop asking questions until he'd wormed the whole story out of her. She needed something to distract him from that purpose. Her nose wrinkled when she noticed a pungent odor surrounding him. "Is that whiskey I smell?"

She followed her nose, and it led her to Ethan's navy wool shirt. "You stink like a saloon on a Saturday night." She rose up on her knees to sniff his breath. Surprisingly, there was no whiskey smell.

Her brow furrowed. That didn't make any sense at all. "How come your clothes smell like whiskey but your breath doesn't?"

Ethan set his foot down from his knee and started the rocker in motion. "I dropped by the Medicine Bow planning to have a drink. Before I could order, a freightman stumbled and spilled his drink down the front of me. Then Dora came up to wipe me off and"—he grinned—"my plans changed."

Patch made a moue of distaste. "Consarn it! I don't see why you or Pa want to have anything to do with that Dora Deveraux. That red-headed floozy is a—"

Abruptly, Ethan caught Patch by the chin and said, "Don't be calling names, Patch. It's not something a lady does."

Patch recoiled at Ethan's rebuke. She jerked herself out of his hold and scooted over to where she'd made her pallet. She turned her back on him and pulled the quilt up over her shoulder. As she stared into the fire, her eyes blurred. Her chest felt achy deep inside. It hurt to swallow.

Why did Ethan's disapproval always seem so much worse than Pa's? And he had used that word again. *Lady.* Dora Deveraux wasn't a lady, but both Pa and Ethan gave the dang woman plenty of attention.

"I heard tell you're going to be getting a new dress," Ethan said.

"I got measured for one," she admitted.

"That's something I'd like to see," he mused. "I bet you'd be a sight all gussied up."

Patch rolled over to face Ethan. "A dress won't make me a lady," she said, "if that's what you're thinking."

"I was only thinking that you'd be awful pretty in a dress," he said in a soft voice. "And it'd make your father happy."

"All right. I'll wear the stupid dress. But only for Pa's sake."

He smiled, and she was glad she'd agreed.

Ethan stood to go to bed. On his way past, he bent over and tousled her hair. He paused and let a strand or two slide through his fingers.

"Why, this is like cornsilk," he said. "What'd you do to it?"

"I washed it," Patch said, slapping his hand aside.

"You oughta wash it more often."

It was one insult too many. Patch attacked, throwing her weight against Ethan's legs and tripping him. Ethan just laughed as he rolled into the fall. She quickly pinned him down on his back by sitting on him. The harder he laughed, the madder she got.

Patch hit at whatever part of him she could reach with her fists. "Durn you, Ethan! Smelling like you do, how dare you say that *I* need to bathe more often."

He did little to defend himself, just parried the worst of her blows and laughed. "If the shoe fits, wear it," he managed to say. Then added, "That is, if you haven't dumped them all in the river."

Even the mention of shoes was like rubbing salt in an open wound. Patch used every swear word she knew and several new ones she made up for the occasion. Ethan just roared with laughter.

"That's enough games for now, Patch," he said at last, capturing both her hands in one of his. "It's way past your bedtime."

"I'm not a child," she huffed. "I can stay up as long as I like."

"Yeah, well, you're acting awful cranky."

"Yeah, well, maybe I've got good reason."

He shoved her off onto her fanny on the floor and got to his feet. "Suit yourself. I'm dead on my feet." He ruffled her hair once more and dodged her hand when she swung at him.

Patch watched him walk out of the room without giving her a backward look. She could still hear him chuckling as his boots hit the floor.

Oh, the indignity of it all! Patch didn't understand why his cavalier treatment galled her so. She only knew it did. She felt peeved, put-upon, and provoked. But she would get her revenge. Just let Ethan try finding his boots tomorrow morning. She'd take great pleasure in telling him he could go fish for them!

The creak of floorboards in the hall woke Molly. It was still pitch dark, and she wondered who was wandering around at this time of night. She quickly rose and put on a robe to investigate. To her surprise, she caught Whit stealthily opening the door to Seth's room.

"What are you doing out of bed?"

Whit flattened guiltily against the wall. "I was just—I just . . . I went out to use the necessary," he said.

"Oh. Well, be careful you don't wake up Seth when you get in bed."

"That's no problem," Whit said. "Because he's not in there."

"He's not?"

"He never came to bed," Whit said.

"Go on, then, and get back to sleep." Molly made sure Whit got into bed and waited to tuck him in before she left. But instead of going back to bed, she walked over to the lace-curtained window. For a long while she stood watching as the sky slowly turned from a dark cocoon into a brilliant pastel butterfly of color.

Where was Seth? she wondered. Why hadn't he said he was leaving? And why should it upset her so much to know he had disappeared without telling her where he was going? More important, did she really want to be there to confront him when he returned?

Suddenly, the door opened, and he was standing there.

"Molly? Is something wrong?"

She kept her voice carefully under control as she replied, "You tell me. Where were you, Seth?"

"I was . . . with a patient. Mrs. Gulliver."

"All night?"

"I didn't intend to be gone so long, but she was having trouble. So I stayed."

He was lying. She could see it in his eyes, hear it in his tone of voice. But why would he lie? What could he possibly have been doing that he couldn't tell her about? The possibilities were endless and distressing, to say the least.

Molly wasn't sure what she would have said next, but she was never given the chance. There was a sharp rap on the door, and when Seth opened it, a heavy-set man wearing overalls and workboots stood there. His hair was standing on end and going every which way, and he was nervously curling the brim on a battered brown hat.

"It's Iris," the man said. "It's her time."

"I'll get my bag," Seth replied. He explained to Molly, "It's Iris Marsh, our closest neighbor. She's having labor pains at last. The baby's late coming. I've got to go. We'll have to postpone our trip into town."

Molly saw the worried look on Seth's face and said, "I'll go with you. Maybe I can help."

"The children—"

"I'll wake up Whit. He can take care of Nessie. Just give me a minute to get dressed."

Seth was waiting outside with the buggy harnessed when Molly came through the front door. "Let's go," she said.

It was a quick five miles to the Marsh place, which turned out to be a sod house cut into the side of a hill. Molly was astonished when she entered to see how many people were living in the small, dark space. There were identical twin boys about Whit's age, an older girl with deep-set brown eyes who held a year-old baby in her arms, and a pig-tailed girl about Nessie's age. Five children. And Iris Marsh was expecting a sixth.

"You kids stay out of Doc Kendrick's way, you hear?" their father said. "How's that boilin' water comin'?" he asked the oldest girl.

"It's ready, Pa," she said. "Whenever Doc Kendrick needs it."

"I'll leave you to it, Doc," Henry Marsh said. "I've got some plowing to do." He called the twin boys to come with him and left the room.

Molly couldn't believe he would simply walk away like that. Didn't he want to be near his wife in case something went wrong? But then, he wasn't going far—no farther than a voice could call.

Molly had experienced childbirth with and without her husband present. James had been at sea when Whit was born. She had cried out in vain for him when the pains were at their worst. She had wept tears of joy when she saw their son for the first time. How she wished James had been there to share the moment with her! Whit had been two when James finally came home. Her son had been frightened of James's enthusiastic homecoming, but he had soon come to love his father. He was inconsolable when James took to the sea again.

When Nessie was born, James had been home, but he had been no more a part of the birthing process than he had when he was gone. Oh, he had come upstairs when she called. But when Molly saw how much her pain distressed him, she had sent him away again. Perhaps that was the case with Henry Marsh. At any rate, as many times as Iris had been through this ordeal, the two of them must have worked out this arrangement between them.

Molly met Seth's eyes and smiled. This must be the most rewarding part of his work, she thought. To help bring new life into the world.

A small portion of the room had been curtained off with a blanket hung from a rope. A constant low moan was coming from behind the partition. Molly stepped behind the blanket and was immediately drawn to the woman who lay there.

Iris Marsh was rail thin, except for her immense belly. She had a piece of leather clenched between her teeth through which guttural groans were escaping. Her hands gripped the brass bedstead above her as her body strained to disgorge its burden. Her chambray nightgown was draped at her waist, and her knees were up and widespread. To Molly's amazement, the woman's abdomen rippled under the powerful contraction.

As soon as the contraction was over, Iris let go of the bedrail, heaved a sigh of relief, and reached out to shake Molly's hand. "You must be the new Mrs. Kendrick. Heard the doc got hitched. It's a pleasure meetin' you, ma'am."

Molly responded to the woman's overture with equal warmth. "I'm pleased to meet you, too, Mrs. Marsh."

"Call me Iris. Everybody does."

"And I'm Molly. You have a lovely family, Iris. Are you wishing for a girl or a boy?"

"Henry wants a boy. But I'd like to have me another little girl. Heard you brought a couple kids with you. How are they taking to the west?"

Molly looked up at Seth, wondering where all this information had come from, but he just smiled and shrugged. "The children are adjusting very well," she said. If it was a lie, it was in a good cause.

"I know you ladies would like to chat some more, but there's some business needs tending," Seth said. "Molly, see if you can find a clean sheet to put under Iris. And get me some of that boiling water for my instruments. I don't think it's going to be long now."

Molly did as she was told. But long after the sheets had been changed and the boiling water had cooled, the child still had not been born. More than five long hours had passed since they had arrived. Molly now knew more about Iris Marsh than she had learned about Aunt Hattie in the six months she'd lived with her.

She knew Iris and Henry had come west from a farm in Kansas trying to escape memories of atrocities that had occurred in their town during the war. That Henry preferred suspenders to a belt and that he wore false teeth. That Iris had always wanted a red satin dress and had dreamed of performing on a steamboat traversing the Missouri. That they had named their girls after flowers—Rose, Amaryllis, and Daisy—and their boys after trees—Ash and Alder. This baby would be called Lily if it was a girl, and Birch if it was a boy.

If Molly had even suspected something might go wrong, she

wouldn't have let herself get so involved with the other woman. But it had seemed when they arrived that everything would be over very quickly. The baby's head had crowned some time ago, yet it refused to be born. Molly didn't dare voice the fear that had been growing over the past several hours because she didn't want to frighten Iris. But in that, she had underestimated the older woman.

"Something's wrong, Doc," Iris said. "I been straining, but the babe just won't come. Ain't there something you kin do?"

Seth took the woman's hand in his to check her pulse. It was weak; Iris was tiring. "I can try using forceps to pull the baby out. Don't know if it'll work. But it's all I know to do."

"You won't crush its skull or nothing like that, will you, Doc?"

Molly saw Seth swallow hard. "I'll be careful, Iris. As though it were my own child."

"I trust you, Doc," the exhausted woman said as her eyes fell closed. "Don't know how much longer I can hang on. Better go ahead and give it a try."

"Don't give up," Molly said as she squeezed Iris's hand.

"Don't you worry none about me," Iris murmured. "I ain't forgot you promised to throw me a christenin' party at your place."

In fact, they had planned the entire party down to the date and the guest list. Molly only hoped there would be a reason to celebrate.

"I'll need your help," Seth said to Molly. "I'm going to try and situate the head a little better for what I need to do. And I may have to cut a little. Be ready to hand me the scalpel and forceps."

Molly saw Seth's hands trembling, and she realized suddenly the tremendous courage it must take to play God. What followed happened mercifully quickly. He made a small incision, and the forceps did what all Iris's hours of pushing hadn't. Moments later, the baby was lying on the sheet between Iris's legs. Molly watched with growing respect for Seth's skill as he cleaned the mucus from the baby's throat and gave it a slap on the rump that forced out a lusty cry.

Molly felt the sting of joyful tears as she met Seth's jubilant gray eyes. She wondered at that moment what it would be like to have Seth's child, to see the joy on his face at the moment of birth.

"You have a daughter, Iris," Seth said. "Lily looks just fine."

Seth cut the cord and laid the baby beside her mother, while he waited for the afterbirth and disposed of it. He made sure there wasn't any additional bleeding, then stitched up the cut he'd made.

Iris was too tired even to open her eyes to look at her new daughter. But Molly saw her feel the tiny fingers and toes, and smile when she realized they were all there.

"I guess I owe you that christening party," Molly said. "I'll take care of sending out the invitations."

Iris just nodded and kept on smiling.

A moment later, Henry appeared at his wife's bedside. He looked harried, worried, and Molly realized that even though he hadn't been present in the room, he had never really left it.

"She looks awful pale, Doc," Henry said.

"It was a hard birth," Seth said. "But give her a little rest, and she'll be fine. By the way, you have a daughter."

Henry grinned, exposing the full set of false teeth. "She's purty as her mama, ain't she, Doc."

"Sure is, Henry. Guess we'll be going. I hoped to get to town today. May still be able to make the trip if I hurry."

It was shortly after noon, and Molly felt wrung out. And exhilarated. As Seth headed the buggy back toward home, Molly put her arm on his sleeve and said, "I don't pretend to know much about you, Seth Kendrick. But you aren't a coward. That was the most courageous act I've ever seen in my life. I am so proud of you, and proud to be your wife. You saved Iris's life. And you brought Lily into this world whole and healthy."

Seth was more moved than he could say. Molly's belief in him was a balm for his battered soul. He wanted to reward her confidence in him by telling her everything. The first words were on his lips when he bit them back. He couldn't tell her the truth. Not without taking the chance that she would despise him for it.

And now that he'd had a taste of it, he wanted, craved his wife's admiration. So he sat still and stolid and saw her expression cool when he didn't respond to what she had said.

"Do you still want to go to town today?" he asked.

"Why, yes, if we have the time before dark."

"You aren't too tired?"

Discouraged, yes. Tired, no. "I'll be fine. Besides, I'd like to get a present for the baby."

"All right. We'll drop by the house and exchange the buggy for the buckboard and then go on."

Molly removed her hand from Seth's sleeve and folded it together with the other one in her lap. She looked at Seth from under her lashes, trying to decipher the expression on his face. But his features were stony. There was nothing to see.

Only now, Molly was more curious than ever about the man she had married. She had a thousand things she wanted to ask Seth but couldn't think how to begin the conversation. At long last she simply said, "Tell me about Patch's mother."

At first she thought he wasn't going to answer. Then he took a deep breath and said, "What do you want to know?"

"What was her name?"

"Annarose."

"What was she like?"

"She was blond and blue-eyed. Tall. And her left cheek dimpled when she smiled." Which had been often.

Molly tucked a strand of hair behind her ear that had blown loose in the wind. She pulled her straw bonnet down and retied the bow a little tighter under her chin. "That's what she looked like. Tell me something else about her."

For a long time he just stared off over the grassy plains. At last he said, "She was terrified when she found out she was going to have a child. Her mother had told her that birthing a baby was a painful ordeal. But as the baby grew inside her and started to move, she became fascinated and excited by the whole idea.

"As she grew more confident, I became more terrified. I didn't want to lose her. Annarose had become the light of my world, my happiness, my heart. It turned out that I was right to be afraid. It was a hard birth."

Seth cleared his throat and continued. "After Patch was born, Annarose's skin was white as chalk, she had lost so much blood."

"Is that how she died? In childbirth?"

He shook his head. "Annarose cheated the Devil. Two days later, she was on her feet. She took to mothering like a kid to hard candy and nursed Patch for almost a year. I never got tired of watching. I learned what it meant to be father and husband. I was their protector; it was up to me to keep them safe from harm."

"It must have been a comfort to have all that knowledge of medicine."

"I wasn't a doctor then," he said flatly.

That surprised Molly. "What did you do?"

He hesitated, then said, "It doesn't matter. That's all in the past."

Molly had opened her mouth to ask just how and when Annarose *had* died, when Seth cut her off.

"Anyway, it's my turn to ask some questions." He looked her straight in the eye and said, "Tell me about James—and I don't mean what he looked like."

The first words out of Molly's mouth surprised her. "He was hardly ever home." They sounded resentful, even to her ears. She hadn't felt that way at the time—or had she? She tried to explain away the condemning inflection in her voice. "He was the captain of a whaling vessel, you see, and had to be gone for years at a time."

Seth cocked his head to look at her. "You say that as though he had no choice."

"He didn't, really. The men in his family had been whalers for a hundred years. He was born and bred to it. And he loved it."

"More than he loved you?"

Molly drew in a hissing breath. "I don't think that's a fair question. He loved me, and he loved whaling."

"So he had both a wife and a mistress."

Molly frowned. "I don't understand."

"You and the sea," Seth said.

"He loved me more," Molly insisted.

"But he always chose the sea."

Molly was silent for the rest of the trip home. In the eleven years she had been married, it had never occurred to her to question the fact that James had spent seven of those years at sea. Gallaghers were whaling men. They came home to unload the whale oil in their holds, to impregnate their wives, and to spend what they'd earned. Then they repaired their ships, restocked them with provisions, and set sail again. It had never occurred to her to be jealous of the sea. Until now. When it was much too late.

Maybe with Seth she ought not to take things so much for granted. Maybe this time around, she should not be so indulgent of her husband. Maybe on the trip to Fort Benton, she would just have to ask Seth where he had gone last night, and demand an honest answer.

❋9❋

"THAT DAMNED MASKED MARAUDER has been at it again!"

Drake Bassett kicked at one of several broken whiskey kegs that littered the ground. Pike Hardesty had brought him up to the butte overlooking town to see for himself the damage that had been done. Drake was used to opposition; he had learned how to crush it. But this Masked Marauder was turning out to be as hard to pin down as campfire smoke.

The man Bassett had hired to sell whiskey to the Blackfeet lay on the grass groaning. He hadn't been shot—just forced to drink a great deal of the alcohol-turpentine-tar mixture he'd been selling. The poor sot might have been better off dead, Bassett thought. The whiskey concoction had blinded him.

"Get him into town and see if Doc Kendrick can do anything for him," Bassett told his henchman.

Pike leaned against a scrub juniper, cleaning his teeth with a broken twig. "Sure, boss. Whatever you say."

"I want you to find a way to stop this Marauder," Bassett said. "He's costing me a fortune, dumping whiskey faster than I can make it. I'm paying you for protection, Pike. If you can't do the job, I'll get someone who can."

Pike scratched the stubble under his chin with the twig he'd been using on his teeth. "Just can't figure out who this Marauder fella could be," he said. "Isn't a man in town I can name with the balls to do a thing like this."

"It's damned certain somebody was here. I want him caught."

"That Masked Marauder don't hang around long enough to get caught," Pike protested.

"That's your problem," Bassett said. "Clean up this mess. And I don't want to see that ugly face of yours again until you've come up with a way to get rid of that damned Masked Marauder!"

———————

The instant Patch saw her father drive up in the buggy, she sought out Whit. He was just pulling his suspenders up over his shoulders after leaving the outhouse when Patch intercepted him. "Come on. It's time."

In the bright light of day, Whit had begun having doubts. He dragged his feet as she hauled him toward the buckboard. "I'm not so sure—"

"Look, when I talked to you last night, you said you wanted to run away. Now do you, or don't you?"

Whit's brow furrowed. "I do. But I've been thinking. Maybe I need to plan some more. What if I get hungry on the trip?"

"I'll pack you a tin full of sandwiches and some dried apples. That ought to hold you till the steamboat's a fair distance from Fort Benton. Then you can let the captain know you're on board and work your way to St. Louis."

Whit thought of the severe punishment for a stowaway on board a sailing ship and wondered if the same treatment applied on the river.

"Do you want to stay here in Montana for the rest of your life?" Patch asked.

"No."

"Then what are we waiting for? I thought you wanted to be a sailor—and get back to the sea," she taunted.

"All right," Whit said, his jaw firming as she whipped at his pride. "Let's go."

Patch hid Whit under the canvas tarp that covered the bed of the buckboard, then went to the kitchen to pack a lunch for him. She thought the game was up when Ethan caught her wrapping sandwiches in brown paper.

"What are you doing?"

"I'm—uh . . . packing some food for me and Whit. We're going fishing. Is that all right with you?" she asked with just enough belligerence to back him off.

Ethan stuck his thumbs in the front of his jeans. "I think it's nice of you to take Whit under your wing like this."

"Who said I—" Patch cut herself off. Let Ethan think what he wanted. The truth would be out soon enough. "I gotta go. Tell Pa where we are, will you?"

"Sure, be glad to." He grinned and added, "By the way, you might see if you can hook your shoes while you're at it."

Patch grimaced and looked down at her bare feet. After Ethan had retrieved his black leather boots that morning, he had retaliated for the trick she'd played on him. Her oldest, most worn-out—most comfortably worn-in—pair of shoes had been pitched into the pond. She had newer shoes, but on general principle she chose not to wear them. It wasn't the first time, and wouldn't be the last, that she had gone barefoot.

Patch wasn't even out the door when she saw Ethan pick up Nessie and rub noses with her. That baby definitely had to go! She hurried to the wagon, looked around to make sure she wasn't observed, then slipped underneath the canvas to join Whit. A second later the dog-wolf, Maverick, jumped under the tarp to join her. Standing up as he was, the dog's figure was clearly outlined under the canvas.

"Hey! What's he doing here?" Whit demanded. "He's going to ruin everything."

"Go away, Maverick," Patch said, shoving at the dog's haunches. He didn't budge.

"Come here and help," she ordered Whit.

"He'll bite me."

"No, he won't. Come on, hurry. Before they come."

The two of them shoved with all their might, but the most they accomplished was to get Maverick to lie down.

"This is just great," Whit said in a voice that made it clear that he thought it was anything but. "What do we do now?"

"This isn't really such a bad thing," Patch said. "Nobody's gonna come around asking us any questions in town with Maverick along."

Whit pursed his lips. "Yeah, maybe you're right. Just make sure you keep him quiet till we get there."

Patch lay down with her head on Maverick's fur. She settled herself none too soon. A moment later, she heard her father helping Molly up onto the buckboard.

"What an awful message to find waiting for you," Molly said. "Do you think you'll be able to help that poor man who was blinded?"

"Won't know till I see him. You sure you still want to go along? We're liable to end up spending the night."

"Yes. I just wish I'd had a chance to talk to Whit," Molly said. "I wanted to ask him to help Ethan with Nessie."

"Don't worry. Ethan'll take care of everything. Look at the bright side. Patch and Whit are doing something together for a change."

If only he knew, Patch thought, eyeing Whit in the shadows across from her. *If only he knew.*

Indeed, if Seth and Molly had realized their children were hidden in the back of the buckboard, they might have guarded their conversation more carefully. As it was, Patch's ears burned, and Whit's face turned scarlet as their parents exchanged humorous yet personally revealing stories about their children.

"I'll bet you'd never guess how Patch got her nickname," Seth said.

"I thought it was a shortened name for Patricia."

Seth grinned. "It could be, but it isn't. Ethan gave her the nickname when she was just three."

"Uh-oh," Molly said with a smile. "I think I know where this story is heading."

"Patch had this habit of crawling up on Ethan's chest when he was sleeping. Every time he woke up, there was this patch on his long johns where Patch's wet bottom had been. He took to calling her Patch, and the name stuck."

"That's almost as bad as how Whit got his name," Molly said.

"What's Whit short for?" Seth asked. "Whitley? Whittaker, Whitcomb?"

"Whittling."

"You're kidding."

Molly grinned and shook her head. "When we were first married, James spent time every evening after dinner sitting on the back stoop whittling. He was gone to sea when I found out I was expecting a child, and I had no idea what I should name the baby. The one thing I knew James loved was—"

"Whittling," Seth said with a laugh.

Whit rolled his eyes, and Patch grimaced back at him. They didn't think their parents were the least bit funny. To make matters worse, the heat was stifling under the canvas. Ticklish rivulets of sweat inched their way down into embarrassing places that couldn't be scratched with someone else watching. When Maverick started to stand up halfway through the trip, it took their combined weights, and overlapping body parts, to hold him down. By the time they reached the town limits of Fort Benton, neither Patch nor Whit could look the other in the eye.

Meanwhile, several times during the conversation, Molly had been on the verge of confronting Seth about where he'd spent the previous night. But the mood between them had been so pleasant that she couldn't bear to spoil it. Maybe he had been telling the truth. The least she could do was give him the benefit of the doubt.

What was more worrisome to her was how to deal with the fact that she and Seth would be spending the night together—alone. Her ambivalent feelings toward the man confused her. She admired his courage as a doctor; his physical cowardice baffled her. She desired Seth; she did not love him. She had pledged to love James forever; Seth was her husband and wanted her to be his wife in every way.

With James, everything had been so simple. Love and desire had walked hand in hand. With Seth, she felt adrift in a turbulent sea without oars or a sail, or even a rudder.

"I think it might be a good idea to go ahead and get a room at Schmidt's Hotel when we arrive," Seth said. "That way you'll have a place to rest while I pick up the plate glass for the windows at Carroll & Steell."

Molly refused to think ahead. She would take each step as it came. And do what felt right. She cleared her throat and said, "That sounds just fine."

Seth left the buckboard at the livery, and he and Molly headed for Schmidt's Hotel. While most of the town's businesses were constructed of adobe and logs, or housed in tents, Schmidt's had been the first building made from lumber hauled by bull train from Helena. Jacob Schmidt met them at the front desk. The German was known to have a volatile temper. He had once gotten angry and closed down the dining room just because a freightman had tugged on his coattail and demanded service.

"I'd like a room, Uncle Jake," Seth said.

"For you and the missus?"

"Yes," Seth said, drawing her forward to meet the German. "Molly, meet Jacob Schmidt."

"Call me Uncle Jake," the fat little man said, taking her hand

and shaking it once. "I give you best room in the house. Big bed. You like it."

"Th-thank you, Uncle Jake," Molly said. She couldn't get used to the frankness of westerners. They said what they were thinking and seemed to have no sense of modesty. Seth saved her from having to say anything more by leading her past Jake and up the stairs to their room.

Uncle Jake hadn't lied. The room was lovely, with a big old maple four-poster covered with a star-patterned quilt and a matching maple wardrobe in which to hang their clothes, a brick fireplace, and a dry sink with a flower-patterned pitcher and bowl for washing. From the window she could see most of the levee, including several steamboats pulled up to load freight and disgorge passengers. Molly turned back to Seth, uncertain what to expect from him now that they were alone.

Seth slowly walked over to her. His fingertips caressed her palm as he handed her the key to the room. "I need to go check on that blinded whiskey-seller and run my errands. I'll meet you back here later. Uncle Jake can give you directions to I. G. Baker & Co. They probably have the largest selection of cloth goods."

Then he kissed her.

He took his time about it, kissing one side of her mouth, then the other, then running his tongue along the seam of her lips, slipping it inside for just a taste. He lifted his head and looked at her, and she saw the barely leashed desire that raged in him. He took a step back from her, and another. Then turned without a word and left the room.

Molly realized she was panting. She put a hand against her heart to still its pounding. Her tongue slicked her lips—and found the taste of Seth. Enervated, she sank down on the edge of the bed. Once again, she had yielded to his kisses. Her whole body had responded to the mere touch of his mouth. With very little effort, he had made her want him.

Molly couldn't understand what had happened. When he touched her, all thought of resistance fled. He didn't have to fight her for what he wanted. She willingly surrendered in his arms. Molly wasn't sure whether she felt guilt or euphoria at the prospect of the coming night. She settled the matter by admitting she felt both.

While their parents were otherwise occupied, Patch and Whit had little trouble sneaking out of the livery with Maverick. Patch led Whit up and down alleys heading toward the levee. Everything might have gone as planned, except that when they were passing the back window of one of Drake Bassett's warehouses, Patch clearly heard the words *"Masked Marauder."*

She halted in her tracks. Whit bumped into her, started to complain, and was immediately shushed by Patch. "They're talking about the Masked Marauder. Shut up so I can hear."

Whit hadn't the foggiest notion who the Masked Marauder was, but Patch was captain of the ship, and he had no choice but to follow her orders.

Patch listened only with the expectation of hearing more of the Masked Marauder's heroic exploits. But the more she listened, the wider her eyes got. The men inside weren't praising the Marauder—they were planning to ambush and kill him!

They were just beginning to discuss the details of the plan when Maverick, for no good reason that Patch could see, bared his teeth and growled ferociously. She grabbed the dog's snout, but she was too late to avoid discovery.

"You out there! What are you doing? Hey! That's my dog!"

"Run!" Patch yelled. She gave Whit a shove and took off.

Whit wasn't expecting the push. He stumbled a couple of steps to the end of the alley and fell face-first into the street. Patch came running back to grab him by the seat of his trousers and yank him to his feet. That delay allowed the men inside to reach the street in front of the warehouse.

Whit took off, but rough hands captured Patch. A second later, Maverick attacked the man holding Patch, barking excitedly and snapping at whatever flesh he could reach.

"What the hell? Get down, you damned mongrel!" The man holding Patch lashed out with a boot and gave Maverick a vicious kick in the ribs. Yelping in pain, the dog-wolf tucked its tail between its legs and slunk away.

Outraged, Patch struggled against the man's hold. "Durn you! Leave my dog alone! You pig-faced yellow-belly. You—"

"Shut up, kid," the man snarled. "Who are you? What were you doing listening at the window?"

Patch wasn't about to tell her name. If her pa found out she was in town, she'd be in trouble for sure. Instead of answering, she bit the hand that held her.

Whit hadn't stopped running, figuring Patch was right behind him. When he heard the man howl, he looked back just in time to see Patch being slapped. Whit stopped, not sure whether to run back to help her or go in some other direction for help. The size of the man who held Patch decided him. He whirled to run and collided with a solid object. The force of the impact toppled him into the dirt.

Solicitous hands helped him up. "Where are you going in such a hurry, son?"

If Whit hadn't been so frightened for Patch, he might have been terrified at the grim features on Seth Kendrick's face when he suddenly realized who had just run into him.

Before Seth could say anything else, Whit blurted, "You have to help Patch. There's a man hitting her. Over there. He—"

"Where?"

Whit pointed.

"Your mother should still be at Schmidt's Hotel. Find her and stay with her. Go! Now!"

Seth didn't wait to see whether Whit obeyed him, just headed on the run for Patch.

"That's my daughter you're holding, Pike," Seth said when he was within calling distance. "Put her down."

Pike Hardesty peered at Seth through narrowed eyes. "This brat's yours, Doc?" he asked. "You oughta teach her not to listen at windows."

Patch jerked ineffectually against Pike's grip on the front of her shirt. "Pa, he's planning to—"

Pike shook Patch to shut her up. "Keep your mouth shut, kid. You didn't hear nothin'. Understand?"

"Why not try picking on someone your own size?" Seth said.

"Why, Doc. Didn't know you was a fightin' man." He let Patch go, and she scampered to Seth's side.

Seth's hand traced the growing bruise on Patch's face, and his jaw tautened. "Go find Molly at Schmidt's Hotel. Stay there till I come for you."

"But, Pa—"

"Don't argue with me, Patch. Get out of here."

Patch called Maverick to her side and hurried down the street. She went just far enough away to be out of her father's line of sight, then stopped to watch what was about to happen.

At last! she thought. *He's going to fight at last. My pa is not a coward.*

"Come on over here, Doc, and we'll see how you handle yourself," Pike said.

Seth looked over to the doorway of the building and saw Drake Bassett leaning against the portal, smoking a cigar. Though he was a relatively young man, Bassett had snow-white hair and a salt-and-pepper moustache and brows. His features were ordinary: dark brown eyes spaced wide, a nose that hooked a little, thin lips, and a sloping chin. He was dressed plainly in a gray wool suit, and he wore a single watch fob across his vest. He was a picture of honesty and prosperity.

Drake Bassett was prosperous, all right, Seth thought. It was the honesty he was lacking. The man was so crooked, he could eat nails and spit out corkscrews. Bassett was the brains and Pike was the brawn of what had become a very dirty business. People had begun to gather, and Seth was guessing Bassett wouldn't like calling attention to himself. "Call off your dog, Drake. This has gone far enough, don't you think?"

"Your kid started the trouble," Bassett said, eyeing the growing crowd.

"My daughter meant no harm. She—"

"Figured you'd try to wiggle out of fighting, Doc," Pike said. "Admit it. You're just plain yellow."

Seth felt the eyes of the crowd on him. He had chosen this path, and he had known it wouldn't be easy. But it was hard to endure the disgust and disdain in all those faces. "Think what you like. Just don't ever touch my daughter again."

Pike laughed in his face. "Ooh. I'm scared. What you gonna do to me, Doc? Rap my knuckles with a stick?"

The crowd laughed along with Pike, and some began calling Seth names. Seth just stood there, enduring their raucous jests. He had made a vow, and as hard as it was, he would keep it. He turned and began walking away.

He hadn't taken two steps when a blur came racing past him and leaped onto Pike's back. "Take that, you varmint!"

The crowd went wild, yelling and screaming encouragement to Patch as she attacked the man who had forced her father to back down. Her assault had surprised Pike, so she was able to box his ears and yank his hair before he reached up, grabbed her by the arms, and threw her over his head onto the ground.

Patch landed so hard, all the air came out of her in a huff. Then she lay still.

The crowd quieted instantly and looked at Seth to see what he would do.

Seth knelt beside Patch and checked the pulse at her throat. Although fast, it was strong and steady. She opened her eyes, and he saw she was only dazed.

"Pa?" she said. "I couldn't let him say those things about you."

"It's all right, Patch," he said. He lifted her in his arms and carried her over to Red, who was part of the crowd. He handed her into the other man's arms and said, "Take care of her."

Then he turned to face Pike, who was leering at him.

"Whatcha gonna do now, Doc?"

Seth pulled off his suit coat and draped it over the hitching rail. Then he undid his string tie and pulled it off. Finally, he unbuttoned the throat of his shirt and turned up his cuffs. "All right, Pike," he said. "Whenever you're ready."

Pike grinned at the crowd. "Looks like the doc's finally decided to fight." He put his hands up in fists like a boxer to protect his face. "Here I am, Doc. Come and get me."

Seth took Pike at his word. He marched up to him and put a fist in the burly man's stomach, folding him in half like an empty wallet. He followed that with an uppercut to the chin that straightened Pike back out again.

Pike's fists were still out there in front of him, but somehow they didn't seem to be doing him much good. Seth showed no mercy, hitting Pike in the face, choosing his punches. A right to the eye, another under the chin. A quick left opened a cut in his cheek; another jab widened it.

Pike's right eye was already swelling closed, and his left cheek was dripping blood like a faucet. Pike couldn't understand what had gone wrong. He swung hard, and Seth stepped out of his way. He swung again, and Seth simply wasn't there. He charged and caught Seth in a bear hug. Bigger and stronger, he tried crushing the other man.

But Seth got a hand under Pike's chin and forced his head back. Pike either had to let go or get his neck snapped. As soon as he did, Seth hit him in the solar plexus, knocking the breath clean out of him.

Pike dropped to his knees.

Seth didn't have a mark on him. "I warned you not to touch my daughter. You lay a hand on her again, and I'll finish the job."

Pike heard the crowd murmuring and felt the nausea rise in his stomach at the thought of being beaten by a man everyone knew was too scared to fight. Slowly, his hand inched toward the gun tied down on his leg.

Molly had left Whit at the hotel and come looking for Seth. She had found him in time to see everything. When Seth had refused to fight, she had felt ashamed; when he had effortlessly whipped Pike, she had been astounded. She was shoving her way toward him through the crowd when she saw Pike Hardesty reaching for his gun.

"Seth!" she cried. "Look out behind you!"

Molly was watching Seth when she heard the gunshot. In that instant she realized that her feelings for him were much stronger than she had ever imagined. If she'd had a gun, she would have shot Pike Hardesty herself.

Seth jerked when the bullet hit him, but he didn't fall right away. He shook his head slightly, swayed, then crumpled to the ground.

Molly was the first to reach Seth and dropped to her knees beside him. The gorge rose in her throat when she saw the blood streaming from the wound on his head.

When Patch saw her father fall, she tore herself from Red's grasp and ran toward him. She halted when she realized Molly had gotten there before her. She stood back, feeling shut out. "Pa. Oh, Pa!"

Pike pushed his way clumsily to his feet and crossed to stand over Seth. He grunted when he saw his bullet had gone high and wide, merely creasing Seth's left temple instead of hitting him in the heart.

Bassett was watching the crowd and realized their mood had turned ugly. "You remember that business we talked about, Pike? I think you'd best be on your way."

Pike shoved his way through the crowd, which parted like the Red Sea as he approached them. There was no law in Fort Benton, and no one wanted to face him down. When he saw Patch, he made a detour that took him close to her.

Patch shrank away from the scarred man in horror.

"Keep your mouth shut, kid," Pike warned in a low voice, "or next time, I'll kill him."

Patch gasped, but before she could say anything, Pike Hardesty was gone.

Molly ripped some of her petticoat into strips and used it to try to stop the bleeding. Once her initial shock was over, she was able to see that the wound was not as serious as she had thought. She was greatly encouraged when Seth groaned and raised a hand to his head.

"Don't move," Molly said in a soothing voice. She looked around for a familiar face and spotted Red Dupree. "Could you help me move Seth to Schmidt's Hotel? We have a room there."

"Sure, Mrs. Kendrick," Red said. "Some of you fellas come over here and lend a hand. Take Doc Kendrick over to Uncle Jake's place."

Molly wrung her hands helplessly as she followed behind the men who jostled Seth toward the hotel. Patch had hold of her father's hand and walked beside him.

"Ain't but a crease," Red reassured Molly. "He'll be right as rain in no time."

"Why did it happen at all?" Molly demanded. "Why doesn't somebody arrest that man? How can he get away with shooting an unarmed man like that?"

"Ain't nobody around here as fast with a gun as Pike, ma'am. And he's mean enough to eat raw liver. Closest army is at Fort Shaw, and they're tied up with the Sioux. Got no choice except to put up with him, if you see what I mean."

Red made sure Seth was settled on the four-poster bed before he shooed everybody out of the room and left Molly, Patch, and Whit in peace.

Molly hurried to Seth's side. He started to say something to her, then groaned and lost consciousness again. She took the time to bathe away all the blood on his face. When she was finished, she noted his breathing was shallow but his pulse was steady.

She turned her attention to the two children who were sitting on ladderback chairs that had been brought in and placed in the far corner of the room.

Molly walked up to Patch and waited until the girl looked up at her. "You nearly got your father killed," she accused.

"I know," Patch replied in a frightened voice. "I didn't mean for anything like that to happen."

"It's as much my fault as hers," Whit said.

"Is that so?" Molly asked.

Whit nodded.

"What were the two of you doing in town? How did you get here?"

"It's a long story," Patch said with a sigh. "Are you sure you want to hear it?"

"Every word."

Patch and Whit exchanged worried glances.

"You can start whenever you're ready," Molly said, eyeing first Whit and then Patch. "I'm listening."

✳10✳

When Seth awoke, he thought he was alone. A moment later, a shadowy form materialized beside him on the bed.

"Is that you, Molly?"

"It's Dora Deveraux."

Seth put a tentative hand to his head and winced as he tried to sit up.

Dora pushed him back down and said, "Stay flat. Believe me, you'll feel better. How'd you let Pike get the drop on you like that?"

"My mistake," Seth said dryly. "I should have asked for Marquess of Queensbury rules."

Dora grinned. "I knew somebody would go a step too far with you someday. What did Pike say to make you mad?"

"He struck Patch."

Dora's face lost its humor. "That bastard. You should have killed him."

"Someday I will."

"Look, we don't have much time before your wife comes back."

"Where is she?" Seth asked.

"She took your kids downstairs to the dining room to get something to eat. I saw them come in and snuck up here. I had to tell you, it looks like Bassett is already back in business selling whiskey to the Indians. Same place as before, if you can believe it."

"That man can't take a hint," Seth said.

"Also, three gold miners are coming in on the stage from Virginia City at the end of the week. Think the Masked Marauder will be able to give them an escort?"

"It's a possibility," Seth said. "Thanks for the information, Dora."

"Anytime, Seth. So how do you like that new wife of yours?"

"I like her fine."

"Too bad. I miss you." Dora brushed Seth's hair back from his forehead. She trailed her fingers down the side of his face and passed her thumb across his lips, which parted at her touch. She leaned over to kiss his mouth, but he turned aside at the last second so her lips met his cheek instead.

When the door clicked shut, Dora slowly straightened and looked over her shoulder. Molly was standing there white-faced, holding a tray in her hands.

"Who are you?" Molly asked. "What are you doing here?"

"I'm Dora Deveraux, Mrs. Kendrick. I was just visiting Seth," Dora said, cool as ice. "We're old friends."

Old friends, indeed! More like *kissing cousins*! It was painfully apparent the two of them were very well acquainted.

Molly guessed from Dora's clothing what kind of woman she was. Her full skirt only came to her knees, and the form-fitting bodice left most of her bosom and shoulders bare. Her auburn hair was pinned up in curls, and she wore a garish green feather that matched the color of her spangly dress. The woman sat on the bed snuggled up next to Seth and had a possessive hand on the pillow beside his head. She didn't seem in any hurry to leave. Molly decided to give her a nudge.

"Seth needs his rest," she said, crossing to the table beside the bed to set down the tray.

"Well, he certainly knows how to make the best use of a bed," Dora said, shooting a sly grin in Seth's direction.

Seth flushed. "Dora was just leaving," he said firmly.

Molly wanted to know why the woman had come in the first place. But it was apparent that she wasn't going to get any answers from Dora Deveraux. The woman made a point of touching Seth as she resettled the blankets around him. Then she crossed the room past Molly and stopped at the door to look back toward the bed.

"Come see me when the newness wears off," she said to Seth. She didn't bother to close the door when she left the room.

Molly wanted very much to slam it after her. She resisted the urge and walked over and closed it very carefully and quietly.

Tension sang in the room. Seth pursed his lips and shook his head. "Dora and I aren't . . . that is, we haven't—"

Molly turned and leaned back against the door. "But you did," she said with certainty.

Seth shrugged. "I'm a man, Molly, not a monk."

"She still wants you."

"I can't control what she wants."

Molly didn't realize what she was going to say until the words were out of her mouth. "I won't share you, Seth. I know what it's like to have a husband with a mistress. I won't suffer the same mistake twice. Make a choice, and make it now."

"You don't understand—"

"There's nothing to understand. Do you want her, or do you want me?"

Seth grinned. "I like you when your dander's up, Molly. It makes your eyes sparkle."

"I'm serious, Seth."

He sobered. "I choose you, Molly. Today, tomorrow, always."

For a moment it was hard to believe she had won. The extent of her relief was disturbing, because it meant she cared more than she ought. After all, they had both agreed they could never love each other. They had both agreed this was a marriage of convenience. It shouldn't matter whether he had a mistress. It shouldn't matter whether he was committed to her and her alone.

But it had. It had mattered tremendously whether he chose her or Dora. So maybe her feelings for Seth Kendrick weren't as nonexistent as she had thought.

Molly was very much aware of Seth's eyes on her as she rearranged the pillows behind him to make a backrest. She helped him to sit up, noticing the grimace of pain when he was finally upright. "How does your head feel?"

"Like someone's in there knocking around with a hammer."

"Be thankful for the pain," Molly said with a smile. "It means you're alive." She sat down beside him where Dora had been, and tucked a napkin under his chin. "You could have been killed, Seth."

"Thanks to you, I wasn't." He took her hand in his and squeezed it. "You saved my life, Molly."

Molly looked down at his bruised and torn knuckles and then back at his untouched face. "Why did you let the whole town—and me—think you were afraid of Pike Hardesty, when you could have whipped him anytime?"

He rubbed Molly's palm with his thumb, not consciously seducing but obtaining that result all the same.

"I have my reasons, Molly. That's all I can tell you."

Molly tried not to feel hurt by his secrecy. After all, they had been husband and wife for less than two weeks. She knew he was telling her to drop the subject, but she persisted. "Why don't you carry a gun, Seth?"

His grip tightened on her hand. "I can't give you an answer to that question. Yet."

He was shutting her out. The walls were there, reminding her that however her feelings for Seth might be changing, he was holding to his side of the bargain. Molly didn't know what to say, so she said nothing.

She pulled her hand from his and busied herself setting up the tray on his lap. She expected Seth to make a fuss if she tried to feed him, but for whatever reason, he didn't. He opened his mouth and swallowed a spoonful of the broth she offered him.

"What did you do with Patch and Whit?" he asked.

"I didn't drop them down the bottom of a well, if that's what you're wondering," Molly said with a wry smile. "Although I very much wanted to. Those two rapscallions were in the back of the wagon the whole way into town!"

"I can understand why Patch would hitch a ride, but why did Whit come along?"

Molly paused with the spoon in midair, took a deep breath, and said, "He was running away."

"Patch was helping him?"

Molly nodded.

Seth forked a hand through his hair and winced when he got too close to his wound. "I suppose I should have seen it coming. Whit and I haven't been getting along very well."

"It isn't your fault," Molly said. "Whit never wanted to come here in the first place. If anybody's to blame, it's me, for bringing him here against his will."

They were both silent, thinking about what they had hoped to achieve through this marriage, and how far short of their expectations they had fallen.

"Where do we go from here?" Seth asked.

Molly knew he wasn't only talking about Whit and Patch but about their own relationship as well. She took a deep breath and said, "Maybe we made a mistake getting married."

"No!" Seth replied sharply. "I admit I hadn't bargained on so much resistance from Patch and Whit. But I'm willing to try to wear them down if you are. I'm betting we can outlast them and turn the five of us into a family."

"I don't think you realize what a Herculean task that will be."

"Wouldn't the results be worth the effort?"

Molly imagined them all sitting down to a supper table together, talking about what each had accomplished during the day, sharing their joys and their sorrows. It was a goal worth striving for. But she had her doubts about whether they would ever succeed. "Just how do you suggest we accomplish this miracle?"

Seth grinned. "First of all, we don't let Patch and Whit provoke us into arguing with each other over them."

"Were we doing that?"

Seth just stared, and Molly conceded, "All right. What else?"

"We stop jumping apart and feeling guilty when they see us together. In fact, I'll even go a step further and suggest we act like genuine, couple-in-love married people whenever they're around."

Molly stiffened. "How will that help?"

Seth chose his words with care. "If they see that you and I are committed to each other, that there is no hope that their machinations can succeed, they'll stop trying to push us apart. At least, I hope they will."

The loud knock at the door brought Molly to her feet. "That'll be Patch and Whit," she said. "I left them having dessert in the dining room." She took the tray from Seth's lap and set it on the table beside the bed.

He caught her wrist and said, "What do you say, Molly? Do you want to give it a try?"

"Yes," she said. "Yes, I do."

"Then sit here beside me."

Slowly, Molly sat back down beside him. She allowed Seth to draw her palm up to his mouth, where he kissed it.

"All right," he said. "Are you ready?"

Molly nodded.

He raised his voice and called, "Come in. The door's open."

Patch and Whit tumbled excitedly into the room and drew to a quick halt when they saw the intimate picture their parents presented together on the bed.

Patch frowned.

Whit grimaced.

Seth and Molly exchanged amused glances.

"Come on over here where I can see you both," Seth said.

Reluctantly, Patch and Whit crossed to stand beside the bed.

"I think you two have some explaining to do," he said.

Patch spoke first. "I'm sorry, Pa. I didn't mean for anything bad to happen. Whit made me come along."

Whit stared in disbelief at Patch. It was true he had asked for her help. But he hadn't forced her to come. He turned to his mother and said, "*She* was the one talked *me* into coming. I was having second thoughts about the whole idea of running away when—"

"If you've changed your mind about leaving," Seth interrupted, "then you'll be going back to the ranch with us tomorrow. Is that right?"

Whit stuck his hands in his pockets and scuffed the floor with the toe of his shoe. "I guess so."

"Then you'd better get a good night's sleep. You and I have a lot to get done tomorrow before we leave town."

Whit's eyes narrowed suspiciously. But if that was the extent of the punishment he was to receive, he wasn't about to complain.

"I'll stay here with you tonight, Pa," Patch volunteered. "Whit can get a room with his ma."

"No," Seth contradicted. "You and Whit can get another room. Molly and I will sleep here."

Molly opened her mouth to object, saw Seth's brow rise a fraction, and remembered their discussion. They must present a united front to their children. Their entire future depended on it. She caressed Seth's jaw and said, "I want to be able to keep an eye on your father tonight, Patch."

"But, Pa—"

Seth never took his eyes off Molly's face. "You go talk to Uncle Jake, Patch. He'll make sure you and Whit get settled in," Seth said.

Patch watched her father reach up to push a stray curl behind Molly's ear. With a snort of disgust she turned to Whit and said, "Let's get out of here," then marched out the door. Whit followed her without a backward glance.

Once the two children were gone, Molly let out the breath of air she had been holding. She reached up to grab Seth's hand, which had begun to tease the lobe of her ear. "Patch isn't going to give up without a fight."

"I never expected she would," Seth said. "I'm glad you agreed to have the children take another room. I've wanted to be alone with you for a long time." His hand encircled her nape and drew her toward him. He kissed the edge of her mouth with the enticing beauty mark on it, then groaned and leaned back against the pillows.

Seth's eyes closed, and his hand fell to his side. "Of all the nights to have a headache."

Molly laughed. "This isn't exactly how I pictured us spending our first night together, either." She rearranged the pillows again, helping him to get comfortable.

"Will you lie down with me, Molly, so I can wake up beside you in the morning?" he murmured.

"All right, Seth." Molly stepped behind a screen in the corner and changed into the warm flannel nightgown she had packed earlier in the day. When she was ready for bed, she blew out the lantern and Seth held the covers so she could slip beneath them. He curled a strong arm around her and nestled her back into the niches created by his muscular frame.

It felt different from lying close to James. Seth was leaner, and an inch or two less tall, so when their bodies spooned together she could just feel the rough bristle on his jaw against her face. His warm, moist breath on her nape made her shiver.

"You're cold," he said, pulling her more snugly against him. "Let me warm you up."

Molly felt as if she were on fire, but she wasn't about to tell Seth that when he had just admitted his head ached. There was no sense starting something they couldn't finish. Instead she asked, "What brought you to Fort Benton?"

His hand absently caressed her waist as he spoke. "I was looking for somewhere I could start over fresh. There are wide open spaces in this country where a man can carve out a place for himself."

"Start over from what?"

Seth smiled in the darkness. "You don't miss a thing, do you, Molly? All right, if you want to know, I'll tell you. I was a surgeon for the Confederacy. By the end of the war, I'd seen enough of death and done enough mutilation in the name of medicine to last me a lifetime. I wanted to escape from anything and everything that would remind me of those brutal years. I couldn't do that by going back to Texas. People there will be fighting the war in their hearts and minds for years to come.

"So I headed north with Patch. I ended up taking a steamboat from St. Louis to the end of the line—Fort Benton. I built myself a house here two years ago and started breaking horses for the army. I hadn't intended to let anyone know I was a doctor. But someone got shot once when I was in town and—the rest is history."

"You didn't mention Ethan. I thought he came here with you."

Seth shook his head. "Ethan and I met in Texas before the war, when he was still just a kid. He showed up in Fort Benton last year, just before winter took hold. Ethan's life is his own, Molly. If you have questions you want answered, you'll have to ask him."

Molly made up her mind to do just that. Maybe Ethan would be able to tell her more about the man she had married than Seth was willing to reveal about himself. She was silent, thinking about what Seth had said. He still hadn't told her what he did for a living before he became a doctor.

But when she opened her mouth to ask, she yawned instead.

"Close your eyes, Molly," Seth said, reaching up to gently do it for her. "And get some rest. Morning comes early."

Molly snuggled back against him. The worries of the past weeks and months seemed somehow far away. She felt safe and secure. In moments, she was sound asleep.

Seth's arm tightened about Molly's waist as he felt her body relax. He fought sleep because he wanted to enjoy this moment. He smiled as he thought of how she had demanded that he give up Dora for her. If only she knew! But maybe it was better that she didn't. He didn't expect her to understand why he had done what he'd done. He didn't expect her to care for him.

All the same, he liked the feeling he had gotten when she'd insisted she wouldn't share him with another woman. He hadn't felt like that since Annarose had demanded he take his eyes off the hurdy-gurdy girl at the county fair. He bent over to kiss the petal-soft skin of Molly's nape. Of course, he would never love Molly the way he had loved Annarose. But he had to admit he was starting to care. That wasn't a bad thing. As long as he didn't let it get out of hand.

Confident in his ability to manage his feelings for the woman in his arms, Seth closed his eyes and drifted off to sleep.

Meanwhile, Patch was having nowhere near so easy a time finding peace. It was unsettling to realize that her father had sided with his new wife over his daughter. To add insult to injury, she was stuck spending the night with a stepbrother she loathed. Even now, Whit was twisting and turning restlessly in the twin bed across from her.

"Consarn it! Can't you stay still?" she cried at last.

"This bed feels strange. I can't get comfortable," Whit retorted.

"I can't believe I agreed to come to town with you," Patch ranted, "and got myself in trouble for no good reason that I can see."

Whit bolted upright. "Wasn't my fault you stopped to listen at that window! That's when all the trouble started."

"Yeah? Well, it's a durned good thing I did! Those men are planning to ambush the Masked Marauder."

"So who the heck *is* the Masked Marauder, anyway?" Whit asked.

"Only the bravest, most heroic man on the face of the earth," Patch replied. "Of course, nobody really knows who he is because he wears a black mask."

Whit snickered. "Sounds like you're in love with him or something."

"That's ridiculous! I admire him. Who wouldn't?"

"What'd he do that's so special?" Whit asked.

"Somehow he finds out when the stage is going to be attacked by Indians, and he rides to the rescue."

"So why would those two men want to kill him?" Whit asked.

"From what I heard, the Masked Marauder destroyed some kegs of whiskey those men were selling to the Indians. They don't want him interfering with their business anymore. So they figure to ambush and kill him."

"Golly!" Whit exclaimed. "And you heard their plan? What are you going to do?"

Patch frowned thoughtfully. "If I knew who the Masked Marauder was, I'd tell him, of course. But that fella Pa fought with, that Pike—he said if I tell anyone what I heard, he'll kill Pa."

"How would he ever know you said anything?" Whit asked.

"I suppose if the Masked Marauder didn't fall into their trap, he'd know—or at least suspect," Patch said. "And I can't take the chance. Pa doesn't carry a gun. He wouldn't have a chance if Pike decided to shoot at him again."

"On the other hand," Whit said, "if you warned the Masked Marauder, he'd probably shoot Pike."

"On the other hand," Patch said, "how can I possibly warn the Masked Marauder when I don't know who he is?"

Patch froze as she recognized the significance of something the two plotting men had said. "Wait a minute. Maybe I *do* know who it is!"

"You do?"

"I didn't realize it until just now, but I know the identity of the Masked Marauder."

"So who is it?" Whit demanded.

"Ethan Hawk."

Whit's jaw dropped. "Naw. Really?"

Patch sat up in bed. "Remember when you came to see me the other night, and Ethan came in from outside when he was supposed to be sound asleep in bed?"

"Yeah?"

"*That* was the night those whiskey kegs were supposedly broken to pieces."

"So?"

"Ethan's shirt smelled of whiskey that night, but he hadn't drunk any. He told me somebody spilled whiskey on him, but don't you see? He must have gotten whiskey on himself when he broke up all those kegs!"

"I've never seen Ethan wearing a gun," Whit pointed out.

"But he has one," Patch said. "I've seen it in his cabin. And another thing," Patch said, her voice getting more excited as she became more certain she was right. "The Masked Marauder appeared for the first time about six months ago. Right after Ethan came to live here."

"So are you gonna tell Ethan about the plan to ambush the Masked Marauder?" Whit asked.

Patch thought about it. She was drawing a pretty big conclusion from pretty flimsy evidence. If she was wrong, Ethan would be sure to tell her father. And she didn't want to think about the results of such an eventuality.

However, if she secretly followed Ethan whenever he left the ranch from now on, she would not only be there to warn him about the ambush, but she could also be there to see the Masked Marauder in action.

"I'm going to have to ponder this a little longer," she said, "and decide what I should do. In the meantime, don't you blab anything to anybody."

"I won't," Whit promised.

"Now lie down and leave me be so I can think."

Whit lay back down and covered himself, but soon he began shifting again.

"Garn!" Patch said. She rolled out of bed, stomped over to Whit, and tucked the blanket tight under the mattress all around so he couldn't move. "Now go to sleep!" she ordered.

Whit smiled and did as he was told.

❊ 11 ❊

THE FIRST FEW DAYS home after the disastrous trip to Fort Benton were busy ones for Seth and Molly. He worked with Ethan and Whit to finish the third bedroom. She cooked and cleaned and sewed diligently on a dress for Patch.

On the day the dress was finished, Molly talked Patch into trying it on to surprise the men when they came inside for supper. Nessie watched from the four-poster in Patch's room as the transformation began.

Molly started with Patch's straight blond hair, brushing all the tangles out and taking the scissors to the ends to crop them just below her shoulders. Then she cut a fringe of bangs that fell just above Patch's brows. Finally, she combed Patch's hair back from the sides and gathered it at the crown, securing it with a black grosgrain ribbon, leaving the rest to fall down her back.

Once Patch's hair was done, Molly started from scratch and added layers of clothing. A white chemise with pink ribbons and lace-trimmed cotton drawers came first. Unfortunately, that was as far as Molly got before Patch balked.

Pointing to the corset in Molly's hands, she said, "I ain't gonna put that blasted thing on."

"Every lady wears one," Molly said.

"I ain't a lady."

"Do you want to be one?"

Patch's lids dropped to lay feathery crescents on her cheeks. "Don't matter if I do," she said in a quiet voice. "Ain't got the know-how."

"I'm here to teach you," Molly said.

Patch fidgeted with the ribbon on her chemise, liking the softness of it and the delicate pink color. She kept remembering how Ethan had said she'd look pretty in a dress. She wanted to please him, and to please Pa. But was that instrument of torture really necessary? "Do I hafta wear that durned thing?"

"It'll help your posture and make the dress fit properly."

"All right," Patch said in a resigned voice. "Do your worst."

Molly slipped the white coutil garment over Patch's head and settled it into place before tightening the laces.

"Take a deep breath," Molly ordered.

Patch gasped as Molly pulled the corset laces tighter. "You're squeezing me to death!"

"Just let me tie this off," Molly said, breathless from exertion. "There. All done. Now, hold your arms up and I'll bring this petticoat down over your head. One more."

Molly watched Patch's face in the oval dressing mirror and saw the mulish thrust of her lower lip. She had to work fast, before open rebellion broke out. "Arms up again. Let me slip this dress on." She put a hand against Patch's outthrust hip. "Stand up straight."

Patch uncocked her knee and drew her shoulders back in an exaggerated pose. "Is that straight enough for you?"

"Yes, fine," Molly answered. She disregarded Patch's sarcasm, attributing it to the anxiety that was its source.

Molly had cut off her striped silk dress so it came to midcalf on Patch, revealing a pair of black kid boots trimmed with ribbon. The leftover moss-green-striped material had become a sash for the waist. She had added an overskirt of plain green silk bought at I. G. Baker & Co., caught up at the sides with matching rosettes.

Once she finished buttoning up the bodice of the dress, Molly straightened the sailor collar over the girl's tense shoulders and puffed out the long sleeves. She stood behind Patch and brown eyes met blue in the silvered mirror before them.

"You look lovely, Patch. Every inch a lady."

"Looks can be deceiving."

Molly laughed. "You'll do fine."

Patch tried to sit on the bed in her normal way, but the corset kept her from bending. "Just like I thought. Can't hardly move in this getup."

"You'll learn. Now let Nessie and me get gussied up, and we'll treat the gentlemen to the presence of three ladies for dinner."

Molly couldn't have said who was more nervous when they heard the men washing up on the back porch, she or Patch. But Molly wished she could have had a tintype of Seth's face when he first saw his daughter, to save and show him in the years to come. His gray eyes glittered with emotion as he walked up to Patch and took her hands in his to hold her at arm's length. Seth's eyes met Molly's, and she saw it was a powerfully bittersweet moment for him.

"You look like your mother," he said to Patch. He let go of one hand and held the other over her head so she could turn in a circle for him. "I wish she were here to see you, Patch."

Seth felt grateful to Molly for the metamorphosis she had wrought in Patch. But Annarose should have been the one to dress Patch like this. Annarose should have been the one to share the glorious sight of their daughter looking like a proper young lady.

Patch was pleased at her father's approval. But it was the reaction in a set of bright green eyes that she sought. Ethan didn't disappoint her. His glance was warm with admiration and approbation. She stood still for his inspection as he took her hand from her father. His eyes widened slightly at the small bosom revealed by the fitted bodice of the dress.

"You're quite the young lady," he said with a grin.

Patch flushed. "Do you think so?"

"You're going to be a beautiful woman someday, Patch. Take my word for it."

Patch felt a fluttery feeling in her stomach, sort of like a butterfly inside. Before she could identify its source, he let go of her hand and picked up Nessie.

"Look at this little lady," Ethan said. "Aren't you the pretty one."

As Patch watched Ethan with Nessie, she experienced a startling and most unpleasant revelation. Ethan was using exactly the same tone of voice—and approximately the same words—to praise the four-year-old that he had used with her. She had wanted to look grown up for Ethan. It was agonizing to realize that to him she was just another little girl.

Patch just wanted to get away, to get out of the room and out of these foolish clothes. But as she started to back out of the room, her pa pulled out a chair for her and said, "May I have the pleasure of seating you, Miss Kendrick?"

His eyes glowed. His smile was so broad, it made her throat ache.

How could she disappoint him by running away? She swallowed her bitter letdown and allowed her father to seat her at the table.

The heels on Patch's shoes had only raised her a couple of inches to match Whit's height. But the total visual effect of styled hair, corseted body, and tailored silk dress left Whit feeling that Patch had somehow far outgrown him in a single afternoon. He felt bereft.

"I liked you better in pants," he said flatly as he sat down beside her.

Soon they were all seated at the table, with Nessie in a special raised chair that Seth had constructed for her. Molly had used her rose-patterned china, and with the ladies dressed as they were, supper had a festive air that belied the problems they were dealing with on a daily basis.

"Whit's bedroom ought to be finished by tomorrow," Seth announced. "I figure we can move his things in there by late afternoon. Patch can start sleeping in her own bed again."

Patch opened her mouth to object, but a piercing look from Ethan caused her to shut it again.

Molly glanced at Seth and saw that his gaze was intent on her. Tomorrow they would truly become man and wife. But it was too soon. She needed more time. The patient man had somewhere misplaced his patience.

"By the way," Seth said to Molly, "since we'll be finished with the room tomorrow, I thought maybe you'd like to have your first riding lesson later in the afternoon."

"I—I suppose so," she replied. "What should I wear?"

Seth's brow furrowed. He had planned to teach Molly to ride astride because he didn't have a sidesaddle. "I don't suppose you have a split skirt?"

Molly shook her head.

He grinned. "Then I guess you'll have to wear some of my pants."

Molly laughed. "I'd look ridiculous."

"You'll look adorable," Seth countered in a teasing voice.

"A pair of my pants would fit better," Ethan said. "You're welcome to them."

Patch shook her head in disbelief. Why on earth had her pa gone to such lengths to get her into a dress, when he thought Molly would look *adorable* in a pair of his pants? She would never understand grownups if she lived to be a hundred. "I'm gonna get out of this rig and go frog-hunting down at the pond," she said in disgust. "Anybody want to come along?"

"I do!" Nessie said.

"Me, too," Whit joined in.

"I think I'll help Molly with the dishes," Seth said.

Ethan raised a surprised brow, but when Seth winked at him, he quickly rose and said, "I'll keep you kids company."

"I have to help Patch and Nessie change out of their dresses," Molly said to Seth. "You can clear the table while you're waiting for me."

Seth pursed his lips and looked around at the table. Ethan grinned and scooted out the door after Whit. "Have fun!" he called over his shoulder.

By the time Molly returned, Seth was elbow deep in dishwater. "I'll finish those for you," she said.

"I'm almost done. Why don't you sit down and relax? You've put in a hard day."

"So have you." She set a plate of bones down for Maverick, absently patting the dog-wolf on the head as she did. She picked up a towel and began drying dishes and putting them away.

"I've been meaning to tell you, I have to go into town again later this week."

"Oh?"

"It's Mrs. Gulliver again."

Molly glanced at Seth from the corner of her eye. Was there really a Mrs. Gulliver? She hadn't thought so. But surely Seth wouldn't have brought her up again if she didn't exist. "What's wrong with Mrs. Gulliver, anyway?"

"Bowels," he said.

That was an intimidating enough subject that Molly shied from pursuing it. She lifted Bandit, the raccoon, off the counter, where he had just finished eating a plate of scraps, and set him on the floor. Then she leaned out the open window and set a bowl of milk on the back porch. "Here kitty, kitty," she called. The mountain lion came running.

"How long will you be at Mrs. Gulliver's?" Molly asked as she resumed drying dishes.

"I don't expect to stay the night. But it depends on how poorly the old lady's doing."

"I'll keep a light burning for you," she said.

"I'd like that." Seth leaned over and gave her a quick kiss on the mouth. "Thanks."

"What for?"

"For turning Patch into a lady."

Molly smiled. "I have a ways to go yet."

"Maybe. But getting her into a dress is a major miracle as far as I'm concerned."

Molly focused on the china coffee cup she was drying. "I haven't wanted to mention this, Seth, because I know how attached you are to Patch. But if you really want to make a lady of your daughter, she needs to go to school."

"She attends school in town every fall."

Molly folded the damp dishcloth and laid it over the back of a kitchen chair to dry. She turned to face Seth and said, "I mean she needs to go away to school—to a finishing school for young ladies."

"No."

Molly put a hand on Seth's arm. "It wouldn't be forever. And it would open up a whole new world to her that isn't possible here. Just think about it. Will you?"

"No."

Molly didn't press him further.

"I think I'll go see if I can catch up to the kids," Seth said. "Do you want to come along?"

"I need to change my clothes. And it has been a long day. Why don't you go on," Molly said.

She wasn't surprised when Seth turned and left her without another word. It was a lot to spring on him in one night—to see his daughter as a young woman, and then to tell him that he had to send her away.

But Molly knew there was only so much she could accomplish with Patch. Seth's daughter had been forced to become independent at a very early age. It wasn't easy for Patch to take advice or direction from anyone. Molly could polish off the rough edges, but Patch very likely wouldn't allow more change than that.

Seth got no farther than the back porch when he spied a figure huddled near the woodpile. "Who's out there?"

"It's me, Whit."

Seth crossed over to sit down beside the boy on a pile of split logs that was stacked to be cut for firewood. "What are you doing out here?"

Whit held up a stick in one hand and a knife in the other. "Whittling."

Seth perused the knife Whit held out to him. "Mighty fine knife. Sharp."

"My da gave it to me. He taught me how to whittle. Said it helps a sailor pass the time at sea."

Seth pulled a Bowie knife from the scabbard at his belt. "My pa taught me to whittle too," he said. He searched around till he found a stick the right size, then began to shave the bark from it. "It does a fine job of passing the time around the campfire, too."

"When you whittle, you don't have to think about anything," Whit said.

"Nope," Seth agreed.

"And however you're feeling, why, you can take it out on the wood."

"Yep," Seth agreed. Wood shavings began to pile up in front of him.

"My mother says it's silly to whittle. 'Cause you don't have anything to show for it when you're done."

"Shows how much she knows," Seth muttered under his breath.

"What?"

"Nothing."

"I especially like whittling 'cause I can do it alone," Whit said.

"Me, too," Seth agreed. "But I'm glad you let me join you tonight."

"Yeah, well, I'm getting kind of used to having you around."

———————————

Molly had stood by the kitchen window and listened shamelessly to the conversation by the woodpile. Seth Kendrick was a kind, caring man. What woman wouldn't fall in love with him?

A grieving widow.

Clamoring voices announced the return of Patch, Nessie, and Ethan. Molly pulled her robe more closely around herself and stepped out of the kitchen door to join them on the back porch.

Nessie came running up to her and held out both hands. "See my frog, Mama?"

Molly bent down just as Nessie opened her hands. The frog she was holding leaped straight up in the air, actually grazing Molly's cheek on its way past. She yelped in surprise, to the accompaniment of laughter from everyone on the porch, including Nessie.

Molly collapsed in a heap on the porch step and pulled Nessie into her lap with a breathless laugh of her own. "I nearly had a seizure!"

The dog-wolf, Maverick, and Rebel, the mountain lion, soon appeared to stalk Nessie's frog, which was finding the porch a much less safe place than the pond.

Molly sat quietly and held Nessie while she listened to Patch tell her father about the huge bullfrog she had almost caught.

"But he got away," she said at last. "No thanks to Ethan."

"I didn't think your pa'd want you to go swimming in the dark," Ethan said.

"I ain't afraid."

"Never said you were," Ethan replied. "But it'd be a shame to get that pretty hair of yours all wet."

Patch reached up and patted the ribbon in her hair, as though to make sure it was still there. "Yeah, well, it would have dried."

"I think maybe it's time for you kids to get to bed," Seth said.

"I'll be waiting for you, Patch," Ethan said as he headed off toward his cabin.

In a tradition as old as the ages, Seth's and Molly's children wheedled and fought against the end of the day as their parents readied them for bed. Molly insisted on removing the ribbon and brushing Patch's hair fifty strokes before she would allow the girl to escape to Ethan's cabin. Whit and Nessie had passed the stage of exhaustion, yet they resisted the pull of sleep that sought to claim their consciousness.

At long last, the bedroom lamps were out, the children tucked in and kissed and told they were loved. And Molly and Seth were alone, and awake, and very much aware of each other.

"Would you like to go for a walk now?" Seth asked. "Or just sit and talk?"

Molly began to back away from him. "I really ought to go to bed. I—"

"Please don't go."

Seth reached out and grasped her hand.

Molly felt a slow warmth travel up her arm and spread throughout her body. She looked up into Seth's eyes and found them avid with desire. His nostrils were flared for the scent of her, and his body was taut with need.

"Come with me," he said.

"Where?"

"To the stable. You can see the mare you'll be riding tomorrow."

And make love to me.

Seth didn't say the words, but Molly heard them all the same. Somehow she found herself following him. When they reached the stable, he lit a lantern and hung it at the head of a stall. A pretty black mare with a white diamond on her forehead stuck her nose out over the half-door and nuzzled Seth's shirt.

"I usually have something for her—a dried apple or a carrot."

Molly patted the mare's silky nose. "She's beautiful."

"She's also very gentle."

I can be too.

"You don't have to worry about getting thrown," Seth said.

Molly looked up into Seth's eyes and read his thoughts.

It's all right, Molly. I won't hurt you.

"Would you like to see the hayloft?" he asked.

It's more private up there. We won't have to worry about being interrupted.

"All right," she said.

Seth took the lantern and climbed up the ladder ahead of her. Molly saw he must have been thinking about this for a while, because in the corner of the loft lay a quilt she had last seen packed away in the top of the wardrobe in Seth's room. He set the lantern down on an empty crate and spread the blanket on a crunchy bed of hay. Then he turned and faced her.

You can still say no. We can stop here and now.

Molly took a step toward him. It was all the response he needed. She was swept up in his arms and pulled into a strong embrace. His mouth found hers, his tongue seeking entrance.

She groaned once in despair—or desire—and parted her lips.

His tongue was gentle but thorough, reaching behind her upper lip for the sensitive flesh there. He searched the ridged roof of her mouth before drawing her tongue into a duel with his and asking—demanding—that she return the favor.

He untied her robe and impatiently pushed it off her shoulders, then stopped and looked at her in the shadowed light of the lantern. Her nipples had peaked beneath the soft flannel gown and were clearly visible. He slowly unbuttoned the gown, kissing his way down, making her flesh catch fire from the warmth of his lips.

"Molly, Molly. I want you so much!" His voice was guttural with need. Urgent. Excited.

Molly caught the fever in his flesh and fed upon it. She reached out a hand and unbuttoned his shirt and shoved it away from his shoulders. He quickly skinned out of his long john shirt, leaving him naked to the waist. Molly did something she had wanted to do for a long time. She put her hands around him and, leaning her cheek against the wiry hair on his chest, felt with her hands for the scars on his back.

"How did you get these?" she asked.

"They're gunshot wounds, Molly. Part of my past."

He didn't let her ask another question, just covered her mouth and took what he needed.

Molly's knees refused to hold her, and as she felt herself falling, Seth caught her and lowered them both to the quilt. His hands caught the hem of Molly's nightgown and slipped up under it, pushing it out of his way as he caressed her calves and the insides of her thighs, coming ever closer to the heat of her, yet not touching. Waiting.

Molly shivered.

Seth took her hand and placed it over the front of his jeans. "Feel that, Molly. That's what you do to me."

Molly shivered.

"You're cold, sweetheart. Let me warm you." He mantled her body with his, fitting his hips into the cradle of her thighs, letting her know how much she was wanted.

Molly thrust her hands into Seth's hair and pulled his head down to kiss him. She breathed his name. "Seth."

She teased his lips, playing a game of taste and touch, but never staying in one place so that he could put his tongue in her mouth and mime the dance of lovers.

Abruptly, Seth grabbed her gown at the neck and edged it down, revealing her breasts but trapping her arms. Slowly, as though he had all the time in the world, he leaned over and kissed one breast, then the other. He caressed her with his mouth, sucking and biting, and then soothing with more kisses.

"Seth," Molly begged. "I want to touch you."

He stopped long enough to pull the gown down to free her arms, then pulled it off over her feet. He stopped again to look at her.

Molly felt self-conscious. No man had ever seen her thus. Not even James. She was grateful for the dim light that she hoped would hide the marks left by the children she had borne.

But Seth's eyes saw only perfection. "You're beautiful, Molly." He laid a hand reverently on her womb and let it trail down to the nest of dark hair between her legs.

Molly started to close her eyes, but Seth said, "Look at me. I want to see what you're feeling."

So much. She was feeling so much. Molly groaned as Seth slid a finger inside her.

He lay beside her, and his mouth found hers and tasted honey as he gloried in the feel of her mouth on his.

Molly arched toward him, opened to him, felt him put another finger inside her.

She put her hands on his face and ended the kiss. "Seth. Stop. Please."

He gasped with the effort, but he did. "What's wrong?"

Molly reached down to the buttons on the front of his jeans. "Take off your clothes. So I can touch you."

Seth's entire body tautened at the thought of her hands on him.

Molly smiled at the haste with which Seth's trousers and long johns found their way to the bottom of the quilt to join her night-gown. She put a hand on his flat belly and trailed her fingers down the crease between his thigh and the place where his desire for her was abundantly evident. She surrounded him with her hand, surrounded the heat, the softness, and the hardness.

Molly drew him toward her and led him inside.

Seth sighed with pleasure as he pushed deep inside Molly, all the way, until there was none of him that was not a part of her. He felt her heels grasp his buttocks and pull him tight against her. He began to move, slowly, and mimed with his tongue in her mouth what his body did below.

Molly's fingernails made crescents in Seth's flesh as she clutched him and held on, while her spirit soared and her body shuddered with its release.

Seth's face looked more in agony than ecstasy, but his final cry was one of triumph as he spilled his seed in her and made her his wife.

❉12❉

Pᴀᴛᴄʜ ᴡᴀs ɴᴇᴀʀʟʏ ᴀsʟᴇᴇᴘ on her pallet in front of Ethan's fireplace when she heard him moving stealthily through the room. She opened her eyes just a crack and saw in the banked light of the fire that he was dressed in dark clothes. She tried to remember whether the Masked Marauder had ever rescued anyone at night. She didn't think so. But she couldn't take any chances.

As soon as he was gone, she dressed quickly and followed after him, riding bareback with a halter she'd grabbed at the corral because she thought he would get too far ahead of her if she stopped to saddle her horse. After an hour of following him, Patch still hadn't figured out where Ethan could possibly be going. Patch looked on that as a positive sign that he must be the Masked Marauder. Why else would he be wandering around in the dark?

He changed direction again, and this time Patch saw in the distance the soft yellow glow where Fort Benton was situated. He continued on through town, beyond the last warehouse on the levee to a wooden barnlike building. Patch pulled her horse to a stop in the shadows and watched nervously as Ethan went inside the darkened building. A few moments later, he came out leading a large, coal-black horse on a halter and carrying a small saddle roll. He mounted again and, leading the black, rode back the way he had come.

Patch slipped into a nearby alley and stared with eyes rounded big as saucers as he rode past her.

Ethan really was the Masked Marauder!

She wondered why he kept the big black in town, where it might be found. Although the townspeople would hardly think to look for the Masked Marauder's horse right under their noses. At least, they hadn't so far.

Patch wanted to confront Ethan with what she knew and beg him to allow her to go along on his next adventure. But if Ethan wouldn't let her go swimming in the pond after dark, he would hardly be likely to take her along when there was real danger. She didn't dare let him know she had found out his secret.

Although he took a circuitous route, Ethan ended up right back at the ranch. Patch followed him to a copse of pine not far from his cabin, where a lean-to stood. She had never even known it was there! When he took the horse and the saddle roll inside, she turned and left, racing for the corral to return her horse before he returned and discovered it missing.

She headed back to his cabin on foot, stripped off her clothes, lay down with her back to the door, and covered herself with the quilt. A few minutes later, she heard the door squeak as Ethan pushed it open. She marveled at how quietly he made his way across the room.

To her surprise, he made a detour over to her. She held her breath, then realized that was sure to give her away. She forced herself to take slow, deep, even breaths as Ethan knelt beside her and pulled the covers up over her shoulders. He brushed aside her bangs, his hands gentle, his touch slow and easy, so as not to disturb her sleep.

Patch nearly died when she felt the touch of his lips on her forehead. She fought to keep from opening her eyes to look at him. Whyever had he done such a thing? Fortunately for her thudding heart, a moment later he stood and walked away. Patch wondered if he had ever done anything like that before. She didn't understand what she was feeling, but it upset her to think that Ethan felt free to just kiss her like she was some baby or something.

She couldn't confront him about it without revealing she was wide awake—a fact for which she had no easy explanation. Patch lay there and fumed about it for a while, until she decided what he'd done wasn't so terrible and maybe best forgotten. Except she didn't really want to forget it. In fact, she was probably going to remember it for the rest of her life.

Patch fell asleep thinking about the best way of saving the Masked Marauder from the ambush that Drake Bassett and Pike Hardesty were planning for him. All she really knew was that the ambush was supposed to happen on the butte west of town where the two men had set up a whiskey-selling operation. She wondered whether she at least ought to let that information slip to Ethan. She decided to sleep on it and make her decision in the morning.

Only when she woke up in the morning, Ethan was gone. And so was the big black stallion.

Patch realized she couldn't take the chance that Ethan might slip away like that sometime and end up getting ambushed. So when he returned, she immediately confronted him.

"I know you're the Masked Marauder, Ethan."

His eyes never blinked. He never moved at all. "What makes you think that, Patch?"

"Don't try to pretend. I saw you go to town last night and get your black stallion. I saw the saddle roll—which probably has your mask inside. The reason I'm telling you I know is—"

"You're wrong about the stallion, Patch. Your pa is paying for the use of that black for stud. That's where I was this morning. I took him up to service the mares in the box canyon."

"What about the saddle roll?" Patch queried.

"Just some tack for the stallion."

"Tell me the truth, Ethan. It's important. Are you the Masked Marauder?"

"You'll have to look elsewhere for a hero, Patch. I'm not the man you're searching for." He turned and walked away.

Patch had been so sure it was Ethan that the letdown was tremendous. Now she was no closer to knowing who the Masked Marauder was than anybody else in town. But she had information that was vitally important for the Masked Marauder to know. What on earth was she supposed to do now?

———— • ————

Molly was worried about Patch. Seth's daughter had been wandering around all morning with a hangdog expression. Right now she was sitting at the kitchen table with an uneaten sandwich from lunch in front of her, turning her glass of buttermilk in circles on the table-cloth. Nessie was down for her nap, and Whit was putting the finishing touches on his room with Seth. Ethan had gone scouting for more wild horses that could be captured and sold to the army.

"Is there anything you'd like to talk about?" Molly asked.

Patch shook her head no.

"Do you want to go outside for a while?"

Patch shrugged. "I guess so." She rose and scuffed her way out the door.

Molly decided Patch's distraction was probably due to the fact that she would be moving back into her own bedroom tonight. When she did, Nessie would still be there. It was going to be an adjustment for Seth's daughter to share her room with somebody else. If Molly could have arranged things differently, she would have. But Seth had said it wasn't practical to build a fourth bedroom for Nessie when the two girls could easily share. Molly could sympathize with Patch because she had a difficult situation of her own to face this evening.

Last night, after she and Seth had made love, they had lain for a long while in each other's arms. At first, Molly had felt content. Making love to Seth had felt right and good, and it had been more than just a little wonderful. But soon she had begun to think of all the things Seth hadn't told her about himself . . . and to wonder.

Who had shot him in the back? And why? What had he done before he became a doctor? How had Annarose Kendrick died? Why had he allowed the town of Fort Benton to think him a coward? Where had he learned to be so handy with his fists? What kind of relationship did he *really* have with Dora Deveraux? And why did he want to keep so much of his past a secret from her?

Molly had learned a great deal about patience from being married to a man who was gone to sea for years at a time. It should have been a simple matter for her to let Seth's secrets unfold over time. But the existence of a dark, unknown side to her husband frightened her. She had already surrendered her body to the stranger beside her. Molly was haunted by the fear of committing her heart and soul to a man who was not worthy of them. She was determined to know what Seth seemed equally determined to keep to himself.

Molly cleared her throat and said, "Seth, I think we need to have a talk."

Seth lazily ran his fingertips across the crest of her breasts. "I'm listening."

Molly grabbed his hand to still its sensuous journey. "I want to know what you did before you became a doctor. And I want to know how Annarose died."

He tensed. "I've told you those things aren't important."

"They are to me."

Seth tried distracting her by nibbling on her ear.

Molly jerked away. "Seth, please. I want some answers."

Seth sighed and lay down flat. He raised an arm to shield his eyes. "Why do you want to know?"

"I want to understand who you are."

"By finding out what I used to be?"

"Yes. By finding out everything I can about you."

He sat up abruptly and leaned over her, his eyes fierce and smoldering in the light of the lantern. "What if I told you I've killed men, Molly? Not just a few. What if I told you I'm good with a gun—fast. What if I told you Annarose died a violent death? Will those answers satisfy you?"

He lurched to his feet and began stuffing his legs into his pants. He yanked on his boots and threw his shirt and long johns over his shoulder. "Come on, get dressed."

Molly grabbed at her nightgown and hurriedly poked her arms into the sleeves. She stood and began gathering the quilt.

"Leave it," he snarled. "I might need a place to bed down sometime."

As Molly followed Seth down the ladder, she realized that much of his fury had been directed at himself. Was he regretting what he had been? What he had done?

Unfortunately, the answers he had given her had only raised more questions. Tonight, when she joined him in the bedroom they would be sharing from now on, she had to decide whether to ask for more answers. Or whether to simply go forward from here, accepting and loving the man Seth was—the man he had become, shaped by the violence in his past.

Molly had been staring out the kitchen window, and she saw Seth come out of the barn headed for the house.

She had completely forgotten about her riding lesson! She was still wearing the dress she'd put on first thing this morning. Ethan had brought her a pair of his jeans earlier in the day, and she ran to Seth's bedroom now to put them on. She hurried because she didn't want him coming into the bedroom after her.

"Molly? Where are you? Are you ready to learn how to ride?"

Molly was embarrassed by the way Ethan's pants conformed to the contours of her hips and legs. But she hadn't time to find something else to wear. She furiously rolled up the hems and pulled on a pair of boots Seth had bought for her in town. She checked to make sure Nessie was still sleeping soundly and moments later arrived breathless in the kitchen doorway. "I'm here."

Seth whistled appreciatively. "Those jeans do more for you than they ever did for Ethan."

Molly smoothed her hands down over her hips. "I'm hoping to get a riding skirt sewn in another day or so. But I've been planning and cooking for the christening party tomorrow for Iris's new baby. I just haven't had time—"

"You look fine. Don't worry about it. Come on."

The black mare, Star, hadn't looked particularly large when Molly stood beside her in the corral. However, the view was somewhat different from atop the animal. Molly was very much aware of how far off the ground she was. She clutched the saddle horn for dear life while Seth adjusted the stirrups.

"You're going to do fine," Seth assured her. "Just relax."

With Seth's hands positioning her, touching her at the waist, on her back, at the knee and the ankle, that was impossible.

"Just walk Star around the corral so you can see how it feels. Let your body move with the rhythm of the horse."

At first Molly was stiff, but with Seth's encouragement she was soon surprisingly comfortable. "This isn't so bad," she said.

The trot was more difficult, but she soon mastered it, and finally the canter, which although it was a faster gait, was smoother. Molly was loping Star around the corral, confident in her ability to control the animal, when Bandit darted across Star's path.

Molly was thrown up on Star's neck as the mare went stiff-legged, shying away from the raccoon. Just as Molly regained her seat and her footing in the stirrups, Nessie crossed practically under Star's feet, oblivious to the danger, intent on catching Bandit.

This time Star reared. Nessie froze, suddenly aware of the animal towering over her. Molly sawed on the reins, hoping to turn Star so the animal's hooves would not come down and crush her daughter. Star backed sideways on her hind legs and jerked against the reins. For a moment it appeared the mare would lose her balance and topple over backward.

Molly's mouth was open, but the scream was caught in her throat.

Seth was halfway across the corral when he realized he wasn't going to get there in time. His heart was in his throat. Everything seemed to move in slow motion. There was nothing he could do to prevent the tragedy that was about to occur.

The mare's hooves were on their downward arc when a blur of color—Patch!—rolled under the lower rail of the corral, grabbed Nessie, and kept on rolling. Even so, Star's hooves struck a glancing blow on Patch's shoulder.

Suddenly everything was moving at full speed again. Molly and Seth reached the two girls almost at the same moment. Nessie was sitting in the dirt beside Patch, crying. Molly dropped onto her knees and scooped her daughter into her arms. She squeezed Nessie tight, reassuring herself that the little girl was whole and safe.

Patch lay sprawled on the ground where she had landed. She inched her shoulder up slightly and groaned.

"Is she all right?" Molly asked Seth in a choked voice.

With shaking hands, Seth felt for broken bones and torn skin at the point where the mare's hoof had landed. He lifted Patch's right arm to see the range of movement, and she groaned again.

"I don't think her shoulder's broken, but she's good and bruised," he said. He gently lifted Patch into his arms and carried her inside to her bedroom. Molly came along and pulled the covers down and took off Patch's shoes before Seth laid her down.

"Get some cool water," Seth ordered. "A compress will help ease the bruising."

Molly picked up Nessie, unwilling to let her out of her sight, and headed into the kitchen.

Seth sat down beside Patch and started unbuttoning her blouse. He put a hand behind her and sat her up so he could take her shirt off. When he saw the pink ribbons on her chemise, it occurred to him that he might be embarrassing her—again.

Patch's eyes were closed, her face flushed. "I'd leave you to do this for yourself," he said in a constricted voice, "but I expect you won't have much use of that shoulder for a while." He skimmed the shirt off her, had her turn over on her stomach, and covered her up to the waist.

Molly returned with a bowl of cool water and several cotton cloths which Seth used to ease Patch's pain.

"Good thing I was wearing pants," Patch mumbled against the pillow.

"What's that?" Molly asked.

"Couldn't've made it to Nessie in time if I'd been dressed up like a lady."

Molly met Seth's eyes. "No, I guess this country isn't made for ladies," she said. She smoothed the bangs back from Patch's face and said, "I want to thank you for risking your life for Nessie."

"Woulda done it for anybody," Patch said ungraciously. She didn't know herself why she'd risked life and limb for that little intruder. But she didn't want praise for doing it. She just wanted everybody to go away. She closed her eyes and shut them out.

"I think she's sleeping," Nessie said, leaning close and peering into Patch's face.

Molly took Nessie by the hand. "Let's leave her alone and let her rest." She put a comforting hand on Seth's shoulder as she passed by him.

"I think I'll sit with her for a few minutes," he said.

As Molly turned to leave the room, Whit arrived in the doorway, having just put the finishing touches on his new room. "What's going on?" he asked. "Why is Patch in bed?"

"Star almost kilt me," Nessie said importantly. "But Patch saved my life."

"Golly!" Whit said. "I miss all the fun!"

When Ethan showed up at suppertime, Whit treated him to an embellished version of Patch's heroic efforts to save Nessie from Star's thundering hooves. The object of all this praise was, of course, still asleep in bed.

After supper everyone marched out to Whit's new room, which had its own outside entrance as well as a door cut through to Patch's room, which connected it to the rest of the house.

Seth had made a bed with rope springs, and a table and chair. The table already held a lantern, several books Whit had brought from Massachusetts, and a pitcher and bowl for washing. There were pegs on the wall for his clothes. It had a dirt floor right now, but Seth eventually planned to cover it over with wooden planks. A stone fireplace graced one wall and was necessary to heat the room through the frigid winter.

Molly's contribution was green-checked gingham curtains for the glass windows. Right now they were tied back to allow the last of the sun's rays to light the room.

Molly left the three men talking about whittling while she ushered

Nessie through the connecting door into Patch's bedroom. "You be careful not to roll over during the night and hurt Patch's shoulder," she admonished her daughter as she tucked her into bed.

"I won't hurt Patch," Nessie said. "I *love* her."

Molly looked to see whether Patch might have heard this confession, but Seth's daughter seemed still to be sleeping. "I love her, too," she whispered to Nessie. "Now go to sleep."

After Molly left the room, Patch's eyes blinked open in the darkness. All this talk about love was getting pretty sickening. That Gallagher woman and her kid hardly knew her. How could they care? Only, Patch had to admit the little girl had a way of getting under your skin. When she had seen Nessie under Star's hooves, she hadn't hesitated to risk her life for the kid. It was all pretty confusing, actually.

Patch froze when she felt Nessie's fingers curl around her hand and squeeze gently. Patch grimaced. The little intruder had a way about her all right. She closed her eyes and sighed and gently squeezed back.

Molly had stepped into Whit's bedroom in time to catch Seth tucking her son—toes and all—under the covers. Ethan had already gone to his cabin. She quickly kissed her flustered son good night in front of Seth, followed Seth outside, and closed the door behind her.

"He's excited about having his own room," Molly said as they walked around to the kitchen door. "You did a wonderful job with all the furniture."

"I'm glad you're feeling so charitable with me, because I'm afraid I have some bad news for you."

"Oh?"

"Ethan dropped by Fort Benton while he was gone. Seems Mrs. Gulliver can't wait. I'm afraid I have to go see her tonight."

"Oh." Molly hadn't realized she would feel so disappointed. But she did. "Maybe you won't be gone long."

"I hope not," he said. "But don't wait up for me."

Molly managed a smile. "I'll leave a light in the window for you."

"Thanks, Molly." He pulled her into his arms and kissed her hard. And just as quickly let her go. "I'll be back as soon as I can."

———— · ————

Pike Hardesty had been watching in hiding for the better part of a week, waiting for the Masked Marauder to show his face. The Blackfeet had been coming and going every day, buying their firewater, with no sign of any masked rider on a big black horse. It had seemed so provoking an act to begin selling whiskey again in the exact same place that he had been sure the Masked Marauder would be back. But he hadn't come.

There was a campfire over by the kegs, where the whiskey-seller could warm himself. But Pike was hidden up a hill behind some rocks. It was damned cold. This was the last night he planned to sit out here all alone waiting. If the Masked Marauder didn't show up tonight, he would just have to come up with some other plan to get rid of him.

When a rider suddenly appeared in the eerie light of the campfire, his black cloak flowing out behind him, Pike's skin crawled. A mask covered the man's face from the nose up, and a black hat sat low on his brow. Pike saw the metal gleam of two guns, one tied down on each leg.

Pike realized the man had picked his moment carefully. The only Indians near the campfire had already passed out from the whiskey they'd drunk. The whiskey-seller already had his hands up. If Pike hadn't been there, a repeat of the past destruction most certainly would have occurred.

But Pike was there. He raised his rifle and sighted on the Masked Marauder's heart. The way the man was silhouetted in the light of the fire, he couldn't miss. Just pull the trigger, and it would all be over. But Pike had spent a week in the cold to catch the Masked Marauder, and he ought to at least get to watch the man squirm before he died.

The Marauder had already tied up the whiskey-seller and taken an ax to the first of the barrels of whiskey when Pike came sauntering down the hill with his rifle trained on him.

"You might want to stop what you're doing for a minute," Pike said, "and think about meetin' your maker."

When the Marauder started to drop the ax from his right hand, Pike said, "Don't make a move. I'm going to shoot you anyway, but if you're real careful, I might let you live a little longer."

"Well, well, Pike. I always thought this day would come," the Marauder said.

"How do you know my name?"

"Everybody knows you, Pike. You make a habit of shooting unarmed men. Only, I guess this'll spoil your record, seeing as how I'm wearing a gun—two guns."

Pike lifted the rifle and sighted along the barrel. "You're gonna die."

"Everybody's gotta die sometime."

Pike was getting nervous. He had the rifle aimed right at that Marauder, had the drop on him plain as red paint, but the masked devil wasn't showing scared. What kind of man was he? More to the point, who was he? "Take off that mask," Pike ordered.

"Can't do that, Pike."

"I'll shoot if you don't."

"You'll shoot if I do."

Pike knew he ought to just shoot the Marauder and get it over with, but he wanted the man to grovel before he killed him. "I figure you're all gurgle and no guts," Pike said. "So I tell you what I'm gonna do. I'm gonna start shooting at parts of you, and when you decide to take off that mask, you just tell me and I'll stop."

"I expected as much from you, Pike. Your kind—"

Pike was listening, watching the Marauder's mouth move as he spoke, so he was startled when a gun magically appeared in the man's left hand. Pike pulled the trigger on his rifle as soon as he saw it, and he knew his bullet hit the man. But the Marauder shot at the same time.

Pike saw the yellow flash before he heard the six-gun roar. He stumbled backward—his jaw dropping in surprise—as a bullet smashed into his rifle, splintering it and driving the weapon out of his grasp.

The Marauder dropped the ax and pulled his other gun faster than Pike had ever seen anyone move in his life. But the masked man didn't shoot. He just stood there with both guns aimed at Pike.

Pike felt the sweat break out on his brow. His stomach curled up and forced bile into his throat.

"I ought to kill you," the Marauder said. "But I'll give you a warning instead. Get out of town, Pike. Get out of Montana. Because if I ever see you again, I'm going to put a bullet through your black heart."

Pike watched impotently as the Marauder backed away into the darkness. A moment later, he heard the thunder of hoofbeats as the Marauder made his escape. Pike grabbed the Colt in his holster and shot into the darkness, hoping he would get lucky, but knowing he was just wasting bullets.

Pike ranted and raved for several minutes after the Marauder was long gone. Not only had he failed to kill the masked man, he'd been made to look a fool in front of the whiskey-seller, who was bound to spread the story in Fort Benton. Drake Bassett wasn't going to be happy when he heard what had happened here tonight. Hell, he wasn't too damn delighted himself!

First the defeat at the hands of that yellow-bellied doctor, and now this! Pike was in a mean mood by the time he hit the outskirts of Fort Benton. He headed for the Medicine Bow Saloon and stomped over to the table in the corner he considered his own private property, bullied the men sitting there out of their seats, and proceeded to drink three glasses of rye in brooding silence.

What he needed was a woman, Pike decided at last. And only one woman would do. He searched the smoky saloon for Dora Deveraux, and when he didn't see her, he headed up the stairs to her room, knowing full well she was probably with another customer. It was going to mean a fight, but he was itching for one.

He twisted the doorknob planning to walk right in, but the damn thing was locked. "Open up, Dora, and let me in!" Pike yelled.

Dora came to the door, but instead of opening it she spoke through the wood. "I've got a customer, Pike. Come back later."

"Send him on his way, Dora. Or I'll do it for you."

"Wait your turn. I'll make it worth your while."

"I don't wanta wait. Now open this damn door before I kick it in!" he shouted at the top of his voice.

When Dora opened the door, Pike shoved past her, wanting to get his hands on the man he knew would be in her bed. He stopped, gape-mouthed at what he found. A slow red flush worked its way up his neck. For there in Dora's bed, with pillows plumped up behind his back and covered only in a sheet, sat his nemesis—Doc Kendrick.

"Evening, Pike," Seth said. "Sorry to inconvenience you, but I got here first."

Pike took one step toward the bed before he heard the snick of a gun being cocked. He stopped dead. The doc held both hands up and wiggled his fingers to show he was unarmed. Pike turned and saw Dora standing with a small derringer. It wasn't much as guns go, but she couldn't miss at this range, and even a small slug was enough to kill a man if it landed in the right spot. Dora was holding the gun aimed right between his eyes.

"Get out, Pike. And don't come back tonight," Dora said.

Pike looked from the gun in Dora's hand to the amused expression on Doc Kendrick's face. "Hiding behind petticoats this time, Doc?"

Seth shrugged.

"Bet that new wife of yours'd sure be interested to know where you are right now."

The doc didn't bat an eyelash, but his face paled, so Pike realized he'd hit a nerve. "Yeah," he said. "Next time I see her, I 'spect I'll just have to have a little talk with her."

"Stay away from my wife," Seth said in a deadly voice.

"Whatever you say, Doc," Pike said. He looked from the unwavering gun in Dora's hand to the doc and back again. It wasn't worth dying just to get laid by Dora. He'd use one of the other girls.

But he'd make Dora sorry. And Doc Kendrick would pay as well.

Pike tipped his hat and said, "Be seein' you, Doc." Both his eyes and his voice hardened when he added, "And you, too, Dora."

❋13❋

Seth RETURNED IN THE early hours of the morning. Molly awoke immediately when she heard him moving around in their bedroom.

"Seth?"

"Go back to sleep," he said.

She turned over and sat up in bed, watching as he undressed. His movements were weary. "You must be exhausted," she said.

"I am." He stripped down to his white long-john shirt and drawers and eased into the bed beside her, releasing a hissing breath as he did.

Molly waited for him to reach out for her, to pull her into his arms. When he didn't, she wondered whether he might still be angry from the incident in the loft. "How is Mrs. Gulliver?" she asked.

"What? Oh, fine."

Molly turned over and inched closer to him. She tentatively put a hand on his side.

He grabbed her wrist and held it away from him.

"Seth, you're hurting me."

Abruptly, he released her. "Leave me be," he said. "I'm whipped, Molly. It's been a long day."

Molly knew she shouldn't take his rejection to heart. After all, he was used to coming back to this room and being alone. Even though he had known she would be there, it still must be an adjustment. Besides, the man had been up all night nursing a woman with troubled bowels. That was bound to make anyone grouchy and brusque.

Molly made all the excuses for Seth she needed to feel better, then made up her mind to turn over and go to sleep. She flipped the covers up over her shoulder—and distinctly smelled perfume.

At first she thought she must be mistaken. She lay there and inhaled slowly and deeply. There was something in the air, all right. She inched over to face Seth again, leaned a little closer, and sniffed the shoulder of his long johns. Just honest male sweat there. But as she lifted her face, her nose brushed against the back of his head. His hair reeked of the pungent female scent.

Blood thrummed in Molly's veins as she absorbed the implications of what she had discovered. Was it possible that the reason he had wanted nothing to do with her tonight was that he had already lain with another woman? Had he really been with Mrs. Gulliver, as he had claimed? Or had he been with Dora Deveraux?

Molly hated herself for being so suspicious. Probably Mrs. Gulliver was one of those eccentric old ladies who smothered herself in expensive colognes. So why not just ask him why he'd come home from nursing an old lady smelling like a French doxy?

Molly had opened her mouth to confront Seth when she heard a loud snore. He was asleep. Was it the sleep of the guiltless? Or the sexually sated? For certain, it was the sleep of an absolutely exhausted man. If he wasn't guilty, she would feel like a fool for waking him up.

Maybe now was the time for some of that patience she had learned over the years. All she had to do was wait and watch to see how Seth acted in the morning. She would know if he had been with another woman. Surely the truth would be written all over his face.

Besides, the mysterious Mrs. Gulliver had been invited to the christening party tomorrow for Iris Marsh's new baby. If Mrs. Gulliver showed up, all Molly's questions might be answered.

Unfortunately, Mrs. Gulliver sent her regrets through her niece, Mrs. Biddle, who came and brought her five-year-old daughter to play with Nessie. Molly had also invited Red Dupree and Jacob Schmidt to the party. Everyone else present had been suggested by Iris, including members of the Methodist congregation in Fort Benton where Iris and Henry attended. Among them were the saddler and his wife, the proprietor of I. G. Baker & Co., the tinsmith and his wife, and three freightmen.

That many people wouldn't have fit in the house comfortably, and Molly was glad the day had turned out sunny and warm, because she could hold the party outside. She had talked Seth into making a table out of a few split logs and two sawhorses and covered it with a piece of the same checked gingham material she had used to make Whit's curtains. Everyone had been asked to bring a covered dish and dessert for the table and a blanket to spread out in the shade of the cotton-woods near the house. Besides her own covered dish and dessert, she was providing iced tea and lemonade for everyone.

Molly noticed that the wives liked Seth and spoke cordially to him. The men nodded politely, but they didn't willingly include him in their circles of conversation. Doc Kendrick was a necessary man to have around when they were ailing, but otherwise, they knew little about him. In the west, one didn't ask questions; information had to be volunteered. Over the past two years Seth had remained aloof from them. Molly saw the strain around her husband's mouth and eyes as he smiled and pretended their indifferent treatment of him didn't matter.

But there was no reason why Seth's relationships with his neighbors couldn't be improved. Molly walked right up to the tinsmith and said, "Your wife tells me you're thinking of adding another room to your home, Mr. Grimbald. I'm sure Seth would be willing to lend a hand if you need it."

Mr. Grimbald tugged at the neck of his collar and said, "Why, I wouldn't want to impose."

Molly looped her arm through Mr. Grimbald's and walked him over to where Seth was talking with Ethan.

"I was just telling Mr. Grimbald that you'd be glad to help him build the extra bedroom on his house," Molly said with a bright smile on her face.

Seth's face looked ominous, and for a moment Molly thought Mr. Grimbald was going to pull her arm out of the socket trying to escape. But she held on as a slow smile spread across Seth's face. He took off his hat, forked a hand through his black hair, and settled the hat again.

"Look, Doc," Grimbald began in a effort to ease the tension, "I never said I wanted you—"

"I'd be glad to help you, Isaiah," Seth said. "Matter of fact, I just added a bedroom on here."

"You did?" Grimbald said. "How'd you cut the door through to the rest of the house?"

"If you want to come with me, I can show you."

Molly smiled as Grimbald wandered off with Seth.

When she turned to join the rest of the party, Ethan blocked her way.

"Neatest thing I ever saw," he said with a grin.

"What's that?"

"Don't play dumb with me, missy. I saw you grab Grimbald. And I saw him nearly jumping out of his drawers to escape your clutches. That's as smooth a manipulation of two men as I've ever seen."

Molly lifted her chin. "If these people knew Seth, they wouldn't ignore him like they do."

"I couldn't agree with you more. I just never thought I'd see the day when Seth would rejoin the human race."

"I didn't know he'd ever left it!" Molly responded tartly.

"Maybe not in body, but in spirit he resigned himself to being alone a long time ago. You're good for him, Molly. He won't thank you for dragging him back among the living, but I will."

Molly relaxed. "You're a good friend, Ethan. How did Seth ever find you?"

He smiled sardonically. "I found him. Come on over and sit down with me out of the sun, and I'll tell you about it."

Once they were settled on a quilt under a shady cottonwood, Ethan said, "I was fifteen and on the run from the law when I met Seth for the first time."

Molly's eyes widened. Was Ethan an outlaw?

He leaned close and whispered, "Yes."

"Yes what?"

"I'm still wanted by the law, Molly. Not here in Montana," he reassured her. "Back in Texas."

"What did you do?"

"I killed a man who deserved to die. I was wounded in the shoot-out. Dora dug the bullet out of my leg, but—"

"Dora Deveraux?" Molly asked in amazement.

Ethan grinned. "Small world, huh?"

"I'll say," Molly muttered. "Go on."

"Anyway, Dora dug the bullet out, but I was still losing a lot of blood when I saw what I thought was an abandoned line shack. I managed to slide off my horse and get myself inside. Turned out Seth was there. He had Patch with him. Lord, she was only about three years old then and tiny as can be."

"What was Seth doing there? Was he hurt?"

"Drunk."

"*Drunk?* Seth?"

"And looking at the moon through the neck of a bottle."

"I can't believe it. And Patch was there while he was in that condition? Was she all right?"

"Curled up on the bunk and sleeping like an angel."

"What did you do?"

"Took the bottle and the guns away from Seth and laid him on the bed with Patch."

"*Guns?* Seth?"

"Two of the nicest Colts you ever saw. Found me a comfortable spot on the floor and went to sleep. Come morning, woke up to find Patch sitting on my chest. Saw the kid was hungry and fed her. Figured I couldn't just leave her there with Seth passed out like that. I hung around till Seth woke up, then hung around a little longer till I convinced him he owed it to the kid to stay sober."

That wasn't the whole story, but Ethan didn't feel he could say more than that without revealing Seth's secrets.

"I stayed with Seth and Patch for almost six months while my leg healed—at least as much as it was ever going to. Then the family of the man I'd killed found out Seth was hiding me. I didn't want to put him or Patch in any danger, so one night I lit out.

"I saw Seth again during the war, when he was doctoring. It turned out the family of the man I'd killed had hired detectives to watch Seth in case I showed up, and they came after me again. I had to run. I've been running ever since. I came here last fall because Dora said she needed my help. I'll stay until I have to move on again."

"I thank you for helping Seth," Molly said. "And I hope you don't ever have to leave."

Ethan grinned. "I hope so too. I kind of like it around here. Besides, Patch needs looking after as much now as she ever did."

Molly saw Iris gesturing to her and realized it was time for the christening ceremony to begin. "I've got to go," she said. "Thanks again for taking care of Seth, Ethan." She leaned over and kissed him lightly on the cheek and then ran to join Iris.

The christening itself was lovely. Iris and Henry Marsh had asked Molly and Seth to stand as godparents for their sixth child. Molly held the baby while the Reverend Adams baptized her. Then she and Seth took their vows as godparents to the baby, and the celebration began.

Of course everyone fawned on Lily. But the main topic of conversation at the party was the Masked Marauder's encounter with Pike Hardesty the previous evening.

Drake Bassett's whiskey-seller had come running back into town and spread the word at the Medicine Bow Saloon. He had seen it all, he said. How Pike Hardesty had the Masked Marauder dead in his rifle sights, and the Marauder had drawn his gun and beat Pike "slicker than butter on a teaspoon." However, the rumor was that the Marauder had been wounded.

"Anybody asked you to treat a gunshot wound lately, Doc?" Grimbald asked.

"Not lately," Seth replied. "Maybe the Marauder didn't get shot after all. Could be that's just brag on Pike's part. Or maybe it was only a scratch, and he took care of it himself."

"Could be," Grimbald agreed, and turned to discuss the possibilities with someone else.

This was the first time Patch had been dressed up in company, and Molly kept a close eye on her to see how she was managing. It was comical to see Patch come face to face with Ferdie Adams, the preacher's middle boy. Ferdie's eyes nearly bugged out of his face. He yanked his hat off his head and rolled it nervously in front of him. His eyes remained glued on Patch's two small feminine accomplishments.

"What're you looking at?" Patch demanded, fists on hips. "Didn't you ever see anybody in a dress before?"

"Ain't never seen *you* in one," Ferdie pointed out.

"Yeah, well, watch what you say about it. Just 'cause I'm all gussied up don't mean I can't use my fists if I have to."

"Yes, ma'am," Ferdie said.

Patch snorted in disgust. "I ain't a ma'am, Ferdie."

"Whatever you say, Patch." He put a finger into his collar, which seemed to have gotten tighter in the past few minutes. "You, uh, wanta go down to the pond and catch frogs?"

"Can't hardly move in this getup," she confessed. "How about a game of marbles, instead?"

"Sure," Ferdie said. "You got any?"

"I got a whole bag. I'll go get them and meet you around back."

Whit had been standing nearby throughout their conversation and asked, "Can I play too?"

"Who're you?" Ferdie asked.

"That's my dumb old stepbrother," Patch said.

"Name's Whit."

"You any good at marbles?" Ferdie asked.

"I was a champion player in New Bedford."

"Patch is the best player around here," Ferdie said. "You better than she is?"

Whit met Patch's eyes and said, "Could be. Don't really know."

Ferdie's eyes gleamed as he sensed the possibility of a challenge. "Go get your marbles, Patch, and let's find out."

Molly started to follow after them, to intervene if necessary, but she was waylaid by Mrs. Gulliver's niece.

"I want to think you for inviting me," Mrs. Biddle said. "We don't have many entertainments in Fort Benton. I hope this is just the first of many."

Molly smiled. "I'm glad you could come. I'm only sorry Mrs. Gulliver isn't here." At least now she knew the woman really existed.

"Aunt Judith didn't feel well enough to leave the house today. Your husband has been a godsend, Mrs. Kendrick. Why, Doc Kendrick sat with my aunt for an entire half-hour last night, bless his soul."

"A half-hour?"

"Can you imagine such a thing? And him such a busy man, with a family of his own to come home to now."

Molly felt sick to her stomach, but her facial expression didn't change a hair. In a perfectly pleasant voice she said, "Did he say where he was going when he left your aunt's house last night?"

"Why, no he didn't. Home, I expect. Where else would he go with a pretty wife like you waiting for him?"

Where else, indeed? Molly very much feared she knew the answer. She'd seen for herself that Dora Deveraux didn't think much of Seth's marriage vows. But she couldn't understand what he found so attractive about the woman.

"I'd better go check on my daughter," Mrs. Biddle said.

Molly didn't see the woman leave, though she was staring right at her. She had turned her glance inward.

"Penny for your thoughts?"

Molly was jerked back to reality by Iris's voice. "You wouldn't much care for them, I'm afraid."

"I noticed you frowning after you talked to Mrs. Biddle. Bad news?"

"No. Yes. Not really."

Iris smiled. "You seem to be perfectly clear on that."

Molly laughed. "I wish you lived closer. I could use someone to talk with who could make me laugh."

"Come visiting anytime. It gets a mite lonesome without someone to talk to. Not that my oldest girl isn't a comfort to me, but sometimes a woman just likes to have another woman to share her thoughts with. You know what I mean?"

"I know exactly what you mean," Molly said.

"Anyhow, I been wanting to tell you what a good job you've done with Patch. Never seen her look so pretty nor act so nice. She's turning into a real little lady. Why—"

"Fight! Fight! It's the doc's brat, Patch, she—"

Molly didn't hear the rest. She was already running toward the back porch. When she rounded the corner of the house, it wasn't the preacher's middle boy rolling around in the dirt with Patch—it was Whit.

Both their faces were red with exertion. Whit had a swollen eye. Patch had a split lip. Their arms and legs were tangled together, and it was hard to see where one began and the other ended. As Molly arrived from one direction, Seth arrived from the other. He reached down, hauled Whit up by the scruff of his shirt, and grabbed one of Patch's arms—the one with the sore shoulder, from the yelp she let out—and held both children at arm's length.

"I'm not a cheater!" Whit yelled.

"You durned sure didn't win fair and square!" Patch yelled back.

"Shut up!" Seth shouted over both of them.

Both Patch and Whit seemed to realize at the same time that they were surrounded by adults watching with various levels of amusement. The two adults that mattered most—her father and his mother—weren't laughing.

"Whit! How could you?" Molly cried.

"Just look at yourself!" Seth said to Patch.

"He started it!" Patch said.

"She hit me first!" Whit argued.

"You're both to blame," Seth said. "And I'm ashamed of both of you."

"I hate him!" Patch cried.

"I hate her back!" Whit shouted.

"Stop it, both of you!" Molly said. She turned her back on the children, in hopes of concealing their misbehavior behind her skirt, and met the eyes of the crowd. "Just a little family squabble," she said with a crooked smile. "We'll have it settled in no time. Why don't you all go see what kind of dessert is on the table."

No one moved for a moment, until Iris said, "Come on, folks. Let's give this family some privacy so they can settle their differences."

The preacher breathed a sigh of relief that Ferdie was not involved, as he laid a hand on his middle son's shoulder and ushered him away from the fray. Ferdie looked back over his shoulder and grinned at Whit. "You sure showed her," he whispered to the other boy.

"I'll take Nessie with me," Iris said to Molly. "She can play with Amaryllis."

A few moments later, only Ethan remained to watch the confrontation of parents and children.

Molly looked at the remains of the dress she had so lovingly sewn for Patch. The sash was gone. One sleeve was ripped from the shoulder, the hem was down, and there was a tear in the skirt. A fine powdery dust covered the whole of it, and blood from Patch's cut lip stained the bodice. The ribbon had come undone in her hair, and one blond curl hung down over her eye.

"What am I going to do with you?" Seth said. "Look at you. Look at your dress."

Patch's fingertips covered the tear in her skirt and fitted the material back in place. When she looked up again, Ethan was staring at her with pity in his eyes.

Molly's heart went out to Patch when she saw the stricken look on the girl's face.

"I just ain't cut out to be a lady, Pa," Patch said in a woeful voice. "And I don't care if I never become one."

She tore herself from her father's grasp and ran off in the direction of the pond. Seth started to go after her but realized he still had hold of Whit. "What do you have to say for yourself?"

"It wasn't my fault!" Whit retorted. "I hate her. I hate you. And I hate living here! Let me go!" He jerked himself free and ran toward his room.

A moment later, Molly heard the door slam.

Ethan took his hat off, forked a hand through his hair, and put his hat back on again. He cleared his throat and said, "I think I'll go see if I can find Patch," then turned and walked away.

Seth stood across from Molly, unyielding, stony-faced. Molly had absolutely no idea what he was thinking. If she had felt secure in her relationship with him, it would have been easier to contend with the upsetting scene she had just witnessed. She would have gone to Seth for succor and given it as well. Enfolded in his strong arms, they could have laughed over this perfectly normal incident of sibling rivalry and reassured each other that everything would be all right.

But Molly didn't take a step toward Seth and was thus denied the consolation they could have provided each other. She was frozen in place by the certain knowledge that her husband had lied to her about where he had been last night.

Molly was very much afraid that she had made a horrible mistake in coming to Montana. That she had made a mistake in marrying this secretive man with his violent past. That was not the worst of it. The biggest mistake of all was that she had fallen in love with a man who did not—could not—love her back.

Molly gritted her teeth to still her trembling chin. She balled her hands into fists and hid them in her skirts. "I'm going to return to our guests," she said in a controlled voice. "Do you want to come with me?"

"Do you want me to come?"

"I can face them by myself. But it would be easier if you came with me."

"Then I'll come with you." Seth took her elbow in his hand to lead her around to the shade of the cottonwoods. "Smile," he said.

Molly put a bright smile on her face.

"Everything all settled down?" Henry Marsh asked as they approached.

"It's quiet for the moment," Seth said. "But with kids you never know what's coming next."

Henry grinned. "You said it. The wife and I sure do appreciate your having this party for us, Doc, Mrs. Kendrick. And we're proud as punch to have the two of you stand godparents to our Lily."

"It's our pleasure," Molly said. But she wondered if she and Seth would still be together when and if the time ever came that they were needed as godparents for the child.

Molly slipped away during the afternoon to speak with Whit and found him sitting on the edge of his bed, whittling. A pile of wood shavings had collected on the dirt floor at his feet.

When he saw his mother, his lips compressed, but he didn't stop what he was doing.

"I brought a steak to put on your eye, for the swelling," Molly said. "Lie back on the bed." She didn't give Whit a chance to protest, just pressed him down. He lay with the knife on one side of his body and the whittling stick on the other. She dabbed at his eye with a cool, wet cloth, then laid the steak on. "I can think of better uses for a good steak," she said with a tentative smile.

"I'm sorry, Mother," Whit blurted. "I didn't mean all those things I said. I don't hate it here. I don't want to leave. I don't even hate Patch. I get mad at her a lot, but mostly she's okay."

"Then maybe the next time you see her, you can apologize."

Whit's chin jutted. "It wasn't my fault."

Molly brushed a lock of sweat-damp hair away from Whit's brow. "You weren't just a wee tiny bit to blame?"

"Maybe," he admitted grudgingly. "All right. I'll say I'm sorry." Under his breath he added, "But I'm only gonna half mean it, 'cause it was half her fault."

Meanwhile, Patch had found a secluded spot near the pond and was stripping off the tattered dress—and along with it all pretenses of being a lady. It was foolish even to try, she thought, when she was so certain of failing. She stood there fingering the feminine chemise and drawers while tears dripped off her cheeks and her nose began to run. Just as she lifted her arm to swipe it off, someone thrust a bandanna in her face.

Patch took it and blew her nose. Assuming her pa had come to tell her how disappointed he was in her, she kept her face hidden behind the handkerchief.

"I'm sorry, Pa. I didn't mean to cause a ruckus. It just happened. I never lost at marbles before. And when Whit beat me—well, I got angry."

Patch felt a shirt being settled around her bare shoulders, and a pair of arms comfortingly surrounded her.

"Oh, Pa, I—"

"It's Ethan."

Patch dropped the kerchief and looked aghast through watery eyes at Ethan's sympathetic face. She shoved against his chest, pushing him away, mortified to think he had seen her standing there in her underwear. She quickly poked her hands through the arms of his shirt and tried buttoning it up. But her fingers were shaking too badly.

Ethan pushed her hands out of the way and did it for her.

Patch couldn't look him in the eye. But he wasn't content to let her suffer in peace. He lifted her chin and made her look at him.

"It isn't what you wear that makes you a lady, Patch. It's how you handle yourself around other folks. It's more than manners—although you have to learn them. It's knowing you're entitled to respect, and respecting the rights of other people. Your stepmother is that kind of lady."

Patch bristled, but Ethan didn't let her pull away. He lifted the tail of his shirt and wiped the blood from the edge of her mouth. "You don't have to keep fighting against everyone and everything. The people who care about you most are already on your side."

"I can't face Pa," Patch admitted.

"There's nothing you can do that your pa won't forgive and forget."

Patch sighed. "I hope you're right."

He pulled her into his arms and gave her a quick, hard hug. "You know I am."

She looked up into his green eyes and said, "Thanks for coming, Ethan."

He grinned. "It's a good thing I did. How were you planning to get back into the house past all those people when you're stripped down to nothing like that?"

"I guess I wasn't thinking too straight." Patch had her arms around Ethan, and it suddenly dawned on her that the only mark on his upper body was a thin red scratch. Either Pike Hardesty hadn't wounded the Masked Marauder, or Ethan wasn't him.

"Now what's wrong?" Ethan asked as he saw her perplexed look.

"Nothing. Only, haven't you ever wondered who the Masked Marauder is?"

Ethan's lids shuttered his eyes. "Sure I've wondered. Doesn't everybody?"

Patch shrugged. "I really thought it was you. I don't know how I could have been so wrong."

Ethan stiffened imperceptibly. "Come on, Patch. Let's get you back to my place and get you into some clothes."

As much as Molly wanted the party to be over and their guests gone, everyone stayed until the last possible moment, squeezing the most fun and joy they could from times spent together that were too few and too far between. It was after dark and Nessie was asleep in her bed before Seth and Molly finally bade the last of their guests farewell.

"Have you seen Patch or Whit since early this afternoon?" Molly asked as she eased down onto the front-porch step.

"Ethan had a talk with Patch. She's bedding down at his place tonight. I checked, and Whit is asleep in his bed."

Molly heaved a sigh of relief. "At least neither of them ran away."

Seth sat down on the lower step, evoking memories of the last time they had been here together. "That's counting small blessings indeed. Besides, if you want my honest opinion, I don't think either one of them wants to run away."

"I hope you're right." She pulled at a stray thread on the sleeve of her cambric dress. "Seth, do you think Pike really shot the Masked Marauder? I mean, if he had, the Marauder would have come to you for help, wouldn't he?"

"I'll tell you, Molly, even if I'd doctored the Masked Marauder, I wouldn't have said anything today."

"Does that mean you did take care of him?"

Seth smiled. "Anything's possible."

Molly's eyes widened. A relieved smile touched the corners of her mouth. There it was—the explanation for where Seth had been last night. He had already as much as told her he knew who the Masked Marauder was. And if the Masked Marauder had been wounded, of course Seth would have had to treat him. And the perfume—why, what more perfect hideout for the Masked Marauder than some Soiled Dove's boudoir?

If Molly was grasping at straws, well, she had made herself a haystack. She didn't want to believe Seth had lied to her about Dora. It hurt too much. Because she cared too much.

She took Seth's hand and said, "Come with me." She grabbed a quilt hanging over the porch railing and tucked it under her arm. She led him away from the house, down toward the pond.

"Where are we going?" Seth asked.

"Someplace quiet. Someplace private. Someplace where I can have you all to myself."

Molly spread the quilt over the dew-soaked grass beneath a cottonwood. It was dark; the only light came from a quarter moon and the stars.

"Now," she said. "Take off all your clothes."

"What?"

"We'll have a race to see who can finish first."

Seth laughed and tore the buttons off his shirt as he ripped it from his shoulders. All Molly saw was flashes of white as Seth skinned out of his jeans and long johns.

"I win," he said a minute later. "Now I can help you."

Molly laughed as he began tugging at petticoat strings that needed to be untied. She was breathless by the time he had unlaced her corset. He simply ripped her chemise down the front and skimmed it down off her arms.

She backed away from him, laughing as she pulled down her lace-trimmed drawers. When he stopped coming, she pulled them back up again. "Fooled you!"

A second later she was lying flat on her back on the quilt, and he was lying on top of her. His hand cupped the heart of her, and she could feel the warmth of him through the cotton cloth.

"Seth. Make love to me."

His mouth found hers and teased it open so his tongue could come inside and ravish her. He searched out the beauty mark on her face and kissed her there. Then his kisses went seeking and found places she hadn't known were so sensitive to the touch. A moment later, his hand was inside her lacy cotton drawers, and she moaned as he teased her with his fingertips. But soon the cotton was in his way, and he pulled the lacy garment down and off and tossed it aside.

"Molly?" Seth pulled her into his arms, and the touch of warm flesh against flesh in the cold night air was exquisite. The hair on his chest was slightly abrasive as he rubbed himself slowly against her. His mouth found the place where her neck joined her shoulders, and he kissed his way up to her ears. His breath was hot and moist, and the sensation sent shivers down her spine.

Molly wanted to return the pleasure he was giving her, so she let her hands go wandering and found the muscles across his shoulders, the crease of his spine, his taut buttocks, and his long, lean flanks. She listened for the sounds he made—the moans and groans and hissed-in breaths of air—that taught her how to please him. As she slid her fingertips down his side, he gasped and bolted upright.

"What's wrong?" Molly asked. "What did I do?"

"I'm a little ticklish," he said.

Molly grinned. "That's an awful thing to admit." She reached up to tickle him on purpose, and this time he grabbed her hand at the same time he gasped.

Only it wasn't a funny kind of gasp, it was a painful kind of gasp. "Seth?"

He took her hand and brought it back to his body, then gently ran it across a scab along his ribs. "I had an accident with an ax. I didn't want to worry you. It's just a scratch, but it's still pretty sensitive."

"You should have told me. I would have been more careful." Then Molly grinned impishly. "I guess I'll just have to find some less-sensitive spot to handle." Whereupon she reached over and cupped him in her hands.

Seth groaned. But there was no mistaking this as anything but a sound of pleasure. He didn't move, just let her touch him however she wanted. And Molly tried everything to see what made him moan the loudest.

Seth didn't last long before she was flat on her back, and he was deep inside her.

"Love me, Seth," she whispered. Her body arched into his, seeking fulfillment.

His body thrust into hers, seeking the same.

And in the darkness, under the wide Montana skies, they found the peace and contentment each had been seeking.

Afterward, Seth pulled Molly into his arms and levered a leg over her to keep her close. They were quiet for a long while, listening to the katydids and frogs. "I guess I should have listened when you said Patch needs to go away to school to become a lady. I thought—I hoped she could do all her changing right here. I can see maybe it might not be a bad idea after all to send her away."

Seth laid his head against Molly's breast, and she smoothed his hair with her hands. "It doesn't have to be right away," she said. "And it doesn't have to be for long. Don't worry, Seth." She kissed the top of his head. "Everything will turn out fine."

"Tomorrow—"

"I don't want to think about tomorrow," Molly said, kissing Seth's eyes closed. "I want to enjoy tonight."

It was nearly dawn before they crept back into the house, wrapped together in the quilt and giggling like children.

❊14❊

IT HAD BEEN NEARLY three weeks since the christening party, during which time Seth had gone into town twice to treat Mrs. Gulliver. Both times, he had come home very late. Both times, he had made love to Molly after he slipped into bed. He had never again smelled of a tart's perfume. But Molly couldn't help wondering why he was gone so long, and where he went when he wasn't with Mrs. Gulliver. She might have ignored her nagging unease except for one thing: Molly was fairly certain she was pregnant.

The signs were there: tenderness in her breasts, a slight dizziness if she stood too fast, fatigue, and most telling of all, she had missed her monthly course. She wasn't sure how she felt about having another child. The thought of having a baby—Seth's baby—was wonderful. But were they—all of them—ready for another addition to the family?

Patch and Whit were speaking again, although *snarling* would be more descriptive of their communication. Patch seemed to tolerate having Nessie in her room well enough. But every night at supper, Molly waited for an eruption of the tempers that never seemed far beneath the surface.

That was why she had so much looked forward to the trip she was making this afternoon to visit Iris Marsh. She wanted to talk to the other woman and get some advice. When she had thought she might be pregnant, she had talked Seth into teaching her how to drive the buggy. Now she was glad she had.

Seth didn't want to let her go on her own. "You might get lost. Or lose a wheel. The horse might bolt. There are always Indians around. Or—"

Molly had interrupted, "I'll be fine. The trail you use to reach the Marsh place is easy to follow. And the distance is short enough that if I lose a wheel, I can walk home or to the Marshes' whichever is closer. You taught me to drive, so you know I can handle the rig under any circumstances. And you must admit the likelihood of anything else"—she specifically did not mention an Indian attack—"happening is slim."

It was slim, but it was there. When Seth frowned, Molly put her arms around him and kissed him on the mouth. "You have work to do here. I'll be fine."

Reluctantly, he had agreed.

Whit and Patch decided to stay home to help Seth and Ethan with gentling a couple of wild horses that were scheduled to be delivered to the army later in the summer. Molly settled Nessie beside her on the front seat and waved at them all as she cheerfully drove away.

Molly felt pretty proud of herself when she pulled the buggy up in front of Iris's sod house. Iris was outside leaning over an elevated tin tub, scrubbing clothes on a washboard. Her oldest daughter was working a wringer and hanging the clothes on a line that had been strung between two trees. The pig-tailed girl, Amaryllis, was sitting at her mother's feet playing with several calico kittens. The older baby, Daisy, had inched her way to the edge of a blanket and was eating a handful of grass. Molly's godchild, Lily, lay in a wooden cradle placed in the shade of the hill. Molly assumed the twin boys were with their father working in the fields.

"Why, what a surprise!" Iris said, wiping her hands dry on her apron as she approached the buggy. "Step down and come inside for something cool to drink."

As soon as Nessie was out of the buggy, she raced over to play with the kittens.

"Rose," Iris called to her oldest daughter, "keep an eye on things out here while I go sit and visit with Mrs. Kendrick."

"Yes, Mama."

Molly made a detour to admire Lily before she followed Iris into the sod house. The coolness of the earthen room was a relief after the heat of the afternoon sun. It took Molly a second to get her bearings in the dimness before she settled into a chair Iris held for her at the table. Iris poured them each a glass of sun-brewed tea and sat down across from Molly.

"Now, what brings you visiting in the middle of the week?" she asked.

"Do I have to have a reason for coming?"

"Most people do."

Molly smiled. "You're right. I wanted some advice."

"Ain't much I know about you don't know better yourself," Iris said. "But fire away."

"It's about Seth."

Iris smiled. "Guessed as much. There's more to that man than meets the eye."

"Do you think he would keep a mistress in town?" Molly blurted.

Iris was silent for a moment before she asked, "What makes you think such a thing?"

Molly explained that Seth had gone to town to check on Mrs. Gulliver, but that Mrs. Biddle had said he didn't stay there very long. "But he's usually gone from home the better part of the evening," she finished.

"And you think he's seeing another woman?"

Molly nodded. "Dora Deveraux."

"Tell me, when he comes home these nights he's gone, does he make love to you?"

Molly flushed. "Yes."

"Does he take his time?"

"Yes."

"Then I don't reckon it's another woman. Which leaves you looking for another reason why he stays in town," Iris said, tapping her chin thoughtfully. "Any thoughts?"

"He might be meeting the Masked Marauder."

Iris's eyes widened. "Does he know who it is?"

Molly leaned forward eagerly. "From things he's said to me, I think so. I just wish I knew for sure one way or the other what he's doing in town. Because . . . because I think I'm pregnant."

"Lordy, lordy, girl. That's great news!"

"I don't know," Molly said with a worried frown. "Patch and Whit are having enough trouble accepting things the way they are."

Iris took a swallow of tea to give herself time to think. "I see what you mean. But maybe a new baby is exactly what your family needs."

"It is?"

"How can they not love the baby? It'll be Patch's kin through Seth, and Whit's kin through you."

Molly smiled. "I knew there was a reason I came to see you, Iris. You talk such good sense."

"Glad you think so, Molly. You'd better get going so you're home in time to make supper for that man of yours."

Molly hadn't gone very far when she got the idea to go to town before she drove back to the ranch. The more she thought about it, the better she liked it. She could buy some material to make Patch a new dress and pick up a pair of trousers for Whit. And she would buy something special for Seth, a present to give him when she told him about the baby. At the crossroads, instead of continuing east toward the ranch, she turned north toward Fort Benton.

Pike Hardesty could hardly believe his eyes when he saw Doc Kendrick's wife come driving into town perched up on top of that buggy seat. He looked for the doc on horseback following her, but unbelievable as it seemed, she was alone. Well, well, maybe he was going to get a chance to get back at Doc Kendrick sooner than he'd thought.

Molly found everything she wanted at I. G. Baker and was feeling quite pleased with herself when she walked out of the store, loaded down with packages. She was conscious of someone following too close behind her and looked over her shoulder to see who it was.

Pike lifted his hat and said, "Afternoon, purty lady. Let me help you with those packages."

Before Molly could protest, he had taken the parcels out of her hands. There was nothing she could do without making a scene. She took Nessie's hand and, with her back stiff, and chin high, began walking toward where she'd left the buggy.

Pike walked beside her. "Been wondering when you'd come to town, purty lady. Guess that yellow-bellied husband of yours was scared to show his face."

"My husband seemed to come away well enough from his last encounter with you," Molly said. She had arrived at the buggy. "I'll take those packages now."

Pike dumped them in the buggy.

Molly lifted Nessie up into the front seat, but when she tried to join her daughter, Pike stepped in front of her, barring the way.

"Seems kinda strange you defending the doc after what he done to you."

"And what is that?" Molly asked.

"Caught him myself in Dora Deveraux's bed, not more'n two weeks after you was married," Pike said.

Molly's face blanched. "You're lying."

"Come along and ask Dora yourself if you don't believe me."

Pike had hold of Molly's arm and wouldn't let go. He started dragging her away from the buggy toward the Medicine Bow Saloon, halfway down the street.

"Wait here for me, Nessie," Molly called over her shoulder. "I'll be right back."

Molly looked around at the townspeople they passed, for someone she knew, someone who would help her. But when Pike glared at them, they all looked down at the ground. Molly wasn't sure what Pike had in mind for her, but the thought of going upstairs in the Medicine Bow Saloon with him sent her heart into her throat.

She wasn't without hope. She was sure that if Red Dupree saw her come into the saloon with Pike, he would intercede. Only Pike didn't go in the front door. When they reached the shadowed alley alongside Bassett's saloon, he headed through it to the back of the building.

It was then that Molly realized that if she was going to escape, she had to do it on her own. Just as they reached a set of back stairs to the second floor, she stomped on Pike's foot and yanked hard to free her arm. He was so surprised at her attack that he let her go and grabbed his foot.

When Pike saw her start to run toward the street, he came after her. Molly had nearly reached sunlight when she was caught from behind. Pike grabbed her by the shoulder and swung her around so she slammed against the wood-slatted building. His fisted hand swung around and hit her hard in the chin. Everything went black as Molly slid down the side of the building onto the ground.

When she came to, Molly was terrified, because she was in a strange bed. A quick look at her surroundings left her confused. The entire room was littered with dolls. A cherubic doll with a ceramic face lay on the pillow next to her. Molly sat up and put a hand to her sore jaw, working it carefully until she was sure nothing was broken. She heard voices arguing outside the room—a man and a woman— and looked around for a weapon. She opened a drawer in a bedside table and found a small gun. At first she was afraid to touch it, but as the voices got louder and angrier, she took it out and held it in her hand.

When the door opened, the derringer was pointed at Dora Deveraux.

"It's not loaded," Dora said. She walked over to Molly and took the gun out of her hand. Then, to Molly's chagrin, she unloaded the bullets into her palm and dropped both gun and ammunition onto the bedside table.

Molly stared wide-eyed at the woman, wondering what her part was in this kidnapping.

"I sent Red out to keep an eye on your kid," Dora said. "You wanta tell me what you're doing in town without Seth?"

"I came to get some material for a dress," Molly said, "and to get a present for Seth. I wanted to surprise him."

Dora put a hand on Molly's chin and turned her bruised face to the light. "He's gonna be surprised, all right."

"Were you arguing with Pike Hardesty?" Molly asked.

Dora clucked her tongue in disgust. "Stupid fool. If any of those men down there knew he'd hit you, they'd lynch him to the nearest tree. Don't know that Seth won't kill him anyway when he sees what Pike did to your face. I told Pike he oughta get out of town for a while. He didn't like gettin' advice from a woman. But at least he wasn't dumb enough not to take it."

Molly very much feared it was Seth who would be killed in any encounter between the two men. Pike had already shot at Seth once. The next time, he might not miss. She would just have to come up with some story about what had caused her bruise that didn't involve Pike Hardesty.

"Please don't tell Seth about this," she said to Dora.

"He's gonna find out."

"Not if you don't say anything."

"Why did Pike wanta haul you up here, anyway?"

Molly cleared her throat. "I called him a liar when he said Seth was here in bed with you right after we were married."

"Ain't that a sack of hell," Dora said. "I told Seth he should've explained to you about that."

All the blood drained from Molly's face. "Then he *was* here?"

"Why, sure he was, honey. But that's because—Hey! Don't you go fainting on me now." Dora put a hand on Molly's head and forced it down between her knees.

Molly felt dizzy. She could hear a buzzing sound in the background that she knew must be Dora talking, but she couldn't understand any of the words. Her chest hurt. And her eyes burned. And her stomach felt nauseous.

"I'm going to throw up," she said.

"Now, now—"

"I'm going to throw up," Molly repeated.

Dora ran to get a basin from the dressing table and held it while Molly was sick. She dampened a cloth with water from the pitcher and wiped Molly's mouth.

"You don't look so good. Maybe I better ask Red to drive you home."

"No!" Molly knew there was no way she would be able to explain things to Seth if Red came along. "I'll be fine." She got to her feet and was none to steady. "I think if I could just have a sip of water, I'd be fine."

"Haven't got any more water, honey. But how about a little shot of something stronger? Probably be just what you need."

Molly nodded and held out her hand for the shot glass full of whiskey Dora poured for her. She took a tentative sip and felt it burn all the way down. It warmed her inside, where she was so terribly, terribly cold. She sipped again, but got too much, coughed, then swallowed the rest. She handed the empty glass back to Dora and said, "Thank you."

Molly walked very carefully, though unsteadily, to the door. When she got there, she turned and said to Dora in a perfectly calm voice, "Stay away from my husband. If you go near him again, I'll scratch your eyes out."

She left the room, then realized she had no idea which door led to the back stairs. She opened Dora's door again and asked, "Which way to the stairs?"

The beautiful Soiled Dove was grinning ear to ear when she said, "Last door on your left."

When Molly got back to the buggy, Red took one look at her and said, "Son of a bitch. What happened to you?"

Molly had yet to think of what reason she was going to give Seth for her bruised face. What popped to mind was, "Some yard goods fell on me from the top shelf at I. G. Baker."

"Lordy mercy. Looks like that smarts," Red said as he helped her up into the buggy. "You gonna be able to get home all right?"

"I'll be fine," Molly said.

And she was. In fact, she was so dead inside that she didn't even feel the pain of her jaw. When she arrived home it was after dark, and every lantern in the house was lit. As soon as she drove up, Ethan, Patch and Whit came running out to greet her.

"Where have you been?" Whit demanded anxiously. "I got worried when you didn't come home."

"Where's Seth?" Molly asked.

"He went looking for you after it got dark," Ethan said. "I expect he'll be back when he doesn't find you somewhere on the road between here and the Marsh place."

"I decided to go to town to get some things."

Ethan didn't say anything, just looked at her in a way that spoke volumes. Molly nearly fell as she got down from the buggy. Ethan caught her in his arms and carried her inside.

"Mother!" Whit cried. "Is she all right?"

"I think she's just worn out," Ethan said. "Why don't you go help get Nessie to bed and then you can come say good night to your mother."

Ethan laid Molly on Seth's bed and reached down to take her shoes off. Her eyes were closed when he started undoing the buttons on her dress. They flashed open in alarm, and she grabbed at his hand.

"Figured you better loosen the laces on that corset you're wearing," he said.

Molly tried to get up to go behind the screen to change and slumped back down again. Tears slid out of the corners of her eyes. "Go ahead," she said.

Impersonally, deftly, Ethan unbuttoned Molly's dress. He lifted her and slipped the bodice off her shoulders, then turned her over and untied the laces on her corset. Molly sighed in relief. He put his hands on her shoulders and began to rub the tension out. "Would you like to talk about how you got that bruise on your face?"

"It happened in town," Molly said.

"I figured that. How?"

"Some yard goods fell on me."

"Uh-huh."

"Did you know Seth was seeing Dora Deveraux?"

Ethan's hands froze. "Who told you that?"

A shuddering sigh escaped Molly. "I had it right from the horse's mouth."

"You saw Dora?"

"Thanks to Pike Hardesty."

"What does Pike have to do with this?"

"He's the one who told me Seth was seeing Dora."

Ethan swore under his breath and began to rub Molly's shoulders again. "Everything isn't always what it seems, Molly."

"I should hope the hell not," Seth said from the doorway.

Molly pushed herself up on her hands, realized she was only half-dressed, and pulled her dress up to cover her chemise as she scrambled into a more presentable position on the bed.

"What are you doing in my bedroom with my wife?" Seth demanded in a cold voice.

"Molly wasn't feeling well when she got home. I carried her in here."

"And took half her clothes off? That was mighty considerate of you."

Ethan stood and said, "Listen, Seth—"

"Get out of here, Ethan."

Ethan's lips pressed flat. He looked from Molly to Seth and back again.

"It's all right, Ethan," Molly said. "I'll handle this."

"You're a fool, Seth," Ethan muttered as he stalked out the door.

Seth closed the door behind Ethan and turned to Molly. "Where were you?"

"I went to town."

"Without telling anyone? Do you know how dangerous that is?"

"I do now. I'm sorry, Seth. I—"

"Sorry?" Seth grabbed her by the shoulders and shook her hard. "Do you have any idea how I felt when you didn't come back before dark? Do you have any idea what kind of crazy thoughts went through my head when Iris said you'd left hours ago? Do you?"

"Seth! Stop! I'm going to be sick."

Before he could do anything to help, she leaned over the side of the bed and heaved. But she had lost everything in her stomach at Dora's. Molly retched and retched until tears squeezed from her eyes, but nothing came up. At last her body released her from the awful spasms, and she slumped forward, sobbing.

Seth lifted her up in his arms and pulled her face to his chest. When he did, she cried out and grabbed her jaw. For the first time he saw the terrible bruise that had previously been hidden in the shadows created by the single lantern.

"What happened to you? Who did this?"

Molly knew that Seth's life might depend on how well she told her story. She tried to keep her voice casual and light as she explained, "It was just a silly accident. I was buying material for a new dress for Patch at I. G. Baker. A heavy bolt of material fell from the top shelf and hit me in the jaw. Really, it looks worse than it feels."

Molly held her breath for a second, waiting to see whether Seth would accept her story. When he pulled her tighter into his arms, she let out a silent sight of relief and closed her eyes.

"I was so worried about you, Molly. If anything had happened to you . . ." He smoothed the hair back from her face and kissed her eyes closed. It frightened him to see her so pale. "What made you sick, Molly? Do you know? Was it something you ate?"

He had given her the perfect opening to tell him she was sick because she was pregnant with their child. But how could she tell him that joyous news in light of what she had learned this afternoon? "I didn't have anything to eat today," she said. "I guess I was just exhausted."

He hugged her tight. Seth had discovered something in those awful hours when he had searched for her that had at first astonished him, then left him terrified. How awful it would be to find out he loved Molly, only to lose her before he had a chance to tell her so. Now look what he had done. He had accused his best friend of having taken advantage of his wife. And instead of being glad that Molly was home safe, he had shaken her within an inch of her life. She had been so sick! Lord, his body ached for the wretchedness he had seen in her face.

"Molly, I just wanted to tell you—"

"Not tonight, Seth. I'm so tired. I can't talk anymore tonight."

There were several knocks on the door, and it opened to reveal Whit and Patch.

Whit crossed to the foot of the bed. "We just wanted to see if you're all right, Mother."

"I'm fine," Molly said. "I'll tell you both all about everything in the morning."

"Let's go, Whit," Patch said. "Your mother needs to rest."

"I know that," Whit snapped. "I was just leaving."

The two of them left the room arguing over which one of them was being more considerate of Molly's feelings.

Seth finished undressing Molly and laid her carefully in bed. He joined her and pulled her into his arms. First thing tomorrow morning, he would tell her he loved her. And they would start over from there.

✳15✳

WHEN SETH WOKE UP early the next morning, Molly still had dark circles of exhaustion under her eyes. He decided it didn't make sense to wake up an exhausted woman to tell her he loved her. He was careful to be quiet in the kitchen as he made coffee so as not to wake anyone, but as he turned from the stove, Nessie stood at the kitchen door.

"You woke me up," she accused. The very next words out of her mouth were, "Where's Mama?"

Seth hurried over to scoop Nessie up in his arms. He laid a finger across his mouth and said, "Shh. Your mother's still sleeping. She's tired from her trip into town."

"I went to town too," Nessie said.

"I know."

"I didn't like the bad man."

Seth froze. "What bad man?"

"The man with the hurt on his face. Here." Nessie laid her hand against Seth's cheek.

"What did the bad man do?"

"He took Mama away. But she didn't want to go."

"Where did he take her, sweetheart?"

"I don't know. Mama told me to stay in the buggy. I got scared."

"But you were a good girl and stayed in the buggy?"

"Uh-huh. Red came and said Mama would be coming in a minute. But it felt like a whole *hour*," Nessie said. "And when she came back, she had a hurt on her face too. Here." Nessie put her hand on Seth's jaw, which had tautened as the little girl spoke.

Seth set Nessie down and said, "I want you to go get back in bed with Patch and stay there until your mother wakes up."

"But Da—"

"What did you call me?"

"Uh . . . Seth?"

Seth gave her a quick hug. "I like Da better. Now do as I said, Nessie."

She made a face but said, "All right, Da."

Seth crept into his bedroom and sat down on the bed beside his sleeping wife. His fingertips lightly grazed the bruise Pike Hardesty had put there. His face paled with fury. "I'll kill him this time," he whispered.

He rose and silently left the room.

———————

Molly swatted at the itch on her face for the second time. When it came back again, she opened her eyes. Nessie was sitting beside her on the bed. She had a strand of Molly's hair in her hand and was using it to tickle her mother under the nose.

Molly rolled over and said, "Go away, Nessie, and let me sleep. It's too early to be up."

"Da is up."

Molly squinted over at the other side of the bed. "So he is. Did you just call Seth 'Da'?"

"Uh-huh. He said I could. After I told him about the bad man."

Molly tensed. "What bad man?"

"The bad man who took you away."

Molly sat up and pulled Nessie into her lap. "What did you tell Da?"

"That you didn't want to leave me, but the bad man made you go away."

Molly set Nessie on the bed and started dressing, yanking on the new split riding skirt she had made for herself. "What did Da say when you told him that?"

"He told me to go back to bed."

"Where is Da now?"

"I don't know."

"Patch!" Molly shouted as she ran into the next room. "Patch! Wake up!"

Patch sat bolt upright at the sound of her name being screamed through the house. A second later, Molly arrived in her bedroom doorway.

"Go get Ethan, quick!"

"What's the matter?"

"Your father's gone to town to fight Pike Hardesty again."

"Why would he do that?"

"Because Nessie told your father that Pike put this bruise on my face."

Molly turned her head, and Patch gasped at the black and blue mark on Molly's jaw.

"Garn! You look awful!" Patch said.

Molly tried not to sound as frantic as she felt. "We have to go after your father. Pike doesn't fight clean, and he doesn't fight fair. He'll kill Seth."

"I'll be back with Ethan in the flick of a horse's tail. He'll know what to do."

Molly woke up Whit and told him to watch Nessie while she was gone to town. When Ethan arrived at the house moments later, she explained the facts to him as quickly and calmly as she could.

"Now he's gone to meet Pike. We have to stop him."

To Molly's surprise, Ethan seemed reluctant to go after Seth. "He can handle himself. He doesn't need you in town. And I don't think he'd appreciate you coming after him."

"I don't care what he'd appreciate," Molly retorted. "I am not going to let this baby be born without a father!"

"Baby?" everyone said at once.

Molly closed her eyes and clenched her teeth. "I wanted to tell Seth first. But yes, I'm going to have a baby."

"I guess it couldn't hurt to go and keep an eye on things," Ethan said. "But *I'll* go. The rest of you stay here."

Molly wrung her hands in indecision.

"There's nothing you can do in town that I can't. You're exhausted. You have to take care of yourself. Think about the baby," Ethan said.

For the baby's sake and no other reason, Molly nodded.

Patch and Whit exchanged looks. They hadn't agreed to anything. The instant Ethan was out of sight, they slipped out of the house to the barn and saddled their horses.

"We gotta be there," Patch said. "Pa might need us."

"Right," Whit said. "We can warn Da in case there's an ambush or anything."

Patch arched a brow at Whit. "He ain't your Da."

"He is so. You wanta make something of it?"

Patch tightened the cinch on her saddle. "Ask me again when I have more time to argue."

Nessie was watching out the front window when Whit and Patch rode away. "There they go."

Molly was sitting at the kitchen table with her head in her hands. "There who goes?"

"Whit and Patch. They're riding *fast*."

Molly jumped to her feet. "They're what?"

Nessie pointed. "See."

"I'll wring their disobedient little necks!" Molly grabbed Nessie by the hand and ran all the way to the barn. She harnessed the buggy and shoved Nessie up into the front seat. "Hang on," Molly said. "We're going to town!"

———————

Pike had stayed out of town for twenty-four hours and figured that was long enough. Nobody was going to come after him for hitting Doc Kendrick's wife. They were too scared of him to do anything. Dora had just said that to get rid of him. He still owed Dora for that business with the doc. Now was as good a time as any for her to pay.

Despite Pike's belief that there was no danger for him in town, it never hurt to be careful. He used the back way upstairs to Dora's room.

Dora was just ushering a customer out, and Pike waited until she was closing the door to shove his way into her room.

Dora turned and walked away from him. "Hello, Pike."

"Don't touch nothin', Dora. I ain't forgot how you pulled a gun on me."

Dora draped herself across the bed and pulled her black negligée aside to show off her red satin chemise and drawers. She pulled a knee up and adjusted the red garter on one of her black silk stockings. "You come here for a reason, Pike?"

"I figure you owe me some time under the covers, Dora. I'm here to collect."

"You know I never turn down a payin' customer, Pike. Only, before you drop your drawers, maybe you'd like to know the Masked Marauder is waiting for you downstairs."

"What?"

"Came in about three hours ago. Been sittin' at your table downstairs playing solitaire ever since."

Pike felt the sweat break out on his brow. "What's he want with me?"

"How should I know, Pike? Why don't you go downstairs and find out?"

Pike thought seriously about sneaking out the way he'd come in. Then he thought again. The Marauder would be expecting him to walk in the front door of the saloon, not to come down the stairs. He'd have the drop on that masked devil this time for sure. He'd lay all that talk to rest about him getting out-gunned by the Masked Marauder when he shot that sonofabitch dead.

By now, the town of Fort Benton knew there was going to be a showdown of some kind. A crowd had gathered in the saloon, although no one had worked up the nerve actually to speak to the Masked Marauder. There was a constant irritating noise, like a mosquito buzzing an ear at bedtime, as they talked low amongst themselves. Most of the speculation centered on why the Marauder had finally decided to show himself in public. And whether he would, at last, reveal his identity.

The Marauder had ridden up to the Medicine Bow Saloon on a big black stallion looking more sinister than anyone had expected. His shirt, pants, and boots were all black. He wore a black leather vest with the outline of a Texas star stitched in red on the pocket.

Movement on Front Street came to a standstill as he dismounted. He was tall, broad-shouldered, and slim-hipped. Tied-down twin Colts rested in tooled black leather holsters that looked well used. His black mask was tied in a knot behind his head and covered his face down to his nose, with only slits for his eyes. It wasn't even possible to tell the color of his eyes because his high-crowned black hat was pulled low and shadowed his face. He sported no beard or moustache, but he had a strong jaw and a grim-lipped mouth. An aura of danger and mystery surrounded him.

It was hard to believe this man might be someone they knew, someone who worked beside them day to day. Try as they might, it was impossible to imagine any one of their ordinary friends as this mythical hero. Yet here he was in their midst. The Masked Marauder had come to life.

Men had stepped aside as he shouldered through the batwing doors of the saloon and looked around. Apparently he hadn't found whoever it was he'd been looking for, because he sauntered over to the table against the wall—Pike Hardesty's table—and sat down. He had asked Red in a low, raspy voice—obviously disguised—for a deck of cards and a glass of rye. Since then, he had played solitaire and ignored the rest of the room.

When Pike started down the stairs, a hush settled over the saloon. Hardesty had his Colt revolver drawn and aimed at the Marauder. He walked right up to the masked man and said, "This time I aim to find out who's under that mask."

"You will, Pike," the Marauder said.

Since all eyes were focused on the confrontation across the room, it was easy for Patch and Whit to slip in under the batwing doors of the saloon. They sidled along the wall trying to be inconspicuous.

"I don't see Pa," Patch whispered, searching the barroom.

"Maybe he ain't here yet."

Patch shot Whit a look of disdain. "We're here. And he left before we did."

"Maybe he's upstairs," Whit suggested.

At that moment Patch caught sight of the Masked Marauder. She grabbed Whit's arm and said, "He's here."

"Where? I don't see him."

"Not Pa, you idiot! The Masked Marauder!"

Whit's eyes rounded when he spied the masked man dressed all in black. "What's he doing here?"

"Looks like he's facing down Pike Hardesty."

Patch looked up the stairs. If Pa was up there, he'd be with Dora. She didn't think he'd had much to do with Dora since Molly came along. If she went upstairs, she could warn Pa not to come down. But if she left the barroom, she might miss the Masked Marauder in action. She finally decided to station herself at the bottom of the stairs. That way, she'd be able to warn her pa if he showed up.

Patch's heart was thudding as she watched the Masked Marauder play his game of solitaire, despite the gun trained on him by Pike Hardesty. She could see him talking but couldn't hear what he was saying.

I don't care what he told me. The Masked Marauder has to be Ethan, she thought.

He had left the ranch right after Pa, riding to the rescue. He could have stopped to get his mask from the warehouse at the edge of town. Why else would the Masked Marauder have appeared in public like this and forced Pike Hardesty into a confrontation, except to save her pa?

"Why don't you take off that mask and let all these fine folks see who you are?" Pike said.

The Marauder turned another card. "Does it really matter who I am, Pike?"

"Naw. I'd just like to see your face when I kill you," Pike said with a grin. "Now get up slow and easy, and keep your hands where I can see them."

Everyone in the saloon held their breath, waiting to see if the Marauder would go for his guns. There was a murmur of surprise when he stood up, just as Pike had ordered.

Abruptly, Red spoke from behind the bar. "Do your killing outside, Pike. I've laid down enough fresh sawdust on your account."

Pike slowly backed away from the Marauder to bring Red into his line of sight. The bartender had a shotgun aimed at him. "Whatever you say, Red. Just don't go gettin' an itchy trigger finger."

"Come on, you," Pike said, gesturing the Marauder out from behind the table with his gun. "Outside."

Patch and Whit melted into the wall as the Masked Marauder passed by them. Patch could have reached out and touched him, he was so close. It wasn't until he had nearly reached the batwing doors that Patch realized he didn't have Ethan's hitching gait. But if the Masked Marauder wasn't Ethan Hawk, who was it?

"That's Da," Whit croaked.

"What?" Patch hissed.

"Da is the Masked Marauder!" he hissed back. "Look at him. At his hands. At his mouth. It's him!"

Patch's eyes rounded, and her jaw dropped. It wasn't possible. It couldn't be. Ethan was—But Ethan *wasn't* the Masked Marauder. The Marauder didn't have Ethan's limp. If Whit was right, her father was about to face down Pike Hardesty in a gunfight!

She shoved Whit ahead of her and urged, "Let's go! We have to help him if we can!"

They were caught up in the crowd that poured from the saloon into the street after the two gunmen. The onlookers backed up against the buildings on either side of Front Street, out of the line of fire. Patch and Whit found a spot behind the horse trough from which to watch the showdown.

"We have to do something!" Patch said.

"Da doesn't need our help," Whit said confidently. "He can handle this with one hand tied behind his back."

Patch stared at Whit for a moment, then out at the masked man before her, whom she now recognized as her father. Whit seemed confident that her pa could save himself despite the fact Pike Hardesty was standing there holding a gun on him. Patch thought of the reverence she had always felt for the capabilities of the mythical masked hero. She cringed at the memory of all the unnecessary battles she had fought on her father's behalf. He was not a coward. Never had been. She was the one who had been afraid—of what people would think. Patch felt a welling of emotion in her throat.

"You're right," she said to Whit. "Pa can take care of himself."

In fact, the Marauder didn't seem the least perturbed by the fact Pike held a gun on him. When he reached the middle of the street, he turned to Pike and said, "I warned you what would happen if you didn't get out of town. I'm willing to make this a fair fight."

Pike snickered. "I ain't."

When Molly drove into Fort Benton, she saw the crowd gathered on Front Street. She saw the two men in the distance faced off against one another and knew what she had to do.

She stopped the buggy and said, "Climb down, Nessie, and wait here for me." She helped her daughter out of the buggy, then lashed the buckskin gelding with the whip, sending him galloping down the street straight for the two men.

Pike heard the excited roar of the crowd behind him and took his eyes off the Marauder for one second to see what had caused it.

In that moment the Marauder drew his gun and fired.

Pike saw his own shot go wide in the same instant he felt a bullet strike him in the chest. He staggered, then his knees crumpled and he fell on his face. The Marauder walked over and knelt down beside him.

"Who are you?" Pike rasped.

The masked man leaned over to whisper in his ear.

Pike's eyes widened. "Bullshit! You can't be—" It was the last thing he ever said.

The crowd converged on the Marauder, shaking his hand, patting him on the back, and begging him to take off his mask.

Molly had pulled the buggy to an abrupt stop when she heard the gunshots and saw a man fall. She sat in the buggy seat, heart pounding, hands tight on the reins to restrain the excited buckskin, and stared at the scene before her. At last she realized it was Pike Hardesty on the ground and that the Masked Marauder was kneeling beside him.

She felt relieved that Pike was dead, but where was Seth? She searched the crowd and found Patch and Whit peeking over the horse trough in front of the saloon. She would tan their hides when she got them home! She backed the buckskin up and headed the buggy toward them.

Among those watching the events on Front Street with avid interest was Drake Bassett. He was not at all happy with what he had seen. He had counted on Pike to get rid of the Masked Marauder. But usually, if one wanted something done right, one had to do it oneself. Bassett took a Winchester down off the wall mount beside his desk and balanced it on the windowsill to take aim on the Marauder. He had to wait for the shot because the crowd had converged on the masked man.

"I sort of suspected this might happen."

Bassett froze.

"If you want to live, I suggest you drop that rifle."

"Who's there?" Bassett stood as the rifle clattered to the floor.

"Turn around and find out," the voice said.

When Bassett turned, he felt his skin get up and crawl all over him. "It can't be—"

He looked out the window at the man who had shot Pike Hardesty, then back at the masked man standing in front of him—unarmed. "Is this some kind of joke? A trick? Which one of you is the real Masked Marauder?"

The masked man flashed a smile. "Both of us."

"Who are you?" Bassett demanded. "And who is he?" He pointed out the window.

"The bane of your existence," the masked man said in a hard voice.

"I don't think I—" Bassett pulled the gun he kept inside his coat, certain he could kill the unarmed man standing before him. Only, before he even had the gun out of his coat, the man had pulled a knife from behind his back and thrown it. Bassett looked down and saw the hilt protruding from his belly.

"How did you do that?"

"Lots of practice," the masked man said with a cynical twist of his mouth.

Bassett fell on his side, the lifeblood ebbing out of him.

The masked man stood there for a moment staring at the dead man before him. He tensed as he heard someone at the door, then relaxed when he saw who it was.

"Is he dead?" Dora asked.

"Yes."

"I'm glad, Ethan."

Ethan reached up and untied the mask from his face and shoved it into his pocket. "I'll be moving on now, Dora."

"But I'm glad you came, Ethan. I'm glad you remembered, and that you came."

"I owe you, Dora. If you ever need me, Seth will know how to find me."

"Do you think you'll ever settle down somewhere, Ethan?"

"A man with a price on his head never can." Ethan looked bleakly out at the Masked Marauder being cheered by the townspeople. "I have to say my good-byes to Seth, but then I'll be on my way."

Down on the street, Molly was starting to get worried. She had retrieved Nessie, and she had Patch and Whit in tow, but nowhere did she see Seth. Where was he? Had Pike somehow gotten to Seth before the Marauder confronted him?

Patch suddenly jerked free. "There's Pa! Pa!"

Molly turned to see where Patch was pointing. Her jaw dropped as she saw the man standing in the center of the crowd, the man dressed all in black who removed his mask at last to reveal who he was.

Patch and Whit grinned at each other as sheer amazement quieted the crowd. An instant later, a babble of excited voices erupted.

"Who'd have thought it?"

"Sure had us all fooled, Doc!"

"My God, and we all thought you was a—"

Coward.

Stillness descended for a sobering instant as they all thought the word. Then the babble began again.

"That sure was some fancy shootin', Doc!"

"You were something else! Just something else!"

Molly felt herself pushed forward by the crowd, who had recognized her and the children and were anxious to reunite them with Seth.

Seth looked sheepish. "I'm sorry I couldn't tell you sooner, Molly," he said. "It just wasn't possible."

"We're having a baby, Pa," Patch said. "That is, Molly's having a baby."

The crowd laughed, and someone shouted, "Seems like you been a pretty busy man lately, Doc."

Molly flushed bright red.

"You gonna keep on wearing a gun, Doc?" someone yelled.

"We need a sheriff here in Fort Benton," another said. "Seems you'd do a good job."

"I just want to be a doctor," Seth said in a quiet voice.

"Come on, Doc. Will you at least think about it?"

"All right," Seth said. "I'll think about it. Right now, I'm taking my wife and kids home."

"Sure, Doc, sure."

Seth wrapped an arm around Molly's shoulders. She remained stiff against him. He had known she would be upset when she found out he had been sneaking out at night to be the Masked Marauder. But he had thought she would at least see the humor in the situation.

Molly wasn't laughing. She wasn't even smiling. As he lifted her up into the buggy seat, she arched a brow and said, "When we get home, we have to talk."

Ethan joined them at the buggy with Seth's big black horse, which he tied on behind.

Patch leaned out of the buggy and asked, "Did you know Pa was the Masked Marauder, Ethan?"

"How about that!" Ethan said.

Prompted by Ethan's enthusiasm, Patch launched into a litany of accolades for the Masked Marauder.

It was easy for Seth and Molly to avoid talking on the way home because Patch and Whit never shut up. They argued vociferously over which was the most dangerous exploit of the Masked Marauder. And whether Whit was going to help Patch build a ship in the whiskey bottle she had taken from the saloon. At last Patch said, "For a while I thought Ethan was the Masked Marauder, Pa. Can you imagine that?"

Seth turned and shared a smile with Ethan, who was riding along beside the buggy. "Oh, I can see how you might have been fooled."

When they got home, Molly took the children inside and fed them supper. Seth unharnessed the buggy and rubbed down the buckskin. Ethan joined him in the barn.

"I wanted to thank you for being a friend when I needed one," Ethan said.

"Anytime."

"That Masked Marauder idea of yours worked just fine. You should have seen the look on Bassett's face when he realized there were two of us."

"How is Drake?"

"Dead," Ethan said. "Dora's gonna make up some story about a drifter passing through to account for the stab wound in his belly."

Ethan straightened the buckskin's mane. "It's time I moved on, Seth. Especially now that the town has seen you use a gun. Eventually, they'll find out who you are. And then *they'll* know where I am."

"Maybe not."

Ethan shook his head. "Can't take the chance. Might put you and your family in danger." Ethan grinned. "Speaking of families, it looks like you're going to be a proud papa again."

Seth grinned back. "How about that?"

"With another mouth to feed, you might want to take that sheriff's job they offered you in town," Ethan said.

"I'll think about it."

"You know, Seth, the past is over and done. It was an accident."

Seth heaved a sigh. "Yeah."

"I guess I'd better go say good-bye to Patch before I leave."

Ethan found Patch sitting on the back porch. "Hello, there."

"Sit down, Ethan. I was just counting my marbles. I'm going to have a rematch tomorrow with Whit."

"I'm sorry I won't be here to see you win," he said.

"You have to go scouting for wild horses again?"

"No." He took a deep breath and said, "I'm leaving, Patch. For good."

"But you're Pa's partner. You have a cabin here. You can't leave."

"I'm a drifting man. And it's time to move on."

"Why?"

He put a hand on her shoulder. "I have my reasons, Patch. I have to go."

"No you don't!" she said, jerking away from his touch, refusing to be mollified. "You could stay if you wanted to." She damned her pride and grabbed his shirt in both fists. "Don't leave, Ethan. I love you! Someday I want to be your wife!"

"Dammit, Patch. You don't know what you're saying. You're just a kid!"

Patch recoiled as though he had slapped her.

Suddenly aware that he had hurt her feelings, Ethan sought to mend fences. "You've got your whole life ahead of you, Patch. And plenty of time to find the man who'll be right for you."

"I don't want anybody else. I want you," she said stubbornly.

He took her hand and brushed his thumb across her grimy knuckles. "I tell you what I'll do, Patch. I promise someday, when you're all grown up, I'll come back and find you. If you still think you want to marry me—" He shrugged. "Well, we'll see."

"Do you promise?" Patch said.

Ethan nodded.

"Cross your heart and hope to die?"

Ethan crossed his heart with his finger.

"Dang it, Ethan, I'm going to miss you so much!" Patch launched herself into Ethan's open arms and hugged him hard enough to last her the long years she would have to wait for him to return.

Patch didn't try to stop the tears. *Ethan was leaving. He didn't believe she loved him. He thought she was just a kid!* Well, she wasn't going to change her mind about marrying him. She would wait a lifetime if she had to! When he came back—Ethan wouldn't dare break his promise—she would be waiting. And she would be his wife.

Ethan handed Patch a handkerchief to wipe her runny nose. She started to hand it back, but he folded her fingers around the wadded-up ball of material. "Keep it for me till I come back." He stood and said, "Now I have to go say good-bye to your ma."

"She ain't my—"

"She is. And you're lucky to have her," Ethan said.

"Maybe I am," Patch agreed.

"That's the first sign I've seen that you're starting to grow up," Ethan said. "Now give me another hug and say good-bye."

Patch put her arms around Ethan's waist and held on until he removed them.

"Good-bye, Patch."

"Good-bye, Ethan. Don't forget I love you."

He smiled. "I won't."

He turned his back on her and walked away.

❋16❋

SETH'S PATH BACK TO the house from the barn crossed Whit's door. He knocked, and when Whit called out to him, he stepped inside.

"I thought I'd check to see that you were tucked in for the night."

"Mother was already here," Whit said.

"All right. Sleep well, then."

When Seth turned to leave, Whit said, "I wouldn't mind if you tucked me in too."

Seth sat down beside Whit and performed what had become a ritual for them over the past weeks. Then he did something he hadn't done before. He leaned over and kissed Whit on the forehead.

Whit stared at him with probing eyes. "What did you do that for?"

"Because I wanted to show that I love you," Seth said.

"I'm not your son. Why do you care?" Whit challenged.

Seth smiled. "I don't think I can give you a reason. Love just is. I want to help you grow up to be a good man. And I want you to be happy." Seth shrugged. "I can't explain it any better than that."

Whit cleared his throat. "I might love you too."

Seth smiled again. "I wouldn't mind if you did." He leaned over and blew out the lantern beside the bed. "Go to sleep, son."

Whit turned over and did as he was told.

Seth wasn't consciously avoiding the coming confrontation with Molly. But when he headed through the connecting doorway, it seemed a good idea to stop and say good night to Patch and Nessie, too.

The instant he walked through the door, Nessie stood up on the four-poster bed and leaped for him. He barely caught her before she hit the floor.

"Whoa there, girl! What're you doing jumping out of bed like that?"

Nessie wrapped her arms around Seth's neck and laid her head on his chest. "I knew you'd catch me."

Seth's heart was still pounding from the near miss. "Just give me a little more warning next time," he said with a chuckle.

Nessie was easy to love, Seth thought, because she gave love so freely. He should have mentioned that to Whit, but he hadn't thought of it at the time. "It's bedtime, little one. Lie down now and get some sleep."

He laid her down and pulled the quilt up to her chin, then leaned over and kissed her teasingly on the nose.

Seth looked over at Patch, who was leaning on her elbow watching him. Before Annarose died, when Patch was still a baby, he had spent time with her like this every night. He had forgotten about that until now.

As Seth crossed to Patch, she lay down flat and pulled her own covers up, leaving nothing for him to do.

He sat down beside her anyway. He felt awkward with his daughter, not sure how he should treat her. She seemed too grown up for the kind of teasing he had done with Nessie. In fact, the expression on her face dared him to try something like that with her. Which was how he knew that was exactly what he should do.

He leaned over and kissed her on the nose, but as he sat up, he licked his lips. "Mmmm. Those freckles tasted distinctly of brown sugar."

"Oh, Pa!" Patch said. "Don't be ridiculous."

"Maybe I was wrong. Let me see." He kissed her nose again. "Definitely brown sugar," he said. "And you know how I love sweets." He began kissing Patch all over her face, everywhere he could find a freckle.

Soon she was laughing, fighting him off—not too hard—and loving every breathless minute of it.

"What is all the noise in here?"

Seth stopped what he was doing and grinned at Molly, who was standing in the doorway. "I was just kissing all the brown sugar off Patch's face."

Molly smiled. "Pretty sweet, is she?"

Seth looked at Patch and said, "The sweetest."

Patch turned a bright shade of scarlet and pulled the covers up over her head. "Paaaa."

"Come on out, Patch," Seth whispered to the covers that hid her face.

Only her twinkling blue eyes appeared. "Huh-uh."

He held up his hand and said, "I promise to swear off brown sugar for the rest of the evening."

The blanket came down, revealing a shy smile on Patch's face.

Seth carefully tucked the blanket around her as though she weren't already a young woman with budding breasts. "Sleep well, Patch. I'll see you in the morning. I love you."

He blew out the lantern and joined Molly at the door.

"Good night, Da," Nessie said.

"Good night, Pa," Patch whispered. And then, very quietly, "I love you too."

Seth slipped an arm around Molly's waist and headed for the front door. "Let's go sit on the porch," he said. "I have some things I want to say to you."

But when they were settled on the front porch, Molly on the top step and Seth on the bottom, it was Molly who asked the first question.

"Where have you been on the nights when you were supposed to be with Mrs. Gulliver?"

"With Dora Deveraux."

Molly groaned. "Why, Seth?"

"She was giving me information about where Bassett set up his whiskey-selling operation so the Masked Marauder could raid and destroy it. Also, Bassett had someone in Virginia City tipping him off when miners carrying gold were taking the stage to Fort Benton. He'd leak that information to Blackfoot renegades, who robbed the stage. Dora gave me the same information—"

"—so the Masked Marauder could ride to the rescue," Molly said in amazement.

"There was never anything between me and Dora after I married you."

"Pike said he saw you in her bed."

"There were extenuating circumstances."

"This I have to hear," Molly muttered.

"Remember the rumor going around at the christening party that Pike had shot the Masked Marauder?"

Molly nodded.

"Well, he did. I just had a flesh wound, but it was pretty bloody. I couldn't come home to you like that. When Pike showed up at Dora's room, the only excuse I had for being there was that I was making use of her services."

Molly frowned. "So that's why you grabbed my hand that night when I touched your ribs!"

Seth grinned crookedly. "It hurt."

"Wouldn't it have been simpler if you'd just explained everything to me in the first place?"

Seth brushed at some dust on the toe of his boot. "I didn't know you very well when I married you, Molly. I had no idea how you'd react if I told you the truth."

"But later—"

"I couldn't stop until I'd finished the job. I thought you wouldn't worry if you didn't know the truth. But it looks like you worried anyway. I'm sorry for that."

"Does what happened to Annarose have anything to do with the Masked Marauder?"

"No."

"Then why wouldn't you tell me how she died?"

Seth took a shuddering breath and covered his face with his hands. "I didn't want to talk about it."

Molly scooted down to the bottom step to sit beside Seth. She laid a comforting hand on his knee. "I'm sorry. You must have painful memories. It's none of my business how she died."

Seth dropped his hands and said, "I shot her. I killed Annarose."

Seth waited for Molly to cringe away from him. But her hand stayed on his knee, and her eyes never wavered from his agonized face.

He found himself explaining, seeking her understanding and absolution from the horrible nightmare that had plagued him for the past nine years.

"Nine years ago I was a Texas Ranger, Molly."

"A Ranger!" she exclaimed. "With all that talk of killing, I thought you'd been an *outlaw*!"

"I chased enough of them," Seth said grimly. "Once I was ambushed, shot in the back by some rustlers and left for dead. Annarose nursed me back to health and never said a word about my quitting the Rangers.

"Not that I would have. I loved the danger. I loved the challenge of tracking down desperados, of pitting my wits against theirs.

"Nine years ago, when Patch was three, I went after some Mexican bandidos who had robbed a stage and killed the driver. There were three of them. They fled toward the nearest town, a place not far from my ranch. It was dark by the time I rode into town. I knew I should have waited till morning. They had the advantage in the dark.

"But one of them started talking to me, taunting me, saying I was chicken-livered, afraid to fight. When I stepped out of the shadows, they were waiting for me.

"If I hadn't tripped, the first shot would have killed me. I fired at the powder flash and killed one of them. Then I heard someone move behind me.

"You don't forget being backshot, Molly. I wasn't about to let it happen again. I turned and fired into the darkness—toward the noise I'd heard. There was another flash of gunfire in front of me, and I turned and shot at that.

"The next thing I heard was a horse galloping away. I would have gone after him, but I was still shaking. I went to check on the two bodies I'd seen fall. One of the bandidos was dead. The other body—the one behind me—was Annarose.

"I had shot her twice in the chest, but she was still breathing. She was in town to find a doctor because Patch was sick. She'd come running toward me to warn me about the ambush."

There were tears on Seth's cheeks, and he turned away from Molly to wipe them away with his sleeve.

"It wasn't your fault," Molly said. "It was an accident."

"Yeah. I've been telling myself that for nine years. I wanted to die with Annarose. For a couple of months after that, I did my best to get killed. I'm a notorious man in Texas, Molly. An outlaw killer. The meanest, most deadly Ranger around.

"I would probably be long dead now if it hadn't been for Ethan. He convinced me I had something—someone—to live for."

"Patch," Molly whispered.

Seth nodded. "I quit wearing a gun and learned how to heal folks instead."

"So why did you create the Masked Marauder?"

Seth shrugged. "Drake Bassett and his henchman had to be stopped. I didn't want to be known as a gunman, Molly. I didn't want to be dragged back into the life I'd left behind."

"Did you have to let people think you were afraid to fight?"

He shrugged again. "I couldn't kill anyone else if I walked away."

Molly put a hand on Seth's cheek, which was rough with a day's growth of whiskers. "As I said once before, you're an unusual man, Doctor Kendrick. And for the record, I love you very much."

Seth dragged Molly into his arms and hugged her tight. "And I love you."

"Seth, I can't breathe," she laughed. "The baby—"

He turned her in his lap so he could put his hand on her womb. "-Were your other two births easy, Molly? Will having this baby be hard on you?"

"I'll be fine, Seth. I get a little sick in the beginning—"

"I'll say!"

"—but in a few months I'll feel wonderful, I'm sure."

"If anything happened to you—I love you so much, Molly." He kissed her until they were both breathless.

Molly laid her head against Seth's chest and gasped for air. "Is that quilt still in the loft, Seth?" she asked.

"It was the last time I looked," he said with a crooked grin.

"Let's go." She entwined her fingers with his and led him toward the barn.

He lit a lantern, and she raced ahead of him up the ladder to the loft. She was shaking the blanket out when he lifted her into his arms and kissed her hard.

She laughed and thrust her hands into his hair to hold him close. "You crazy, crazy man! Put me down."

"I want to hold you in my arms forever."

"You're going to get awfully tired over the next nine months," she said, "as I get bigger."

Seth grinned. "I'll look forward to it."

He set her on her feet and took the blanket from her. "I'll do that."

But as he shook the blanket to spread it on the straw, he heard a growl and saw two golden eyes reflected in the lamplight.

"Is that you, Rebel?" Seth said. He started to shoo the mountain lion away. "You may have gotten here first, but I've got the better claim."

When Rebel growled another warning, Molly put her hand on Seth's arm. "Seth, look." She lifted the lantern and held it so it shed more light on the corner of the loft. There in the corner was a litter of tiny cubs.

"Oh, Seth," Molly said. "Aren't they adorable. Wait until Patch sees them!"

Seth swore under his breath. "I had plans for that stack of hay," he muttered.

"Let's leave her alone. We can go down to the pond. It's lovely there," she said. "Come on. Grab the quilt, and let's go."

Seth hadn't forgotten their night together down by the pond, under the stars. If they couldn't make love in the loft, the soft grass by the pond was a good substitute.

They ran nearly the whole way, and Molly couldn't breathe because she was laughing so hard. She sought out the spot where they'd made love once before. Seth had both hands on the blanket, shaking it out, when Molly teasingly reached up between his legs from behind.

Seth let the blanket hang from his hands, just stood there and waited to see what she would do.

Molly cupped him in her hand and felt him growing, felt the softness pulse and harden. She put her other hand around him so she held him from before and behind.

Seth gritted his teeth to keep from groaning, but he lost the battle, and a long, low moan issued from his lips.

And was answered by a moan from the shadows under the trees.

"What was that?" Seth said.

"What? I didn't hear anything."

He pulled Molly's hands off him and put her behind him. "Who's out there?" he demanded.

Something moved out from the shadows.

"Maverick!"

The dog-wolf sat down in front of Seth, cocked his head and looked up at him.

"Scat!" Seth said, waving the beast away.

Maverick ran a little bit away and came back with a stick. And sat down in front of Seth.

Molly giggled.

"This isn't funny," Seth said.

"I know," Molly said, and giggled again.

Seth took the stick and threw it as far out into the pond as he could. "That ought to take care of him for a while. Now, where were we?"

He took Molly's hands and put them on the front of his jeans and rubbed them up and down. Then he left her to her own devices while he returned the favor.

While their hands teased, taunted, aroused, Seth leaned down and joined his mouth to Molly's. They played with each other, lips and hands, until their knees were weak. They sank to the quilt, and Seth pushed her skirt up out of the way and let his hands glide up her legs.

"Molly, Molly, let me love you."

"Seth, I—"

Maverick barked to announce his arrival. It was all the warning Seth and Molly got before the wet dog shook himself, spraying them with a whole pond's worth of water. Then he sat down beside Seth and let the stick drop on the quilt.

Molly looked at Seth.

Seth looked at Molly. He grabbed her and roared with laughter. They rolled around the quilt, laughing until their ribs hurt.

"I can't believe he did that," Molly said through gusts of laughter. "I'm soaked."

"So am I," Seth said, stripping himself out of his shirt and using it to wipe their faces dry. "I give up. Let's go inside and go to bed."

Maverick followed them all the way to the kitchen door, but Seth shut him firmly outside. They tiptoed past Patch's door to their own bedroom.

"Shall we light a lantern?" Molly said.

"I don't need any light," Seth said. "I'm perfectly willing to feel my way around." He promptly demonstrated by cupping Molly's breasts in his hands and letting his thumbs brush the tips, which immediately hardened into pebbled tips.

Molly gasped in pleasure. "That sounds like a wonderful idea," she said. She leaned over and kissed her way across Seth's chest until she found a male nipple. She closed her teeth around it and nipped him, then used her tongue to soothe the hurt.

Seth mimicked her action, taking her breast in his mouth, teasing the nipple with his tongue, biting just enough for her to feel his teeth, then sucking until Molly moaned her pleasure and thrust her hands into his hair to hold him there.

Slowly, taking their time, they stripped each other bare. In the dark, every sensation was magnified. They were lovers, celebrating their love for each other. Gentle touches, adoring caresses, teasing hands and laughter. Lots of laughter as they searched in the dark for the edge of the quilt and sheets and pulled them down.

Then Seth lifted Molly into his arms, held her close, and kissed her gently. "Come to bed, wife, and let me love you."

He laid her down, and Molly slipped her feet under the covers—and leaped back up into Seth's arms with a screech.

"There's something down there!"

"Where?"

"Under the covers. Something *alive*!"

Seth tried to put Molly down so he could light the lantern, but she was having no part of that. "Molly, if you'll just let me put you down—"

"I'm not setting one foot on the ground until you get that *thing* out of here!"

Seth finally managed to get the lantern lit. Sure enough, there was a lump under the covers, about in the spot where Molly's feet had been. Seth reached over and yanked the covers away in one fell swoop.

Bandit was curled up in a ball. As soon as the covers were pulled away, he began to chatter angrily.

"You think you're upset," Seth muttered under his breath. "Patch!" he yelled. "Patch, get in here!"

Enough was enough. A frustrated man could take only so much. Then, of course, he realized that both he and Molly were stark naked. He dragged his jeans on, while Molly grabbed a robe and drew it around her.

A second later, Patch opened the door. Nessie was with her, and so was Whit. "What's wrong, Pa?" she asked anxiously.

He pointed to the raccoon curled up on the foot of the bed. "Get that animal out of here before I shoot it."

"I wondered where he'd gotten to."

She scooped the animal up in her arms. "Anything else, Pa?"

"No, just go to bed, all of you. *And go to sleep!*"

When the door closed behind the children, Seth turned to Molly. He smiled crookedly. "I guess I lost my temper."

She walked into his arms and hugged him. "I can understand

why," she said. She kissed him on the chin, the cheeks, the eyes, and finally the lips.

The kiss grew, and maybe because they'd been interrupted so many times, they let their mouths say everything they were feeling. Seth took Molly's lower lip between his teeth and nibbled it, then sucked it into his mouth. His tongue teased the sensitive underside of her upper lip. Their mouths touched tentatively, as passion built slowly but surely.

"Dare we try this again?" Seth asked. He could feel Molly's smile against his lips when she answered, "Sure. Why not?"

Seth didn't waste time taking off his jeans, simply lifted her into his arms and carried her over to the bed. He laid her down, then blew out the lantern and joined her. He slipped a hand up under her robe—

And there was a knock at the door.

"Don't answer it," Seth hissed.

"We have to," Molly whispered back, straightening her robe. "The children—"

Seth levered himself off the bed and lit the lantern. Then he stalked over to the door and yanked it open. "What is it?" he demanded.

Nessie stood there, her thumb in her mouth. "I can't sleep."

Seth sighed. "Would it help if you lie down with us for a little while?"

"Uh-huh."

Seth picked her up, shut the door, and carried her over to the bed. He set her down and went back over to stand beside the door. A second later there was another knock. When he opened the door, Whit and Patch stood there.

"Where's Nessie?" they asked.

Seth pointed to the bed. "Would you like to join us?"

Patch and Whit jumped into the bed beside Nessie and scooched down under the covers.

Seth didn't try to get next to Molly, just took the space that was left on the opposite side of the bed. He sat there and met Molly's eyes over the top of the children's heads. "You realize," he said, "that this sort of thing could severely limit the size of our family."

Molly grinned. "For the next eight months that isn't a problem."

Seth groaned. "Good night, Molly."

"Good night, Seth." Molly blew out the lantern and scooted down under the covers.

Then three sets of loving hands gently tucked their parents into bed.

OUTLAW'S BRIDE

*This book is dedicated to all the
readers, fans, and bookstore owners
who read* The Barefoot Bride
*and asked for Patch and Ethan's story.
Here it is.*

ACKNOWLEDGMENTS

I want to thank romantic suspense author Sherryl Woods for her invaluable assistance in keeping the mystery in *Outlaw's Bride*.

I would also like to thank Mark Bledsoe, owner of the present-day Oakville Mercantile, for his helpful background history and information about the town of Oakville, Texas.

❧ 1 ❧

SHE WAS A LADY. Ethan recognized the breed, though it had been a long time since he had seen one quite so fresh from finishing school—feathers in her hat, gloves on her hands, and a steel rod running down her spine. He was hidden from view, sitting in a high-backed chair in the lobby of the Oakville Hotel. Waiting. Every so often his green eyes flicked to the dusty street outside. Watching.

His eyes were drawn back to the lady. The soft complexion of peaches and cream and a short, uptilted nose contrasted with a strong, determined chin. His lip curled cynically. A lady used to getting her own way, he amended. She looked up at the hotel clerk from under long, feathery lashes that concealed big blue—not quite innocent, he thought—eyes. Her voice was melodious, not demanding, but not demure, either.

"I'd like a room, please," she said.

"For how long?" the clerk asked.

Ethan watched the lady's brow furrow. Her black-gloved hand reached up to smooth already perfectly arranged golden tresses bound up in a very ladylike bun at her nape. "I don't know," she said. "I'm looking for someone who—" She cut herself off.

Ethan was distracted by something on the registration desk. The lady's velvet drawstring purse, which exactly matched her rose red dress, seemed to be moving of its own accord. A moment later a pointed pink nose and long whiskers appeared at the center of the drawstring opening. Ethan grinned. Somehow a field mouse had gotten into the lady's purse.

He started to call a warning but looked out the plate glass window first. He didn't want to let them know where he was any sooner than necessary. Instead of speaking, he leaned back into the comfortable winged chair and waited for the fun to start.

To his amazement, elegant gloved hands surreptitiously poked the mouse back into the purse and once again drew the strings tight. Ethan's brow arched in speculation. She wasn't quite what she seemed, then. No lady in his experience had ever carried a mouse around in her purse.

"I don't know how long I'll be here," the lady repeated. "I would love to have a bath sent up to my room. It's been a long trip."

From where? Ethan wondered. And who had she come to find in Oakville, Texas? Lucky man. Because besides being a lady, she was also a woman. Full breasts that would overflow a man's hands, a tiny waist—unfortunately corseted—and long legs that he could imagine wrapped tight around him while he thrust deep inside her.

Ethan felt his body respond, felt the heavy pulse in his throat, the tightness in his groin. He reminded himself that the steel rod down a lady's back didn't usually bend for the finer pleasures in life. Besides, he thought bitterly, no *lady* was going to want anything to do with him—ever again.

"Hawk! Ethan Hawk! We know you're in there. Come on out!"

Ethan rose slowly from the high-backed chair. He saw the stunned look on the lady's face as she turned to stare at him. He grinned and tipped his Stetson to her. From the corner of his eye he saw the flash of sunlight on blue steel out on the street. He launched himself at the lady and yelled to the clerk, "Duck, Gilley!"

Ethan twisted in midair, trying to keep the lady from being crushed beneath him as he snatched her out of harm's way. Several bullets crashed through the hotel window, sending glass flying. He landed on his shoulder and rolled several times away from the splintering glass.

The lady was a lovely package, but enough to knock the wind from him. He knew every second counted, but he lay frozen for a moment, infinitely aware of the curves lying beneath him. Her hat had come off, and her hair had come loose from its tight bun. A stray curl was tickling his nose, which was pressed against her throat. He blew it away, and felt her shiver.

Ethan lifted his head and looked into big blue eyes that seemed to swallow him in their depths. Her hair lay like a golden nimbus around a heart-shaped face. She had her lower lip caught in straight white teeth. He surveyed that perfect complexion—now pale with fright— and realized that powder half hid a dozen freckles across her nose. So he had exposed another of the lady's secrets. He wished he had time to discover them all. But there were men waiting outside for him. Dangerous men.

He reached across her for his Stetson, which lay amid scattered glass on the tapestry carpet, and settled it back on his head. He was aware of her femininity as firm breasts cushioned his chest. His body naturally slipped into the cradle of her thighs. He swore at his instantaneous reaction to such intimate contact. From the way her eyes widened and darkened, she felt it, too.

She struggled to get up, but he put a hand to her shoulder to hold her down. "Stay here," he warned. "Don't move!"

He started to slide off her but stopped when she said his name.

"Ethan?"

Her eyes searched his face and for a moment he thought she looked familiar. Especially with those freckles and a strand of that glorious golden hair falling over one eye. "Do I know you?"

Her eyes showed pain, as though a shard of glass had cut her deep. "Are you all right?" he asked. His hands quickly roamed her body, searching for some wound.

That perked her up. Her face got that indignant look he might have expected from a lady not used to having a man handle her like a woman. She opened her mouth to speak, but before she could, there was another cry from the street.

"Hawk! Come on out, Hawk!"

He grinned and touched the brim of his hat to her. "Sorry I can't stay to get better acquainted. If you're smart, darlin', you'll get out of Oakville while there's still some starch in your drawers."

She gasped, but his attention was already focused on the men out in the street, hired killers who wanted him dead so they could collect their blood money from Jefferson Trahern. Ethan had learned that he couldn't expect help from the sheriff. Careless Lachlan owed his livelihood to the town council. And the town council was owned by the richest rancher in Oak County, Texas—Jefferson Trahern.

Ethan realized the lady was trying to wriggle out from under him. "Keep your head down!" he snapped, grabbing a handful of those golden tresses to hold her still.

"Ethan, it's me! It's Patch!" she hissed at him, her head bobbing up again. "Patch Kendrick."

He stared with dawning horror at the once impeccably groomed lady lying beneath him, the beautiful stranger who had stirred his lust.

He released her hair and rolled off her as though she had become a mass of angry ants.

"Don't move! Not an inch! Your pa'll kill me if anything happens to you!"

He crawled quickly toward the side window and slithered out into the dark alley before another call came from the street.

What the devil was Seth Kendrick's tomboy daughter doing in Oak County, Texas? And when, by God, had she become a *lady*? Ethan stood in the shadows of the alley near the front of the hotel and waited for the hired guns to make their move. And remembered.

The last time he had seen Patch Kendrick was eight years earlier in Fort Benton, Montana. She had been a pugnacious twelve-year-old brat with elfin features, budding breasts—and the crazy idea that she was in love with him! He had been twenty-five, her father's best friend—and on the run from the law.

Jefferson Trahern had been hunting him even then. Ethan had ridden hard and fast out of Fort Benton to avoid the detectives Trahern constantly had trailing him. He hadn't been caught—not for another year, anyway. Then . . .

What was it Patch had made him promise her when he had left Fort Benton eight years ago? That he would marry her when she was grown up? No, he wouldn't have—couldn't have—promised that! Not, leastways, to a kid who spent more time sporting a black eye than any three prize fighters, who collected wild animals like marbles, and who swore like a bullwhacker who had been to Sunday meeting. He could hear her ranting now with her *garns* and *durns*. Danged if he didn't!

Ethan smiled at the memory of the precocious child she had been. So what had he promised that rumpled hoyden—now elegant lady— the last time he had seen her? She had made him cross his heart, he remembered that. He frowned, trying to dredge up the memory of that long-ago conversation.

But he couldn't recall it. She had just been a kid with romantic notions. He hadn't paid much attention to exactly what he had said to her, something about returning to Fort Benton when she was all grown up. His mouth flattened and his eyes narrowed as he thought of the reason he hadn't gone back to see her again.

Otherwise, he had promised her . . . nothing. Which was a damned good thing, considering the fact that no decent woman would have anything to do with him now. Whatever she might once have been, now Patch Kendrick was one helluva lady.

Ethan couldn't believe the carnal thoughts he'd had about her. And the way he had touched her! Ethan felt the heat in his face. How was he ever going to look Seth Kendrick in the eye? Ethan grimaced. Reluctant as he was to admit it, Patch Kendrick was about the most arousing piece of femininity he had ever held in his arms. Even thinking about her had his body thrumming with desire.

Unfortunately, if Seth ever got wind of the thoughts Ethan was having about his daughter, Ethan wouldn't have to wait for Trahern's vengeance to put him six feet under. Seth would kill him first!

"Come out and get what's comin' to ya, Hawk!"

Ethan pulled his Colt and fanned the hammer as he charged out of the alley, spraying bullets at the five men who converged on him from all sides of Main Street.

He saw one go down near the horse trough. Another fell on the wooden porch of the mercantile. A third dropped where he stood in the center of the rutted street. The fourth dove for cover behind the livery. The fifth got off one shot before he pitched headlong through the plate glass window of the Silver Buckle Saloon.

By then, even with his awkward gait—long step, halting step, long step, halting step—Ethan had reached his horse. He launched himself into the saddle and spurred the big black stallion. The animal hit his stride long before the mass confusion Ethan had left behind him cleared enough for anyone to grab a rifle.

"Ethan! Ethan Hawk!"

He heard Patch Kendrick calling him from the front porch of the hotel and reined his horse to an abrupt stop at the end of the short main street. The urge to answer her was strong. But she could have no idea of the trouble he was in. And he wasn't about to let her get involved. The instant Trahern found out Ethan cared anything about her, Patch would become a target for the old man's revenge.

He pulled off his hat, letting his sun-streaked hair blow in the wind, and gave her a gentleman's bow from the saddle. Then he spurred the black stud and raced out of town, disappearing in a cloud of Texas dust.

Patricia Wallis Kendrick had watched the gunfight unfold with a mixture of terror and awe. She had traveled all the way from Fort Benton, Montana, to find the man who had just ridden hell-for-leather out of this godforsaken south Texas town. She had an old debt to settle with Ethan Hawk. Years ago he had promised to return to court her when she was a grown woman—and to marry her. Patch was here to hold him to his promise.

She angled her hat in a rakish tilt over her brow and tucked a stray blond curl back into the mass of hair she had repinned into a stylish bun. Then she marched down the front steps of the hotel toward the man who had arrived on the scene—well after the gunfight—wearing a badge on his brown leather vest. There was no need to elbow her way through the crowd of gawkers who had converged on the street, because it parted like the Red Sea before her.

"Are you the sheriff?" she demanded.

Sheriff Careless Lachlan was bent over Johnny Two Toes, who was deader than a doornail. He looked up over his shoulder. Startled by the imposing dignity of the woman behind him, he snapped up like a bent willow branch and yanked his hat off his head.

"I'm Sheriff Lachlan." He smiled, exposing tobacco-stained teeth. "What can I do for you, ma'am?"

"Why didn't you stop this gunfight before it started?"

"Why, uh . . ." He scratched his balding pate and said, "Someone mighta got hurt."

She stared down at the dead man at her feet, then toward the other three men who lay sprawled in various postures on the street, her pointed gaze finally landing on the broken window of the Silver Buckle Saloon. "It seems to me someone did get hurt, Sheriff."

His face turned beet red. "Only this riffraff, ma'am." He frowned and muttered, "I told Mr. Trahern this wasn't a good idea."

"You *knew* these men were hired killers, and yet you did nothing to stop them?"

The sheriff pulled at the neck of his shirt and loosened a string tie that was already half undone. "Now I wouldn't exactly say that, ma'am. I did warn the boy they was after him," he said. "Told Ethan he oughta get outta town and go back to that ranch of his'n. But Hawk, he insisted on stayin' in town, facin' 'em down." Careless shrugged in a characteristic way that showed how little he cared, which was, in fact, what had gotten him his name. "You see how it turned out."

"What if Mr. Hawk had been hurt?" Patch asked.

"Nobody can kill that son of Satan," the sheriff muttered. "Not that they ain't been tryin' more years than I can count. Ever since . . ."

"Ever since what?" Patch asked.

"That's history now. The boy's paid for what he done."

"What do you mean?" Patch asked. "How has he paid? And for what?"

"Why, for killing Jefferson Trahern's boy, Dorne. Claimed it was self-defense, Ethan did. Only thing that kept him from gettin' hung was Boyd spoke up for him."

"Boyd?"

"Boyd Stuckey. Old friend of Ethan's from when they was kids. Boyd's near rich as Trahern these days. Anyway, that Hawk boy finally got out of prison 'bout a month ago. Been there nigh on to seven years. I say he's paid his debt. Oughtta be able to walk the streets like a free man. Only . . ." He frowned up at the sun and put his hat back on—lady or no—to keep off the noonday heat.

"Only what?" Patch asked, impatient to hear the rest.

"Only Trahern don't figure it that way."

"So Trahern hired these men to kill Ethan—because Ethan killed his son? Even though Ethan has paid his debt to society by spending seven years in prison?"

"Jefferson Trahern don't forgive nor forget."

"How do I get to Ethan's ranch from town?" Patch asked.

"Head southwest 'bout five miles, you'll find it right along the Neuces River. But you don't want to go there, ma'am."

Patch arched her most intimidating brow. "Why not?"

"Ain't safe."

"Why not?"

The sheriff grimaced. "Lady like you has no business bein' 'round a fella like him. Convicted murderer and all."

Patch squared her shoulders and lifted her chin. "I'll have you know that Ethan Hawk is—" Patch cut herself off. She couldn't call Ethan her fiancé, not without stretching the truth. Nothing had been settled that day eight years ago when Ethan had said good-bye.

Patch had waited as long as she could for Ethan to return to Fort

Benton. Both her father and stepmother had advised her to keep on waiting. "He'll come back when the time is right," her pa had said. But Patch hadn't been satisfied with that.

When her parents began planning a trip to Boston for her to visit her stepbrother, Whit, she realized it was the chance she had been waiting for. She had smiled a guilty good-bye, knowing she was heading for Texas, not Boston.

She had come to this small south Texas town because Ethan had once told her he was born and raised in Oakville, Texas. It was where she had planned to start her search. Darned if she hadn't found him!

Only her journey wasn't quite over yet.

"Can you tell me where I might purchase some gentlemen's clothing?"

Sheriff Lachlan pulled the scruffy hairs on his chin. "Suppose you could check at the Oakville Mercantile, ma'am. Only, why you wantin' men's duds?"

"I could hardly ride five miles cross-country dressed like this." Patch turned her back on the sheriff, stepped up onto the shaded boardwalk, and marched straight into the Oakville Hotel.

Knowing Ethan was an ex-convict didn't change Patch's intentions toward him one whit. She had known he was on the run from the law when she first fell in love with him. Ethan had once told Patch's stepmother, Molly, that he'd had a good reason for killing the man he had killed. Patch wasn't about to pass judgment until she heard Ethan's reasons herself. Assuming Ethan didn't throw her out before she had a chance to ask for them.

Patch felt the color skating up her throat as she remembered what had happened in the Oakville Hotel. She wasn't very experienced in such matters, but it seemed to her Ethan found her at least a little bit attractive. She was ready now to approach him as a woman rather than a child. Surely he would give her the chance to convince him they belonged together.

As Patch entered the hotel lobby, the clerk Ethan had called Gilley said, "You'll have to wait for that bath until I get this glass swept up."

"That's all right," Patch said. "I have some errands to do first." The first thing she did was to retrieve her purse from the registration desk. She gave it a little pat and was relieved to discover that Max was still inside. She had rescued the mouse from a hungry cat at the stage depot in Three Rivers. As soon as she found a catless barn, she planned to release him.

"I'd like to write a letter. Do you have stationery and a pen I can use?" Patch asked.

"You can sit over there at that table," Gilley said. "You should find everything you need."

Patch made her way to the table and chair in the corner Gilley had indicated. She found pen, paper, and ink and sat down to let her parents know she had arrived safely in Oakville—especially since they thought she was on her way to Boston—and that she had found Ethan Hawk.

She laid her purse carefully on the polished cherry surface, then placed a piece of paper in front of her and took pen in hand. She smiled as she thought how much she owed to her stepmother, Molly Gallagher Kendrick.

When Patch was twelve, Molly had come to Montana from Boston to be Seth Kendrick's mail-order bride—and brought along her ten-year-old son, Whit, and six-year-old daughter, Nessie. If Molly hadn't come into her life, Patch knew she would still be wearing scruffy shirts and torn jeans and fighting everyone in town to prove her father wasn't a coward. Instead, she was a lady close to realizing a childhood dream.

> Dear Ma and Pa,
>
> You don't need to worry about me. Everything is fine. I know you both wanted me to wait for Ethan to return to Montana on his own. I hope you'll understand that I couldn't wait any longer.
>
> So, when I got off the steamship in St. Louis, instead of taking the train to Boston to see Whit, I exchanged my ticket and headed south to the town where Ethan told me he grew up. I arrived safely in Oakville, Texas, today—and found Ethan!
>
> Oh, by the way, there was a very good reason why he didn't keep his promise to me. He was in prison!
>
> Ethan has a ranch not far from here, and I'll be going there early tomorrow morning. You can write to me care of the Oakville Post Office.
>
> All my love,
> Patch

P.S. Please give my love to Nessie and my favorite little brother, Jeremy. Will you write Whit for me and explain everything. Tell him I'll see the whaling ship bequeathed to him by Captain Sturgis some other time, and I'm sorry I'm going to miss all those Boston society parties he's attending now that he's a rich nabob.

P.P.S. I'll write again soon! *Don't worry about me!*

P.P.P.S. I think Ethan was a little surprised to see me, but I know everything will work out just fine.

Love and brown sugar kisses,
Patch

Patch folded the letter and addressed it to her father and step-mother. She put everything away and retrieved her purse as she stood and turned to the clerk. "Can you direct me to the post office?"

"It's at the end of Main Street," Gilley said. "In the rear of the Oakville Mercantile."

"I'll be back soon."

"I'll have that bath ready," Gilley promised.

Patch stepped out into the sunlight once more and headed toward the mercantile. She walked as though she had an egg in each hand and a stack of books on her head—the way they had taught her at the fancy school she had attended in Boston. What she didn't realize was that her natural physical grace made her body sway in a way that had every cowhand up and down the boardwalk gawking at her.

Patch had learned a lot of rules in Boston, most of which began with *A Lady Never* . . . Patch figured she had broken about ten of them in the past twenty minutes. She found it difficult to always act like a lady, but she was determined that for Ethan's sake she would epitomize that feminine ideal. No matter how hard it was, she would follow the rules—except when it was absolutely necessary to break them.

Patch politely nodded her head to the local ladies and kept her eyes straight ahead when she passed the cowboys on her way to the mercantile. She didn't care to be accosted by any of them. It was a little harder to ignore the trickle of sweat that snaked down her back. But she was a lady now, and that meant enduring certain discomforts.

Oakville's main street wasn't very long and consisted of two saloons, two hotels, the livery, a jail, a bank, several eateries, and the mercantile. Patch welcomed the cool difference in temperature when she stepped inside the oak-shaded one-story wood-frame building that Gilley had told her housed the Oakville Post Office. She introduced herself to Mr. Felber, the postmaster and owner of the store, and was assured that her letter would be on its way to Montana on the next stage.

"I'd also like to buy a few things," she said.

"Help yourself, Miss Kendrick," Mr. Felber said. "Help yourself."

Since Patch had supposedly been heading for Boston, she didn't have the sort of clothes packed in her trunks that she needed for a jaunt on horseback. Fortunately, her parents had given her enough funds for the trip to Boston so that she could afford to buy what she needed.

As Patch discovered, Mr. Felber never came out from behind the counter. When he'd said, "Help yourself," it was because he couldn't be bothered. While she searched out a pair of Levi's, a chambray shirt, socks, and boots, she watched Mr. Felber sit on his stool and play solitaire. He stopped only long enough to take payment from a lady who bought pins and another who bought peaches.

Patch's attention was drawn to the door when the bell rang to announce another customer, mainly because Mr. Felber got up off his stool and walked all the way to the end of the counter. Apparently, whoever was entering the mercantile was a person of some importance.

The tiny young woman who stepped inside had hair as black as coal, dark brown eyes, and the face of an angel. She was dressed every bit as modishly as Patch herself. Patch had never in her life seen such a beautiful woman. She knew she was staring, but she couldn't help herself.

Patch was chagrined when the woman not only noticed her stare but smiled and walked right up to her.

"Hello," the beauty said. "My name is Merielle. What's yours?"

"Patch—Patricia Kendrick."

"I haven't seen you before," Merielle said.

"I just got into town today."

"Would you like to come to my house to play?"

"To play?" Patch was confused by the invitation, which made no sense. To play what?

"Merielle!"

The tiny woman jumped at the shout from the door. She turned and her smile widened as she hurried up to the sun-browned cowboy standing in the doorway, his hat in his hand, his black hair awry. "Frank! I've found a new friend. Come and meet her."

Merielle took the cowboy's hand and drew him into the store. Patch stared again, because the cowboy was as tall and handsome as the woman was tiny and beautiful. He also had black hair, but his eyes were gray. There were lines beside his eyes and around his mouth, but Patch didn't think he had gotten them smiling.

"Howdy, ma'am," the cowboy said, nodding his head in a jerky motion. He turned his attention to the young woman. "I've been looking everywhere for you, Merielle. I wish you wouldn't run off like that."

Patch frowned as she listened to the way the cowboy was speaking to the woman—as though she were a child. Merielle was tiny, but she had a woman's body. As Patch watched the man and the woman together, it became increasingly apparent, however, that Merielle had a child's mind.

"Can Miss Kendrick come home and play with me?"

Patch saw the cowboy's jaw harden, saw his lids drop to cover the melancholy in his eyes.

"Maybe we could get together another time," Patch said to Merielle, hoping to smooth things over.

The cowboy slanted Patch a grateful look before he focused his eyes on Merielle. His features were troubled. "I don't think your pa wants you bringing home company today."

"But we could have fun. I just know it!" Merielle said.

Patch set her purchases on the counter, then reached out and took both of Merielle's hands in her own. "I promise I'll come visit soon," she said. "You go with Frank now."

"You promise?" Merielle asked worriedly.

Patch wondered why Merielle didn't also have a child's trust. She smiled at the other woman. "I promise."

Merielle's whole face brightened. "All right. I'll see you soon." She turned and linked her arm through Frank's. He nodded to Patch, then slipped his hat on. Patch noticed that he leaned down to listen earnestly to Merielle as he led her from the store.

When Patch turned around to pick up her purchases again, she found Mr. Felber shaking his head and *tsk*ing.

"Such a shame," he said. "Poor Trahern."

That name struck a strident chord with Patch. "Trahern?"

"That was Merielle Trahern. Jefferson Trahern's daughter. I don't know how Frank can stand to see her like that."

"What is Frank's relationship to her?"

"He's Trahern's foreman. He and Merielle used to be sweethearts a long time ago. Whole town knew those two kids were in love. Wasn't ever going to come to anything, though."

"Why not?"

Mr. Felber played a red nine on a black ten. "Frank Meade was dirt poor. Trahern would never have let his daughter marry a sod farmer's son."

Patch told herself she wasn't going to ask, but the words were out before she could stop them. "Has she always been like that? Childlike, I mean?"

"Nope. And that's the shame of it."

Patch felt the gooseflesh on her arms but forced herself to ask anyway. "What happened? What made her like that?"

"Poor girl lost her mind when Ethan Hawk raped her."

❊2❊

"Hold it right there!"

A towheaded hoyden in hitched-up trousers stood on the porch of a rundown ranch house, holding a rifle aimed at Patch's heart. The girl reminded Patch vividly of herself at twelve or thirteen—except she had never carried a gun. The shadow of fear in the girl's hazel eyes was countered by the pugnacious thrust of the youngster's chin.

Patch shifted in the saddle but didn't attempt to dismount. "I'm looking for Ethan Hawk's place," she said with a smile meant to ease the child's anxiety.

"You found it."

"Do you know Ethan?" Patch asked.

"Guess I do. I'm his sister."

Patch was stunned. She had never thought of Ethan as having a family. He had always seemed so . . . alone. Obviously, she didn't know as much about Ethan Hawk as she had thought. She met the girl's brazen stare and asked, "What's your name?"

"Don't think I'm gonna tell you."

Patch bit back a retort and asked with ladylike calm, "Is he here?"

"Who wants to know?" the girl demanded.

"My name is Patri—Patch Kendrick. I'm a friend of your brother's."

The girl harrumphed in disbelief. "Ethan don't have no friends in this town."

"I came here all the way from Montana especially to see him."

The ragamuffin's eyes narrowed. "What if I say I don't believe you?"

Patch issued an unladylike snort. "How many females have come here hunting for Ethan?"

The girl shrugged. "You got me there. He usually tracks down

Jewell at the saloon if he needs a woman." She kept the gun aimed at Patch.

Patch forced down a stab of jealousy at the mention of another woman's name. It had never occurred to her that Ethan might be involved with somebody else. Her common sense rescued her from further distress. No Soiled Dove could hope to compete with an honest-to-goodness lady when it came to claiming a man's love. Could she?

"Do you mind if I get down off this horse?" Patch asked. "It's been a while since I did a lot of riding. I have to admit I'm discovering muscles I'd forgotten about. I can explain everything, if you'll let me."

A weak voice from inside the house called out, "Leah, let her come on in."

"But Ma! What if Trahern sent her here to spy on us?"

"Leah! Do as I say!" the voice from inside commanded.

Patch let out a breath she hadn't realized she was holding as Ethan's sister lowered the Winchester.

"You can come in," Leah said, "but don't try anything, 'cause I'll be watching you."

Patch had been appalled at the decrepit condition of the ranch house and outlying buildings, but even the sorry state of affairs outside hadn't prepared her for the shambles the house was in. Patch stepped into a parlor that reminded her of the days when she had been a runny-nosed kid keeping house for her widowed father. Unkempt didn't half describe it.

The horsehair sofa was threadbare, but it was barely visible beneath the collection of dirty clothes, leather tack, and yellowed newspapers that were strewn across it. A hat rack held a filthy saddle blanket and a pair of spurs. The rolltop desk provided a snug haven for a calico cat and a litter of nursing kittens.

Through an open doorway Patch could see pots and pans stacked around the pump in the kitchen. The trestle table still held plates and silverware from a previous meal. A baby raccoon played with a coffee mug on the kitchen floor, tracking through the puddle of coffee that had apparently been spilled when the cup landed.

Patch had spent enough time at Ethan's cabin when he lived in Montana to know he hadn't put up with such squalor then. So she didn't understand the mess now, especially since it appeared there were at least two females, mother and daughter, living here with him.

"Leah, bring her in here," Ethan's mother called.

"Ma's sick," Leah said. "Don't you go bothering her," she warned.

"Is it serious?"

Patch saw the flash of panic that shifted across Leah's face despite the girl's confident, "Ma'll be fine. Just a little upset stomach she can't seem to shake."

When Patch stepped through the bedroom door and saw the older woman's sickly pallor, she knew Leah's mother was every bit as ill as the girl feared. The delicate-looking, white-haired woman lay in the center of a maple four-poster bed. She was dressed in a plain chambray nightgown that was tied primly at the neck. Her skin was stretched thin across high cheekbones, and her silvery gray eyes looked sunken in their sockets.

Despite the chaos in the rest of the house, here everything was clean and neat. The lace curtains had been drawn aside and sunlight streamed across the patterned quilt that was pulled up under the older lady's arms.

Patch crossed to stand beside the bed. "How do you do, Mrs. Hawk. I'm Patricia Kendrick. My friends call me Patch. I hope you will, too."

"Call me Nell, please," the old woman said. "Sit down, Patch, and let me look at you."

Patch sat in the only chair available, a well-used rocker beside the bed. It wasn't the kind of seat a lady normally chose. She forced herself to sit forward and put her feet flat on the floor. Patch wished she were dressed like a lady, but since she wasn't, she settled for putting the steel rod down her spine, tipping her chin up, and squaring her shoulders. Once her fingers were laced together and settled on her lap, she faced Nell, ready to endure the older woman's scrutiny.

Patch quickly began to fret under Nell's regard. She would have resented the thoroughness of the examination if it had been anyone else. But she wanted Ethan's mother to like her. After all, she planned to become the woman's daughter-in-law. She resisted the urge to reach back and scratch as a devilish drop of perspiration trickled down her spine.

"You look like your mother," Nell said at last.

Patch froze. Her mother had died when she was three, and her father had rarely spoken about her. "You knew my mother?"

"Why sure, girl. Your pa's place wasn't far from here. Annarose and I crossed paths in town now and then. Your mother had beautiful bluebonnet eyes and silky blond hair—just like you. Your father adored her. Your grandfather could show you a picture of her if you go visit him."

Patch lurched to her feet. "My *grandfather*?"

"He lives in town now. You mean to say your father never told you about him?"

"No." Patch was still stunned. "Never."

"I suppose I should have guessed. Your grandfather was pretty hard on your pa when Annarose died. He blamed your father for your mother's death. Corwin Marshall never was a forgiving man. I'm sorry if I've upset you."

Patch's head was whirling. She had come to Texas with a precise plan: locate Ethan and get married. She hadn't expected to find Ethan accused of rape. She hadn't expected him to have a family he obviously supported. She hadn't expected to find a grandfather. She sank back down into the rocker. What other surprises were in store for her?

"Did Ethan ever tell you anything about me?" Patch asked.

Nell smiled. "I'm not likely to forget the Kendrick name. My son told me how your father hid him from Jefferson Trahern seventeen years ago, how he tended the wound in Ethan's leg until he was well enough to ride again. Ethan mentioned Seth had a little girl, only three years old. He called her Patch, because she was always leaving wet spots . . ."

Nell chuckled. "Oh, well, I suppose that isn't the sort of story a lovely young lady wants to hear about herself. But my, how the time flies. You're certainly all grown up now."

"Yes, ma'am." Patch was mortified that Ethan's mother knew how she had gotten her nickname. She was downright concerned that Nell apparently knew nothing about the time Ethan had spent at her father's ranch in Montana. "Did Ethan say anything about meeting me again, years later?"

"Later?"

Patch cleared her throat. "When I was twelve, Ethan came to Montana to visit us. He stayed for six months and worked with my father in Fort Benton, breaking horses for the army. The law was closing in on him, so he had to leave. He promised he would come back." *To marry me.* "But he never did."

Nell's fingertips worried a loose diamond shape on the quilt. Her voice was bitter when she spoke. "I never had a chance to speak at any length with Ethan after he was finally caught by that detective Trahern hired to hunt him down. And he never wrote to me from prison."

"Ethan hasn't mentioned me at all during the month he's been home?" Patch asked in a voice that surprised her by its breathlessness.

Nell looked at Patch curiously. "I'm afraid not, dear. Is there something I should know?"

"Uh . . . no . . . that is . . . No." Patch felt the blush at her throat work its way up to stain her cheeks.

"What, exactly, brought you all the way to Texas to see my scapegrace son?" Nell asked.

Did she dare reveal to Nell what she was doing here in Oakville? Patch's stomach clenched. What if Nell forced her to leave the house before she saw Ethan? But she didn't dare tell Ethan's mother why she was here before she had told him! There had to be something she could say that would convince Nell to let her stay around until Ethan returned.

Patch felt the presence of Ethan's sister behind her, like a cat waiting to pounce. "I . . . uh . . ."

"Don't trust her, Ma." Leah slid past Patch and seated herself cross-legged at the foot of her mother's bed, the rifle braced across her knees. "She has a shifty look to her."

Patch watched Nell shake her head at the sight of Leah's dirty boots on her quilt, but it was a sign of just how ill she was that she didn't chastise her daughter. "Let's hear what Patch has to say before we condemn her, Leah."

"Ethan wrote to me that you weren't well, and I volunteered to come and help keep house until you're on your feet again," Patch blurted.

"The heck he did!" Leah retorted as she clambered off the bed. "I do the housekeeping around here." Leah pointed the Winchester at Patch and gestured toward the door. "You can take yourself back wherever you came from, lady. We don't want you here!"

Patch hurried to speak before Leah forced her from the room. "I don't know how long it's been since you've left your bed, Nell, but I can tell you the rest of the house looks nothing like this room."

Nell appeared genuinely surprised. "It doesn't? But Leah has been taking care of everything."

Patch shook her head in denial. "Everything is a shambles. There are dishes and clothes that need to be washed and floors that need to be swept and mopped. Ethan wrote me that he's been too busy with the work outside to be able to handle things in the house, too."

"Leah? Is what Patch says true?" Nell asked.

Leah shot a mutinous look at Patch. "Dirty stinking tattletale!"

"Leah! Apologize to Miss Kendrick."

"I won't!" Leah shouted. "It ain't as bad as she says, Ma."

"Leah, perhaps—"

Leah interrupted her mother. "I ain't hanging around to listen to more of her tall tales." Leah shoved her way past Patch and broke into a run. Her boots could be heard on the wooden-planked floors, followed by the slam of the door at the back of the house.

"I'm sorry, Patch," Nell said.

Patch smiled ruefully. "She reminds me a lot of myself at the same age."

"I knew I was asking too much of her, but . . ." Nell shrugged helplessly. "There was no one else."

"I'm here now." Patch crossed to Nell and fluffed the pillow up behind her. "You just rest and don't worry about a thing. Cleaning up this place will be as easy as throwing a two-day calf."

Patch saw the visible relief in Nell's eyes, the way her body relaxed back into the feather mattress. "Thank you, Patch."

"Thank Ethan," Patch countered with a smile. "He's the one who contacted me."

Patch hadn't told a whopper like that one in a long time, and she was surprised at how guilty she felt. "Get some rest, Nell." She closed the door behind her as she left so Nell could sleep.

The house felt empty, forsaken, and neglected. Actually, the whole ranch gave Patch an eerie feeling. Something was terribly wrong here. She wanted Ethan home, so he could explain just what disaster had befallen him.

Patch heard the raccoon shoving the cup around on the floor in the kitchen. The tiny, sightless kittens were mewing for the calico cat, which had momentarily abandoned them. She looked around at the mess and heaved a giant sigh. Since she had told Nell she was the new housekeeper, she had better do a little housekeeping. She shoved up her sleeves and set to work.

"First things first," Patch muttered as she headed for the kitchen.

She had once had a pet raccoon herself, so she wasn't the least bit afraid of the animal. It was simple to grab the raccoon by the scruff of its neck. To her chagrin, the kitchen door that Leah had slammed was stuck closed. She shoved it open with her shoulder and dropped the raccoon on the back porch. No sooner had she pulled the door shut again than the raccoon was back inside.

"Durn it! How'd you do that?" Patch grimaced when she realized what she had said. Over time, that fancy finishing school in Boston had soaped all the *garns* and *dangs* and *durns* right out of her. It was amazing how they came back to haunt her in moments of stress. She had worked hard to become a lady. She didn't want to have a lapse now, when it was important to impress Ethan with what a good wife she would make.

She stooped down to examine the place where the raccoon had snuck back in and discovered that a section of the floor board had rotted away, leaving a hole that led under the house. Obviously both the cat and the raccoon used the convenient opening as a way in and out.

Patch picked up several of the split logs from beside the stove and stacked them over the hole to block the entrance. No animal was coming through there anytime soon. "That ought to keep you out from now on, you little bandit," she murmured to herself.

Patch was unused to the heat of a Texas spring, and found herself already wet under the arms. The window above the pump was open, and she walked over to it, placed her palms on either side of the frame, and let the steady breeze cool her. It felt wonderful.

But standing in the kitchen like a scarecrow in the field wasn't getting the house cleaned up. She turned to survey the mess and saw the raccoon had climbed up on the table and was eating scraps.

"Come on, Bandit," she crooned to the masked animal. "It's back outside for you."

This time the raccoon wasn't as easy to catch. The animal anticipated her attempts to snare him and evaded her. He hopped off the table and ran behind the stove. At last she had him cornered under the trestle table. He stood up on his hind legs and chattered at her.

"All right, you little bandit, let's—go—now!" She lunged and grabbed the raccoon by one paw, which she used to reel it in. However, she sat up too quickly and banged her head against the bottom of the table.

"Garn!"

"Serves you right!"

That was the first inkling Patch had that Leah was back in the house.

Patch scooted out from under the table, wishing she could rub her head where she had bumped it, but needing both hands to hold the wriggling raccoon.

"I thought you left," Patch said.

Leah eyed her suspiciously. "I came back."

"To help?"

"To make sure you don't steal the silverware!" Leah retorted. "After all, we only have your word that you're who you say you are. The minute Ethan gets home, I'm going to ask him if what you said is true."

"That's fine with me." Patch worked hard to keep the dismay she felt from showing on her face. She was going to have to find a way to head off Ethan and speak to him before Leah revealed her lie. "I don't suppose I could talk you into taking this little bandit outside."

"Give him to me." Leah was halfway to the door when she turned and asked, "How did you know his name is Bandit?"

Patch laughed.

"What's so funny?"

"I had a pet raccoon named Bandit when I was your age."

"But you're a lady!" Leah protested.

"Thank you, Leah. That's the first nice thing you've said to me."

Leah bristled. "Yeah, well, don't get used to it."

Patch was standing by the door to close it after Leah came back in minus the raccoon.

The belligerent child leaned against the kitchen wall and crossed both arms and ankles. "Now what?" she demanded.

"Now we clean."

Patch set Leah to work putting away anything that had a place. Meanwhile, Patch took the time to stable her horse. Then she used Leah's room as a place to change into a calico skirt and starched white shirtwaist that were among the clothes she had brought with her in her saddlebags. She wasn't taking any chances that Ethan might turn up and find her looking like anything less than the perfect lady she had worked so hard to become.

Patch checked to make sure her bun was neat and covered her golden hair with a kerchief. Then she confiscated one of Nell's aprons to save wear and tear on her clothes and carefully transferred her mouse, Max, from the pocket of her shirt to the deep pocket on one side of the apron. "I'm afraid there's one too many calico cats around here to let you go yet," she murmured as she patted the mouse.

Patch couldn't remember the last time she had worked so hard. From the time she was twelve and her stepmother had moved in, the Kendrick home had been a model of order and cleanliness. Patch unconsciously mimicked all the things she had learned over the years from Molly Gallagher Kendrick.

Instead of sweeping the dust from the floor into the corner, she swept it out the door. Instead of stacking the dirty clothes into a neat heap on the chair, she carted them out back and laid them over the washtub for later attention.

Leah grumbled.

Patch praised.

Leah griped.

Patch placated.

Leah groaned.

Patch played deaf and dumb.

When the parlor finally sparkled, Leah slumped down on the horsehair sofa. "I thought we'd never get this place clean enough to please you. Who you expecting to come visit, President Grant?"

"I'm only doing what your mother would do if she were able," Patch said in a quiet voice.

Leah's face scrunched up, and her chin trembled. For a moment Patch thought the girl was going to cry. Patch was learning that Leah felt much more than she wanted anyone to know. The young girl was much more aware—and afraid—that her mother was seriously ill, maybe even dying, than she let on. As quickly as the instant of vulnerability appeared, it was gone. "Yeah, well, we'll see what Ethan has to say about all this cleaning when he comes home."

Which reminded Patch she had dang well better catch Ethan before Leah got to him.

"No rest for the weary," Patch said. "We'd better clear a path in the kitchen if we hope to have supper ready when Ethan gets here."

"Aw, Ethan won't expect—"

"Whether he expects it or not," Patch said firmly, "supper will be ready and waiting when he gets home."

Leah eyed the huge stack of dirty dishes askance. "How you gonna clean up that mess?"

"One dish at a time."

Patch washed, while Leah dried and put the dishes away.

"I used to do this with Ma," Leah said wistfully as she stuffed a towel down into a cup and swished it around.

"How long has your mother been sick?"

"Since about a month before Ethan got out of prison."

Maybe Ethan hadn't forgotten his promise to her, Patch mused. Maybe he had only been waiting until his mother was well before he came for her. If so, she had saved him the time and trouble of going to Montana after her.

"Has a doctor examined your mother?"

Leah stiffened. "Doc Carter took a look at her."

"Did he say what's wrong with her?" Patch asked.

"Nothing he can fix," Leah replied in an agonized voice.

Patch dropped the subject. It would be better to ask Ethan the questions she wanted answered than to distress Leah any further.

While Leah dried the last of the dishes, Patch started looking for something to make for supper. "As I recall, Ethan used to love biscuits."

"He still does," Leah said. "Only, the ones I make taste more like shoe leather."

"Those used to be my favorite kind," Patch said with a chuckle.

Patch found the flour and began looking for the other ingredients she needed. Every step of the way Leah said, "That's not how Ma does it." Or, "Ma always does it this way." Patch obligingly changed her methods, each time involving Leah in the preparation of the biscuits. Before long, Patch had the dough ready to cut into circles.

"Ma always let me do that," Leah mumbled.

Patch handed over the cup she had intended to use. "I'll get some beans started."

Before long there were biscuits in the oven and beans on the pot-bellied stove. Leah showed Patch where she could find a smoked ham. Between them they set the table.

"Too bad we don't have some flowers for the table," Patch murmured.

"There's some black-eyed Susans out back. I mean, if you gotta have flowers."

"Thanks, Leah." Patch put a hand on Leah's shoulder, but Leah stepped out from under the caress.

"I better go pick those flowers."

"I'll check on your mother."

Leah paused on her way out the door. "Ma would like what you did to the house," she conceded.

"Thanks, Leah."

"Yeah, well, don't thank me. You did most of the work." A moment later she was out the kitchen door and had shoved it closed behind her.

Patch shook her head. She knew some of the things Leah must be feeling. She remembered her own turmoil when her father had advertised for a mail-order bride and Molly Gallagher had shown up with her two children. Patch had bitterly resented their intrusion. She had hated Molly on sight and felt an equal animosity toward Whit. She remembered labeling Nessie a whining crybaby.

But she hadn't come here to be Leah's mother. Leah already had a mother.

Who might be dying.

Patch wondered what was wrong with Nell that a doctor couldn't fix. She hoped it wasn't as serious as it appeared. From her little acquaintance with Nell Hawk, she already liked her.

Patch eased Nell's bedroom door open slowly, but the hinges obviously hadn't been oiled in a while, because they squeaked loudly.

"Is that you, Leah?"

"It's me," Patch answered.

There was a moment of silence.

Patch stepped into the room. The old woman was obviously agitated, but Patch wasn't sure why.

Nell sniffed the air, frowned, then sniffed again. "How long have I been asleep?" she asked irritably.

Patch glanced out the window at the unbroken view of rolling prairie. The sun was low in the sky. "Most of the afternoon. It's nearly suppertime. In fact, I came to see if I can bring you something."

"I'm not hungry."

Patch raised a brow. "When was the last time you ate?"

"I had a glass of milk and some mush for breakfast. I . . . I don't remember what I ate for lunch."

Patch was alarmed. Ethan's mother certainly couldn't get well if she didn't eat. "Could you manage some ham and beans and biscuits."

"Is that what smells so good?"

"Yes."

Nell smiled with relief. "Oh, dear. I thought I'd gone crazy for sure. I smelled ham and biscuits, and I couldn't figure out how that was possible since I haven't been out of this bed to cook for weeks."

"Leah helped me."

Nell's eyes went wide. "She did? My Leah?"

"She insisted I make the biscuits just the way you would."

Nell's chin began to quiver.

Patch was desperate for a diversion that would take Nell's mind off the illness that kept her bedridden and unable to take care of her family. Just at that moment, Max moved in her apron pocket. Patch reached down and pulled him out to display him in the palm of her hand.

"Look what I have. His name is Max."

Patch didn't see Leah come in behind her. Leah peered around Patch, curious to see what Patch was showing her mother.

"It's a mouse!"

Leah's excited cry frightened Max, who scrambled up the arm of Patch's shirtwaist. Patch grabbed for him, but he shot off her shoulder onto Nell's pillow.

Nell shrieked "Catch him!" and covered her head with the quilt.

"He's gone off the other side!" Leah shouted as she leapt over the bed in pursuit. "I think he dropped to the floor!"

Patch fell to her knees and peered under the bed, but all she saw was Leah on the other side.

Drawn by the commotion, the calico cat appeared at the bedroom door and let out a loud *"Mrrrrrow!"*

"How did the cat get in here?" Patch cried. "She was still outside when I covered up that hole in the kitchen floor."

"I brought Calico in," Leah replied. "Her babies were crying for her."

Patch met Leah's hazel eyes across the bed. "That cat of yours will kill Max if she catches him. You get her, and I'll try to catch Max."

Nell lowered the covers enough to ask, "Have you found him yet?"

"No, but—"

"There he is!" Nell pointed at the mouse as it ran along the foot of the bedstead and shot off onto the quilt and down over the side of the bed again. Nell shouted orders as Patch and Leah scooted under the bed.

"Get the cat!" Patch screeched at Leah.

Patch and Leah found themselves face-to-face under the bed. The calico cat had the mouse cornered between the carved leg of the bed and the wall.

Leah grabbed the spitting, clawing cat by the scruff of the neck and dragged her away. "Ow! Hurry up, Patch. She's scratching me!"

Patch caught Max as he made a break for it. "Got him!" She wriggled back out from under the bed, fanny first. She lifted her head too soon and caught it on the edge of the bed. "Garn! That hurts!"

She sat up triumphantly on the floor at the side of Nell's bed and held the mouse aloft in her hand. Her scarf had come off and pulled her hair down with it. Blond tresses dangled over one eye. A piece of fuzz was stuck on her nose, and she could feel grit on her cheek. Obviously, Leah hadn't cleaned under her mother's bed lately. But at least Max was safe. The ridiculousness of the situation hit her all at once and a silly grin split her face.

Patch heard a footstep behind her. She looked up and found herself staring into a pair of disbelieving male eyes.

"What on God's green earth are you doing down there, Patch?"

It was Ethan. He was home.

✳3✳

Eᴛʜᴀɴ ʜᴀᴅ sᴘᴇɴᴛ ᴛʜᴇ better part of the day rounding up stray cattle. He was appalled at how few there were to gather. The only way he had survived the seven miserable years he had spent in prison was by imagining how wonderful it would be when he returned to his family and the Double Diamond a free man. His homecoming had been an awful disappointment, a rude awakening to the cold light of reality.

His father was dead. The ranch was in ruins. His mother was sick. His sister was a stranger who watched him with wary eyes. He had felt like crying. But he hadn't. He had gone instead to see Boyd Stuckey, who had been his best friend when they were kids growing up. He had shared everything with Boyd, both his joys and his troubles. In the face of the disaster he had found on his release from prison, he had needed a friend.

Boyd had welcomed him like a long-lost brother. "Ethan! It's great to have you home!"

They had shaken hands, and Ethan wasn't sure which of them had made the first move, but a moment later they were hugging and patting each other on the back. They parted and grinned at each other. They were men now, but the friendship they had forged as boys was a bond that had never been broken. Each knew he could trust his life in the other's hands. In the West, that was about as deep as friendship got.

"You've changed," Boyd said.

"You haven't," Ethan said.

Boyd gestured Ethan to a brass-studded leather chair, one of two situated across from each other in front of the stone fireplace in Boyd's parlor. Once Ethan was seated, Boyd took the other chair.

"Can I get you something to drink?"

"Whiskey, if you have it."

"Theresa," Boyd called. "Some whiskey, *por favor.*"

A pretty Mexican girl brought a tray with a bottle of whiskey and two glasses and set it on a nearby table before she disappeared.

Ethan whistled his approval. "Very nice."

"My housekeeper," Boyd said with a dimpled grin as he poured them each a whiskey. "What shall we drink to?"

"Freedom," Ethan said.

When their glasses were empty, Boyd refilled Ethan's and settled back in his chair. "How have you been?"

Ethan hesitated. A man kept his hardships to himself. And there wasn't much good to share.

"That was a stupid question," Boyd said. He turned his empty glass in his hands. "I'm sorry about your pa."

"It's hard for me to believe he's been dead for two years." Ethan shook his head. "And I can't believe what bad shape the ranch is in."

"Careless never did find out who rustled all your pa's cattle," Boyd said. "I did the best I could to help your ma, but she said she'd never taken charity and never would. Wish I could've done more."

"I thank you for being there for both of them while I was gone."

Neither man spoke about the events of seventeen years ago that had forced them to go their separate ways, to lead separate lives, and put their friendship in abeyance.

"I never had a chance to thank you for speaking up for me at the trial," Ethan said.

"It was the least I could do. You're the best friend I ever had." Boyd paused and added, "I missed you, Ethan."

The moment might have gotten maudlin, but neither man could have tolerated that.

Boyd grinned. "With you gone, it's been as peaceful around here as a thumb in a baby's mouth. Maybe there'll be a little excitement now that you're home."

Ethan grinned back. "Likely you'll see so much of me now that you'll start barring the door when you hear me coming."

They had laughed and talked about other, happier, things and finally, when he had worn out his welcome, Ethan left. He felt better. And he felt worse.

Ethan had shared everything with Boyd when they were children, because Boyd had owned nothing. Their circumstances were nearly reversed now. Boyd was obviously very well off, while Ethan was barely making ends meet. It was a sign of what good friends they had been—still were—that Ethan could be happy for Boyd, rather than jealous of him. But after that first visit, he avoided Boyd because seeing his friend reminded him too much of all he had lost.

Sometimes, when Ethan saw how much work it would take to bring the Double Diamond back to what it had been, he wished his mother had sold out. She'd had several offers for the ranch, including one from Boyd, back when it had been in better condition. Then he would look around him, at the land he and his father had worked together, and feel a well of emotion so great he almost couldn't breathe. In those moments he was glad—and grateful—that his mother had struggled, tooth and claw, to save his heritage for him.

But he wondered about the cost of her sacrifice. She had been confined to her bed constantly since he had returned home. Lately he had come to believe that Doc Carter was right, that his mother was dying of the same wasting sickness that had claimed his father. And, though he fought against admitting it, he was afraid she hadn't much longer to live.

It was plain to see the effects of all that calamity on Leah. His younger sister had sad, wise old eyes that belied her tender age. Leah hadn't even been born when he had been forced to flee his home. He had seen her briefly when he was on trial—a spindly child of five, all eyes and ears, hands and feet. But now, seven years later, she was a stranger to him, and it felt awkward treating her like the sister she was.

Leah was so tough on the outside that it had taken him a while to see how frightened she was inside. She kept to herself, and he was having a hard time breaching her defenses. His sister reminded him a great deal of another rebellious tomboy he had known.

Patch.

Ethan had tried not to think about Patch, but the image of her as she lay beneath him at the Oakville Hotel kept creeping back. He had spent the day wondering what she was doing in south Texas and wishing that his life were in better shape than it was. She had grown up into a beautiful, desirable woman.

Ethan swore as his body tightened in response to the mere thought of her. He had no business thinking about any lady in those terms. Least of all Patch!

Even if he were not a convicted murderer, it was becoming

increasingly clear that Jefferson Trahern was never going to let him be free to marry and settle down. Ethan always had to watch his back for an ambush.

As he approached the ranch house, the sun was nearly down. He was dog-tired, but there was work yet to be done. The horses and hogs and chickens had to be fed. He didn't keep a milk cow because he was never sure he would be around to milk it. He hoped Leah had made some supper, but it wasn't always a sure thing. Maybe tonight he could make some headway on the mess in the house.

Dusk had reduced the landscape to shadows by the time Ethan had brushed down his horse and fed the animals. He trudged to the house, wondering why Leah had lit so many lamps. When he shoved open the front door, he stopped dead.

The parlor was immaculate. The cat and her litter of kittens had been consigned to a basket in the corner. The top was down on his rolltop desk. The hole in the arm of the horsehair sofa had been covered with a neatly pressed doily. His spurs still hung from the hat rack, but his old saddle blanket was nowhere to be seen. There wasn't a speck of dust to be found. And he could smell food. Delicious food.

Biscuits and . . . ham?

Ethan's first thought was that his mother must have made a miraculous recovery. She was the only one he knew who could have wrought such an astonishing change in the state of things in a single day. He looked for her first in the kitchen, but when he didn't find her there, he figured she must have lain down for a rest after all that effort.

Ethan headed for her bedroom, his stride confident despite his limp. He felt really, truly happy for the first time in the month since he had come home.

He shoved open the door and was treated to the appalling—but utterly appealing—sight of a woman's fanny wriggling out from under his mother's bed. You could have knocked him over with a feather when he saw who it was.

"What on God's green earth are you doing down there, Patch?"

Patch reached up to tuck in the hank of hair that had fallen across her brow. She brushed her nose where the piece of lint she had picked up under the bed tickled her. "Hello, Ethan."

Patch's heart was beating lickety-split in her chest. Of all the times for Ethan to arrive! She knew she ought to get up, dust herself off, *do something*! But she sat there like a bump on a log, just staring at him.

His hair was darker than she remembered. That was to be expected after all the years he had spent confined in a cell. Lines bracketed his mouth, and deep crow's feet fanned out from piercing green eyes that had seen too much sorrow and disillusion and disappointment. His angular face showed the harshness of a life spent running from the law. But to her, every line, every wrinkle was dear.

His features were blunt, his nose straight, his chin strong, his cheekbones high and wide. Right at this moment his eyes were wide with worry and surprise and . . . confusion. She had the sneakiest suspicion that he wasn't glad to see her.

"Hi, Ethan!" Leah jumped up, the snarling calico cat hanging by the scruff of its neck from her hand. "This lady says she knows you!"

"What are you doing here, Patch?" Ethan said in a harsh, very unwelcoming voice.

Patch's heart was in her throat, so she cleared it before she spoke. "Looking for you." She tucked the mouse back in her apron pocket and struggled to her feet.

Ethan reached down a hand to help her, and Patch was aware of a stirring warmth where he touched her arm.

"I'm here now. What do you want?" he demanded.

Patch was aware of the two interested parties listening with bated breath. "Is there somewhere we can be alone?"

"Ethan doesn't keep secrets from us," Leah piped up.

Patch shot a pleading glance in Ethan's direction. He grabbed her by the hand and headed out the bedroom door. When Leah started after them, he turned and said, "Let us be, Leah."

"Aw, Ethan—"

Nell called Leah back to her side. "I need some help getting my quilts straightened up, girl."

Leah groaned, but she turned back toward her mother.

Ethan yanked Patch through the immaculate parlor, through the kitchen, with its enticing smells and table set for supper, and out the back door. He kicked the door twice before it would close in the frame.

Ethan stopped beneath a tin roof that looked like it might collapse at any moment and swung Patch around in front of him. "Give me the mouse."

Patch reached down and pulled Max from her apron pocket. Ethan picked up the mouse by its tail, dropped it in the wooden box that held his mother's gardening tools, and slapped the lid closed.

He turned to Patch, crossed his arms, and snapped, "I want to know what the hell is going on! What are you doing in Oakville, Texas? Does your father know why you're here? How did you find this place?"

"Looking for you. Not yet. And Mr. Felber gave me directions," Patch snapped back.

"What are you doing here, Patch?"

"I think that should be perfectly obvious."

"Not to me, so spit it out."

"I'm here to marry you."

Ethan glared at her from beneath lowered brows. He didn't look at all like a happy groom.

Patch's heart dropped to her feet. "You don't have to look so surprised. You promised to marry me, and here I am."

"I don't remember doing any such thing!"

"When you left Fort Benton—"

"When I left Montana seven years ago—"

"It's been nearly eight, but who's counting?" Patch replied flippantly.

Ethan ground his teeth and repeated, "When I left Montana, you were just a kid! I sure as hell didn't propose marriage to a twelve-year-old with tangles in her hair and holes in her britches and a mouth that could use soaping every time she opened it!"

Patch was mortified by Ethan's description of her. The words of protest and explanation were spoken before she could stop them. "I loved you!"

A red flush crawled up Ethan's neck all the way to the tips of his ears. "Hell, Patch. You were just a kid." He shook his head in disbelief. "What you felt must have been hero worship or something."

"Hero worship?" This time it was Patch's face that reddened, but with fury, not embarrassment. Her forefinger seemed to have a life of its own as it poked away at Ethan's chest, punctuating her verbal rampage. "Why you *vain*glorious, *cock*-strutting, *mule*-eared *jackass*! Of all the hogwash I ever heard spouted, that was the worst!

"You made me a promise, Ethan Hawk. And durn it all, you're going to keep it!"

Ethan grabbed Patch's wrist and twisted the offending finger behind her. When her other hand came up, he grabbed that too, and suddenly he had both her arms snagged behind her. Only she wouldn't stay still, so he backed her up against the unpainted wall of the house and held her there with his body. Which hardened like a rock when it met her softness.

Ethan felt his heart pounding. He had thrown a lasso expecting a kitten and caught a wildcat instead. His whole body was alive with expectation. He could feel generous breasts crushed against his chest, and his loins were cradled by soft, feminine flesh. He had the craziest urge to rub himself against her.

Then he remembered who she was. And who he was. And why what he wanted was ludicrous, not to mention impossible, stupid, and just plain idiotic.

"What does your father have to say about your being here?" Ethan demanded in a voice harsh with the passion he was struggling to control.

"I'm sure he'd approve."

"And I'm sure he wouldn't! Does Seth even know you're here?"

"He will when he gets my letter."

Ethan groaned. "He'll kill me."

"Not if you're my husband."

"I'm not going to marry you, Patch," Ethan said through his teeth.

"Why not? I love—"

"Stop saying that!" Ethan found himself unable to look away from the blue eyes staring back at him. Her nose was tipped up in defiance and her chin jutted with stubborn determination.

"You're just a kid!" he said in desperation.

"I'll be twenty next month."

Ethan sneered. "And already a sophisticated woman of the world, I see."

Patch's eyes slipped down to the soiled apron. She blew out a puff of air to remove the strand of hair that had caught on her lips. If only she'd had the time to repair the damage caused by that fracas between Max and the calico cat before Ethan had shown up. Then he would be treating her like the lady she had struggled so hard to become. For him. Because of him.

"I'm a grown woman, Ethan. A lady, to be precise. And I deserve to be treated like one."

Ethan purposely chose to misunderstand her. "You want to be treated like a woman? Well, this is how I treat the only kind of woman I have anything to do with these days."

Ethan ground his hips against hers the way he had been wanting to do. The surprised, satisfied sound she made in her throat drew his flesh up tight.

He hardened his jaw. Seduction wasn't his intent. He transferred both her wrists to one hand and grasped her chin, angling her face up to his. Her eyes went wide with surprise and—heaven help him—anticipation.

Ethan lowered his mouth toward hers, determined on teaching her a lesson about girls playing with men that she wouldn't soon forget. His mouth closed over hers and his tongue thrust its way past her sealed lips.

Only they weren't sealed.

Her whole body swayed toward him.

Ethan jerked himself free. "Oh, no you don't! I'm not going to get caught in that trap."

Still dazed by the effects of Ethan's closeness, Patch stared at him in confusion. "What are you talking about?"

"I know what you're trying to do. It won't work."

"What is that?"

"You're trying to seduce me. Then I'll be honor-bound to marry you. Or else have your father hound my tail for the rest of my life. Where's your sense, girl? You'd have to be crazy to want to marry a man like me."

"Why?"

"I'm an ex-convict," he said flatly.

"I knew you were wanted by the law when I fell in love with you," she countered.

"You weren't old enough to know what that meant." Ethan yanked off his Stetson and forked his fingers through sun-streaked chestnut hair that badly needed a trim. His eyes were bleak when they sought Patch's again. "I spent time in prison for murdering Dorne Trahern."

"But—"

"Don't interrupt. Let me finish. If it were only that, I could maybe think about asking some woman someday to be my wife. But it's far worse than that, Patch." Ethan took a deep breath and let it out. He tried to look at her, but found he couldn't face her expectant—devoted—expression and say what had to be said.

"I've paid for Dorne's death with seven hard years in prison, so most people around here don't hold that against me anymore. But the whole town of Oakville still believes I raped a girl so brutally that she lost her mind.

"There's no hope of me marrying you—ever." He turned and brushed the lock of hair away from her eyes with a touch as gentle as one he might use for a newborn filly. "I care enough about you—and your ma and pa—not to make you an object of pity and scorn by marrying you."

"Are you done?"

Ethan nodded grimly.

"In the first place, I might have been a child when I first fell in love with you, but I'm grown up now." She took a deep breath and, searching his troubled eyes, admitted, "I still love you, Ethan. I always will.

"In the second place, I don't believe you raped Merielle Trahern."

Ethan grimaced. "You're the only one who doesn't."

Patch put a hand across his lips to shut him up and found them still damp from kissing her. And soft. She knew just how soft, because those lips had been pressed to hers. Ethan's first kiss had been everything she had ever imagined, and some things she hadn't.

She hadn't expected her knees to go weak. She hadn't expected him to put his tongue in her mouth. She hadn't expected to taste him. Despite all her talk of being a woman, she had been amazed at the new sensations that had bombarded her, making her feel like a bowl of jelly left too long in the sun. But she had liked it all. And she wanted more.

"I know you're worried about what Pa will say. But Pa only wants me to be happy, Ethan. And marrying you will make me happy."

Patch saw the denial in Ethan's features and hurried to finish before he cut her off. "You need a wife, Ethan. Or at least this ranch needs a woman's touch. Your mother obviously isn't well, and your sister . . ." Patch smiled ruefully. "Your sister reminds me of myself at the same age." Patch grinned. "She's no housekeeper."

"Patch—"

Patch put her whole hand across his mouth. "You can't say I'm not attractive to you, Ethan." Patch felt the flush skating across her cheekbones at such plain speaking. "I . . . uh . . . could feel the evidence that would make any denial a lie."

Ethan would never know how frightening that had been for her, to feel the shape of him pressed hard against her and to know what it meant he wanted from her. Her father raised horses, so she had seen more than one stallion cover a mare. Their coupling was always a wild and savage thing. When the time came, she couldn't imagine how she was going to survive the embarrassment of it all. But with Ethan, she darn sure was willing to give it a try.

Having nothing more to say, Patch dropped her hand from Ethan's face. She threaded her fingers together before her and waited for his response. It wasn't long coming.

"You're forgetting the most important reason why I can't—won't—make you my wife."

"I haven't forgotten," Patch said. "I simply don't believe a word of the accusation against you. You'd never rape a woman, Ethan." She swallowed and said, "You wouldn't have to."

Ethan felt a painful tightening in his chest. He wasn't sure whether it was gratitude for her blind faith in him or the awful knowledge that he had forfeited any chance of ever having a decent woman for his wife when he had fled so many years ago. Now he saw the folly of running instead of staying to seek out the truth.

He had been only fifteen when someone raped Merielle Trahern. He had found her after the fact, but when her brother, Dorne, discovered them together, he hadn't waited for explanations. By the time Jefferson Trahern arrived on the scene to find Ethan wounded in the leg by Dorne's bullet, and Dorne accidentally shot dead, Ethan had known nobody was going to listen to his side of the story before they hung him.

So he had run, and kept on running for ten years, until one of Trahern's private detectives finally caught him. The trial had been a farce, but at least he hadn't been convicted of raping Merielle, for which he had his friend, Boyd, to thank.

Now, *seventeen years* later, he still wasn't free of his nightmare. He had been out of prison only one month—four short weeks—and judging from the hired guns he had faced today, Jefferson Trahern was planning to pick up his quest for vengeance where he had left off when Ethan went to prison. It was quickly becoming apparent that, although the townspeople might be willing to tolerate his presence in Oakville, Jefferson Trahern was not.

In fact, the man seemed obsessed with seeing him dead. Ethan supposed if he had spent the past seventeen years watching a beautiful daughter become a woman, yet remain a child, he might be a little crazed and unforgiving, too.

Ethan closed his eyes so Patch wouldn't see the regret he felt when he thought of what she wanted from him. The events of the past prevented any thought of marriage to her. Even so, his feelings about finding her here were confused, to say the least. On the one hand, he found her incredibly desirable as a woman. On the other hand, he couldn't separate the woman from the spirited, yet vulnerable tomboy in raggedy clothes for whom he felt a big-brotherly affection. It was the younger Patch he felt he had to protect. For her own good, he had to make her go home.

"You're forgetting one other thing," Ethan said in a grating voice.

"What is that?"

"I don't love you."

Patch felt her stomach shift sideways. She lowered her lashes to hide the sharp pain she felt at Ethan's admission. Patch had believed when she left Montana that she had enough love for both of them. She hadn't realized how it would feel to hear Ethan say those crushing words denying any feelings for her.

Patch didn't know there were tears in her eyes until Ethan drew her into his arms and murmured, "Don't cry, Patch. I can't stand to see you cry."

She buried her face in his shirt, clinging to him, to the dream that had brought her all the way to Texas from Montana, the dream of being loved by Ethan, of loving him in return. But he didn't love her. He didn't want to marry her. He—

Patch stiffened as a startling thought occurred to her. Ethan had said he didn't love her in one breath, and in the next had pulled her into his arms and was, unless she was very much mistaken, kissing away her tears at this very moment.

Patch jerked herself from Ethan's embrace. "Liar!" she accused.

"What?"

"You're lying, Ethan Hawk, about not loving me. You *do* love me.

That's why you don't want to marry me. You want to protect me from the scandal of marrying an ex-convict, an accused rapist."

"Patch, I—"

"I appreciate those feelings," Patch said. "Really, I do. Which is why I'm going to stay here and help you find the *real* culprit."

"Patch, I—"

"When your name is cleared, we can be married and live happily ever after."

"Patch, I—"

"Yes, Ethan?"

Ethan took one look at her glowing eyes and forgot what he was going to say. She smiled at him and his body started thinking what it would be like nestled up close to hers. His hands had already reached for her when his brain started functioning again.

"No." Then, because her smile remained firmly in place, he repeated, "No, Patch. It's been seventeen years since Merielle Trahern was violated. It could have been anyone, even some cowhand passing through town. It could have been—" Ethan cut himself off because he had his own ideas about who had done it. He'd had seventeen long years to think about it.

Patch took advantage of Ethan's hesitation. "You do have some idea who might have done it! I knew you would!"

"It's water under the dam. Knowing—suspecting—who did it won't change what's happened. Merielle will still be a child forever," he said, his eyes bleak. His voice was bitter as he added, "And it won't bring back all the years that were stolen from me."

Patch reached out a tentative hand and placed it on Ethan's forearm. She felt his muscles bunch under her touch. "If we find the man responsible, your name will be cleared."

"And if we don't? You'll be stirring ashes that have been banked a long time." There was liable to be a fire down there somewhere that would burn them both.

Ethan voiced another reason it would be foolhardy, not to mention dangerous, to go digging up the past. "Trahern hasn't stopped hounding me, Patch. He wants me dead. He won't care if you get caught in the crossfire."

"But you do." Patch took a step closer to Ethan. He did care. Probably more than he knew. She was sure of it when he folded her into his arms and held her tight. She would just give him a little hand clearing his name. Could she help it if, during the process, he fell deeply, hopelessly in love with her?

"We can find out the truth, Ethan. The two of us, together."

"Patch, I—"

"We'll be a team, hunting down clues to the mystery. Meanwhile, I'll be here to help take care of your mother and sister. By the way, I told them you wrote me in Montana and asked me to come help with the housekeeping. Leah suspects I wasn't telling the truth. You won't give me away, will you?"

Ethan groaned.

"I love you, Ethan."

His arms tightened around her. "All right, dammit," he said in a guttural voice. "You can stay long enough for me to do some investigation. But if I don't discover any new information about the rape, you'll have to abide by my decision not to marry you and go home to Montana. Is that clear?"

"Yes, Ethan," Patch said meekly.

"And meanwhile, you're not to say anything to anybody about this crazy idea you have that I promised to marry you. Understand?"

"Yes, Ethan. You forbid me to tell anyone why I'm really here in Oakville. Is that right?"

Ethan *hmmed* his assent.

"And I promise"—Patch crossed her heart—"that if you don't find the real culprit, I'll leave."

If Ethan could have seen Patch's face, he would have put her on the next stage back to Montana. Fortunately for Patch, her face was safely, happily, snuggled against Ethan's chest.

"Ethan!" Leah shouted from the house. "Someone's coming!"

Leah's warning cry set Ethan in motion. He set Patch aside and grabbed the doorknob. The kitchen door wouldn't budge.

"I don't believe this!" The door was wedged tight in the frame. "Can you see who it is, Leah?" Ethan shouted through the kitchen window.

"Why don't you just walk around the house and see for yourself?" Patch asked.

Ethan turned a scowling face toward Patch. "You might have noticed in town that the sight of me tends to draw bullets. I'd just as soon know who's out there before I show my face."

"I'll go see who it is."

Before Ethan could stop her, Patch scooted around the side of the house through the weeds that had grown up in the yard and headed for the front porch.

"Damn, damn, damn!" Ethan exploded. "That woman is going to be the death of me yet!"

He slammed his palm against the door and it popped open. He shoved it wide and raced—long step, halting step, long step, halting step—for the front of the house.

❋4❋

Pᴀᴛᴄʜ ᴛᴏʟᴅ ʜᴇʀsᴇʟꜰ sʜᴇ wasn't in any danger. Even if the two men riding toward her in the deepening shadows of sundown meant some harm to Ethan, they wouldn't bother her. That made it easier to wait on the front porch with a smile on her face for the arrival of the intruders. The forced curve became more natural when she recognized one of the riders as the handsome young man who had come looking for Merielle Trahern in the mercantile. Her stomach rolled when she remembered he was also Jefferson Trahern's foreman.

"Hello, Mr. Meade," she called out when the two men were within hailing distance. "What brings you here?"

Frank tipped his hat. "Miz Kendrick. Came looking for Ethan."

"He's not—"

"We know he's here," the other man said.

Patch's attention was drawn to the man on Frank's left. She considered Frank handsome. The stranger beside him could only be called striking. His features might have been appealing viewed one at a time, but they were combined in a way that gave the man a fierce, unrelenting look, more intriguing than attractive. If she hadn't been in love with Ethan, her heart might have taken a few quick beats.

He was wearing a Stetson shoved back off his brow, and a hank of dark hair hung down over his forehead. His eyes were mesmerizing, a tawny gold that reminded her of the cougar she had kept as a pet in Montana. She could almost feel the tension radiating from the man. She held her breath waiting for something—she wasn't sure what—to happen.

He smiled.

He had dimples. One, actually, on the left side.

Patch couldn't help smiling back. She had the strangest urge to laugh with relief. He hadn't said a word, yet she was ready to like him.

He wasn't done charming her. While she stood there grinning like an idiot, his mouth tilted up on one side, skewing his smile and giving him a rakish look. His eyes warmed as they focused on her. Even worse, she warmed as his eyes surveyed her from top to toe. She was left in no doubt that he liked what he was seeing.

It dawned on her that she was meeting these two cowmen still wearing the apron she had put on to clean house, with her hair tumbling down and her face smudged with dirt.

"Garn!" she muttered.

"What's that you said, ma'am?" Frank asked.

"Nothing," Patch replied. "What can I do to help you gentlemen?"

"We came to make sure Ethan's all right," Frank answered.

Patch's eyes narrowed suspiciously. "Don't you work for Jefferson Trahern?"

Frank ran the reins through his fingers nervously. "Yes, ma'am. I do."

Her mouth twisted in disdain. "And you call yourself Ethan's friend?"

"I'll personally vouch for him," the stranger said.

"And who are you?" Patch demanded.

The cowboy stepped down off his horse, tipped his hat, and said, "Boyd Stuckey, at your service, ma'am. I'm a friend of Ethan's, too. Whom do I have the honor of addressing?"

Patch was flattered and flustered by his formal speech. It belonged in a drawing room back East. Then she remembered that she had spent more than a couple of years learning how to respond when addressed in such a manner. "I'm Patricia Kendrick. It's a pleasure to meet you, sir."

Patch realized too late that she had extended her hand as though she were wearing elbow-length gloves and a satin ballgown. To her surprise, Boyd Stuckey knew exactly how to treat a lady. He marched up two of the three front porch steps, took her hand in his, and raised it to his lips.

When his mouth touched the back of her hand, she got goose bumps all the way up her arm. She snatched her hand back, bewildered by feelings she had previously been certain no man except Ethan could have incited.

"It's a pure delight meeting you, Miss Kendrick," Boyd said. "To what do we owe the pleasure of your company?"

The sound of his voice, husky and low, sent an astonishing chill down her spine. Patch was confused and upset by what was happening to her. How could a perfect stranger make her feel like this, when she was already in love with another man!

She hurried into speech to cover her feelings. "Ethan worked with my father in Montana years ago. Since we're such old friends, he asked me to come and help out around the house until Mrs. Hawk is feeling better." She arched a brow, eyed both men, and said, "What's your real reason for being here? I have it on good authority that Ethan doesn't have any friends in town."

Frank answered before Boyd could. "Me and Boyd and Ethan grew up together here in Oakville. We've been best friends since we were in short pants. Just ask Ethan. He'll tell you. The three of us have always been tighter than ticks on a dog."

Frank looked so honest and sounded so earnest that Patch was inclined to believe him. "In that case—"

The squeal of hinges as the front door opened interrupted her. Patch turned and saw that Ethan was joining them.

"I was just about to invite your friends to stay for supper," she said.

"We wouldn't want to put you out, ma'am," Frank said.

"It's no trouble at all," Patch replied. "Please, won't you both join us?"

"I have some things to talk over with Ethan that'll sit better on a full stomach," Boyd said.

"Then it's settled," Patch said. "You'll stay."

"Patch, it's not necessary—"

Patch patted Ethan's arm on her way past him. "Invite your friends into the parlor, Ethan. I'll get Leah to help me set some more places at the table." She was gone before Ethan could protest further.

Ethan watched with narrowed eyes as Boyd and Frank ogled Patch's swaying rear end all the way into the house.

"Come on inside before your eyeballs drop out," he said, glaring at his friends. The two men followed sheepishly.

"Looks a little different in here from the last time I saw it," Boyd said as he settled himself on the horsehair sofa.

"Patch has taken things in hand."

"Patch?" Boyd asked.

"That's her nickname."

"I like Patricia better," Boyd said.

"Suit yourself."

Frank edged into a rawhide chair across from the sofa and accepted the glass of whiskey Ethan poured from the bottle his father had always kept along with some glasses on a table near his desk.

"None for me, Ethan," Boyd said.

"What shall we drink to?" Frank asked.

"Freedom," Ethan said grimly.

"To freedom," Frank echoed.

Boyd laid one ankle on the opposite knee and drummed his boot with his fingertips, eyeing Ethan speculatively. "I wish I had a few *old* friends who look like Miss Kendrick."

"I last saw her seven—almost eight—years ago when I worked with her father in Montana." Ethan was irritated by Boyd's interest in Patch, but unwilling to tell his friend to back off. After all, Boyd Stuckey was exactly the sort of man a lady like Patricia Kendrick deserved.

"Patch couldn't have been much more than a kid eight years ago," Frank said.

"She *was* a kid," Ethan retorted. "Hell, when she was three, I changed her wet drawers! Her father, Seth, was the man who hid me out after Dorne shot me, until my leg healed."

The other two men sobered at this reminder of the awful events of the past that had changed all of their lives.

"Pretty nice of her to come all this way to help you out," Boyd said. "Is she staying here at the house with you, or does she have a room in town?"

"I'm staying right here," Patch answered.

All three men stood at the sight of her. Patch had put on the rose red dress she had worn at the hotel. The velvet hugged every womanly curve, emphasizing her femaleness. Her hair was twisted into a neat bun at her nape, and she had powdered away the freckles on her nose. Her back was ramrod straight, but she moved with feline grace. She was as elegant a lady as any of them had ever seen.

Ethan was awed by the transformation from frazzled housekeeper to flawless female, but he wasn't by any means alone in his admiration.

"Well, well," Boyd murmured. "This is a rare treat indeed."

"Shall we go in to supper, gentlemen?"

Boyd was quick to offer Patch his arm, and although she would rather have walked the few steps to the trestle table in the kitchen with Ethan, she was unable to avoid Boyd without being rude.

"Certainly," she said with slight nod.

Ethan was left to trail behind his friends, pondering the way Patch Kendrick had turned his household inside out and his friends upside down.

The kitchen looked homey in the glow from several lanterns Patch had placed around the room. Patch was sitting on the right side of the table. Boyd had seated himself across from her—so he could look at her throughout supper without seeming to stare, Ethan thought wryly. Frank had taken the seat beside Patch. Leah was sitting at the foot of the table. Although *sitting* perhaps wasn't the right word. Leah had her feet doubled under her on the chair, her dirty elbows on the table, and her chin resting in her hands.

Before he sat down, Ethan surveyed the table in amazement. Hot, buttered biscuits. Baked ham. Boiled beans and bacon. A pot of steaming hot coffee. His mouth hadn't watered like this in a month of Sundays. But it wasn't just the food, it was the fact that silverware had been precisely placed on either side of the plates, which held cloth napkins. He hadn't even known his mother owned cloth napkins! Somewhere, Patch had found five cups that matched. In the center of it all stood a fruit jar jam-packed with fresh-picked black-eyed Susans.

As Ethan took his seat at the head of the table, he eyed Patch surreptitiously. The troublemaking hoyden he had known in Montana wouldn't even have used silverware, let alone been capable of arranging it on the table. He watched her place the napkin precisely in her lap. His stomach knotted when she smiled at Boyd across the table.

Then she turned to him, the smile still on her face, and said, "Do you still like biscuits as much as you used to?"

"Yeah, I do." It took Ethan a moment to realize she was holding the basketful of biscuits out to him. He took one, felt how soft it was, and reached for two more. He took a quick bite and through a mouthful of biscuit said, "These are great! Not at all like the ones you used to make." He stopped chewing and looked up guiltily.

Patch laughed. "You mean these don't taste like shoe leather," she said with a twinkle in her eye. "Molly taught me how to make them." She turned to Leah. "And I had a lot of help from your sister."

Ethan's look was nothing short of incredulous. He quickly recovered himself and said, "Then my compliments to you, too, Leah."

Leah flushed to the roots of her hair. "You're welcome, Ethan," she muttered.

Ethan passed the basket on to Boyd, who helped himself to several and passed it across to Frank, who passed it down to Leah. By the time the basket got back to Patch, there was one biscuit left. She took it and was grateful, knowing the typical cowboy's appetite, that they had left her any at all.

If Patch had hoped for civil conversation at the table, she was doomed to disappointment. These were working cattlemen, and their appetites showed it. Once their plates were full, they concentrated totally on eating. It was only after they had demolished the ham and scraped the bowl of beans and poured themselves a third cup of coffee that they sat back ready to talk.

"That was a close call you had this morning," Boyd said to Ethan.

"Yeah, it was." Ethan settled his gaze on Leah. "It's bedtime, kid."

"I'm not tired."

"Then you can go check on Ma."

"Aw, Ethan—"

"Get going, brat."

"I always miss the good stuff," Leah grumbled.

"Tell Ma I'll be in to say good night soon."

Patch was amazed when Ethan's sister obeyed him. She had felt the tension between them all evening. But Patch had also seen the girl's occasional furtive glances at her brother throughout supper. She remembered the painful flush when Ethan had complimented Leah on the biscuits. Patch suspected the girl idolized her brother and wanted his approval, while Ethan, though indulgent, kept her at a distant arm's length.

That wasn't so hard to understand. After all, the brother and sister barely knew each other. They had been robbed of a lifetime together by the catastrophe that had occurred seventeen years ago. Fortunately, once Ethan's name was cleared, they would have the rest of their lives to get well acquainted.

When Leah was gone, Ethan turned to Patch and said, "Maybe you'd like to clear the table."

"Maybe I wouldn't," Patch retorted. "You're not going to get rid of me as easily as you got rid of Leah. I'm staying right here. I think I'd like to hear what your friends have to say."

Ethan frowned. "Don't blame me if you hear something you don't like. Go ahead, Boyd."

Boyd took a sip of coffee and set down his cup. "How's your ma doing?"

"About the same," Ethan replied. "I've had Doc Carter in to see her, but he says there's nothing wrong with her that he can fix. He said just make sure she gets plenty of rest and get her to eat whatever she will."

"Too bad. With your ma so sick, your kid sister would be in a bad way if anything ever happened to you."

"Don't you think I know that?" Ethan snapped.

"One of these days Trahern is going to get lucky. Wouldn't it be better to sell this place and head for greener pastures?"

"These pastures are plenty green for me," Ethan retorted.

"Boyd is right," Frank said. "It's too dangerous for you to stay here, Ethan. Trahern isn't going to give up. He wants you dead."

Ethan smiled grimly. "I'm still alive."

"But for how long? You've only been back home a month, and he's already sicced a pack of killer dogs on you," Boyd said.

Patch cleared her throat. "What would happen if Trahern found out who really raped his daughter? Do you think he would give up his quest for vengeance against Ethan?"

Boyd and Frank stared at Patch as though she had grown another eye in the center of her forehead. Then they stared at Ethan.

Ethan felt his ears getting red. "Patch has this crazy idea about hunting down the rapist."

"After seventeen years?" Frank asked incredulously. "We looked for clues at the time, and there weren't any!"

"If there weren't any clues, why does everyone believe Ethan is guilty?" Patch asked.

Patch couldn't get any of the three men to meet her gaze. At last Ethan said, "Because Merielle's father found me a half mile from his house holding his daughter in my arms, her face all bloody and her clothes half ripped off."

Patch felt queasy. That was certainly damning evidence. But not enough by itself to condemn a man to a lifetime on the run. Her brow furrowed as she thought aloud. "How did you come to find her? I mean, what were you doing there?"

Ethan shoved his chair back from the table and stood in agitation. "Are you so sure I didn't do it?" he challenged.

Patch shoved her own chair back and stood facing him nose to nose. "Absolutely, positively sure."

The tension in the room was palpable. Suddenly, Ethan collapsed back into his chair and dropped his head into his hands. He made a frustrated, growling sound in his throat. "Aw, hell," he muttered in disgust. "Believe what you want. It won't change what everyone else thinks."

Patch sat back down. Before Ethan had spoken, she had convinced herself that he hadn't been anywhere near Merielle Trahern when she was raped. Obviously, she had been deluding herself. Proving his innocence might be a bit more difficult than she had thought. "We have to find out the truth," she croaked past the sudden lump in her throat.

"It's too late," Boyd said flatly. "You're both kidding yourselves if you think you'll find the culprit after all these years."

"We certainly won't if we don't try!" Patch retorted. Her fear that Ethan might somehow be involved after all caused her voice to come out sounding shrill. The look of shock on Boyd's face at her outburst made her realize that her ladylike facade had slipped. But she was fighting for her life. Being a lady came a distant second.

"What about Merielle?" Patch asked. "Is there any chance she'll ever regain her memory?"

Boyd shook his head. "After seventeen years? I'd say it's damned unlikely."

Patch turned to Frank, who hadn't said a word. "Frank? What do you think?"

Patch wished she hadn't asked when she saw the wounded look in Frank's gray eyes.

"For a long time I kept hoping . . ." He knotted his hands and swallowed so hard his Adam's apple bobbed up and down. "I try to take as much pleasure as I can from her company just the way she is." He paused and added in a harsh voice, "Because I don't think she's ever going to be any different."

Everyone at the table was silent, and Patch realized they were all willing to give up before they had even started. "There's no reason why we can't ask some questions," she said.

"To what purpose?" Boyd asked.

"To find some answers!" Patch said in exasperation.

Boyd shrugged. "You'd be wasting your time."

"I agree," Frank said in a quiet voice. "It's ancient history."

"Not to Jefferson Trahern," Patch insisted.

Silence fell again.

At last Ethan raised his head. "Patch is right about one thing. We'll never know if we don't try. I'm sick and tired of having to watch my back. Now Trahern has decided to wage war another way. He's making it impossible for me to borrow money from the bank. Without credit I can't buy feed. I'll be out of business in six months. I don't have any choice. I need to make peace with Trahern. The only way to do that is to find out who really raped Merielle."

Boyd sighed. "I think you're wasting your time—"

"Boyd—" Ethan interrupted.

"—but I'll do what I can to help," Boyd finished.

The two men exchanged glances, then grinned. Boyd slapped Ethan on the back. "Hell, what have we got to lose?"

"When do we start?" Frank asked.

"How about now?" Patch said.

Ethan gave her a sideways look. "What did you have in mind?"

"How about filling me in on everything you can remember that happened the day Merielle was raped?"

The three men looked at each other warily. Because of Ethan's flight and the years he had spent running, they had never spoken about that day.

"All right," Ethan said. "Who wants to go first?"

Frank's Adam's apple bobbed again. "I will."

Patch settled back in her chair to listen.

"It was Merielle's birthday," Frank began, "so we made arrangements to meet in our secret place."

"You met in secret?" Patch asked.

Frank's face contorted in lines so savage he could no longer be called handsome. "Jefferson Trahern didn't approve of his daughter seeing a no-account dirt farmer's son."

"So you and Merielle met behind his back," Patch concluded.

"We were in love," Frank said. "We planned to be married some-day. Somehow."

"Where was this secret place?" Patch asked.

"I can tell you that," Ethan said. "The three of us used to meet there. It's a cave along the Neuces River about a mile from Trahern's ranch house. The entrance is hidden by brush and cactus."

"So all of you knew where it was?"

Ethan nodded. "But we stayed away when Frank asked us to."

"What time did you meet Merielle?" Patch asked.

"Her father was having a party for her that evening, so we decided to see each other right after school. She had to go home first, but she promised to come as soon as she could. I had a present for her . . . a ring." Frank twisted the braided horsehair ring on his little finger.

"What happened?"

"She never showed up."

"Why not?" Patch asked.

"Because some bastard stopped her on the way and beat her up and raped her!"

Patch forced herself to remain calm in the face of Frank's all-too-apparent rage. "When did you realize she wasn't coming?"

"I waited there till the sun had almost set. I figured her father must have caught her trying to sneak out of the house and stopped her. Just in case something else had gone wrong, I backtracked the trail to her house. That's when I found her. She was . . ." Frank's voice broke.

"*You* found her?" Patch asked. "Why weren't *you* suspected of raping her?"

Patch watched as Ethan and Frank exchanged guilty glances.

"You might as well tell her," Ethan said. "It's way past time we spilled the whole story."

Boyd sat up straighter. "You boys been keeping secrets from me?"

"It didn't concern you," Ethan said curtly.

Boyd's face shadowed. "I can leave if you'd rather not include me now."

Frank fidgeted in his seat. "Hell, Boyd, I always wanted to tell you, but Ethan—"

"I figured the less you knew, the less you'd have to lie," Ethan said baldly.

"So what happened?" Patch asked impatiently.

"My family had been invited to the Trahern house for Merielle's birthday party," Ethan began. "When we got there, Merielle was missing. Everybody was out searching for her. I knew she was supposed to be meeting Frank, because he'd warned me at school earlier in the day to stay away from the hideout.

"I headed in the direction of the cave. I didn't get far before I found Merielle. Frank was with her. Her torn underclothes were on the ground beside her. Her nose was bloody, and she wasn't conscious that I could tell. Frank had her in his lap, rocking her in his arms."

He was also crying like a baby, Ethan remembered. He flashed a look at Frank, took a deep breath, and said, "I didn't know what to think. Before I could say a word, Dorne Trahern came riding over the hill. He saw the same thing I did. Only he came to a different conclusion about what had happened."

"He thought Frank had raped Merielle!" Patch said.

"Dorne was always hotheaded, but he went plain loco. And with good reason, I suppose. If it had been Leah . . ." Ethan lowered his eyes to concentrate on the stray thread in his Levi's he was twisting between his fingers.

Patch looked from Ethan to Frank and back again. "How do you know Frank didn't do it?" she asked.

Patch watched Ethan chew on his lower lip. When he raised his eyes, she could see they were troubled. Suddenly she realized that *Frank* was the one Ethan suspected!

"Merielle loved Frank," Ethan said. "I don't think he would have needed to use force with her."

"What if she said yes at first and changed her mind later?" Patch asked. "Would Frank have been willing to stop?"

Ethan thrust all ten fingers through his hair. That was the question he had been asking himself for more years than he cared to count. "Hell, Patch. I don't know. Ask Frank!"

"Frank?"

"I loved Merielle. I would have cut off my hand before I hurt her. But there's no way I can prove my innocence."

"If you were there, why was the rape blamed on Ethan?" Patch asked.

"No one ever knew I was there," Frank said.

"What?"

Ethan picked up the story where he had left off.

"Dorne didn't stop to ask questions. He came off his horse with his gun in his hand. At first I thought he was going to shoot Frank in cold blood. At the last instant he turned the gun and started pistol-whipping Frank.

"Frank was hanging on to Merielle, so he wasn't in a position to defend himself. I tried to stop Dorne, but he was ten years older than me and forty pounds heavier. The best I could do was grab his wrist and hang on. I . . . I didn't realize he had his finger on the trigger.

"I was just trying to get him to leave Frank alone. Only the gun went off. Twice. One shot hit me in the leg and crippled me. The other caught Dorne in the thigh. His wound shouldn't have been fatal, but the bullet cut an artery, and blood spurted out so fast . . . he never had a chance. He bled to death before our eyes.

"For years afterward I tried to convince myself that Dorne deserved what had happened to him. Now I see his death for what it was. A tragic, avoidable accident.

"Anyway, I talked Frank into leaving while I stayed there to try and smooth things over."

"You left Ethan to take the blame?" Patch demanded of Frank. "How could you?"

Frank flushed. "I wanted to stay—"

"It was my idea," Ethan said. "Because of all the gossip about Merielle and Frank, Trahern would have been willing to believe Frank was guilty—and Frank had told me he wasn't. I figured I had a better chance of explaining things and avoiding more bloodshed if I was alone."

His lips twisted into a rueful smile. "Neither of us ever dreamed Trahern would accuse me of Merielle's rape."

Ethan laced his hands behind his head and stared at the ceiling. He remembered everything that had gone through his mind at the time. It had been like a nightmare from which he was going to wake up any second. Only it wasn't a dream. He could recall every word he had said, everything he had done as though it were yesterday.

He had known the bang and echo of the gunshots would bring all those searchers on the run. They weren't going to give Frank Meade any more chance to explain than Dorne had.

Ethan had dragged himself on hands and knees to Frank and yanked on his friend's bloodied shirt. "Frank, you've got to get out of here. People will be coming soon."

"I can't leave Merielle," Frank had said, sobbing.

"Don't you understand? You'll only make things worse if you stay."

"I'll tell them I found her like this."

"You think they're going to give you time to explain, considering who you are and with the picture of you holding her like that staring them right in the face? If they find you with Merielle, they're going to start jumping to the wrong conclusions. You've got to get out of here!"

"I can't just leave her here all alone!" Frank protested.

"Give her to me," Ethan said. "I'll take care of her for you. Go to the cave and wait for me. I'll meet you there when I can."

"I want to stay here," Frank said stubbornly.

"Dammit, Frank! Don't argue with me. Just get out of here. Now!"

Frank had barely stumbled to his feet when they heard the sound of hoofbeats. "Run! Run! Merielle will need you by her side when she's well again," Ethan had shouted.

Frank had taken one last, anguished look at Merielle and fled.

Ethan had stayed, believing that the adults descending on the scene would recognize Dorne's death was an accident. He planned to substitute himself for Frank in the scene where Dorne attacked with his weapon. It never occurred to him that anyone would even consider the possibility that he had raped Merielle Trahern.

It was only later that he realized how stupid, how childishly naive, he had been. Jefferson Trahern had been the first to arrive. Ethan's father, Alex, had been riding at his side.

Frank interrupted Ethan's reminiscence to ask, "What happened after I left Merielle, Ethan? You never said."

Ethan continued his reflections aloud. "Jefferson Trahern came riding over the hill. If my father hadn't been with him, I'd be dead now."

Boyd whistled his appreciation of the life and death situation Ethan had found himself in. "So that's why Trahern tried to ruin your pa. I always wondered why he blamed the father for the sins of the son."

Ethan continued as though Boyd hadn't spoken. "By now it was nearly dark. Trahern was crazed with grief when he realized Dorne was dead. When he saw Merielle . . . I don't think I've ever seen a man so wild. His eyes bugged out, and he started foaming at the mouth. His fists were clenched so hard he was drawing blood with his nails.

"He hit me hard enough in the jaw to roll me over. I lost my hold on Merielle, and she slid a little way down the hill from us. He completely ignored her, just grabbed hold of my shirt and pulled me up far enough so he could reach my face to hit me again.

"Pa dragged him off a little, and pretty soon they were fighting. Pa yelled at me to take Dorne's horse and get away. I didn't know where to go. I figured they'd look for me at home. And I was afraid the cave was too close, so I didn't even stop to tell Frank what had happened, because someone might have found me there. So I just started riding.

"I didn't realize I was heading in any particular direction, but I ended up at Boyd's place. You weren't there, Boyd, but one of the women from the Silver Buckle, Dora Deveraux, had come to spend the night with your pa. Dora dug the bullet out and put on a bandage. But I couldn't stay at your place. They'd be sure to look for me there.

"So I took off. My leg started bleeding again and I was damn near bleached white by the time I came upon what I thought was an empty line shack. I staggered inside, and that's when I found Seth Kendrick and his daughter. A day or so later we rode on to Seth's ranch.

"Seth hid me until my leg healed. At least, as well as it was ever going to. One of Trahern's hired detectives found me there six months later, and I had to run again. I kept running until Trahern's men caught up with me seven years ago. You know the rest."

Patch had listened carefully to Ethan's story, but it raised more questions than it answered. "Sheriff Lachlan told me that Boyd testified on your behalf at the trial. But if Boyd wasn't at home, how could he know anything about what happened that night? Was he invited to Merielle's birthday party, too?"

Boyd snorted. "Hell, no. My father was just a hired hand on Trahern's ranch, a regular drunk, who worked when he was sober for enough money to get drunk again."

"But you're rich now!" Patch blushed a furious red. Imagine saying such a thing, and with such disbelief, to Boyd's face, as though no one who had come from such humble beginnings could have turned his life around so completely. It was just that she hadn't expected such a past from a man as suave and well-mannered as Boyd had shown himself to be.

"I've made the most of life's opportunities," Boyd said with a rueful grin.

"So where were you when all this happened?" Patch queried.

"I was out hunting down my pa to bring him home."

"Where, exactly, was your home?"

"A line shack on the edge of Trahern's property."

"Was anyone with you who could give you an alibi?" Patch asked.

"My father. But he wouldn't make much of a witness."

"Why not?"

"He was drunk then, and he's dead now."

Patch let her gaze shift from one man to the other around the table. Any one of them might have raped Merielle Trahern. They all had opportunity. None had an iron-clad alibi. However, with just the little she knew of them, she couldn't imagine any of these three men doing such a thing.

"I guess that's that," she said.

Ethan cocked a brow. "What's what?"

"We need some more suspects."

Ethan laughed. He couldn't help it. "More suspects? Who did you have in mind?"

Patch shrugged. "I don't know. But they're out there. All we have to do is find them."

"Do you have someplace in mind to start?" Boyd asked.

Ethan rubbed the stubble on his chin. "We could start with Careless Lachlan. He conducted the investigation."

Boyd snorted. "What investigation? It was an open and shut case."

"The sheriff will have whatever information there is," Ethan said.

"Do you want me to talk to him?" Boyd asked.

"I'll do it," Ethan said. "You can start making a list of every man in town at the time who was old enough to do the deed."

"What about me?" Frank asked.

"Have you ever talked to Merielle about what happened that day?" Ethan asked.

Frank shook his head. "I couldn't."

"Try. It may be my only hope."

"All right," Frank said, his Adam's apple bobbing. "I'll try."

A brief, awkward silence followed, broken finally when Boyd rose and said, "Guess I'd better be heading home."

Frank stood as well. "Me, too. Thanks for the supper, Miz Kendrick."

"You're welcome, Frank. And you, too, Boyd."

"If you're going to call me Boyd, I hope you'll allow me to call you Patricia," Boyd said with a smile meant to charm.

Patch was charmed. "Of course," she said.

Ethan gritted his teeth.

"You don't have to see us out," Boyd said. "We know the way."

Once they were gone, Patch and Ethan sat back down at the table. Neither of them looked at the other, but they were both very aware that his fingertips lay only an inch or so from hers on the scarred tabletop.

"Well," Ethan said. "You got what you wanted."

"Only the first part," Patch replied. "There's more to what I want from you, Ethan Hawk. Much more."

Ethan caught himself reaching for her and abruptly rose to his feet. He had no business getting involved with Patch Kendrick, no matter what she wanted from him. "You need any help clearing the table?"

Patch stood and gathered up a handful of dishes. "Sure, if you don't mind."

Ethan's willingness to help was one of the things she had liked about him when she was a child. As a woman, having learned over the years how rare such helpfulness was, she admired him all the more.

They worked together in surprising harmony.

He made sure to treat her like a younger sister.

She made sure to act like a lady.

Because Patch had first loved Ethan when she was a child and he was an adult, there had been none of the sexual nuances that sprang up between them now. She was pleased when Ethan made an effort to ease the tension by reminiscing about the time he had spent with her in Montana and teasing her about her infatuation with the Masked Marauder, who had been a sort of local Robin Hood.

Patch had forgotten how easy it was to talk to Ethan. She had confided often in him as a child. Now she wanted the opportunity to share with him her hopes and dreams as a woman. Only there were matters that had to be settled first before he would be ready to contemplate a future that included her.

They were both sorry when the dishes were done, because they had enjoyed the time together. Patch lifted her arms over her head and stretched, unaware of how much Ethan was enjoying the view. She caught him staring and dropped her arms, realizing she had been caught in unladylike behavior.

However, Ethan didn't seem to mind. His green eyes were warm with approval. "Where do you plan to sleep?"

"I've made a place for myself in Leah's room. We're going to share a bed."

Ethan's lips pursed ruefully. "Does Leah know about your plans?"

Patch smiled, remembering a time when her stepmother, Molly, had suggested that Patch share her room with her brand-new six-year-old stepsister. Patch had fled to Ethan's cabin and spent the night wrapped up in a buffalo skin in front of his fireplace. "I spoke with Leah earlier in the day. She was agreeable . . . after your mother had a talk with her."

"Then I guess we'd better say good night."

"Oh, my Lord, I forgot all about him!"

"Him? Who?" Ethan demanded, his neck hairs rising at the thought of Patch so concerned about another man.

Patch ignored Ethan and headed for the kitchen door, which, once again, was stuck fast.

Ethan held his hand over hers to keep her from opening the door. "Who is it you're going out to meet at this hour of the night?"

Patch looked at him over her shoulder and smiled coyly. "Max!"

Ethan wasn't amused. "Who's Max?"

"My mouse."

Ethan felt like an idiot. "Let me help you." He leaned across her and pried the door loose. For a moment he didn't move. He was conscious of the scent of some kind of flower in her hair, and he could feel the heat of her all down his front. "Do you need a light?"

"It would help if you'd get a lantern so I can see what I'm doing."

Ethan fetched the lantern from the table and held it aloft while Patch retrieved Max, who had remained safe and sound in the gardening tool box all evening.

"Why don't you just let him go?"

"That calico cat would make dinner of him for sure!" Patch responded tartly. She crossed past Ethan back into the house and only waited for him to come inside and drag the door closed before she said, "Good night, Ethan."

Patch resisted the urge to look back at him as she headed for Leah's bedroom.

Ethan stood where he was without moving, because if he took one step, he was going to have her in his arms. And that was not—absolutely not—part of his plans for Patch Kendrick.

He would have to make some time soon to sneak through the back alleys into town and talk with Careless Lachlan. Once Patch realized there was no hope of clearing his name, she would be on her way back to Montana. And his body would stop responding like he was some teenage kid in the throes of calf love. Because he was not—absolutely not—going to make love to any lady with marriage on her mind, especially Seth Kendrick's daughter.

❧5❧

When a week had come and gone in which Ethan had made no move to start his investigation, Patch decided to get things rolling on her own. She told Ethan she needed to take a wagon into town to pick up her trunks from the hotel, which was true, of course. What she failed to mention was that she also planned to have a talk with the sheriff while she was there. It occurred to her that this might also be an opportunity to finagle an introduction to her grandfather.

She decided to do her pleasant business first. Since small towns were notorious for gossip, she thought news of her presence might already have reached her grandfather. Apparently he lived like a hermit, because he was both disbelieving and disgruntled when he opened the door to his room at Pearlie Mae's Boardinghouse and found her standing there.

"Who the hell are you?" he demanded.

Patch revised her expectation that this was going to be a pleasant visit. She realized she was nervous, and her pulse fluttered erratically as she announced, "I'm Patricia Kendrick. Your granddaughter."

She saw a brief spark of acknowledgment in his eyes. Then he scowled. "What do you want?"

"I want to talk to you."

"Well, you've talked to me."

If Patch hadn't put her foot in the door, she would have found herself standing in the hall with the door slammed in her face. "How do you think my mother, Annarose, would feel if she knew you were treating me like this?"

His eyes flickered to a framed picture on the dry sink, then back to her. "All right. You can come in. But if you once mention your father's name, I swear I'll throw you out on your fanny so fast the wind'll whistle."

Once she had bullied her way inside by invoking Annarose's

277

name, Patch closed the door behind her and stood toe to toe with her grandfather, matching him glare for glare. Which gave her a good chance to look him over.

Corwin Marshall had aged as lean as she suspected he must have been as a young man. He stood tall and proud and obstinate before her, dressed in a plaid shirt and store-bought trousers held up by bright red suspenders. His full head of white hair needed a trim. His lips were thin, his nose prominent, his eyebrows as bushy white as his hair. His eyes reminded her of her own. They were a startlingly vivid blue. His face was lined, craggy almost, and his jowls sagged a bit. Otherwise, he looked as hard as she suspected his life had been.

Patch had worn her rose red traveling outfit, complete with gloves and feathered hat and iron rod down her spine, because she had wanted to impress her grandfather with how well she had turned out. She had never dared to ask her father how her mother had died, because any mention of Annarose always made him so sad. But she intended to find out the details from her grandfather. And she wanted very much to see that picture the old man had glanced at before he let her in.

"You are my grandfather, aren't you?" Patch asked when it seemed the old man had no intention of speaking.

He searched her face, looking for familiar features. "I suppose I must be."

"May I sit down?"

There was a small, square table by the window with a chair on either side of it. Her grandfather gestured her toward it. "Be my guest."

He seated her and took the chair on the other side of the table for himself. He began packing a pipe with tobacco from a small pouch. He didn't seem in any hurry to talk.

A checkerboard and checkers sat on the table, along with a deck of cards. A quick survey of the room revealed that her grandfather lived a neat, if Spartan, life. His bed was made, a pair of Sunday boots stood against the wall, and his clothes hung on pegs on the back of the door. A kerosene lamp stood on the table beside the bed, which also held a book. Patch tried to make out the title, but it was turned the wrong way.

On the other side of the room stood a dry sink with his shaving equipment and a pitcher and bowl. A framed photograph of a woman was angled toward the bed. Patch hoped it was her mother, Annarose. Nell had said her grandfather had a picture he could show her. She resisted the urge to get up and go over and look at it and purposely turned her head to gaze out the window. She didn't want her grandfather to think that seeing a picture of her mother was the only reason she had come.

Sunlight streamed through faded gingham curtains that Patch supposed had been put there by the landlady. The window was open, and she could hear sounds from the street a floor below her—a bawling bullock, the creak and rattle of a wagon, the stomp of boots echoing on the boardwalk. The smell of fresh manure swept in on the breeze. She peered down and saw a hitching rail to the left of the window with a bay gelding canted on three legs. The swish of its tail kept a swarm of flies from enjoying the manure without constant interruption.

She could feel the loneliness in this room. It was almost a presence. How sad that Corwin Marshall was living the last years of his life in this solitary way. She wondered why her father had never mentioned her grandfather's existence. And whether the old man would even want to know her now.

When she turned her attention back to her grandfather, she caught him staring at her. Unfortunately, she had no idea whether he liked what he saw. "Well," she said. "Where shall we begin?"

"You look like your mother."

Patch forced a smile. "Nell said the same thing."

Her grandfather's brow furrowed. "Nell who?"

"I'm sorry. I thought you two knew each other. Nell Hawk. I'm staying at the Double Diamond, keeping house for Mrs. Hawk until she's feeling better."

"That's not a fit place for you to be."

Patch's neck hairs bristled. "Why not? Nell is a perfectly respectable—"

"It ain't Nell Hawk I'm concerned about, it's that no-good, gunslinging outlaw son of hers."

Patch leapt from her chair, ready to do battle on Ethan's behalf. "You take that back!" she shouted. "Ethan is as fine a man—" Patch cut herself off. She had risen to Ethan's defense just as she had to her pa's when she was twelve and the whole town had believed Seth Kendrick was a coward. But she wasn't twelve anymore. And her grandfather had a point. Ethan Hawk was a man fresh from prison with a years-old crime still hanging over his head.

She slumped back down into her chair. "I'm sorry for flaring up at you like that. Only, you see, I love Ethan Hawk. I'm convinced he's innocent of everything he was accused of doing. And I'm going to do my best to see that his name is cleared before I marry him. Even if it isn't, I'm going to marry him anyway," she said defiantly.

Patch was breathless by the time she had finished. Her grandfather said nothing, simply struck a match and puffed at his pipe until it was lit. He shook the match out and laid it on the table in a spot that she could see had been blackened by the practice.

"How is Nell Hawk? I didn't know she was sick."

Patch was disconcerted by the change of subject but answered, "She says it's just an upset stomach." Patch leaned forward to confide in her grandfather. "But I think it's something much worse. She doesn't look good, and she's been ill for almost two months without getting better."

Corwin Marshall grunted. And changed the subject again. "How'd you find out about me? When he left town, your father swore I'd never see hide nor hair of you again. Did he have a change of heart?"

Patch fiddled with the strings of her velvet reticule. "Well, no, he didn't." She could almost feel the old man stiffen on the other side of the table. "He probably knew you didn't want to see me," Patch ventured.

"Not want to see you? When Annarose died, I begged him to let me have you. He was no fit—"

Patch had already started to rise from her chair again when her grandfather stopped himself. She sank back down. "I don't know what went on between you and my father," she began, "but don't you think it's time you settled things between you?"

"Your pa murdered my girl. I'll never forgive him for that!"

Patch was appalled at the fury and vindictiveness of the old man's voice. Her grandfather seemed so sure of what he was saying, yet she knew it had to be impossible. She rose immediately to her father's defense. "My father loved Annarose Marshall so much that when he finally married again, he did so with the understanding that his heart was already taken. Are you telling me he *murdered* the one person he loved above anything else in this world? I don't believe it!"

"He never told you, did he?"

"Told me what?"

"Your father shot Annarose and killed her," he said flatly.

Patch gasped. "If he did, it must have been an accident, he—"

"Oh, he claimed it was an accident, all right. I suppose he didn't see her in the dark," the old man conceded grudgingly.

"Can you tell me what happened?"

"Your pa was a Texas Ranger, and some Mexican bandidos he'd been chasing ambushed him here in town. Your ma was supposed to be safe at home. But you'd gotten sick, and she'd come into town hunting the doctor. Your pa was standing on the boardwalk in front of Doc Carter's office when he heard something behind him and thought it was one of the bandidos. To keep from being backshot, he turned and fired into the dark.

"When the Mexicans fled on horseback, your pa discovered that when he'd fired into the dark, the person he'd hit was your mother. She'd been shot twice in the chest. My daughter was still breathing when your father found her, but it didn't take her long to die."

"Oh, my God. How horrible for him!"

"For him! What about me?" Corwin said in a ragged voice. "I lost my girl, and then he took you away, all because I threatened . . ."

Patch waited for him to finish. When he didn't, she prompted, "Threatened what?"

"To take you away from him. After Annarose died, he was never without a bottle. He left you alone, sometimes all day. Come to find out later he was hiding Ethan Hawk at that place of his, letting that murdering rapist take care of you!"

"Ethan is not—"

"Be that as it may," her grandfather interrupted, "your pa disappeared without a trace. Where did he take you?"

"We moved around for a while, especially during the war. We ended up in Fort Benton, Montana. It's as far north as the Missouri River runs, practically to Canada. Pa's a doctor now. He's remarried and has two stepchildren and a seven-year-old son by his wife, Molly."

"Grandpa Corwin . . ." Patch hesitated, waiting to see if he would object to the familiarity of the address. When he didn't, she continued, "Grandpa Corwin, I thought you might like to be my grandfather for real. I mean, now that I'm going to be living in Oakville, we could see each other often."

The old man harrumphed. "What is it you want from me?"

"I don't really know," Patch said. "I've never had a grandfather before." She gave him a gamine smile and said, "I thought you might have some ideas."

"Grandpas usually dandle the young'uns on their knee." He gave her a look and said, "That'd be a bit of a chore now."

Patch laughed. "I promise you can dandle your great-grandchildren on your knee. I'd like us to be friends. Is that all right with you?"

He stared out the window and puffed on his pipe, creating a cloud of cherry-scented smoke. "All right," he said through teeth clenched on the pipe stem. "Friends."

"Thank you, Grandpa Corwin!" Patch was around the table and on her knees beside her grandfather before she thought about what she was doing. She put her arms around his waist and hugged him tight. His shirt smelled of cherry tobacco.

When his hands folded around her shoulders, she felt a band tighten in her chest. "There's one more thing," she said, her voice muffled against his shirt.

He reached out with a shaking hand and gently smoothed her hair. "What's that, girl?"

She leaned her head back and met his eyes, which looked rheumy now with age. "Nell said you had a picture of my mother. May I see it?"

He dropped his hands and sat back, staring out the window. "It's on the dry sink."

She rose and crossed the room. She picked up the daguerreotype in its brass frame. "Oh," she said in a trembly voice, "she does look like me."

Patch turned to her grandfather and saw through a blur of tears that he had set down his pipe. His eyes were closed tightly, and he was pinching the bridge of his nose as though he were in pain.

"You must miss her terribly," she whispered.

"Every day," the old man grated in a hoarse voice.

A moment later she was on her knees again at his feet with her arms wrapped tightly around his waist.

She said nothing.

Neither did he.

Patch made a silent vow to get her grandfather out of this lonely place. She wasn't sure how she was going to accomplish that goal, but she knew she had to try.

"Will you come visit me sometime at the Double Diamond?" she asked.

"I don't know . . ."

"I won't leave until you promise."

"All right," he said with a sigh of resignation. "I'll come."

Patch took leave of her grandfather shortly thereafter and headed for the hotel. She sat down at the desk in the lobby and wrote a quick letter to her parents, letting them know she had met her grandfather and chastising her father for not telling her about him sooner.

Meanwhile, Gilley hauled her trunks from the room where she had left them when she arrived in Oakville and put them in the wagon she had brought to town for that purpose.

Patch realized she had spent more time with her grandfather than she had intended, and that she would have to hurry if she didn't want to worry Ethan by a too-long absence. He had given her strict orders not to dally in town. "There's no telling how Trahern will react to the news you're staying at the Double Diamond," he had warned. "So finish your business and get back here as quick as you can."

It wasn't that Patch had ignored his counsel on purpose. But once she had started talking to her grandfather, the time had simply gotten away from her. She still had one more stop to make before she was ready to head back to the ranch. Actually, two stops. First the post office to mail her letter and then the sheriff's office.

She folded her letter and addressed the envelope, then stood and adjusted her hat. "Everything all set, Gilley?" she asked the clerk, who was once again manning his post behind the hotel desk.

"All finished, Miss Kendrick," the clerk answered. "Two trunks, three carpetbags, and five hatboxes all loaded into the wagon."

Patch remembered how much trouble it had been to keep secret from Molly the things she was packing in the bottom of her trunks that had nothing to do with her trip to Boston. She hadn't planned on coming back to Montana, so she had brought a few mementos of her past, as well as some items from her hope chest to start her new life with Ethan. In those trunks, under all the fashionable clothes Molly had insisted she would need for her social life in Boston, were the treasures she had collected for the home she planned to make with her new husband.

Some of the things she could use right away, the linens and such. There were other things—Patch blushed at the thought of the lacy nightgown she had bought in St. Louis—that would have to wait until she was married. Because she had packed so much extra, there hadn't been room to hide boots and trousers. Thus, her necessary stop at the mercantile her first day in town.

Patch crossed to the desk to give Gilley something for his trouble. "Thank you, Gilley. By the way," she said, "where will I find the sheriff this time of day?"

"Careless? Probably be in his office. He usually eats at his desk, mostly 'cause the town pays for his meal if he's working at noontime."

Patch smiled. "Thanks, Gilley."

The jail was across the street from the mercantile. It was made of rock and surrounded by three huge live oaks, one of which, Ethan had told her, had actually been used for hangings in the past. Patch wasn't superstitious, but she just knew there had to be ghosts that haunted the place at night.

Patch decided to post her letter before she paid her visit to Careless Lachlan. As far as she knew, Ethan hadn't been in to see him yet, and it couldn't hurt to let the sheriff know that the investigation of that long-ago incident was being reopened.

Patch had stepped off the boardwalk where it ended to allow access to an alley when a hand reached out and grabbed her by the wrist. She was yanked into the cool, murky shadows and slammed up against the wall. A hard male body pressed up against her and a callused hand stifled the scream on her lips. The abrupt change from sunlight to darkness momentarily blinded her. She was terrified until she heard a familiar male voice.

"What the hell do you think you're doing, Patch?"

"*Mmmmp,*" Patch replied. The hand came away and she snapped, "I was walking down the street! Or at least I was until you yanked me into this alley. What's got into you, Ethan? What's wrong?"

"I told you to get your bags and get back to the ranch. You left right after breakfast. It's practically noon. What the hell have you been doing all day?"

Patch relaxed. He was worried about her. She played with a button on his shirt with her gloved fingers. "I went to see my grandfather."

Ethan had the oddest sensation he was being undressed, even

though the buttons remained in place. It was a fantasy he had been fighting the past week, Patch undressing him. Here she was doing it— or rather, not doing it—in the middle of town. He forced his mind back to the subject at hand. "I thought Corwin Marshall was dead."

"No, he just sold his ranch and moved into town. And guess what, Ethan?"

"I'm afraid to ask."

"He's going to come visit me at the ranch sometime."

"Patch, there's no sense getting any more people involved in my situation than already are."

"He's not involved. He's just a lonely old man, Ethan, and I want to spend some time with him."

"Patch—"

"Have you talked to the sheriff yet, Ethan?"

"No, but—"

Her gloved fingers walked up his shirt toward his collar. "Could I go with you?"

He grabbed her wrist. "No."

Her lips pouted. "Why not?"

He smoothed them out with his thumb. "I told you, it isn't safe."

She stared up at him, her eyes pleading even though she wasn't saying a word.

"Patch . . ."

Ethan hadn't intended to kiss her. That had been the last thing on his mind when he dragged her into this alley. In fact, he had been ready to wring her neck. But he lowered his face and she lifted hers and, sure enough, their lips met.

It was just a touch of flesh to flesh, but it made his blood hum and his spirit soar. He rubbed his lips against hers, and her mouth came open. Lord, Lord! How could he resist that sort of temptation? His tongue slid along the crease of her mouth, and he felt her quiver.

He wasn't aware of what his hands were doing until she froze. He had her breast cupped in his hand! He started to let go, but she hesitantly arched toward him. She made a low, animal sound in her throat that caused his groin to draw up tight.

Ethan brushed his thumb delicately across her nipple and heard her gasp as it tightened into a bud. He thrust his tongue into her mouth and groaned when she sucked on it.

It was the sound of two women talking that brought him to his senses. He jerked away from Patch, put a hand across her mouth to keep her from making any noise, and pulled her deeper into the alley.

"It's shameless, that's what it is, a lady like her staying in the same house with the likes of him," one woman said.

"His mother is there, and his sister," the other answered.

"A sick woman and a little girl," the first woman retorted. "What's to keep him from forcing himself on her the way he did that poor Trahern girl?" The woman *tsk*ed and continued speaking, but by then they were well past the alley, and their voices were no longer clear.

"See what you're in for if you hang around me," Ethan whispered in the darkness. "Misery and unhappiness, that's what's in store! You'll be a source of gossip on the tongue of every old harpy in town. Get out of here, Patch. Now, while you can."

Patch dropped her forehead against Ethan's shoulder and rubbed her cheek against his chest. She liked the feel of him and wanted to be closer. Her fingers curled themselves into his shirt reflexively, like a kitten's claws. "No, Ethan. Whatever happens, I want to stay here with you."

Patch felt him shudder.

"Then heaven help you, little one. Because I can't help myself."

He tipped her chin up and kissed her, only this time he wasn't gentle. The fervent kiss frightened her, but she reminded herself this was Ethan, that she loved him, and he would never do anything to hurt her. Sure enough, the pressure on her mouth eased, then gentled, then persuaded.

Patch found herself responding. Her arms slid up around Ethan's neck, and her tongue slipped out tentatively to meet his. Ethan's arms tightened around her, and he pressed his lower body against her. She could feel the hard length of his shaft.

She slowly arched her body into his and heard him groan.

His hands grasped her hips and held her still. "Don't, Patch. Or I'll end up having you right here, standing against an alley wall in the middle of town."

Patch lowered her hands to his shoulders and leaned against him. All she heard for the next several moments was the sound of her own ragged breathing and the heavy beat of Ethan's heart.

"Let's get married now, Ethan. Let's not wait." Patch lifted her face to his. She could easily see his features now that her eyes had adjusted to the dark. "I don't care what the old biddies say. I don't care what the town thinks of you. I only know I love you. And you want me, Ethan. You can't deny it."

Ethan used his hold on her hips to lever her a good foot away from him. Maybe with distance he could keep his senses. "You're only making this harder for both of us, Patch. I won't deny I want you. *But I don't love you.* And I absolutely will *not* marry you with the whole town thinking I'm the kind of man who could beat up a woman and take her innocence and leave her bleeding on the ground."

Patch turned her head away. "All right, Ethan," she said. "I won't mention marriage again."

He caught her chin in his hand and forced her to face him. "You know I'm right, Patch."

She avoided agreeing with him. Because she didn't. "As long as you're in town, wouldn't this be a good opportunity to see the sheriff?"

Ethan gave in gracefully. "I suppose so."

"Good," Patch said. "Let's go."

"Whoa!" Ethan said. "I can't just go marching into his office."

"Why not?"

"Because . . ." Ethan realized that the threat of being bushwhacked was probably pretty slim in the sheriff's office. "All right," he said. "Let's go. You let me do all the talking."

"Of course, Ethan," Patch replied. "You're the boss."

Ethan laughed at the totally un-Patchlike meekness of her reply. He hugged her quickly and just as quickly let her go. The temptation was too great to do more. "Come on, you shameless minx. Let's go see what Careless has to say."

❋6❋

Ever since ethan had suggested that Frank talk to Merielle about the rape, he hadn't been able to think about anything else. Every day for a week Frank had been trying to get up the courage to broach the subject. The truth was, he was terrified. What if she got hysterical? What if she stopped talking altogether? What if she went completely out of her mind?

What if she remembered what had happened?

Greater than his fear was his desire to have Merielle as she had been seventeen years ago. Laughing. Smiling at him. Loving him. He wanted to kiss her and hold her in his arms and have her touch him with wonder as he touched her.

They had been naive and innocent then. He was only fifteen, she barely thirteen, and each of them in love for the first time. Generally they understood what was supposed to happen between lovers. But they had both been as shy as they were eager to discover the secrets of each other's body.

He had touched her breasts only once. Her cheeks had burned red with embarrassment the whole time he was unbuttoning her dress, and she had clenched fistfuls of his shirt to keep herself from shoving his hands away. He had pushed the dress down off her shoulders until it caught on her elbows and felt her shiver as her flesh was exposed to the sunlight in the loft of her father's barn. Her eyes, oh, God, her eyes had blazed with ecstasy and joy when his callused fingertips brushed against her flesh for the first time.

Her breasts had been small, only half-developed, the nipples tight, tiny pink buds. His chest had been banded with awe. His whole body had trembled with need. That other part of him, the part he hadn't yet used as a man with a woman, had surged to life, hardening in readiness for an act he could only imagine.

Frank had wanted to put his mouth on her flesh. He had dreamed of it. Before he could garner the courage to act on his desire, she had asked, "Could I touch you, Frank?"

"What?"

It had never occurred to him that she had the same sorts of fantasies he did. After all, she was a lady, or would be in a very few years. But there was no mistaking the longing in her eyes. He had reluctantly let go of the precious part of her he was holding and slid his arm around to her back.

"Do you want to unbutton my shirt? Or do you want me to do it?" he asked.

She looked delightfully confused for a moment before she said, "I want to do it."

Her fingers were stiff at first, from having been clenched so tightly on his shirt. She kept her chin down so he could see only the top of her head. He marveled at how she always got the part so straight, evenly dividing the lustrous sheen of black hair. He reveled in the thickness of her braids, their softness. All the while he was trying to think of something else, she was slowly but surely unbuttoning his shirt.

He sucked in his gut reflexively when she tugged on his shirttails to release them from his pants. He laughed nervously when he felt his body shiver. "I sure ain't cold," he said. And he hadn't been.

Shivering in sunlight. In the years to come he would often ponder the phenomenon. That day, his thoughts had been on Merielle. He had held his breath waiting to feel her fingertips on his skin.

A small patch of black curls had formed very recently on his chest, and that was what drew her attention. She reached tentatively and grasped several of the curly hairs.

He winced when she pulled too hard, but he wouldn't for the world have asked her to stop what she was doing. She slid her hand across his flesh, raising goose bumps along the way. Until she found a male nipple. It fascinated her. She traced it with her finger. She tweaked it and laughed when he jerked. She brushed it with her thumb.

Not even in his dreams had Frank imagined such feelings. His body drew up tight. His pulse pounded in his head until he couldn't think. His whole being came alive with wants and needs as old as the ages and as primal as nature.

Then she leaned forward and tasted his nipple with her tongue.

A groan, almost of pain, wrenched its way out of his throat.

She looked up at him, her eyes concerned, questioning. "Did I hurt you, Frank?"

"Oh, no, Merielle," he hurried to assure her. "It was just that . . . I felt like . . . I . . ." His tangled emotions left him tongue-tied. He didn't have words to tell her what he felt.

She demanded them anyway. "Felt like what, Frank?"

"I'd have to show you," he grated out.

He waited to see if she would let him do to her what she had done to him. Her brow furrowed slightly while she thought—it always did—and when it cleared he had his answer.

"All right, Frank."

He felt awkward, like the schoolboy he was. What if she didn't like it? What if she never let him touch her again? His sense of humor rescued him. If he didn't hurry up, she might change her mind, and he would never get to touch her the first time!

Frank was just lowering his head, and it was a ways down, since he was so much taller than she was, when they heard someone coming into her father's barn. They were in the loft, and there was no reason for anyone to come up there, but they waited with bated breath to be discovered. Whoever it was left the barn again almost immediately, but the spell was broken.

The instant it was safe to move again, Merielle pulled away from him and hurriedly yanked her dress back up over her shoulders. She fumbled with her buttons, and he brushed her hands away to do it himself.

"We should have met at the cave," he murmured. "Then we wouldn't have been interrupted."

She blushed, but a mischievous smile teased her lips. "Tomorrow," she promised.

"Tomorrow's your birthday. What about the party your father's having for you? Will you be able to get away?" He hadn't been invited and had been afraid he wouldn't see her alone. He had braided a ring out of black horsetail hair especially for her.

"I'll meet you after school," she said. "I have to come home first, but once Father sees I'm back, he won't pay any attention to where I go."

He buttoned the last button at her throat. "Don't be late. I have a present for you."

"I won't." She stood on tiptoe and pulled his head down to kiss him quickly on the lips, then raced for the ladder and headed down. She flashed him a quick grin of complicity before she disappeared from sight.

His thoughts shied away from what had actually happened the next day. It was too painful to remember. However, his confrontation with Jefferson Trahern the day following Merielle's birthday—the day after she was brutally raped—remained vivid in his mind.

He had gone to the Tumbling T because he couldn't stay away. He had slid off the mule his father used to pull his plow and tied it up along with the assortment of wagons and buggies drawn up at the front of the imposing house. He swallowed hard as he looked, really looked, at Merielle's home.

Merielle lived like a princess in a palace. What had ever made him think they would someday get married? He could never provide her with a grand home like the one she had grown up in. Pillars held up the second story of the house and black shutters framed sparkling windows. There must have been twenty rooms inside.

Merielle had never cared that her father had money and his father never would. Frank knew the town had him pegged as a man who would never get the dirt out from under his fingernails. And the chances of him getting into that great big house to see her the day after she had been brutally raped were slim to none. Nevertheless, he had to try. He had been in agony wondering how she was, whether she was still hurting, whether she would be willing to see him again.

When he knocked on the solid front door, it was answered by Mrs. Felber, whose husband owned the mercantile. She was a big-boned woman, with equally large features. She was wearing black. With her hair scraped back off her face, her nose became the focus of her face. Her mouth opened to reveal large, horsey teeth. Frank knew her son, Chester. He had started school with the other kids, but hadn't progressed far, since he was slow-witted. From the time he was ten, Chester had stood head and shoulders over everybody else. He had never fit in. He had only gotten bigger as he got older. Fortunately, he was a gentle giant.

"Why, Frank, you shouldn't be here," Mrs. Felber admonished.

He stood there, hat in hand, one booted foot digging at a knothole in the porch and muttered, "I came to see Merielle."

Mrs. Felber shook her head emphatically. "That's impossible."

"Can you tell me how she is?"

Mrs. Felber took pity on him. "I'm sorry, Frank. The poor girl . . . she . . . she isn't well."

Frank had figured that out for himself. He wanted more specific information. "Is she awake? Can she talk? Does she know who did it?"

"Oh, dear. I don't think—"

"Can I come in? I need to see her. I—"

"Who's at the door, Mrs. Felber?"

Frank recognized Jefferson Trahern's booming voice. His first thought was to turn tail and run as far as he could as fast as he could. But he would only have to come right back. *He had to know how she was!*

Mrs. Felber stepped aside and Jefferson Trahern stood in the doorway. "What are you doing here?"

In the past month or so Frank had discovered that his Adam's apple had a life of its own when he swallowed. He swallowed now and felt it slide jerkily up and down. "I came to see Merielle."

Trahern stepped out onto the porch and closed the front door behind him. Before Frank realized what the big man was going to do, he had grabbed a handful of Frank's shirt and drawn him up on his toes. "Did you have anything to do with what happened to my girl?"

"I love Merielle, sir."

Trahern shook him like a rat. "Bah! You're not fit to shine her shoes."

"I will be someday, sir."

Trahern's eyes narrowed. "You talking back to me, boy?"

Trahern's fist knotted tighter on his shirt. Frank was starting to choke. "May I see her, sir?"

He met Trahern's penetrating stare, trying to look innocent, even though he knew a lot more than Trahern thought he did about the rape.

"I've heard the gossip about you and my daughter, boy. If I thought for one second that you'd laid a hand on her, I'd hang you myself!"

Frank might have been poor, but he had never begged. He was begging now. "Please, won't you tell me how she is, sir?"

"That's none of your damn business!" Trahern used his hold on Frank to force him backward toward the edge of the porch. When he let go of Frank's shirt, Frank staggered backward down the steps into the dust at the bottom. A horse nearby snorted nervously and shifted sideways.

"Get on your mule and get out of here! I don't ever want to see your face around here again." Trahern turned his back and reached for the doorknob.

Frank scrambled to his feet and headed back up the stairs. He wasn't leaving without finding out what he had come to learn. He grabbed Trahern's arm and pulled him around. "Is she all right? Has she spoken? What did she say?"

Trahern's mask of civility was more fragile than Frank had suspected. Pressed for answers, he exploded. "Hell, no, she's not all right! My baby's been brutalized by some fiend and she . . . she's lost her mind!"

Frank stood stunned. "What do you mean?"

"I mean she doesn't remember a thing! She smiles and smiles like nothing happened, like everything's fine. With one eye so swollen she can't even see, and her mouth so tender it hurts when she talks. She wants to know what I got her for her birthday, and whether I think everyone will show up for her party. It's like yesterday never happened!"

Merielle's father was staring right at Frank, but he wasn't seeing him. Frank knew that when Trahern came to his senses he would be sorry he had spoken. Frank backed away, then ran. He mounted the mule and kicked him hard into a trot. He knew now what he had come to find out.

A month or so after the rape, Merielle started showing up in town, always with her father. She seemed perfectly fine. She smiled and laughed and conversed normally. Frank found a way to cross her path one day and said hello, but it was clear she had no recollection of him or of what they had been to each other. It was all gone. Wiped clean.

Frank had been devastated. He hadn't stopped loving Merielle, hadn't stopped wanting to touch her. But when he looked into her eyes, no hint of the budding woman he had loved could be found. That horror was compounded when it became apparent that Merielle was trapped in time, caught as the young girl she had been when she was violated.

It was nearly a year later, when Frank turned sixteen, that he made up his mind to work for Jefferson Trahern. He worried what Ethan would think of him—working for a man who hated his friend and wanted him dead.

But Frank felt sure Ethan would understand why he had to do whatever was necessary to be close to Merielle. The way things stood, he rarely got to see her. At least if he worked on her father's ranch, he would get a glimpse of her now and then. Only, Frank wasn't at all sure that Trahern would hire him.

When he presented himself once again at the front door to Merielle's home, his heart was pounding in his chest. He couldn't have been more surprised when Merielle herself answered his knock.

"Hello," she said. "Don't I know you?"

For an instant he thought she remembered who he was. Her next words made it clear she didn't. "We met in town, I think." Her brow furrowed. "I don't remember your name."

"Frank Meade," he said.

"Yes, that's right. Come in, Frank."

Frank looked around for someone to stop him. There wasn't anybody, so he stepped inside. Trahern's wealth was even more evident on the inside than the outside.

The house had the standard dogtrot entrance typical in most Texas homes, with a hall down the center and doors leading off to rooms on either side. But there all resemblance to the hovel in which Frank lived ceased.

The walls were paneled with walnut and a chandelier graced the entryway. He saw bits of china and pewter in the dining room on the right. Merielle led him to a parlor on the left where lush green velvet curtains framed the windows. A mahogany piano stood in one corner, with a piece of music on the stand. He wondered if Merielle still played. She had hated her lessons before—

He forced himself to focus again on the room. Two settees faced each other separated by a plush Oriental carpet. One wall held shelves full of leather-bound books. A comfortable reading chair was close by. His jaw dropped when he caught sight of the elaborately carved marble fireplace. It was covered with half-dressed cherubs.

He self-consciously brushed off his trousers before he lowered himself gingerly onto the shiny brocade that covered one of the settees. To his amazement, Merielle sat down right beside him.

"Now, Frank," she began. "Tell me all about yourself."

It had been the strangest conversation of his life. He told her things he had never told her before. He didn't know how long he had been sitting there when Trahern entered the room. When he spotted Frank, the man had murder in his eyes.

Frank stood instantly, looked for the way out, and saw that Trahern had it blocked. Since he couldn't flee, he prepared himself to fight.

Only, Merielle took the fight right out of her father when she said, "Frank has come to ask you for a job, Father. You will give him one, won't you? Frank could hitch up my buggy and drive me to town, and then you wouldn't always have to stop what you're doing to worry about me. And Frank knows all about cattle. Don't you, Frank?"

The two men were helpless to deny her what she wanted. They both loved her more than their own lives. So Trahern agreed to hire Frank. Oh, he watched him like a hawk. But he hired him. In return, Frank had worked hard to make Trahern respect him. And he had spent every spare moment he could with Merielle. Loving her.

But he had never spoken of the past.

Only, now that Ethan had put the thought in his head, Frank couldn't wait to get Merielle alone to talk to her about what had happened all those years ago. He was terrified, because he had found something he thought he had lost.

Hope.

Frank was working in the barn, forking hay into a stall when Merielle suddenly appeared.

"Father and I are going to town. Would you hitch up the buggy for us?"

Frank leaned the pitchfork against the side of the empty stall. "Sure." He pulled a bandanna from his pocket and swiped at his face.

"You missed a spot." Merielle took the bandanna from him and rose up on tiptoes to dab at a spot on his temple. "There. That's better."

When she offered the bandanna back to him, Frank caught her hand in his. "Merielle, there's something I've been wanting to ask you."

She looked guilelessly up at him. "What, Frank?"

Frank opened his mouth and closed it again. "Let's go up into the loft and talk there." Maybe if they were back in the loft together, it would help spark some memory of the past.

Merielle looked uncertainly up the ladder.

"Don't be afraid," Frank said. "I'll make sure you don't fall."

It was a sign of how much time they had spent together, and of how much she trusted him, that Merielle climbed right up the ladder. Once they were at the top, she headed immediately for the open loft door.

"Oh, you can see everything from here," she said as she gazed out over the rolling prairie.

Frank came up behind her and put his hands on her shoulders. It was the first time he had touched more than her hand in seventeen years. His hands were trembling, but she didn't seem to notice.

Merielle looked over her shoulder at him and smiled.

Encouraged by her lack of fear, he said, "You and I were up in this loft together once before. Do you remember?"

Her brow furrowed. He felt her shoulders tense. She shook her head. "No."

He turned her around so she faced him. "It was the day before your thirteenth birthday." Frank's heart was pounding so hard it felt like he had been running. It was hard to breathe. He felt panic building, but he fought it back.

"When we were here the last time, we kissed each other," he said. "We did?"

"We promised to meet the next day, so we could kiss some more."

Her eyes were a dark chocolate brown. He had lost himself in them more than once, years ago. Now they looked wary.

"I don't think I've ever been kissed," she said.

"Oh, but you have. I've kissed you myself. Would you like me to show you how it's done?"

He was holding her hands, waiting for her to pull away. Instead, she lifted her face to his and said, "All right, Frank."

He kissed her. It was the barest touch of lips.

When he lifted his head, she was staring at him strangely. She pulled one hand free and touched her lips in wonder.

Remember! he willed her. *Remember what we had together.*

"I . . ." She put her hand to her forehead as though she were dizzy, then looked up at him as though she had never seen him before. "Would you kiss me again?"

His heart thundered. He lowered his head and pressed his mouth to hers. She made a small sound in her throat, but when he would have ended the kiss, she put a hand on his shoulder to hold him there. He slid his arms around her and pulled her close.

This moment was all his dreams come true. She was in his arms kissing him again, and he was kissing her. He thought he would go crazy when her body arched instinctively toward his.

The instant she came in contact with the hard length of him, she wrenched herself free. He sought her eyes. Instead of the wonder and delight of the past, he found terror and confusion.

"Don't kiss me anymore, Frank. It . . . it scares me. I feel . . . strange inside."

He reached out to her, and she shrank from him.

"It's all right, Merielle," he said. "I just want to hold you."

"You won't . . . you won't hurt me, will you, Frank?"

"Oh, God, no, Merielle," he said, horrified that she could even think such a thing.

She threw herself into his embrace. "You're my best friend, Frank," she said, her cheek pressed against his chest. "Please don't be mad at me."

He slid his hand down her silky hair again and again in a gesture of comfort that brought back the most painful of happy memories. "I'm not mad," he murmured against her temple.

"You won't kiss me again, will you? I didn't like it."

"I promise I won't kiss you again."

Now he knew why he had never spoken with Merielle about that long-ago day. Because before there had always been hope. Hope that she would somehow cast off the childlike demeanor that had protected her from the awful truth and be ready for a life with him as the woman she had become. Now there was nothing to look forward to except endless unfulfilled longing.

"Hey, Frank! You got that buggy hitched up yet?" Trahern called from the front porch of the house.

"Not yet," Frank called back.

"Get a move on! I'm late for a meeting with the sheriff."

Frank grabbed Merielle's hand and headed for the ladder down out of the loft. He went first and she followed quickly after him. He had reached the floor of the barn by the time Trahern barked, "Is Merielle out there?"

"She's here," Frank called back.

"Send her on into the house. I want to talk to her before we leave."

Merielle started for the barn door, but Frank caught her hand to stop her. She kept her back to him and said, "Father wants me. I have to go."

Frank could hear the fear in her voice. He tried to turn her around so he could look at her, but she resisted him.

"No—" She was almost frantic to get away from him.

But he was stronger. When he finally got her turned around, she burst into tears. He drew her into his arms and held her close.

"It's all right, Merielle. It's only me. It's Frank."

"I'm sorry, Frank. I don't know why I got so scared," she confessed.

But he knew.

He could feel her shuddering. "Shhh," he soothed. "I'm not going to hurt you. No one's ever going to hurt you again."

"I . . . I . . . my head hurts," she said. "I think there's something I should remember, but when I try, it hurts!"

"Then don't try," he said in a quiet voice.

Frank cupped Merielle's face in one hand and caressed her damp cheek with the pad of his thumb. "Smile for me," he said in a gentle voice.

Merielle managed a wobbly smile. "I'll always smile for you, Frank."

He turned her toward the barn door. "Go on, now. And tell your father I'll be there in a minute."

The instant she was gone, Frank let out the sob that had been building in his chest. He brushed his eyes roughly with the sleeve of his shirt and tried to get hold of himself. It wasn't the end of the world. She considered him her friend. She smiled for him. He could still love her.

Only not as a woman.

His throat felt raw, swollen so thick it hurt. "God! Do something! Help me!" he pleaded in a raspy voice. "I don't know how long I can keep on seeing her every day, wanting her, and knowing I can never have her."

There was no answering voice. Because he was living in hell. There was no God here.

❧7❧

PATCH PAUSED ONE STEP beyond the shadowed alley and squinted her eyes against the brilliant sunlight. Ethan was more careful. He stopped and stared out into the sunlight from the safety of the alley until his eyes had adjusted to the differing light. He couldn't afford to be blinded even for a second. A bullet was faster than chain lightning with a link snapped.

When Ethan stood at her side, Patch said, "I have to make a stop at the post office first and mail a letter to my family. Why don't you go ahead to the sheriff's office, and I'll meet you there."

"I'm not sure I should let you out of my sight," Ethan replied with a wry smile. "I might not see you again till suppertime."

Patch wrinkled her nose at him. "I'm only going across the street."

"All right. But don't be long." Ethan studied the main street of town with narrowed eyes. "And watch your step."

"I'll be fine," Patch assured him. "You're the one who needs to be careful." She let her gaze follow the same path as his. "Do you really think there's someone waiting out there to shoot you?"

"Crowd the fence and someone's liable to boost you over."

Patch waited for the dust to settle after a wagon loaded with farm tools passed, then began her trek across the rutted dirt road. When she arrived on the other side, she looked for Ethan over her shoulder, but all she saw was the door to the sheriff's office closing.

She walked briskly into the Oakville Mercantile, intending to drop off her letter and leave. After all, she had promised Ethan she would join him as soon as she could. She fully intended to keep that promise. Of course, that was before she ran into Merielle Trahern.

Merielle wasn't alone. Frank was with her. Patch was dying to ask whether Frank had found an opportunity to speak with Merielle about the past, and what the results of that talk might have been.

Merielle hadn't seen her yet, so Patch mouthed to Frank, *Have you talked to her?*

Frank mouthed back, *Yes.*

Does she remember anything?

Frank shook his head once, twice. *No.*

Before Patch had time to register the disappointment she felt, Merielle spied her.

"Patch! My friend, Patch!" Merielle's face was wreathed in a smile of delight. "Where have you been? I wanted to invite you to come to my house, but I didn't know how to find you."

Patch accepted Merielle's embrace and hugged her back. "I'm staying with a friend of mine, and yours too, once upon a time— Ethan Hawk."

Patch ignored the frown Frank aimed at her for bringing up Ethan's name. She was too busy searching Merielle's face for any sign of recognition.

Merielle's pretty brow furrowed. "Ethan Hawk? Do I know him?" She placed a gloved fingertip to her temple.

"Is something wrong?" Patch asked.

"I . . . My head hurts."

Because she's trying to remember, Patch thought. But why did remembering hurt? Obviously, the events of that day were simply too horrible to contemplate. Or maybe it was more than that. What if it had been someone close to Merielle who had violated her trust? Like Frank.

Or Ethan.

Patch shoved that second thought aside. She wouldn't believe that Ethan was capable of such a heinous crime. It occurred to Patch that if it hurt Merielle to try to remember, *the memories were there*!

Obviously, Frank was too protective of Merielle—or worried about the answers she might give—to force her to recall the past. Patch wasn't. Somehow, she had to find a way to be alone with Merielle, to provoke the girl's memory, to force her to confront what had happened and *remember*.

Frank loomed over Merielle's shoulder. "We'd better be leaving now. Your pa—"

Merielle shook her head and stood her ground. "I don't want to leave. I want to talk to Patch."

To Patch's surprise, Mr. Felber appeared at Merielle's other shoulder. "Jefferson Trahern wouldn't take it kindly if you upset his daughter," he warned Patch.

"Patch is my friend," Merielle said to Mr. Felber. "She's coming to my house for supper."

"Miz Kendrick probably has other plans," Frank said. His message to Patch was clear: *Don't come.*

"I'm not doing anything that would keep me from joining Merielle for supper," Patch countered with a beatific smile at Frank.

Frank's lips pressed flat in disapproval. For some reason, Mr. Felber didn't look too happy, either.

"When can you come?" Merielle asked.

"When would you like me to come?"

"Today."

"Your father might have other plans," Frank cautioned Merielle.

"He won't mind if I invite Patch. Do you, Father?"

Patch turned and saw that Jefferson Trahern had entered the store. Her first impressions were of power and pride. He was a big man, both broad and tall, with collar-length white hair and a neatly trimmed salt and pepper mustache. He was wearing a black broadcloth suit with a brocade vest that hid a slight paunch at his waist and a string tie that emphasized the sagging flesh at his throat.

This was the Jefferson Trahern she had imagined, a man who wouldn't hesitate to crush his enemy. This man was easy to hate.

Her second impressions were no less distinct, but gave her a contrary image of Trahern which made her uneasy. Lines of pain and bitterness pinched his nose and bracketed his mouth. When his gaze alighted on his daughter, his dark brown eyes bore a look so sad they made Patch want to weep.

But it would be a cold day in hell before she wept for Jefferson Trahern. This was the man who had hounded Ethan Hawk to hell and back. Trahern had made sure Ethan spent the better part of his youth in prison. Trahern wanted Ethan Hawk dead.

Patch curled her clawed fingers into daintily gloved fists that she kept hidden in her skirt. She wasn't about to let Trahern know what she really thought of him. The smile on her face as she turned to greet Merielle's father was so warm it would have melted butter.

"Why, hello," she said. "I don't believe we've met, Mr. Trahern. I'm Patricia Kendrick."

Trahern tipped his flat-crowned hat. "Nice to make your acquaintance, Miss Kendrick. Merielle has told me about you."

Patch was surprised. "She did?"

Trahern gave Patch a look up and down. She was careful to keep her eyes lowered demurely, to look as mild-mannered and gently bred as she possibly could.

Merielle hurried over to her father and looped her arm through his. "Father, I've invited Patch to supper tonight. You don't mind if she comes, do you?"

Trahern pursed his lips thoughtfully. "I suppose it would be all right."

Merielle stood on her toes and tugged on her father's arm so he knew to bend down for her kiss on his cheek. "Thank you, Father."

Merielle turned to Patch, her face beaming. "See, I told you he wouldn't mind."

"Are you sure it won't be any trouble?" Patch asked Trahern.

"If my daughter wants you to come to supper, you'll come."

Trahern's statement sounded more like an order than an invitation. Patch bit back a scathing retort, told her neck hairs to settle down, and nodded her acquiescence. "What time?" she asked.

"We eat after the sun sets."

"I'll be there," Patch said. "Now, if you'll excuse me, I have another appointment." She swept past Trahern, dropped her letter on the counter for Mr. Felber to send off in the next day's mail, and left the mercantile with her chin up and her shoulders squared.

Once outside, Patch crossed beyond the window out of sight, then quickly backed up against the wooden wall of the building. She took several deep breaths. She unballed her fists and realized her hands were trembling.

Patch knew it was unreasonable to despise Jefferson Trahern. He had lost his beautiful daughter on the same day his only son was killed. His grief must have been awful, overwhelming. She couldn't blame him for wanting justice. She probably would have applauded his efforts, if only he weren't stalking the man she loved. But Jefferson Trahern had to be stopped. And the best way to do that was to find out the truth.

"Miss Kendrick?"

Patch whirled at the sound of Trahern's voice. *Think of the devil, and he lands on your doorstep.*

"Are you all right?"

"You surprised me." Patch put a hand on her heart as though she could slow it down from the outside.

"I wanted a chance to talk to you privately."

"We're alone now." Patch had no intention of going anywhere with Jefferson Trahern.

Trahern looked around him. There was no one coming along the boardwalk in either direction. They stood in the shade of a live oak, so the heat wasn't unbearable. "All right. I can say what I have to say here. I want to know what your relationship is to Ethan Hawk. I want to know why you're staying at the Double Diamond. And I want to know why you've befriended my daughter."

That was plain speaking.

Patch started with the last question, because it was the easiest to answer. "I didn't choose to befriend Merielle, she chose me. I know she isn't . . . quite right. But I think she needs a friend, and I can be that to her.

"I'm staying at the Double Diamond because Mrs. Hawk is ill, and she needs someone to do the cooking and cleaning and to keep an eye on her young daughter."

Patch avoided answering the most difficult question directly. "I know you've sworn vengeance on Ethan Hawk, that you blame him for everything bad that's happened to your children. But I believe you've wronged him. Someday, soon, I hope to prove that to you."

"I plan to see Ethan Hawk dead and buried if it's the last thing I do," Trahern said. "If you know what's good for you, you'll keep your distance from him."

"I won't leave Mrs. Hawk to manage alone," Patch said.

"Suit yourself."

He started across the street, and Patch hurried to catch up with him. "Am I still invited for supper?"

He paused in the middle of the street, and such was his presence that he stopped a dray full of lumber coming one way and a load of cotton coming from the other. "I won't deny my daughter anything she wants. If you wish to come, Miss Kendrick, you're welcome."

He left her standing there, and she was lucky not to be run over when the two wagons swung back into motion. It wasn't until she reached the sidewalk that she realized Trahern's destination.

He was opening the door to the sheriff's office.

Patch experienced a terrifying moment when she imagined what would happen when Jefferson Trahern and Ethan Hawk met face-to-face with only Careless Lachlan to referee. She was frozen in a state of helpless panic. There was no way she could get there in time to prevent what was going to happen.

She was so focused on the door to the sheriff's office that she never saw Ethan until he was beside her.

"What are you doing here? I thought . . ." Her face seesawed from Ethan to the sheriff's office and back.

"Shall we stroll this way?" Ethan placed her arm through his and headed down the boardwalk away from the jail.

"Ethan, what—"

"Later," he said. "I think it's time we headed for home."

———————

Careless Lachlan never looked up from his plate when he heard the front door open and shut. Damn that Ethan Hawk, stirring up trouble, keeping a man from his dinner. It was plumb loco to open up an investigation of a crime committed seventeen years ago. He had told Ethan everything he knew. Which was nothing. What did the damned man want from him now? "What the hell're you doin' back here—"

Careless glanced up to see Jefferson Trahern standing in front of him. The forkful of food he had just shoveled into his mouth came spewing back out. He bobbed to his feet, grabbed the red-checkered cloth tucked under his chin, and swiped at the mashed potatoes on his chin and scattered in clumps across his desk.

Trahern retrieved the gold pocket watch from his vest pocket, extended it the length of the gold chain that held it there, snapped it open, checked the time, and snapped it closed again. "It's exactly one o'clock. Did we, or did we not, have an appointment today?"

Careless stood there looking like a fool and feeling like a jackass. "We did. Have a seat, Mr. Trahern." Careless gestured toward the nearest chair, but it was piled high with posters and flyers. He gestured to another that held a frayed Montgomery Ward catalog. In fact, there wasn't any surface in the room that wasn't covered with something.

"Why don't you clean this place up?" Trahern asked in an irritated voice. "Sheriff of a town ought to be a little neater, don't you think?"

Careless wasn't sure whether that was a warning or a threat. It felt like both. Careless swallowed down his feelings of annoyance. He was the same man now that he had been twenty years ago when Trahern had gotten him hired by the town council. He had felt then as he felt now. Cleaning was a waste of time. Things just got messed up again.

But he served as sheriff of Oakville only so long as it pleased Jefferson Trahern for him to do so. At fifty-four, Careless Lachlan didn't feel like pulling up stakes and moving on. When Trahern said jump, Careless got to hopping like a bunch of tree frogs. "I'll get someone in here to straighten up," he mumbled.

Careless hurried around his desk and shoved a pile of flyers and posters onto the floor from the seat of a ladderback chair. "You can sit here."

Trahern took one look at the uncomfortable chair and said, "I think I'll stand. This won't take long."

Careless felt uncomfortable standing face-to-face with Trahern. But he didn't know any way to retreat behind his desk except by turning his back on the other man. No one with sense and a wish for survival turned his back on Jefferson Trahern.

"Uh . . . what can I do for you, Mr. Trahern?" Careless asked. "You ain't come about that idea of Hawk's, have you? I mean, 'vestigatin' what happened seventeen years ago—that's crazy, right?"

"I have no idea what you're talking about," Trahern said. "Who's investigating what?"

Careless wished he had kept his mouth shut, because it felt damned uncomfortable now that he had his foot in it. He pulled at the hairs on his chin. "Uh . . . ain't you heard?"

"Heard what? Spit it out, Careless. I haven't got all day."

"Had a visit from Hawk. He wanted to know everythin' I 'membered 'bout the 'vestigation of your daughter's ra— 'Bout what happened that day when Miss Trahern got . . ." Careless didn't dare get any more specific because every time he tried, Trahern's face tightened up. Finally, he said, "Anyway, Hawk wants to know what I found out in my 'vestigation."

"What did you tell him?"

"That there weren't no 'vestigation, 'cause we knew who done it."

"What did he say to that?"

"Said we was mistaken. Said he didn't do it. Said the real culprit has been runnin' free all these years. He means to find the man who done it and bring him to justice."

"He won't have to look any farther than his own mirror," Trahern said. "Ruthless son of a bitch."

Careless scratched nervously at his crotch. He caught Trahern's disgusted look and left off what he was doing.

"There isn't anyone else it could be," Trahern muttered.

"Hawk said there's whole bunches of suspects."

"Who?" Trahern demanded.

"Everybody who showed up to your daughter's party. Hawk said it coulda been any one of 'em."

Trahern quickly went through a mental list of everyone who had been invited to Merielle's birthday party. It was a long one because he had just finished his year of mourning for Merielle's mother, who had died unexpectedly of pneumonia the previous winter. He had wanted his daughter to have the kind of shindig her mother had always given. He had asked half the businessmen in town to come, along with everyone in the cattlemen's association. Dorne had invited some of his friends, as well.

But none of them had been anywhere near Merielle when she was found. Ethan had.

There was only one reason why Hawk was raising doubts now about what had happened. He wanted to stop Trahern from hounding him, and he hoped to get public sympathy on his side. By God, that wasn't going to happen!

Every morning when he faced his daughter across the breakfast table, Trahern was reminded of Ethan Hawk's crime. He hadn't been able, even with all his wealth, to undo the damage Ethan had done.

Once, a long time ago, he had brought in some doctors from back East to see if they could help Merielle recover her memory. But their attempts only made her hysterical. For several days afterward she didn't speak at all. He was afraid of losing her completely, so he had sent the doctors back where they came from. He had loved the child she was, and mourned the woman she would never become.

It had cost a fortune to hunt Ethan down. He had frothed at the mouth when a jury sentenced Ethan to a mere seven years in prison instead of hanging him for Dorne's murder. And he had nearly gone mad when they insisted there was insufficient evidence to convict him of Merielle's rape.

It was during the years Ethan spent in prison that Trahern realized the law wasn't going to give him the justice he craved. Of course he couldn't be blatant about taking the law into his own hands, because the town was willing to concede that Ethan had paid his debt in prison. Trahern had to exercise discretion in order to avoid causing trouble for himself.

Ordinarily, he would have ordered his foreman to make whatever arrangements were necessary to solve the problem. But his foreman, Frank Meade, had been Ethan's friend. He didn't trust Frank to look to his boss's interests where Ethan was concerned.

So Trahern had left Frank out of it. To distance himself, he had asked Careless Lachlan to take care of hiring someone to kill Ethan Hawk when he got out of prison. To his chagrin, Ethan had easily dealt with the first bunch of hired guns Careless had found. This time, however, Trahern was bringing in the best. He wanted this business finished once and for all.

His hate for Ethan Hawk had been a boil on his neck for seventeen years, chafing under his collar, the swelling less some days and worse on others. He wanted it cut out.

"Have you contacted that gunman in Wichita?" Trahern asked the sheriff.

Careless had been surreptitiously shifting himself, trying to get comfortable inside his trousers. He hadn't yet succeeded, and his agitation came out in his answer. "It ain't that easy hirin' killers when you're the sheriff!"

"That problem can easily be remedied," Trahern said in a menacing voice.

Careless realized he had crossed the line and mentally stepped back. "Ain't gonna get rid of Ethan Hawk with no hired gun. He's too fast," he said sullenly.

"We'll see. Calloway has a reputation of his own. Now, are you going to take care of it, or do we need a new sheriff in Oakville?"

Careless felt like a pony with his bridle off. He didn't know which way to go, what to do. This had been a good job for a long time. He had done a few favors for Jefferson Trahern over the years, especially when Dorne was alive. Overlooking the boy's pranks in town that resulted in broken windows and damaged property. Calming down Horace Felber when Dorne roughed up Chester. Warning off the father of a sodbuster girl Dorne had made advances to.

He had manipulated the law for Trahern, too. Moving off some drifters who had settled on land that didn't belong to the Tumbling T, but which Trahern used to graze his cattle. Refusing to help Alexander Hawk when masked riders began rustling his cattle. Railroading Ethan Hawk into prison.

He'd had his doubts at the time about whether Ethan was guilty, but he had lacked the guts to face down Jefferson Trahern. Things hadn't changed much in seventeen years. Careless wasn't proud of himself, but he had to live somehow. And this was all he knew.

He faced Trahern with his head hanging like a panting tongue. "I'll take care of it."

"How long before you think he'll get here?"

"I ain't got no control of that," Careless said. "He'll be here when he gets here."

"Just make sure he does the job," Trahern said. "Or you can say good-bye to yours."

Trahern whirled on a booted heel and left Careless standing there.

When the door slammed behind the big man, Careless heaved a sigh so big you could feel the draft.

"Hell," he muttered. "Way things are goin', looks like I might have to shoot Ethan Hawk myself."

❋8❋

ETHAN TIED HIS HORSE to the back of the wagon Patch had brought to town, helped her up onto the wooden seat, then stepped up and across her and seated himself. He grabbed the reins, gave the team a slap, and headed the wagon out of town.

Patch scooted as close to Ethan as she could and threaded her arm through his. "What did the sheriff say?"

"That I'm wasting my time. There never was any investigation, so he doesn't have any information to share with me."

"Did you tell him you plan to do your own investigation?"

Ethan smiled wryly. "He wasn't impressed."

Ethan looked at the spot where Patch's thigh rested against his. The feel of her flesh pressed up close to his was giving him ideas he had no business having. He sidled his leg away, but to his dismay, hers followed.

Ethan glanced at Patch from the corner of his eye. She smiled at him, the soul of innocence. She couldn't know what she was doing to him, he decided, and it would only embarrass them both if he said anything. He gritted his back teeth and tried to ignore his body's response to her nearness.

"I thought surely Trahern was going to catch you in the sheriff's office," Patch said.

"I saw him coming and slipped out the back." Ethan eyed her keenly. "It looked like the two of you were having a discussion. What was that all about?"

"You'll never guess what happened!"

"Knowing you, probably not," Ethan said with a wry twist of his mouth.

Patch playfully hugged his arm tight against her. Ethan felt the weight of her left breast against his arm. He glanced sharply at her, but she seemed oblivious to what she had done.

"It's something wonderful, actually," Patch said. "I got invited to supper by Merielle Trahern."

"You what! Are you out of your mind?" Ethan yanked the team to a quick halt. He set the brake and wrapped the reins around it to leave his hands free to shake the daylights out of Patch. Only she had clutched his arm and was holding on for dear life.

"Give me a chance to explain!"

He grabbed her jaw with his free hand, tipped her chin up, and said, "This had better be good."

"Don't you see? Merielle is the key to everything. What if she could remember what happened? What if she could name the man who attacked her? Trahern would have to leave you alone."

"What does all that have to do with going to dinner at Trahern's place?"

"Merielle likes me, Ethan. I think she might learn to trust me. Maybe I could get her to talk about the past."

"I thought Frank was going to do that."

"Did I happen to mention that I saw Frank with Merielle at the mercantile?

"No, you didn't."

"Well, Frank was there. He already tried talking to Merielle, but she didn't remember anything."

Patch slipped her free hand up to play with the dark curls at Ethan's collar. He shuddered as her gloved finger slid across his nape. He grabbed her wrist and dragged her hand down. His eyes narrowed. That sort of behavior was damned provocative. The lady had to know what she was doing to him.

Patch smiled nonchalantly up at him and continued, "So you see, I have to go to Merielle's house for dinner."

"No, I don't see that at all. I've told you how Trahern feels about me. I don't want you getting caught in the middle."

"Trahern knows I'm staying at the Double Diamond, Ethan. He said if Merielle wants me for a friend, he won't stand in her way. Actually, once he found out Merielle liked me, he practically ordered me to come."

Patch traced the corded muscle that stood out on the back of Ethan's hand. "This is a chance we can't afford to pass up. If Merielle ever gets her memory back—"

"You're shooting at stars, Patch. The chances of Merielle being like she was are slim to none."

"I'll take that chance," Patch retorted.

"I don't want you to go."

"I'm going."

Her chin jutted mulishly, her blue eyes flashed. Her breathing picked up so her breasts rose and fell practically under his nose. Ethan found her absolutely beautiful. Utterly desirable. *Almost* irresistible.

He carefully separated himself from Patch, picked up the reins, and headed the team homeward again. "We'll talk about this later."

"I won't change my mind."

"We'll see."

The team had barely started moving when Patch cried, "Stop the wagon!"

Ethan jerked the team to a halt. The wagon was still rolling when she leapt down from the seat and headed off in the direction of a patch of sagebrush. Ethan wrapped the reins around the brake and raced after her.

"What's the matter?" he yelled as he ran. "Where the hell do you think you're going?"

By the time he caught up to her, Patch had already dropped to the ground in the brush beside a small doe that was trying unsuccessfully to get back on her feet.

"Stay away!" Ethan warned. "Those flailing hooves could slice you to ribbons."

He noticed that Patch was on her knees in the dirt—totally unmindful of the costly red velvet dress she was wearing. Here was the reckless hoyden he remembered from the days in Montana. Careless, carefree, with a heart as big as the sky. Only his hoyden had grown into a woman, the sight of whom left his throat dry and his heart pounding.

"Relax, dearie. Everything's going to be all right," Patch crooned to the wounded animal.

"*Dearie?*" Ethan rolled his eyes.

"Shut up, Ethan, you're scaring her," Patch said in a cooing voice for the benefit of the anxious deer. "She's going to need some help. She's been shot in the leg."

"By someone who expected to have venison for supper," Ethan

replied. "Let me finish the job, and we'll be the ones with fresh meat on the dinner table."

He already had his Colt out when Patch turned on him like an avenging fury. "How could you even *think* of killing this poor, defenseless creature?"

"I like venison steak."

"Ethan Hawk! Are you going to help me get this deer into the wagon, or not?"

"I will, but only because I figure it'll die anyway, and I'll get my steak sooner or later."

Patch glared at him. "You didn't used to be so uncaring of a wild animal forced to flee the hunter's gun."

His features hardened. "That's because, once upon a time, I used to be one myself."

While Patch crooned comfort to the deer, Ethan took off his shirt and draped it over the deer's eyes. Then he picked up the animal and put it in the back of the wagon. Instead of returning to her seat beside him, Patch clambered into the wagon bed.

"You're going to ruin that dress," Ethan warned.

"Garn!" Patch said, looking down at the dust-covered velvet, which now had a small tear in the hem where it had caught on the wagon when she jumped down. "I forgot all about it!"

Ethan gave her a quick kiss. He couldn't help it. She was such a delightful mixture of impatient child and caring woman, minx and starched-up lady. He quickly retreated to his seat on the wagon bench before he was tempted to do more.

Leah was standing on the porch with the Winchester in her hand when they arrived back at the ranch. "Where you been all day? Ma's been askin' for you."

It wasn't clear which of them Leah was speaking to, but both of them reacted to the urgency in Leah's voice.

Patch scrambled down before Ethan could come around the wagon to help her. "She's not any worse, is she?" Patch asked.

"I . . . I don't know," Leah answered.

Patch saw the worried look on the girl's face. She paused to say, "Ethan, put the deer in a stall in the barn, please. I'll get to it as soon as I can." Then she hurried inside to Nell.

"Deer?" Leah said, eyes wide.

Ethan pulled Patch's trunks, bags, and hatboxes off the wagon onto the porch. He barked orders to Leah about taking care of the team as he picked up the doe and hauled her into the barn. Then he followed Patch into the house.

He found Patch sitting on the side of the bed, brushing the damp hair from his mother's forehead.

"There, there, now," Patch was crooning. "You don't have to think about a thing except getting well."

He watched Patch massage his mother's temples.

"Does that feel better?" Patch asked.

Ethan stayed at the foot of the bed, afraid to come any closer. He could see his mother was worse. He couldn't lose her now. Not after everything she had been through to save the ranch for him. Leah needed her. He needed her.

Ethan wasn't aware of the sound of protest he made until Patch turned to look at him.

"Your mother's feeling poorly. She aches all over, and her stomach feels too upset for her to eat what Leah prepared. You sit with her, and I'll go make her some broth."

Patch relinquished her spot, but Ethan stood frozen by the foot of the bed.

Nell called to her son. "Ethan?"

Patch could almost see him bracing himself before he took the few steps to his mother. His eyes pleaded with her not to leave him alone. "I'll be back soon," she promised him.

His mother's eyes slid closed, and Ethan took advantage of the opportunity to look closely at her. He could see her veins through skin that was thin as ice on a Texas pond. Her right hand shook with palsy. Perspiration dotted her forehead and the narrow space beneath her nose. Her lips were dry and cracked. Her breathing was shallow. She was so motionless, he thought she must already have fallen asleep.

Ethan felt suddenly like that boy of fifteen who had been forced to flee his home, confused and alone and frightened of what the future held.

He sat down beside his mother and gently laid his head down on her breast, as though he were a boy again, come to her for solace. The scent of her was familiar, even after all these years. It must be the soap used to wash her nightgown.

He felt his throat squeeze up tight and swallowed over the lump there. When he felt her hand in his hair, he closed his eyes and let her comfort him.

She spoke to him in a voice that was barely a whisper. "During the awful time after Alex died, when you were still in prison, I was tempted to sell this place. Boyd would have given me a fair price. You'll never know how close I came to accepting his offer. But I thought of how much this ranch had meant to you and your father, and I couldn't do it. So I hung on. I wanted you to have a home to come to when you were free."

Nell's fingers tangled in Ethan's hair and stilled.

He put his hand atop hers on his head. "This place and you and Pa were all I thought about in prison," he admitted. "I . . . I think it would have killed me to come back and find it all gone."

"I'm dying, Ethan."

Ethan's nose burned. He closed his eyes against the sting of tears. "Ma, you . . . Ma." He couldn't speak past the pain in his throat.

"You have to leave this place!" she said in a fierce whisper. "I can't bear to wake up another morning wondering whether this will be the day Jefferson Trahern kills my son! Take Leah and Patch and go somewhere far away from here and start over. Please, Ethan. Promise me you'll leave!"

She was clutching at him. Crying. Sobbing.

Ethan sat up and lifted his mother into his arms to comfort her, as though their roles had suddenly changed, and he was now the adult and she the child. He rocked her back and forth, offering the only comfort he could give her.

"Did you know that Patch and I have started to investigate what happened all those years ago? We're going to find the real culprit, Ma. Then Jefferson Trahern can hound him instead of me. Don't worry, Ma. Everything will be all right. I can take care of myself. You just concentrate on getting well."

Fortunately for both of them, Patch arrived at the door, bearing a tray that held a bowl of broth and a glass of milk. Ethan settled his mother back against the pillows and carefully straightened the blankets under her arms. But he didn't look at her. He didn't think he could face the terror and pleading in her eyes. "You eat some soup, Ma, do you hear me?" He leaned over and kissed her on the cheek, then left the room as quickly as he could.

Patch caught a glimpse of the exhaustion and despair on his face before he got away. She had stood outside the door, holding the tray of food for Nell, not willing to intrude on Ethan and his mother. Her heart had gone out to him.

As a child, she had never seen Ethan's vulnerability, only his strength. Needing his mother and being able to comfort her in turn made him seem more human somehow. She saw him suddenly less like a god to be adored from afar. He could feel pain. He could suffer.

Until this moment, Patch hadn't realized how little she knew about the man she had idolized as a child. Only now did she see how much more there was to Ethan Hawk than the friend who had tickled her ribs and ruffled her hair when she was twelve years old.

Patch wished there were something more she could do to help Nell and Ethan. She didn't know how Ethan could stand to watch his mother die. It was killing Patch.

She sat down beside Nell without saying a word and began spooning broth into her mouth, a teaspoon at a time. To her surprise, Nell managed almost half the bowl before she turned her head away. Then Patch held the glass of milk while Nell drank a swallow or two.

Patch set the tray of dishes down on the table beside the bed long enough to be sure Nell was comfortably settled to sleep, then picked it up as she turned to leave the room.

"Patch?"

"Yes, Nell?"

"Take care of him for me. And Leah."

"I will. Rest, Nell. I'll see you in the morning."

"Send Leah to me, will you?"

"All right."

Patch found Leah in the kitchen with Ethan. "Your mother would like to see you." Patch saw the dread in Leah's eyes, but there wasn't much comfort she could give. Nell wasn't getting better. She was much, much worse.

Once Leah was gone, Patch confronted Ethan. "Isn't there something we can do? I feel so helpless!"

"Doc Carter says there's no medicine that will make her better. She has the same thing my father had. There isn't any treatment."

Uncomfortable with Ethan's prognosis, Patch busied herself collecting the things she needed to care for the wounded doe. "After I make a quick change of clothes, I'm going out to the barn to take care of Dearie," she said. "If you'd like, you can send Leah out to join me after she speaks with your mother."

"Thanks, Patch. I will."

Patch was on her knees in the hay when Leah's wide eyes appeared in a space between the slats of the stall.

"I could use some help," Patch said.

"What's wrong with her?" Leah asked as she slipped into the stall and squatted down beside Patch.

"Someone shot her in the leg."

"What are you going to do?"

"First I'm going to take out the bullet and bandage the wound. Then I'm going to take care of her until she's well. You can hold her head down and keep her busy at that end while I work on her leg. Make sure that blindfold stays tight over her eyes."

"All right." Leah reached out a hand to rub the doe's nose. "I've never seen a deer so close up before. I mean, one that wasn't dead."

The doe's nose twitched as she smelled Leah's hand.

"I think she likes me," Leah said with a flashing grin. The grin disappeared as she added, "Ethan will never let us keep her."

Patch noticed the "us" with satisfaction and said, "I'll take care of Ethan."

"You're braver than I am," Leah muttered. She rubbed the doe's coat, keeping her eyes downcast as she said, "Sometimes I don't think Ethan likes me."

Patch wiped the blood off her hands onto a towel she had brought with her and reached for Leah's chin. She tipped it up, forcing the girl to look her in the eyes. "Right now, you and Ethan are still getting to know one another. Love takes time to grow."

"Like a watermelon or a pumpkin?" Leah asked.

"Something like that," Patch replied with a laugh.

Love takes time to grow.

Patch couldn't remember a time when she hadn't loved Ethan. But it was becoming apparent that what she had felt as a child was a mere seedling that had been sprouting leaves and flowering vines since she had come to Texas.

Which made her wonder, as Leah had, about Ethan's feelings for her. She knew he desired her sexually, but beyond that she was as much in the dark as Leah was. It was not a comfortable feeling.

Patch finished what she was doing as quickly and as painlessly for the deer as she could. She left Leah in the barn making friends with Dearie while she headed back to the house. There were some chores she had to do before she left for her supper at the Trahern house.

She tipped most of Nell's leftover milk into a bowl for the calico cat, but saved some for Max. Ethan had made a small wooden-slatted cage for the mouse, which spent its days on the kitchen windowsill. Patch usually moved the cage inside to the counter beside the pump at night. She did so now and poured a small amount of milk into Max's dish.

"I didn't know mice drank milk," Ethan said.

Patch smiled. "I have to admit it's an experiment. I just thought he has as much right to it as the cat."

They both watched while Max sniffed at the bowl, lapped at it once, then stuck both front paws into the milk and began drinking in earnest.

Patch laughed. "I guess he likes it."

The calico cat came bounding over as Patch set the larger bowl of milk on the floor beside the stove. The cat was a lot more dainty—her paws didn't go into the bowl—but she lapped the milk with equal relish.

Patch took off the apron she had donned to fix Nell's supper and laid it over a kitchen chair. "Would you mind hitching up the buggy for me while I finish getting ready."

"I thought it was settled that you're not going."

"I thought it was settled that I am."

Ethan put his hands on his hips and glared at her.

She put her hands on her hips and glared back.

"Ethan, I'm not going to argue with you about this. You're not my father or my brother or . . . or my husband." *Yet.* "There's nothing you can say that will change my mind. So please, just tell me whether you're going to hitch my horse to the buggy, or whether I need to do it myself."

"I'll do it," Ethan said through tight jaws.

"Will you bring my trunks to Leah's room first?"

Ethan nodded abruptly and left the room.

Patch made sure she left something prepared in the kitchen for Leah and Ethan's supper, then headed for Leah's bedroom to change her clothes. Leah was there waiting, her hazel eyes wide with awe at the number of trunks and bags Ethan had brought inside.

"Are all these trunks filled with clothes?"

Patch laughed at the look of amazed reverence on Leah's face. "Mostly." She opened the trunk in which she had packed her wardrobe and sifted through things until she found a princess dress of slate blue silk and a white silk fringed shawl. In another bag she found a pair of riding boots made of kid, with patent leather tops. In a third, smaller bag she found a cameo pendant framed in gold. It had been a graduation gift from her father and stepmother.

"Ooooh." Leah's admiration of the gown was obvious. She reached out to touch the silk, realized her fingers were dirty, and drew back. "I've never seen the likes of that."

"It needs to be pressed before I can wear it. Do you think you can find your mother's iron?"

Leah was clearly reluctant to leave the room for any purpose.

"Go find the iron and wash your hands, and you can help me unpack a few of these things before I go."

Leah rushed to obey. When she returned, she said, "I put the iron on the stove to heat. It'll be ready in a minute."

"You can unpack that bag," Patch said, pointing to a faded carpetbag. "Most of those things can be put in the top drawer of the chest, the one you emptied for me to use."

Leah's eyes were bright with excitement. Most of the items she recognized for what they were, although she had never seen such fine quality. A pair of kid gloves. A muslin fichu. A fan of ivory, embroidered in black silk. And two bolts of cloth, one of dark green wool and another of mint green silk.

Leah fingered the silk lovingly.

Patch draped the silk across Leah's shoulder. She turned the girl to face the oval mirror standing in the corner. "You'd look lovely in a dress made of this silk. Maybe we can—"

Leah sidled away. "Wouldn't have no place to wear it."

Patch saw herself years ago, wishing and wanting till her teeth hurt for a fine silk dress, yet not daring to hope. She made a vow to herself that, whatever happened between her and Ethan, she would make sure Leah had a dress made of mint green silk before the girl got too much older.

Patch was keeping an eye on the sun. It was on its way down when she finished dressing. Before she left the bedroom, she donned a straw bonnet trimmed with blue silk ribbons. The envy in Leah's eyes when she stepped into the parlor was enough to convince Patch she looked fine, but she wanted Ethan's approval. Only he was nowhere to be found in the house.

There had been a day, a long time ago, when Patch had dressed up just for Ethan. It had made her heart soar when he looked her up and down and said, "You're going to be a beautiful woman someday, Patch. Take my word for it."

Patch wanted Ethan to look at her now and tell her she had become everything he desired, and more. More importantly, she wanted him to acknowledge her as a lady. Because back then, she had fallen far short of Ethan's standards for ladylike behavior. In fact, she had gotten into a fight and ruined the beautiful dress she had been wearing. Even now she could remember Ethan's words of comfort and counsel.

"It isn't what you wear that makes you a lady, Patch. It's how you handle yourself around other folks. It's more than manners—although you have to learn them. It's knowing you're entitled to respect, and respecting the rights of other people."

Patch had tried to grow into the kind of woman Ethan could admire. She had spent the past eight years trying to become his ideal. It hadn't been easy.

She hadn't minded giving up fighting. If she never got another black eye, it wouldn't break her heart. She hadn't minded giving up trousers. Too much. Although she still resorted to them when she needed to ride astride. She hadn't even minded learning manners. Having courteous, preplanned responses to every situation helped her immeasurably to maintain her self-control. Because she loved Ethan, she had always thought the sacrifices she had made were well worthwhile.

But she wanted Ethan to notice the changes. And he hadn't. Yet.

Patch pursed her lips, wondering why Ethan hadn't come back inside. It wasn't like him to sulk.

"Do you know where your brother is?" she asked Leah.

"He was out on the porch last time I saw him."

Patch stepped onto the front porch and closed the door behind her. It was that gorgeous soft pink and gray time between daylight and dark. Everything seemed to cast a longer shadow. Patch thought she saw something move beside the house. "Ethan?"

"I'm right here."

Patch whirled to face him. He had stepped onto the porch behind her. Her swinging skirt wrapped around her legs, holding her paralyzed for a moment.

"I'm ready to go," she said.

"You look beautiful." Ethan hadn't known he was going to say the words until they were already out. He walked in a circle around Patch. She stood perfectly still, but he could feel the sexual vibrations radiating from her. He wanted to pick her up and carry her off somewhere, to take his time undressing her and then bury himself deep inside her. He wanted to be as close to her as two human beings could be to each other. He stopped behind her and breathed in the scent of her, something sweet and soft, like she was.

"You can still change your mind," he murmured in her ear. "You can stay here with me."

It was all Patch's dreams come true. Ethan admired her. He wanted her. But the timing couldn't have been worse. "I have to go, Ethan. I won't stay late."

Rationally, Ethan knew why Patch was going to supper at Jefferson Trahern's house. But it was one more piece of straw in the load he had been collecting since he had gotten out of prison. Lately, it seemed like so much of what happened in his life was beyond his control. His mother dying. His persecution by Trahern. His desire for Patch Kendrick. It left him feeling riled and edgy. Loaded to the muzzle with tamped-down rage.

He stalked around her until he was looking her in the eye. "A real lady wouldn't be haring off into the dark all alone," he taunted.

Because he knew Patch so well, his barb stabbed her where she was most vulnerable. "A real lady would never get involved with an outlaw!" she shot back.

"A *rapist* outlaw!" Ethan hissed. "Watch yourself, Miss Kendrick. You never know when I might go crazy and attack you!"

Ethan snaked a hand around her waist and pulled her snug against him. Patch felt more anger than arousal, but Ethan was exhibiting equal measures of both.

Patch could see he was on the edge. She didn't want to push him over. "Let me go, Ethan."

"You came all this way to marry me. Are you saying you don't want me anymore?"

"Not this way!" she spat at him.

He released her as suddenly as he had taken her in his arms. They stood glaring at each other, panting.

"You know why I have to do this, Ethan. It isn't fair to blame me—"

"You're the same reckless brat you always were, Patch. Just dressed up in finer feathers," Ethan accused.

"Durn you for a long-eared—" Patch clapped her hand over her mouth. How had she allowed Ethan to provoke her into swearing at him? "I don't know who set a burr under your saddle," she said. "But I'm not going to hang around to get stomped. I'll be glad to discuss this further with you at another time, when you're calmer."

She tried to cross past him, her head held high, but he snagged her elbow and wrenched her back around.

"Don't walk away from me."

There was something in his voice when he spoke, a layer of need beneath the anger and arrogance, that kept Patch from struggling against his hold. "What do you want from me, Ethan?"

She shouldn't have asked, because he made short work of showing her exactly what he wanted. She was in his arms so fast it made her head spin. His mouth latched on to hers in a savage kiss, and his arms crushed her tight. His hand found her breast and kneaded it through the satin.

God help her, she did nothing to stop him.

No lady Patch knew would have allowed such liberties to a man who wasn't her husband. So maybe Ethan was right. Maybe she was the same shameless hoyden she had always been, dressed up in finer feathers. But she had always known that if it ever came to a choice between meeting Ethan's ideals for a lady, and being the woman in his arms, she would always choose the latter.

At the sound of a horse approaching, Ethan abruptly let her go and slipped back into the shadows closer to the house.

"Patricia? Is that you?"

Patch took a step closer to the edge of the porch. "Boyd? What a surprise! What brings you here?"

"I came to make sure you get to Trahern's place and back home safely," Boyd said as he stepped off his horse.

"Seems to me that's asking the fox to guard the chicken coop," Ethan said as he emerged from the shadows.

Boyd laughed. "You're just jealous."

"This is a very thoughtful gesture," Patch said, "but totally unnecessary. I don't want to take you out of your way."

"It's not out of my way." Boyd smiled, showing off his dimple. "You see, I've been invited to supper, too."

"You mean this wasn't Ethan's idea?" Patch asked, glancing at him from the corner of her eye.

"Hell, no, it wasn't my idea!" Ethan bit out.

Patch turned to Boyd for an explanation, which he quickly gave.

"When Trahern mentioned that Merielle had asked you to join her tonight, I volunteered myself to be your escort."

"Why, thank you, Boyd, I guess," Patch said.

"You don't mind, do you, Ethan?" Boyd asked his friend. "I promise to make sure Patricia gets home safe and sound."

Ethan leaned against the post that held the tin roof up over the porch. "No problem. I'm sure Patch—Patricia—will enjoy your company."

"Are you sure you don't mind, Ethan?" Patch asked.

"Why should I mind?" Ethan smiled, but there was no joy in it that Patch could see. He had his hands stuck in the back of his Levi's and his boots crossed at the ankle. It was a relaxed pose, but Patch could feel the hostility rolling off him in waves.

"Go on, Patch," Ethan said. "Boyd's waiting."

Patch turned and walked away from Ethan. It seemed safer for Boyd if she stepped down off the porch, rather than have Boyd come up to get her. When she reached Boyd's side, he put his arm around her shoulder. He made it seem like the most natural thing in the world. His touch was light, and Patch had the feeling that all she had to do was shrug the slightest bit and it would be gone. So she did nothing to make him remove it.

Boyd led her to the buggy Ethan had brought around to the front of the house and helped her step up to the seat.

"All right if I leave my horse here?" Boyd asked.

"I'll put him in the barn for you," Ethan said.

Once Patch was settled in the buggy, she met Ethan's eyes. They were fierce with emotions that changed from moment to moment. Anger, resentment, need, desire, then anger again.

"Good night, Ethan," she called to him as Boyd turned the buggy away from the house. She had the feeling she was leaving something important behind her. She looked back over her shoulder, wishing she were on the porch with him. Then Boyd said something to her, and she turned to answer him.

Ethan stood watching the buggy until it disappeared into the dark. He fought back the terrible jealousy he felt of his friend. Ethan had seen the look in Boyd's eyes when they followed Patch. It had taken all his restraint not to lay Boyd flat.

But Ethan had to stop thinking about his own wants and needs, and start thinking about Patch. She belonged with a man like Boyd. Boyd could give her all the fine things Ethan couldn't. Boyd would be good to her. If Jewell at the Silver Buckle was to be believed, Boyd was good with a woman in bed. If Boyd offered to marry Patch, she would have everything a woman could want in a husband. Except, that husband wouldn't be him.

He wondered when and how his feelings for Patch had changed. He certainly hadn't been aware of it happening. All he knew was that his need for Patch now didn't all reside behind the buttons of his jean's.

When Ethan turned to go back inside, he found Leah staring at him from the doorway. His heart leapt to his throat. *Ma.* "What is it, Leah? What's wrong."

"It's Calico. Her babies are crying, but she hasn't come to them. I've looked everywhere, but I can't find her."

Ethan's heart started beating normally again. From the distress on her face, Ethan had been afraid Leah was going to tell him their mother was dead. Instead, it was only a missing cat.

Ethan put a hand around Leah's shoulder to reassure her. He was amazed at how thin she was. He pulled her close against his hip. "Let's go look together. She can't have gotten far."

❀9❀

IN THE FIRST MOMENTS after they drove away from the ranch, when Patch realized she was all alone with a virtual stranger—a handsome, debonair man who had let it be known he found her attractive—she felt self-conscious. Boyd didn't allow that feeling to last long.

He relaxed forward with the reins in his hands, spread his knees wide, leaned his forearms on his thighs, stared straight ahead between the horse's ears, and said, "Do you know what my earliest recollection is of Ethan?"

As simply as that, Boyd relieved her discomfort, aroused her curiosity, and gained her complete attention. "What?"

"My pa was drifting around Texas looking for work, and we rode up to the Double Diamond, my pa sitting on this walleyed, goose-rumped, bandy-legged mare that couldn't chase a cow if her life depended on it, and me perched up there behind him, my legs spread wide over the croup of that old cayuse.

"This boy about my age was sitting cross-legged on the front steps of a shiny white house like he owned the place. He was petting a black and white spotted hound dog, and oh, how I envied him!"

"For the house, or for the dog?" Patch asked with a grin.

"Both. And for the parents he had sitting in rockers on the porch behind him. His pa was smoking a pipe, just watching the sun go down, and his ma was knitting something yellow.

"Ethan jumped up and trotted down the porch steps, that hound bitch right beside him. His ma warned him off—my pa wasn't much into shaving or baths, and we must've been a sorry-looking sight—but Ethan kept on coming. That's when his pa joined him.

"Didn't take me long to figure out that the reason Ethan hadn't been worried about coming down those steps to meet us was because he knew his father would be there to help him out if he got into trouble.

"Ethan's pa stood right next to Ethan, even put a hand on his shoulder. Ethan looked up. His pa looked down. Didn't say a word, either one of them. But I could see they were having a whole conversation."

Boyd shifted his head from side to side, playing first one role, then the other.

"*What do you think, son?*"

"I wanta meet that boy, Pa."

"*Don't look too respectable, son.*"

"But I need someone to play with, Pa."

"*We'll see, son. We'll see.*"

"Then the two of them turned to look at us, waiting to hear what my pa had to say."

Boyd slowed the buggy as they came to a particularly rutted section of the road. When they were past it, he flicked the reins and resumed his story.

"That's the picture of Ethan I carried with me when he was gone all those years, running from the law and in prison. Him and his pa standing there together, the two of them against the world. When I was a kid, I used to imagine myself in his place.

"Anyway, my pa asked for work, and Ethan's pa took another look at him and that pitiful excuse for a horse he was riding, and I could see he was going to turn him down.

"Ethan's pa was already making apologies when Ethan's ma interfered. She said sure they had some work for my pa and the two of us were welcome to bed down in a room in the barn."

Patch laid a hand on Boyd's arm. "Your father actually worked for Ethan's?"

Boyd nodded. "We stayed at the Double Diamond for three years. That was longer than my pa had ever been anyplace. You see, Mrs. Hawk took one look at me and saw a motherless waif who needed tending. She wasn't about to send me off alone with my drunken pa.

"During that time, Ethan and I became fast friends. We shared everything." Boyd smiled. "Or rather, he shared everything he had with me. I didn't have much of my own."

"Why did you leave?" Patch asked.

"Pa got drunk once too often and accidentally burned down the barn. We had no place to live anymore. But Ethan's pa made sure my pa got work, and Jefferson Trahern let us use a line shack on the edge of his property to live in. That's where I grew up."

"So Ethan's family and the Traherns really were friends before all this happened."

"Sure were. That one night changed all our lives."

"You've come a long way from being the boy you just described to me. And you don't strike me as being anything like your father. What made the difference?"

Boyd shrugged carelessly. "Funny how it all came about. I had an aunt who died and left me some money. I used it to buy a small place. Over the years, I've managed to make my nest egg grow."

"There's something I don't understand. If you're Ethan's friend, why did Trahern invite you to supper tonight?"

"Purely a business matter," Boyd said.

Because they had reached their destination, Patch didn't have a chance to pry further.

The instant Boyd stopped the buggy, Merielle came running out of the house to greet Patch. "I'm so glad you're here. I was afraid you wouldn't come!"

Patch was impressed anew with Merielle's beauty. She was dressed in an exquisite evening dress that showed off the woman she was. The short-sleeved gown was made of white tulle and trimmed with cloth zinnias of rich, bright colors along the square-necked bodice and in a trailing diagonal spray across the layered skirt. She wore a coronet of real zinnias around her upswept hair and a necklace of gold pendants set off her flawless skin.

The picture of a poised, confident young woman was not what it seemed. Merielle quickly stepped back as Boyd crossed past her on his way to Patch's side of the buggy. Patch realized she was seeing, for the first time, Merielle's reactions to a man she didn't know well. The young woman had plainly put some space between herself and the stranger.

Merielle waited until Patch had taken several steps away from Boyd before she approached and slipped her arm through Patch's. She ignored Boyd and urged Patch inside. "Come on in. Father's waiting for you in the parlor."

The way Merielle had greeted, or rather, *not* greeted Boyd made Patch wonder whether the girl had an aversion to all strange men, or just this one.

Was Boyd the one? He didn't have an alibi. He had known where Merielle would be. Merielle avoided him like the plague.

It couldn't be him.

Why not?

I like him.

Patch saw movement beyond the front porch and recognized Frank Meade standing in the shadows. He threw the stub of a cigarette down and ground it out with his boot. He met her gaze briefly before he turned and walked away toward the bunkhouse. Patch wondered what it must be like for him, always living on the fringes of Merielle's life. Awful, she decided. Just plain awful.

Patch was nervous about meeting Jefferson Trahern again, but hid her anxiety behind a smile. The big man rose as she entered the parlor with Merielle by her side. Boyd followed a few steps behind her.

"Good evening, Mr. Trahern," she said.

He nodded his head. "Miss Kendrick. Would you like some sherry?"

"No, thank you."

"Can I get you a drink, Boyd?"

"No, thanks. A cup of coffee would be welcome," Boyd replied.

Trahern walked to the parlor door and called, "Maria!"

A short, rotund Mexican woman appeared. *"Señor?"*

"Please bring a cup of coffee for the gentleman."

"Sí, señor."

"Make yourself comfortable, Miss Kendrick," Trahern said.

Patch couldn't help seeing the absurdity of the situation. Here she was being asked to sit down and engage in social chitchat with the man who had sworn to kill Ethan. She just couldn't do it. Fortunately, Merielle came to her rescue.

"Father, I'd like to show Patch my room. Would you excuse us for a little while?"

"I'll call you when supper's ready," Trahern said.

Boyd winked conspiratorially at Patch as she made her escape with Merielle, who walked a wide circle around him on her way out of the parlor.

Merielle took Patch's hand and started up the steep stairs in the central hallway. "My room is up here."

In Merielle's room, Patch saw further evidence that the thirty-year-old woman had been caught in a web of time. The room was filled with the playthings of a nine- or ten-year-old child. Merielle showed Patch her favorite rag doll.

"Her name is Emily," Merielle said. "I tell her everything." Merielle sat on the canopied bed and urged Patch onto the counterpane beside her.

Seated on the bed as they were, the two women were reflected in the gilt-framed mirror that hung above a copper-plated dry sink across the room. Patch wondered what Merielle saw when she looked at herself in the mirror. Did she see a woman with breasts and hips made for childbearing? Or did she see the child she was in her mind?

"What are you looking at, Patch?"

"Two lovely ladies."

"Lovely? Who?"

"Us, silly."

Merielle flopped onto her stomach with her chin in her hands and stared at herself in the mirror. The longer she stared, the more confused she got. She knew very well that her nose was too big for her face and covered with freckles, and that her cheeks were too full and made her face look round.

She brushed her hand down the bridge of her nose. *That's strange. The freckles are gone.*

She touched the pale flesh beneath pronounced cheekbones. *Where did the roundness go?*

The face staring back at her *was* lovely. But it wasn't hers!

She stuck out her tongue and crossed her eyes.

Patch laughed at Merielle's antics. "Didn't you like what you saw?"

Merielle sat up with her back to the mirror. "Not really."

"Why not? You're very beautiful."

Merielle frowned. "Not yet. But I will be when I grow up. Father says so. My mother was beautiful. She died when I was twelve. That was . . . that was . . . a long time ago."

"How old are you now, Merielle?"

Merielle opened her mouth to answer, but realized she wasn't sure. "I . . ."

"When is the last birthday you remember?" Patch prompted.

Merielle sought an answer to the question, but it wasn't forthcoming. She felt dizzy and closed her eyes to concentrate. Her mouth was dry, and her tongue felt thick. Her head was pounding, but she furrowed her brow and forced herself to think back.

At first there was nothing. It was like being in a maze. Every road she took led to another blind alley. It was frightening because sometimes she felt trapped. As she traversed the maze, she saw something glowing in the distance. She headed for the light. It was candles. Candles on her birthday cake.

My birthday. It's my birthday. But which one?

She could see her mother smiling at her, urging her to blow out the candles.

Count them. How many candles are there? One, two—

"I'm eleven!" Merielle announced triumphantly. She opened her eyes and smiled at Patch. "I'm eleven."

Patch hadn't realized how farfetched it was to hope that Merielle would regain her memory, until she heard the lovely young woman announce that she was eleven years old. Especially since Merielle had just recollected that her mother had died when she was *twelve*.

There was nothing in Merielle's behavior that led Patch to believe she had any notion of all the years that had passed since she had been violated. Her actions were consistent with the age she believed herself to be, even if the words that came out of her mouth were not.

There just had to be some way to get through to her. All Patch had to do was find it.

Merielle picked up her rag doll and began rebraiding Emily's hair. She leaned close to Patch and said, "I told Emily about Frank."

"What about Frank?"

"That he kissed me."

"Frank kissed you?" Frank hadn't said anything about kissing Merielle. Talking, yes. Kissing, no. But then, they hadn't really had an opportunity to discuss Frank's efforts to help Merielle regain her memory. Maybe he had thought a kiss would do the job.

Merielle put a fingertip to her lips. "Don't tell Father."

"Why not?"

Merielle bit her lower lip as she concentrated on Emily's braid. "I . . ." Merielle knew there was some reason she was not supposed to tell her father about kissing Frank. But she couldn't remember what it was. "I don't know. But I'm not supposed to tell him about kissing Frank."

Patch's eyes lit with excitement. Maybe Merielle was remembering a time in the past when kissing Frank had been forbidden. Frank had said they kept their relationship a secret from Merielle's father. "When did Frank kiss you?"

"The other day we were in the barn, and he asked me if he could kiss me."

"Oh."

Merielle mistook the reason for Patch's disappointment. "It wasn't so bad. At first I liked it." Merielle reached down and put a hand on her stomach. "It made me feel . . . funny."

Merielle tried to remember the sensations. The ticklish feeling that had spread throughout her body. The way her knees had suddenly buckled so she had almost fallen. Then the blackness, swallowing her up, sucking her down, so she felt like she was falling. Even now it made her tremble to remember those other feelings.

"After a little while, I didn't like it," Merielle said abruptly. "It scared me."

"Why were you scared?"

Patch knew she had pressed too hard when she saw the panicked look in Merielle's dark brown eyes.

"It doesn't matter," Patch said.

At that moment Maria knocked on the door and called them to supper. Patch noticed that once again Merielle walked wide circles around Boyd. She made up her mind to ask Boyd if this was the first time he had been around Merielle, or if she always acted this way toward him.

Conversation at the dinner table was surprisingly general. Patch couldn't remember afterward what had been said. She was hoping for a chance to talk to Merielle again after supper, but the young woman pleaded fatigue.

"Will you come again soon?" Merielle asked.

"Maybe we could go on a picnic," Patch suggested.

"That would be fun! May I go, Father?"

Patch couldn't look at Trahern because his eyes gave away too much of what he was feeling, and it was plain that his feelings were sad.

"If you wish," Trahern said. "When is this picnic going to be?" he asked Patch.

"How about next Sunday, after church," Patch suggested.

"Next Sunday," Trahern agreed.

Patch gave Merielle a quick hug before she left.

Once Patch and Boyd were back in the buggy, Boyd sidled closer and quipped, "I like the way you say good night. Am I going to get a hug, too?"

Patch wasn't in any mood to put up with advances from Boyd, especially since she had put him back on her list of parties suspected of raping a vulnerable young woman.

"What you're going to get is a black eye if you don't put some distance between us."

Boyd scooted away, but looked offended. "You didn't mind me getting close earlier tonight."

"Did you rape Merielle Trahern?"

There was a moment of stunned silence before Boyd said, "You're taking an awful chance asking me a question like that when we're all alone in the dark, miles from anyone who could hear you scream for help, don't you think?"

The irony and sarcasm in his voice was enough to convince Patch she had made a mistake. She groaned and looped her arm through Boyd's to make amends. "I'm sorry, Boyd. I'm going crazy wondering who could possibly have done it."

"We may never know," Boyd said.

"Let's talk about something else."

"All right. There's a dance in town on Saturday night. Will you go with me?"

Patch's first thought was to wonder why Ethan hadn't mentioned the dance. The answer was painfully obvious. Ethan couldn't walk freely down the main street of town, let alone attend a social function in Oakville. Patch wished she could tell Boyd that she was committed to Ethan. But Ethan had forbidden it. She was now in the awkward position of having to refuse Boyd without being able to give him the real reason she wouldn't allow him to court her.

"I couldn't leave Mrs. Hawk alone," she said. It sounded like the lame excuse it was.

"You can't leave her for a few hours to go to a dance, yet you're going on an afternoon picnic with Merielle the next day?"

"I don't want to go with you, Boyd."

"That answer sounds more honest, although I'm not any happier with it. Why won't you come with me, Patricia?"

"I'm not attracted to you, Boyd."

Boyd clucked his tongue. "You're lying again, Patricia."

Patch flushed, mortified that Boyd knew she was a little fascinated with him, even though it was Ethan that she loved. She told herself it was merely that she felt unsure of herself with Ethan, who had known her first as a baby whose wet drawers he had changed and then as a coltish child of twelve. Naturally she had relished Boyd's attentions as a sign that she was the kind of woman who could attract a man. But it was Ethan she wanted to attract. Not Boyd.

"I'm flattered that you want to take me to the dance, Boyd. But I wouldn't feel right kicking up my heels when Ethan is still a hunted man."

"That's more honesty, but still leaves me without a partner for the dance."

"I like you, Boyd," Patch admitted to soften her refusal. "But I don't—"

Boyd put a hand to her lips to stop her speech. They were back at the rutted part of the road, so he slowed the buggy down. "All right, Patricia. I'm willing to wait a little while to see whether—how—Ethan's situation gets resolved."

"Boyd, I—"

Boyd kissed her.

It happened so suddenly, Patch didn't see it coming. He just turned his head and laid his mouth on hers. The kiss was over before she had a chance to protest. By the time she realized she should have slapped him, he was already leaning forward again in that harmless pose, his forearms on his thighs, his eyes directed between the horse's ears. He slapped the reins, and the buggy picked up speed again.

Heat burned in her cheeks. "Don't ever do that again!"

"You liked it."

"I didn't! I hardly know you."

Boyd showed her a cheeky grin. "But you like me."

Hoisted on her own petard. Patch was feeling her lack of sophistication in worldly matters. Boyd was Ethan's age, and it seemed he had learned a few tricks in the ten or twelve years he had on her. But Patch knew the time to stop this flirtation was now, before Boyd's feelings got engaged.

Whether Ethan wished it or not, she would have to tell Boyd the truth.

Patch saw lights in the distance that signaled they were nearing the Double Diamond. If she was going to say something, she had to do it now.

"I can't get involved with you because I'm already in love with another man."

Boyd didn't look at her, but she saw a muscle tighten in his jaw.

"Ethan," he said flatly.

Patch said, "Yes."

"Ethan can't—won't—marry you."

"I won't argue with you about this, Boyd. I can't change how I feel."

It didn't happen right away, but she saw the tension ease out of him.

"Ethan's a lucky man," he said at last.

"I wish you'd tell him that," she replied with a wry laugh.

"All right, I will."

"No, don't!" She put a hand over Boyd's and removed it when she felt him flinch.

"Why not?"

Patch laughed to relieve her nervous tension. "I want him to figure it out for himself."

Patch had half expected Ethan to be waiting up for her, but there was no sign of him on the porch when they arrived at the ranch house. She got down on her own, unwilling to give Boyd the opportunity to touch her, afraid he might take liberties again that would cause another confrontation. This time she *would* slap him!

"I'll unharness the buggy and take care of your horse before I leave," Boyd said.

"Thanks." Patch fled into the house before he could say more.

Ethan wasn't waiting on the porch for Patch because he was waiting in the barn for Boyd. He was sitting on a bale of hay just outside the circle of light created by a lantern hung on the end of an empty stall.

"How did it go?" he said as Boyd led the tired horse into the barn.

Though startled, Boyd quickly recovered his composure. "I couldn't figure out why you weren't waiting on the porch for her. I would have been, if she were my girl."

"Patch is not my girl."

"She thinks she is." Boyd walked Patch's gelding into the empty stall, found a brush, and began currying the animal's sweat-flecked hide.

Ethan stayed in the dark. It was easier to speak to Boyd when he didn't have to worry about his friend reading the brittle emotions on his face. "Patch believes my name will be cleared. She thinks we have a future."

"What do you think?"

"I think she's dreaming."

"Why not tell her so?"

"Don't you think I've tried? She was stubborn and willful as a kid, and she hasn't changed a whit! She doesn't know when to give up."

"Then you give up. Sell out, take your mother and sister and go away. Leave Patch behind."

Ethan's heart skipped a beat. It wasn't the loss of the Double Diamond that crossed his mind. It was the thought of a lifetime without Patch that left him feeling bereft. "I can't."

Boyd threw the brush down in the hayrack in disgust. He found his horse in another stall and tightened the cinch on the saddle. "Patricia deserves a chance to be happy. Speaking frankly, I think she'd be happier with me than with you."

"Maybe so. But I'm not giving her up. Not yet."

Boyd led his horse to the barn door and mounted up. "You're my friend, Ethan. So here's a little friendly advice. Do yourself a favor. Leave Oakville while you still can."

"And Patch?"

"She won't miss you. I plan to make her my wife."

—

❊10❊

FRANK GRASPED THE NAKED flanks of the woman beneath him and thrust himself deeper inside her. He withdrew and thrust again. His air-starved lungs, his sweat-streaked body, his pounding heart gave mute testimony to his labor. There was pleasure to be had from the exquisite friction of flesh against slick flesh as he drove himself toward satisfaction. His fingers tightened as he felt the woman struggle for freedom beneath him.

"Don't move," he said through gritted teeth. "Don't move."

She stilled, and he continued his plunder of her body. He kept his eyes closed, squeezed tight, and used his imagination to remake her features into the ones beloved to him. He imagined her with dark eyes alight with desire, her lips full from being bitten in passion, her nostrils flared to catch the scents of lovemaking thick in the air between them. He heard his name whispered by her voice, heard her begging him to fill her full with himself.

He sat up and pulled the woman's legs over his thighs. He slipped his hands under her buttocks and levered her body closer to his. And thrust again. Harder. Deeper. Faster. Wet sounds. Slapping flesh. Harsh breathing. His body drove him to find surcease from the endless craving for one particular woman. He felt as though he would die of wanting. Die of needing. Finally, his body demanded release from its torment. As he spilled his seed, he cried, "Merielle!"

His body slumped forward, drained of its essence. Exhausted. Finished.

Frank wished he could be swallowed up in a void so he wouldn't have to face what happened next. He heard the woman take a breath to speak and tightened his fingers to keep her silent. After so many years, she knew what he wanted. Sometimes she gave him the peace he needed. Sometimes she forced reality back too soon.

"Frank? I've got another customer waiting downstairs."

Frank's breath shuddered out of him. He opened his eyes. The room was dark. But not completely. Harsh yellow light seeped in under the door and up through cracks in the floor along with the noise of the piano from the saloon downstairs. "All right, Jewell. Give me a minute to get my pants on."

Frank liked the dark. It helped the illusion last longer. He didn't want to see Jewell's kohl-blackened eyes and rouged cheeks, her plump, middle-aged body. He didn't want to see the starkness of the room where she did business. He rid himself of the condom Jewell made all her customers wear and left it in the brass spittoon beside the bed.

Jewell had risen and crossed to a dry sink, where she kept water in a pitcher for washing. He heard her wet a washcloth and wring it out in the bowl. He knew she was wiping away all traces of him, of his saliva and sweat and semen, before her next customer came. It was one of the things he appreciated about Jewell. She was clean.

"How is Merielle?"

It was a question Jewell always asked. She knew, as well as anyone, that Frank had always loved the other woman. She knew, better than anyone, just how much.

"I tried talking to her about what happened all those years ago," Frank said.

Jewell sank down onto a bench beside the dry sink. "My, my. What happened?"

"Nothing. Except maybe I scared her."

"How'd you do that?"

"By kissing her," Frank admitted in a taut voice.

"She didn't like it?"

"I think she did, at first. Then she pushed me away."

"So what she's feeling toward you now maybe is at odds with what she remembers happening to her a long time ago?"

Frank frowned. "I never thought of it like that."

"Are you going to kiss her again?"

"No."

"Why not?"

"Because she didn't like it."

Jewell shook her head. "I think maybe you ought to kiss her some more and see what happens. What have you got to lose?"

"She might not want me around anymore."

Jewell laughed. "That girl adores you. You'd have to do something pretty terrible for her to send you packing." Her eyes crinkled as she smiled. "And I'm telling you, Frank, there isn't a woman alive who wouldn't enjoy your kisses."

Frank felt embarrassed by the sexual compliment. He turned his back on Jewell and pulled on his long underwear.

"I haven't seen Ethan in a while," Jewell remarked.

Frank pulled on his jeans over his long johns. "He's been busy."

Jewell laughed, a husky, throaty sound. "Busy with a long-legged blonde, the way I hear it."

"Miz Kendrick is a lady, Jewell."

"A lady's got all the same equipment as a woman, last I heard," Jewell replied.

Frank took some money from his pocket and laid it on the table beside the bed. He reclaimed his shirt from the standing mirror he had thrown it over. He had caught sight of himself in bed with Jewell once, and ever since had made sure the mirror was covered. He slipped on his shirt and began buttoning it. "I think she means to marry Ethan."

"Question is whether Ethan means to marry her," Jewell said. "Or whether he'll get the chance. Saw a man come into the Silver Buckle tonight looked like trouble for Ethan."

"Gunfighter?"

"Think so. Mean, hard-looking son of a bitch. Gonna find out just how hard in a few minutes," she said with a grin.

"He your next customer?"

"Uh-huh. Do me a favor, will you? Ask him to come on up."

Frank stomped his feet to make sure his heels were down in his boots. "Sure. And Jewell?"

"Yes, Frank?"

"Be careful."

"You know me, Frank. I'm always careful."

Once downstairs, Frank searched the bar for the stranger he knew he would find. The gunman was tall and lean. He looked tough as hobnails. His spurred boot was hooked over the footrail, but he wasn't leaning on the bar. He kept his body free, ready to react. Frank met the man's eyes and had the feeling he was seeing death—cold, icy gray orbs that bore no human emotion.

Frank crossed the room quickly, not wanting to give the stranger time to worry that he was looking for a fight. "Jewell says she's ready for you."

Frank felt a chill go down his spine when the stranger said, "I recognize you."

Frank shifted uneasily. "Don't remember us crossing paths before."

"I was here in town a long time ago. Just a kid, really. Came through with my ma. She was looking for work. Didn't find any, so we kept moving. But I remember you."

Frank stood there, waiting to see if he had somehow, in his misspent youth, offended this menacing stranger.

The gunfighter smiled. "You were walking with a black-haired girl in pigtails, and you were both eating off the same apple. She told you not to get near me, because I had sores on my feet and you'd probably catch some horrible disease from me and die.

"But you weren't afraid. You said you'd talk to anybody you pleased."

Frank searched for the incident in his memory. And found it. It was the contrast between the boy and the man that had caused his lapse. "Gloria Violet," he murmured.

"So you remember my mother."

Frank stared at the gunfighter. He remembered now what had drawn him to the barefoot boy. Pity. He had felt sorry for the tall, skinny kid whose mother couldn't even get work as a whore at the Silver Buckle Saloon.

Frank made the mistake of letting the pity he had felt then back into his eyes.

The gunfighter's face hardened like granite. "Name's Calloway. I never forget a friend. Or forgive an enemy." Then the man was gone.

Frank turned to the bartender and asked for a rye. He drank it down when it came and asked for another. The second one he nursed, because he wasn't ready to go back to the Tumbling T and play cards in the bunkhouse with the hands. It was getting harder and harder to pretend that he wouldn't rather be in a home of his own with a wife and some kids playing at his feet.

Frank lost himself in the noise of the saloon, the clink of glass, the rise and fall of conversation, the piano tinkling out "Oh! Susannah!" over and over and Harvey missing the same note each time in the refrain. He was on his fourth rye when Calloway came back down the stairs.

The gunfighter headed straight for Frank. "Jewell told me you work for Jefferson Trahern."

"I'm his foreman," Frank said.

"I need directions to his place."

Frank emptied his glass. "If you care to ride along, I'm going there now."

Calloway nodded his agreement.

Frank had left his horse tied out front. He mounted and followed Calloway to the livery, where he waited while the gunfighter saddled his horse. Frank wasn't in much of a mood to talk, which suited both men just fine.

The ride in the dark was peaceful. There wasn't much to hear but the sound of the wind in the grass, the jingle of the bit and the creak of saddle leather, the clop of horses' hooves, and once in a while, the yip of a coyote. The night was clear, and stars filled the sky as far as a man could see. There were so many they couldn't be counted. Frank had fallen asleep once, trying. A man felt how small he was with so much space around him.

As they neared the ranch, Frank finally broke the silence between them. "Did Trahern say why he hired you?"

"Just that he needed my services," Calloway replied.

"He wants you to kill a friend of mine."

Calloway eyed Frank warily. "I'm real sorry about that."

"I'm asking you to ride out of here, now. Forget you ever heard of this town."

Calloway shook his head. "Can't do it. Got a reputation to keep. I always earn my fee."

Frank felt the hair-trigger tension in the gunfighter. One wrong move, and it would be all over. He didn't intend to draw; he was no match for a fast gun. But Frank owed Ethan what help he could offer. He had to speak on the chance he could head off a showdown. "My friend has done his share of killing, too. You might be the one ends up dead."

Calloway shrugged. "Just makes my job more interesting."

Frank left Calloway in front of Trahern's house and headed for the barn to stable his horse. He knew Ethan could take care of himself. He always had. But Calloway worried him. The man seemed more shrewd, more patient and savvy than the usual gunman Trahern hired.

Frank had spent some time talking to Ethan when he got out of prison, about the awkward situation he found himself in. It hadn't been so bad when he worked for Trahern the first ten years, because Trahern's obsession for vengeance against Ethan—who was nowhere to be found—had come to naught.

He had felt guilty working for Trahern the seven years Ethan was in prison, even though he couldn't see how it hurt Ethan. But he hadn't quit. There was just no reason to keep on living if he could never see Merielle again.

When Ethan had returned recently to Oakville, Frank had realized he couldn't ignore the situation any longer. But after so many years of seeing Merielle day in and day out, he was more attached to her than ever. So he had broached the subject with Ethan.

"If you don't want to be my friend anymore, I'll understand. But I can't give up Merielle. I can't."

"You don't have to," Ethan assured him. "All I ask is that you don't do anything to help Trahern nail my hide to the wall."

"You have my word," Frank said.

And he had kept it.

This latest threat from Trahern, the bounty hunter named Calloway, looked more serious than the last one. Frank made up his mind to ride over to the Double Diamond in the morning and warn Ethan what he was up against.

Inside the barn, Frank heard soft, whimpering cries coming from the loft that sounded like some animal in pain. There were traps in the barn to catch rodents, and he figured he might as well put whatever cat or possum or coon that had fallen prey to one of those vicious traps out of its misery.

As soon as he had unsaddled his horse and forked some hay for him, he climbed the ladder, taking a lantern with him so he could see in the dark.

The noises seemed to be coming from the corner. The closer he got, the more his eyes widened in disbelief. "Merielle? Is that you?"

He hung the lantern on a hook on one of the eaves and knelt beside her in the scattered hay. She was curled into a ball in the corner, her head hidden in her hands. The woeful sounds he had heard were her muffled sobs. When he put a hand on her shoulder, she jerked upright. She took one look at his face in the light and threw herself into his arms.

"Frank! Frank, you came!"

"I'm here, Merielle," he crooned. "I'm here."

"Father wouldn't let me come see you," she said in a choked voice. She levered herself away from his chest with her palms and said in a fierce voice, "I won't let him keep us apart, Frank. I love you. I'll always love you!"

Then she kissed him, her body pressed fervently against his, and her lips like sweet, sweet honey.

Frank kissed her back. If this was a dream, he didn't want to wake up. He thought maybe he had drunk too much, and his mind was making up the words she was speaking, the things she was doing. As much as he wanted to kiss her, he wanted even more to look at her face, to see if her eyes were lucid, to see if what was happening was *real*.

"Merielle," he murmured against her lips. He took her face in his hands and held it steady in the light while he tried to find the girl he had loved in the eyes of the woman in his arms. But Frank had loved Merielle too well and too long. To him, they were one and the same. "I love you, too, Merielle," he whispered.

Her eyes were clear, and she seemed actually to hear and understand what he was saying. The joy she felt was there in her dark eyes for him to see. It was a moment from the past she was remembering, but she *was* remembering. How they had felt toward each other. What they had meant to each other.

Frank hoped like hell his perceptions weren't blurred by the liquor he had drunk. Because this was the first sign he had seen in seventeen years that Merielle had any recollection of their relationship. He was afraid to ask for more, to press her for more. But he recalled Jewell saying "What have you got to lose?"

So he asked, "Merielle, where were we supposed to meet tonight, when your father wouldn't let you leave the house?"

"At the cave."

He pulled her into his arms and hugged her tight. "That's right, at the cave." Just as quickly he put her away from him again. "Do you remember why I wanted you to meet me?"

"You have a present for me," she said with a mischievous grin.

Frank found himself grinning back at her. "Yes, I do." He could hear his heart pounding. He had waited so many years for this moment. He took the ring off his little finger and slipped it onto her middle finger. "I made this for you."

He watched her touch the braided ring he had worn all these years, saw her pleasure in the gift.

Her eyes glowed with warmth and happiness. "I'll always treasure it, Frank."

Suddenly it wasn't enough to watch her relive the past. He needed her here, in the present. So he pushed a little harder. Pressed for more. "What happened, Merielle? Why didn't you come? Who—"

She was gone. As quickly as that, the girl of his childhood was gone, replaced by the childlike person, bereft of memory, who had taken the place of his beloved.

"Frank?" She looked around, obviously upset and confused by her surroundings. "How did I get here? I want to go back to the house."

Frank wanted to bellow with rage. He wanted to howl with despair. He had thought nothing could be worse than Merielle without her memory. He had been wrong. It was far worse to be teased like this. To get a taunting glimpse of the past and have it yanked away again. To think she might be getting better and see it was only an illusion.

"All right, Merielle," he said in a soothing voice. "I'll take you back to the house."

"I can't imagine how I got out here," she said as she followed him down the ladder. "The last thing I remember is saying good night to Father."

Frank wondered if she had snuck out of her room as she had in those days long ago, by shinnying down the live oak outside her window. He looked her over in the light from the lantern and saw the scrapes on her arms and the tear in her skirt. He felt a moment of stark terror. What if she had fallen?

He debated whether to tell Trahern what she had done, but decided against it. The only way to keep Merielle from using the window for escape would be to bar it or nail it shut, and he couldn't bear to think of her locked in like that. She had climbed that tree for years. There was no reason why she should suddenly start falling.

The problem now was how to get her back into the house without letting Trahern know she had been out. He took Merielle's hand and led her from the barn. When they reached the front door, he eased it open and gave her a nudge inside. "Go on upstairs, Merielle."

"Come with me, Frank."

"Merielle, I—"

"Is that you, Merielle?" Trahern called from the parlor.

"Yes, Father. I'm going back upstairs now."

Merielle grabbed Frank's hand and drew him inside. He tried to free himself, then heard Trahern stirring in the parlor. Rather than get caught in the hall, he followed Merielle up the stairs. He felt foolish tiptoeing through the house, but the thought of seeing where Merielle slept kept him moving after her.

She pulled him into her bedroom and closed the door after him. "Come sit down, Frank."

Frank had never seen so many frills, so much lace. Everything looked so fragile, so delicate. He knew if he touched anything it would break. Including Merielle. Especially Merielle.

What was he doing here? Why had she brought him here?

Frank stared at Merielle. What was she thinking now? What did she expect of him?

"This is Emily," Merielle said, holding out a rag doll for his inspection. "She's my best friend."

"I thought I was your best friend," Frank countered.

"Oh. Well, you are. Only I can tell Emily anything."

"You used to tell me everything."

Frank knew he was being contrary, but he couldn't help it. This was an unbearable situation. He didn't belong here. He should leave, but he didn't have the strength to do it on his own. The best he could do was provoke her until she kicked him out.

Merielle's brow furrowed. "Don't you like me anymore, Frank?"

Frank realized the futility of playing games with Merielle. She couldn't keep up with the rules. He sighed. "Of course I like you."

"Are you mad at me?"

"No, I'm not mad at you."

"Then why are you frowning like that?"

Frank forced himself to smile. "There. Is that better?"

She smiled back at him. "Yes." Merielle yawned hugely.

"You're tired," Frank said. "You should go to bed."

"Will you help me get out of this dress? It buttons in back."

Merielle turned her back to him. Frank knew he ought to make her call for Maria. But he told himself he could do this without letting his desire for her get out of control. He undid the buttons as quickly as he could. When he was done, Merielle turned, pulled the dress down over her hips, and stepped out of it.

She stood before him in her undergarments with no more modesty than a newborn babe.

"Would you get me a nightgown from the chest at the foot of the bed?" she asked.

Frank moved as though in a trance. He lifted the lid of the mahogany chest and sorted through the intimate apparel he found there until he came up with a simple chambray gown.

When he looked up again, Merielle had removed the slips and the corset and was standing before him in a thin cotton chemise and lace-trimmed pantalets. When she reached for the bow at the top of the chemise he said, "No, don't."

She looked up at him. "I don't wear anything under my gown."

"You will tonight." Frank slipped the gown over her head and pulled her arms through the sleeves. "There. Now get into bed." He reached over and folded down the counterpane, then pulled down the sheet. Merielle obediently climbed into bed. Frank tucked her in, then sat down beside her.

"Sleep well, my love." He leaned over and kissed her tenderly on the forehead. He started to rise but she grasped his hand.

"Stay with me until I fall asleep," she said.

Frank bit back a groan of frustration. "All right."

She turned over on her side and tucked his hand under her chin. He sat with her until the moon rose. The house was quiet. He gently freed his hand and crossed to the open window. The leaves rustled in the tree. The moss swayed in the wind. He looked at the door, then back at the window. It was safer to climb down than to take the chance of getting caught in the house.

Frank was sitting on a low branch of the tree, seven feet off the ground, when he heard Trahern speaking to someone on the front porch. He figured Calloway was leaving. The longer he listened, the more familiar he found the voice. It wasn't Calloway. It was Boyd Stuckey.

Frank strained to hear, but he couldn't make out what was being said. The two men were speaking too softly, and the rustle of the leaves made the sounds indistinct.

Frank drew his legs up out of sight as Boyd mounted his horse and rode away. He waited until he heard Trahern go back into the house before he lowered himself to the ground.

He leaned against the house with his foot braced on the wooden wall, and rolled himself a cigarette. He struck a match on his jeans and cupped his hand around the tip while he lit it. He inhaled and held the smoke down in his lungs before he breathed it out, along with the tension he felt.

Boyd had been coming to the ranch more frequently of late to speak with Trahern. Frank figured they must be doing some business together. He didn't begrudge Boyd his success, but he didn't understand it, either. Boyd had taken the small inheritance from his aunt and become almost as rich as Trahern. Frank had asked Boyd once the secret of his success.

Boyd had grinned and said, "Calculated risks."

Frank hadn't understood Boyd then. Now he did. It was like what he had done tonight with Merielle. Pushing her to remember. Following her to her room. Staying there to put her to bed. Hoping against hope that a miracle would happen.

He crushed the cigarette under his boot. He was taking his own calculated risks. Only the prize he was hoping to win wasn't wealth and riches. It was Merielle Trahern.

❋11❋

ETHAN HELD A KITTEN in one palm and a leather work glove full of sugar water in the other. He had poked a hole in one finger of the glove and was trying to get the kitten to take suck. Tiny claws dug into his skin as the blind kitten latched on.

"It's working!" Leah cried.

Ethan grinned at her. "Looks like it."

"What's going on?" Patch tied on her apron as she crossed to where Ethan was sitting at the kitchen table. Leah hovered over his shoulder.

"Leah noticed the calico cat was missing last night. We looked for her, but we never found her. I figured she'd come home sometime during the night, but she never did. Leah found these babies crying up a storm this morning and asked if there was anything we could do."

Patch leaned over Ethan's shoulder. "What are you feeding them?"

"Sugar water," Ethan said. "There isn't any more milk."

"Gilley is supposed to deliver some this morning," Leah said.

"Sit down, Leah, and you can take over for me," Ethan said.

Leah quickly settled in the chair next to Ethan. He carefully transferred the kitten into her waiting hand. When he broke the kitten's connection with the glove, it began mewing pitifully. Ethan stood behind Leah and helped her figure out the most comfortable way to hold both the glove and the kitten.

When the kitten latched on once again, Leah looked up at Ethan and smiled shyly. "Thanks, Ethan."

"It was your idea to feed the kittens. I just found a way to do it."

Patch watched as Ethan ruffled Leah's hair. It was the sort of affectionate gesture that brothers the world over used with little sisters. It was a first for both of them, a beginning. Patch felt a sudden lump in her throat when she realized that the way Ethan had just interacted with Leah was exactly the way he had treated Patch in Montana. *Like a little sister!*

Why hadn't she ever realized that before? Was it possible that the affection she had felt for Ethan back then wasn't romantic love? Then what was it she felt for Ethan now? It felt the same. No, that wasn't precisely true. She was able now to admire qualities in Ethan that she hadn't even known existed when she was a child. She needed him in a different way, not just as a friend, but as the missing part of a puzzle she was only beginning to unravel. She was discovering that her happiness was inextricably linked with his.

Patch shook her head slightly. She wanted to share her realization with him, but she was too afraid he would dismiss what she was feeling as fancy. She decided to cherish the feelings and let them grow. There would be time enough to tell Ethan later.

Patch stroked the fur of the kitten in Leah's hand. "What do you think happened to Calico?" she asked Ethan.

"Nothing good, or she'd be here with her kittens," he replied. "I think I'll take another look around for her before breakfast."

Ethan had already kicked the back door open and gone outside to search when Patch made a discovery of her own.

"Max is dead!"

She picked up Max's cage from the counter beside the pump and brought it over to the kitchen table where the light was better. She opened the top and reached in carefully to lift Max out, then sat down across from Leah with the mouse in her palm. She rubbed a finger across his fur. He was stiff and cold, and Patch realized he had been dead for some time.

"I can't believe Max is dead. He seemed perfectly fine last night." Patch laid the mouse back in the cage.

Leah returned the kitten she had been feeding to the basket and picked up another one. "He was just a stupid mouse."

"He kept me company when I was all alone on the journey here. And he made me smile," Patch said in defense of her pet. "I guess I should have let him go sooner. I just didn't want your cat to eat him."

"Cats are supposed to eat mice!" Leah retorted.

There was a knock on the back door. "Patch? Can you let me in?"

Patch shoved the kitchen door open and stepped aside to give Ethan room to enter. He carried something wrapped in his shirt. He lifted the cloth to reveal a patch of calico fur. "I'm sorry, Leah," he said. "I found her under the house. It looks like she died sometime last night."

Leah stared with stricken eyes at the bundle Ethan held in his arms. She hurriedly set down the makeshift feeder and returned the kitten to the basket with the others, then crossed the room to where Ethan stood near the stove. Leah reached out a hand, but couldn't bring herself to touch the dead cat.

Ethan knelt and laid the bundle on the floor beside the stove.

Leah squatted down beside him, her chin on her knees. "What happened to her?"

"I'm not sure. There's not a mark on her. If I had to guess, I'd say maybe she ate something that was poisoned."

"Calico was poisoned?" she asked incredulously. Leah jumped up and pointed an accusing finger at Patch. "You poisoned my cat so she wouldn't eat your mouse!"

"I never did any such thing!" Patch protested.

Ethan rose and stepped between them.

A knock on the kitchen door interrupted what promised to be an ugly showdown. Ethan kicked the back door open and stared in disbelief at the old man standing there.

"You gonna invite me in or let me stand here all day?"

"Come in, Mr. Marshall."

"Grandpa Corwin! What are you doing here?"

"I gotta have a reason to visit my granddaughter?" the old man asked.

"Of course not," Patch said, shooting a quick glance at Ethan to see what he thought of her grandfather's invasion. Ethan leaned back against the counter beside the pump, frankly relieved because the old man's appearance had staved off a fight he hadn't looked forward to refereeing.

Patch gestured her grandfather inside. "Come in, Grandpa Corwin. Sit down. I don't even have the coffeepot on the stove." She settled her grandfather at the table, whisking away the cage with the dead mouse in it and putting it on the windowsill.

Leah sat glaring as Patch hurried around, stirring up the ashes in the stove to make sure it was hot, filling the coffeepot with water from the pump, grinding up coffee beans, and finally putting the coffeepot on the stove to boil. The whole time, Patch was filling in her grandfather on the mysterious deaths of both the cat and the mouse.

Ethan was surprised to hear that Max was dead, too. "It's strange that both animals died the same night. Do you have any idea what killed Max?"

"No. There wasn't a mark on him."

"Same as the cat," Ethan murmured to himself. He had kept to himself his suspicions that someone might have purposely poisoned the cat. It looked now like the mouse might have died of poison as well. However, while the cat had been roaming free outside, the mouse had been in a cage the whole time. So what could have killed both animals?

Corwin Marshall had examined both the cat and the mouse while Patch was bustling around. He sat back down at the table and pronounced, "Most likely poison killed the cat. Probably something it ate. You got any bait out for coyotes?" he asked Ethan.

"Nothing close to the house," Ethan said.

"Your theory might explain what happened to the cat, but what about Max?" Patch said.

"You keep that mouse in a cage all the time?" the old man asked.

"Unless I was holding him."

"What did you feed him last night?"

"Just some milk."

"Milk tainted, maybe?"

"I don't think so," Patch said. "At least, Nell didn't complain about it. But she only drank a swallow or two."

Ethan uncrossed his legs and stood with his hands on his hips. "We fed the same milk to the cat."

"Milk might've been bad," Corwin suggested. "Could've been what killed them both."

"I've never heard of sour milk killing anything," Ethan said.

"Maybe it was tainted with poison," the old man said.

"How is that possible?" Patch asked.

"Cow maybe ate something with poison in it—strychnine, arsenic, lead—and it came through in the milk," Corwin explained.

"I've never heard of such a thing," Ethan scoffed.

"Doesn't happen often, but it happens," Corwin insisted.

Ethan stared at Patch with dawning horror. "Ma's been drinking that milk! *Ma's been drinking poisoned milk!*"

"What's that you're saying?" Corwin asked.

Patch exchanged a glance with Ethan across the room. She could see the wheels turning in his head. "I told you Nell has been ill," Patch explained to her grandfather. "If what you say is true, maybe something in the milk she's been drinking is what's been making her so sick."

"What are Nell's symptoms?" Corwin asked.

"Fatigue, nausea, headaches, palpitations—lots of aches and pains," Patch recited.

"That would fit with arsenic poisoning," Corwin said.

Ethan's brow furrowed. "What I don't understand is why we aren't sick, and why there aren't a lot of other sick folk in town. I mean, if the milk is tainted, wouldn't everyone who drank it get sick?"

"Stands to reason," Corwin said.

"I don't drink milk," Leah volunteered.

"Neither do I," Ethan said. "That would explain why we aren't suffering any symptoms. What about you, Patch?"

"I think I've had one glass of milk in the time I've been here. No more than that."

Ethan turned back to the old man. "How much poison would it take to make a person really sick?"

"Depends on the person. Depends on how much and what kind of poison. Where did you get the tainted milk?"

"Gilley delivers milk every couple of days," Ethan said. "What I still don't understand is why no one else in town has gotten sick."

Corwin pulled his pipe from his pocket and slipped it between his teeth. "Maybe the poison was put in the milk after it was bottled. Maybe someone has been delivering poisoned milk only to your house."

Ethan shook his head. "That doesn't make any sense. Who would want to poison my mother?"

"That's a question worth pondering," Corwin said. "Patch said your ma's been sick since before you got out of prison. Maybe she was supposed to die before you got out. With your ma gone, maybe someone would already have bought this place, put Leah in a home somewhere. Then you'd have no reason to stick around. Who wants you gone from here?"

"Trahern." Ethan spat the name.

Patch's voice was hushed when she said, "Didn't your father die of an illness similar to the one your mother is suffering from?"

Ethan's eyes narrowed as he considered the question. "So whoever is poisoning my mother also *poisoned* my father?"

Corwin nodded. "It fits."

"Pa didn't drink milk," Ethan said flatly.

"But he had a glass of whiskey every evening," Leah said. "Gilley delivered a bottle of whiskey from town every other month."

"Leah, go get that whiskey of Pa's in the parlor," Ethan said.

Leah came running back a moment later with the half-filled bottle.

"Was Pa drinking this when he died?" Ethan asked.

Leah nodded. "He said the whiskey eased the pain."

Ethan held the bottle up to the light. It didn't look any different. He frowned. "Frank and I each had a glass of this the other night. Afterward, I didn't feel sick."

"Probably not enough arsenic in one glass to make you sick," Corwin said. "But after a while, a glass a day every day, and pretty soon you're getting too much arsenic for your body to get rid of it all. You get sick. Eventually, you die."

Ethan shook his head, unable to absorb the monstrous truth—if it was the truth. "I can't believe it. My father *murdered*! My mother— God, if this is true . . ." Ethan balled his hands into fists. He felt a terrifying violence building inside him. It had been possible to accept his father's untimely death, because he had believed it to be an act of God. But if their suppositions about poison were true, someone, some man, had shortened Alex Hawk's life.

Ethan felt strangely breathless as he asked Corwin, "If Ma is being poisoned, would she get well if she stopped drinking the tainted milk?"

"If it's not too late," Corwin said. "If she hasn't taken too much poison already. You could try having her fast and drink lots of water. The effects of the poison would slowly disappear once the poison was gone."

Ethan closed his eyes, afraid to let anyone in the room see the powerful emotions he felt. His mother might not die. She might get well. No wonder old Doc Carter hadn't figured out what was wrong with her. Who would have suspected poison?

"It's not too late," he said fiercely. "I won't let it be too late!"

Without Ethan being quite sure how it happened, Patch was in his arms, and he was hugging her tight. Then he grabbed Leah and lifted her into the air and swung her around until she shrieked with laughter. There was a lightness to Ethan's step and a joy in Leah's eyes that had previously been missing. They had been given hope of a reprieve. Maybe Nell Hawk wasn't going to die just yet.

Patch wanted to tell Nell what they had discovered. Ethan had other thoughts.

"I'd rather wait," he said.

"For what?" Patch asked.

"To see if she gets well. We're just guessing about all this. That the milk was poisoned. That it's the milk that's made Ma sick. I can send samples of both the whiskey and milk to a chemist in San Antonio to be tested for arsenic, but that will take time. What if it isn't the milk?"

Ethan paused. He met Patch's blue eyes and said in a raw voice. "Or what if we didn't catch the poison in time? I couldn't bear to give her hope and then—"

"How will you explain asking her to fast? How am I going to get all that water down her throat without telling her why I'm asking her to drink it?" Patch demanded.

"I'll tell her I wrote a letter to a doctor in San Antonio. That he recommended this treatment," Ethan said.

Patch thought Ethan was being foolish not telling his mother the truth, but she had already figured out that he had difficulty dealing with his mother's illness. "All right, Ethan. We'll try it your way."

They all agreed it wouldn't hurt Nell to get a visit from Corwin Marshall. Patch was surprised at the pleasure in Nell's eyes when she realized who had come to see her. She seemed almost flustered. She reached a frail hand up to check her hair, and her pale face flushed.

"What are you doing here, you old coot?" Nell asked.

"Came to see how you're doing, Nellie."

To Patch's astonishment, Nell laughed like a schoolgirl.

"Hasn't been anyone called me Nellie in more years than I can count," Nell said.

"Time somebody did." Corwin sat down in the rocker beside Nell's bed and settled back with his pipe between his teeth. The two talked like old friends, which, Patch discovered, they were. Patch finally had to make Corwin leave so Nell could get a little rest. He promised when he left the house to come visit again soon.

Patch realized that she had found the perfect means of getting her grandfather to end his self-imposed isolation in that dreary boarding-house room. She would keep him so busy visiting Nell and doing chores around the Double Diamond that pretty soon he wouldn't realize how much time he was spending there.

During the next few hours there was a flurry of activity. The cat and the mouse had to be buried, with appropriate requiems for each. Their deaths were solemnized because they had not been in vain. Leah had to feed the kittens. The sugar water didn't seem to fill them up, and they cried constantly from hunger.

"We'll have to get some milk for them," Patch said.

Leah's eyes looked frightened. "How will we know if it's poisoned or not?"

Ethan's mouth tightened grimly. "I'll go into town myself and get some. And have a talk with Gilley Stephenson."

Patch grabbed Ethan's arm, fearing he would shoot Gilley first and ask questions later. "Gilley only delivered the milk, Ethan. Someone else might have put the poison in it."

"I won't kill him," Ethan promised. "What I want are some answers."

Patch didn't want Ethan to go alone, but he reminded her that his mother and Leah both needed her attention. Patch reluctantly nodded her acquiescence.

Less than a minute after Ethan left the house, she had second thoughts. Patch left Leah in the kitchen and followed Ethan out to the barn. She found him saddling up his horse.

Patch stood at the end of the stall and waited for Ethan to notice her. With instincts honed by years as prey for lawmen and outlaws alike, it only took a second. He spun around, crouched with his gun in his hand. When he saw who it was, his face clouded with anger. He shoved his Colt back in his holster and stalked toward her.

Patch stood her ground.

"What are you doing out here, Patch?"

Ethan put his hands on Patch's shoulders, intending to turn her around and send her back inside. Before he could stop her, she had pressed herself against him and wrapped her arms tight around his waist.

"Promise me you'll be careful, Ethan."

His arms slid naturally around her. "I'm always careful," he murmured in her ear.

She looked up at him. "It'll be more dangerous now. Once you confront Gilley, whoever has been poisoning your mother will know he's been discovered."

"Is there any doubt who's responsible?" Ethan retorted. "Trahern owns the hotel where Gilley works. I wouldn't be surprised if Trahern threatened to fire Gilley if Gilley didn't do what he asked. Not that anything excuses what Gilley's done."

"Maybe Gilley didn't know the milk was poisoned. Maybe Trahern had someone else poison it without telling Gilley about it." Patch stopped. There was no getting around the obvious. Trahern was to blame. Trahern was the one who wanted to ruin Ethan's life.

"Just be careful," she pleaded. "If Trahern knows you've discovered his plot, he'll try something else to get rid of you and your family. Maybe something more direct. More deadly."

Ethan toyed with a stray tendril of hair beside Patch's ear. "Trahern can't try any harder to kill me than he already has. And he won't get another chance to attack my family."

"Let the law—"

"Trahern owns the law in this town! Don't try and stop me, Patch. I intend to make Jefferson Trahern pay for what he's done to my mother. And for killing my father."

Ethan's voice was ruthless, and Patch could see that the years of running, the years of fighting for his life, had made him a dangerous man. "Just don't rush into anything," she begged. "At least give the sheriff a chance to do his job. And come back to me. There's so much we haven't done together. So much I want us to do together."

Her hands slid up his back and, for the first time, down over his buttocks. Because she was pressed close to him, she felt his instantaneous reaction. She turned her face up to his, inviting his kiss.

Patch watched the struggle Ethan waged against his desire. His green eyes blazed with fury and frustration and leaping flames of passion. His arms slowly tightened around her as he pulled her tight against him.

"Damn you, Patch. Damn you for tempting me like Delilah. Daring me to touch what I crave like water in the desert. Begging me to take what I need. I'm just a man, not a saint. And I want you."

Then he was kissing her, his tongue in her mouth, his hands tracing the shape of her body, as though he were a blind man feeling his way in a new world. She was wearing a shirtwaist with buttons that came free—tore free—as he forced his hand into her bodice. Then he was holding her breast in his hand. Flesh against flesh.

The frenzy halted abruptly. His eyes sought hers.

Patch let him see the wonder she felt. The terrible need. The fear and trembling at this new step he had taken.

His fingertips moved slowly, reverently, across her breast, and she purred like one of Leah's kittens as her skin responded to his touch. She bit back a groan when his thumb brushed across her nipple.

"Look at me," he said.

Patch raised eyes that were heavy-lidded, lambent with the fire he fanned within her. There was no voice for the yearning she felt, only her body pulsing with excitement as he cupped her breast and made her feel his need.

"Patch, this is crazy," Ethan murmured against her lips. His hand slid her dress off her shoulders, baring her to his gaze. "Don't let me do this."

Patch was beyond caring what was right or wrong. Her body sang with pleasure as Ethan touched her. When he slid his hand down the front of her, down between her thighs, she grabbed his arms and hung on.

Ethan had no intention of stopping. Nor would Patch have stopped him. She was too afraid something might happen to Ethan and rob her of ever knowing what it felt like to be held naked in his arms, to be loved by him as a man loved a woman.

Patch was immediately aware when Ethan tensed.

"Someone's coming," he whispered.

Patch took one look at the disarray of her clothing and frantically began repairing the damage. Ethan helped her as best he could.

"I'll do it," Patch said when his efforts hindered more than helped her.

Ethan turned to face the intruder, using his body to shield Patch, who wasn't quite finished redressing.

"Leah! What are you doing here?" Ethan realized the ridiculousness of the question. There wasn't any particular reason Leah couldn't be in the barn anytime she pleased. He could hardly expect her to know he was having a tryst with Patch. "I mean, is there something you wanted from me?"

Leah was as upset by the scene she witnessed as the two lovers were by the interruption. She wasn't stupid. She recognized Ethan's protective posture in front of Patch. The way Patch's elbows were moving made it plain she was buttoning buttons.

Leah understood why Ethan wanted to be with Patch. She had her own eye on one of the boys at school. But she'd only had her brother to herself for a short time, and she wasn't ready to share him just yet. It was impossible not to feel jealous of the time Ethan was devoting to Patch. In fact, the way things were going, Patch might soon monopolize all Ethan's time.

"I know what you two were doing," Leah said in a disgusted voice. "I wasn't born yesterday."

Ethan's features hardened. "What Patch and I do is none of your business."

Ethan was immediately sorry for his blunt reprimand when he saw the hurt look that flashed across Leah's face. It was replaced by a mulish cast that boded ill for their budding sibling relationship.

Leah was practically snarling when she spoke again. "I only wanted to remind you that Gilley buys all the milk he delivers to us from Mrs. Felber, at the mercantile. Also, Chester Felber earns his living by milking his mother's cows. So maybe you should talk to all three of them when you're in town. That's all I wanted to say."

Leah backed a few steps, then turned and ran from the barn.

"Damn, damn, damn!" Ethan took off his hat, shoved his hand through his hair, then yanked his hat back on, tugging it down low on his brow. "Just when I thought Leah and I were making some progress, getting to know one another, she gets her nose bent out of joint, and we're back where we started."

Patch slipped her arms around Ethan's waist from behind. "My stepbrother and I fought like cats and dogs. But I love him dearly now, and I know he'd give his life for me." Patch gave Ethan a reassuring hug. "Arguing is a treasured part of being siblings."

"If you say so," Ethan muttered. "I just wish I knew how I'm supposed to act toward Leah. She takes everything I say so seriously. I don't want to hurt her feelings, but I inevitably do."

"Keep on doing what you're doing," Patch advised.

"What's that?"

"Love her. Care for her."

Ethan reached down and unclasped Patch's hands from around his waist, then turned to face her. "How did you get so wise?"

Patch shrugged and grinned. "Trial and error?"

Ethan tucked a stray lock of hair behind her ear. Actually, it was a damned good thing Leah had come along. He wasn't any closer to understanding his feelings for Patch than he had been the day she arrived in Oakville.

He was having trouble differentiating between the child of twelve he had known and the woman she had become. He desired the grown-up Patch, all right. He wasn't denying that. And he admired the way she had pitched in to help with the work that had to be done in the house, her tender care of his mother, and her understanding of Leah.

But every once in a while he saw flashes of the untamed hoyden she had been once upon a time—her flaring temper, her willingness to fight tooth and claw for what she believed, her impatience, her undaunted spirit. To his surprise, he found he admired those traits as much, or more, than her ladylike demeanor.

He wasn't sure which Patch he liked better. He wasn't sure which Patch was the real one. And he was never quite sure which Patch he was dealing with, the lady or the troublemaking minx. But he knew he would hurt them both if he wasn't careful.

Ethan put Patch away from him and picked up the reins to back his horse from the stall. Patch walked beside him as he led his horse from the barn. Once outside, he quickly mounted.

Patch shaded her eyes from the sun as she looked up at him. "I'll be waiting here for you."

"I'll be back when I get some answers."

It was hard for Patch to watch Ethan ride away. She had convinced herself that Ethan Hawk wasn't really an outlaw. He had shot Dorne Trahern in self-defense. Whatever killing he had done while on the run had been necessary to stay alive. She was convinced he had never committed the rape of which he was accused. Now he had gone hunting human quarry. Would he do it within the bounds of the law? Or would the years of being a law unto himself cause him to take vengeance into his own hands?

She had to find out who had raped Merielle Trahern, and soon. There must be a key somewhere that would unlock the secrets of the past. She had to find it. Because without that key, she and Ethan would never be free.

✷12✷

"HELLO, GILLEY."

The hotel clerk nearly jumped out of his skin when he heard the sinister voice behind him. He glanced over his shoulder and visibly relaxed. "Hawk! Why're you sneaking around here like some Injun?"

Gilley turned completely around, which was when he saw the gun in Ethan's hand. Pointed at him. He tugged on his starched collar. He snuck a peek out the brand-new picture window, but the people walking up and down the boardwalk were oblivious to his personal dilemma inside.

Gilley felt the sweat melting the starch in his shirt, making it stick to him. He licked the salty dots of perspiration from his upper lip. "Uh. Something I can do to help you, Ethan?"

"You can tell me why you've been delivering poisoned milk to my house."

"What?" Gilley's eyebrows rose till they nearly met the leftover fringes of hair on his balding head. "I never did such a thing! What makes you think I did?"

Ethan's eyes narrowed as he tried to decide whether Gilley was telling the truth. "Who else, if not you?"

"I get all the milk I deliver to your place from Mrs. Felber. It's already bottled when I put it in my wagon. Maybe she knows something I don't."

"It isn't just the milk that's been poisoned, Gilley. You delivered poisoned whiskey to my father."

Ethan watched the freckles on Gilley's face brighten as his face reddened.

"I swear I don't know a thing about any poisoned whiskey."

"Where'd you get the whiskey you sold to my father, Gilley?"

"From the saloon. I got it from the Silver Buckle."

Ethan frowned. He had been hoping he would find the poisoned drinks had come from the same source. That would mean fewer people were involved in the conspiracy to poison his family. However, now that he had talked to the hotel clerk, Ethan had his doubts whether Gilley was a guilty party. The little man just wasn't terrified enough of the gun in Ethan's hand.

Nevertheless, Ethan said, "Don't leave town, Gilley. Or I'll come after you."

Ethan turned on his heel and headed for the Silver Buckle. It was still early, and there weren't many people in the bar. Slim, the bartender, was sweeping out the old sawdust before laying down new. Ethan was about to seat himself at one of the tables when he noticed the stranger at a table in the corner, with his back to the wall. So Jefferson Trahern had hired another gunfighter to shoot him down.

Ethan seated himself across the room with his back to the opposite wall. He couldn't help smiling at the absurdity of the situation. At least this way they could keep an eye on each other.

In a matter of moments Slim was at Ethan's table. "Can I get you a drink?"

"I'd like a bottle of whiskey."

Slim raised his eyebrows. "A whole bottle?"

Ethan nodded. While he waited for Slim to bring him the whiskey, he studied the stranger. The man wore his gun low, tied down, and the fact he had his back to the wall said a lot about the kind of life he led. He played with a deck of cards, doing tricks, and Ethan suspected that when he wasn't working for hire he played a mean hand of poker.

The stranger didn't bother hiding his interest in Ethan. He stared up from beneath the brim of his Stetson, his eyes glittering intently. He smiled grimly, lifted his glass to Ethan in a toast, and drank it down.

Ethan's sense of humor told him they resembled two mangy dogs walking stiff-legged around each other, sniffing and growling and seeking out a weakness that could mean victory in the inevitable fight to come. Only, he had to hand it to Trahern. This man looked a cut above those who had been sent after him in the past. It sure didn't appear that he planned to rush any fences.

Slim brought the bottle to Ethan's table along with a glass. When he started to open the bottle, Ethan stopped him. "Where do you get this stuff, Slim?"

"Comes from Tennessee, I think."

"No, I mean, do you order it yourself, or do you get it from a supplier somewhere?"

"We get it through Felber at the mercantile."

So the tainted whiskey that had been delivered to his father two years ago had its source at the mercantile. As had the poisoned milk more recently delivered to his mother. It was time he talked with Horace Felber.

"Deliver this bottle of whiskey to the gentleman at the table across the room," Ethan said. "With my compliments."

Slim eyed the gunslinger. "Sure you wanta do that?"

Ethan rose. "I'm sure." He felt the hairs prickle on his nape when he pushed through the batwing doors of the saloon. He half expected a bullet in the back. But it didn't come.

An honorable adversary, Ethan thought with a cynical smile. In days gone by he would have relished the contest. That was before he had recognized his mortality. The several scars on his body were evidence of the lessons he had learned. Ethan didn't want to die. Especially not now, when he had so much to live for.

Patch.

She was never far from his thoughts these days. Every time he believed he had a handle on her, she revealed another facet of her personality. He wondered how many of those different sides of herself she would bring to bed with her. The sprite? The siren? The lady with an iron rod down her spine? Oh, how he would love the chance to melt it down!

He had felt her response to his kisses, her surprise and her surrender. He had felt her tremble at his touch.

She thinks she's in love with you.

What he wondered, what was driving him crazy, was whether her feelings were all left over from her childhood infatuation with him, or whether the woman she had become loved the man he was.

His musings were cut off by his arrival at the door to Horace Felber's store.

The Oakville Mercantile was busy. Several ladies were perusing the notions, while Horace Felber stamped a letter behind the jaillike cage that constituted the Oakville Post Office. The bell over the door jangled, announcing Ethan's arrival. It was almost funny, Ethan thought, how the women shrank from him as though he carried some contagious disease. His mere presence quickly cleared the premises.

Horace Felber didn't bother to hide his agitation at the loss of business. The storekeeper waited until he had closed the door behind the last of his customers before he acknowledged Ethan's presence. He returned to a position of relative safety behind the counter and asked, "What can I do for you, Hawk?"

Ethan fingered a piece of grosgrain ribbon that he thought might look pretty in Patch's hair. "I have a problem, Horace. It seems my mother's been drinking poisoned milk that came from your dairy."

Ethan watched for signs of guilt. Horace didn't twitch an ear or blink an eye. He wasn't even sweating. His chin came up and his palms landed flat on the counter.

"Are you accusing me of something?" Horace demanded.

"I'm asking if you put poison in the milk you gave Gilley to deliver to my mother."

Before Horace could answer, his wife stepped through a dark, heavy curtain that separated the store from the storeroom in back. Mrs. Felber was considerably less composed than her husband. In fact, her face was white as chalk.

It was obvious from her next words that she had overheard Ethan's conversation with her husband. "Is your mother all right?" she asked. "Nell isn't going to die, is she?"

Instead of answering her questions, Ethan asked one of his own. "What do you know about all this, Mrs. Felber?"

"Don't say another word, Lilian," Horace admonished his wife.

"But Horace—"

"If you're going to make accusations like that, you'd better have some proof, young man," Horace said. "Honest citizens like us have rights—"

Ethan had Mr. Felber by the throat in no time flat. He grabbed a handful of the storekeeper's shirt to haul him over the counter and stood him up so he could stare him in the eye. "I want some answers. Now I can get them the easy way or the hard way. It's up to you."

The bell jangling over the door alerted Ethan to the fact someone had entered the store, but he didn't take his eyes off Horace. "Well? What's it going to be?"

"Boyd," Horace croaked. "Make him let me go."

Boyd crossed far enough into the store that he could look Ethan in the face. "Some problem here, Ethan?"

"No problem," Ethan replied. "Horace was just going to tell me what he knows about the poison that turned up in the milk my mother's been drinking."

Boyd's face registered alarm. "Poison? Are you sure? What kind of poison?"

"Marshall Corwin's guessing arsenic. Ma has all the symptoms." Ethan tightened his grip on the storekeeper. "I figure Horace can fill me in on the details."

"I don't know a thing!" Horace bleated.

"Why would Horace want to poison your mother?" Boyd asked. "It doesn't make sense."

"I figure Trahern paid him to do it. What about it, Horace? You on Trahern's payroll?"

"No, I'm not. You're making a mistake. Anyone could have put poison in the milk."

"How do you figure that, Horace?" Ethan asked.

"My boy Chester milks those cows, bottles the milk, then leaves it sitting till it's picked up. Anybody could've put something in the milk and told Chester some story why he was doing it."

"Then maybe I'd better go have a talk with Chester."

"No!" Mrs. Felber cried. "Leave him alone! He's not right in the head. He won't be able to tell you anything."

Ethan loosened his hold on Horace. "It looks like Chester is the one who has all the answers."

"No!" she insisted. "He doesn't understand—"

Mrs. Felber didn't wait to finish her sentence, just shoved her way back through the curtains and out of sight. Ethan heard her heels pounding on the wooden floor, then the slam of the back door.

"Where's Chester now?" Ethan demanded of Horace.

"I don't know. I—"

Ethan leapt over the counter to follow Mrs. Felber.

Boyd was right behind him. "Wait for me, Ethan!"

Ethan damned the badly scarred leg that kept him from moving at a run. Once out the back door of the mercantile, Ethan saw a flash of green gingham that looked like Mrs. Felber's skirt going around a corner at the end of the alley and headed toward it.

When they got there, she had disappeared.

"She probably headed for the Felbers' barn. Chester lives in a room there," Boyd said.

"Let's go."

It took only a matter of minutes to reach the barn on the outskirts of town where Chester milked the cows. Ethan shoved the barn door open and let the sun stream in. The pungent smells of fresh manure and hay assaulted him.

It was long past the morning milking time, and the cows had been driven back out to pasture. He found the tiny room with its simple wooden bed and table where Chester apparently lived. The door hung slack on leather hinges. The only things moving were dust motes in the sunlight. The barn was empty.

"So where are they? Mrs. Felber and her son?" Ethan demanded angrily of Boyd. "You said they'd be here."

"How the hell should I know where they are?" Boyd retorted. "I thought she'd come here. She was headed in this direction."

"Where else could they have gone?" Ethan queried.

"Home, maybe," Boyd suggested.

"I'll go check the Felbers' house," Ethan said. "You take another look around here."

The two men split up and began their search. Ethan knocked and, when there was no answer, let himself in the Felbers' house. There was no one there. Disgusted, but not yet ready to give up the search, he headed out past the houses on the edge of town toward the cow pasture.

He froze when he heard a twig snap behind him. Too late, he remembered the gunman who had been hired to kill him.

"Lucky for you I'm not Calloway. You'd be dead now."

Ethan heaved a sigh of relief. He turned to find Frank lounging against a backyard fence. "Is that his name? Calloway?"

"Yep. Brought him out to the ranch last night myself," Frank said. "Meant to come find you earlier this morning to warn you about him, but I guess it wasn't necessary after all. According to Slim, the two of you already met at the Silver Buckle."

"We did."

"Thought sure you would already have drawn on each other. What's the holdup?"

Ethan grinned. "I'm not ready to die, and I guess he isn't, either."

Frank laughed. "I've been following your trail all morning. Boyd sent me out here from the barn to find you. What's going on?"

"Walk with me while we talk."

Frank slipped into step with Ethan as he stalked—long step, halting step—the streets and alleys of Oakville, searching for his quarry.

"I'm looking for Chester Felber and his mother," Ethan explained. "If I had to guess, I'd say Mrs. Felber ducked into a friend's house somewhere around here. I just wish I knew whether she has Chester with her, and if not, where the hell he is."

"Why are you hunting Chester?"

"I suspect he's the one who's been putting arsenic in Ma's milk. Maybe in the whiskey Pa drank, too. At least, Mrs. Felber acted awful damn suspicious when I started asking questions. She was ranting and raving about how poor Chester doesn't know what he's doing, and how he can't be held responsible. Well, if he isn't responsible, I damn well know who is!"

"Your ma was poisoned? Your pa, too? I can't believe it!"

"Everything points in that direction. I sent some samples off on the stage this morning to a chemist in San Antonio." Ethan stopped. "Hell, I won't find him now unless I start knocking on doors. And I'm not ready to do that. Yet."

He headed back toward the barn as fast as his hitching gait would allow. "Come on, if you're coming."

Frank did a hop-skip to catch up, then matched Ethan's stride as best he could. "Where are we going?"

"I want to see if Boyd found anything in the Felbers' barn. Then I'm going to pay a visit to the sheriff."

"Surely you're not expecting any help from Careless," Frank said. "I mean, not if you're going to accuse who I think you're going to accuse."

"Careless can keep an eye out for Chester. And he can question Horace and his wife."

"What good will that do you?"

"Maybe none," Ethan conceded. "But at least it'll put everyone on notice that I'm through running."

Frank eyed Ethan sideways. "I don't understand."

Ethan paused for a moment and met Frank's glance. "I'm through running from Trahern. From now on, he's the one who'd better watch his back."

Ethan walked through the open barn door, and Frank followed him inside.

The barn was quiet. "Boyd? You in here somewhere?" Ethan called.

"Up here," Boyd said.

"You find anything worth mentioning?"

Boyd came down the ladder from the loft. "I found this." He handed Ethan a small cloth bag that contained a powdery white substance.

"What is it?"

"I'd guess it's arsenic," Boyd said.

Frank whistled. "So Chester really was putting poison in your ma's milk."

"We'd have to get someone to confirm that this is arsenic," Ethan said as he hefted the bag in his hand.

"Even then, you don't have proof it was Chester who did it. Someone else might have kept the poison here and slipped it into the milk when Chester wasn't looking," Boyd suggested.

"I'm sticking with Chester as the guilty party until I get a better suspect," Ethan said. "But even if Chester did put the poison in the milk, I'm betting he didn't act on his own. He doesn't have the brains to think out something like that. Or the motive to do it. Someone told Chester what to do. Someone gave him the poison."

"Trahern?" Boyd asked.

"Who else?" Ethan replied in a harsh voice. "He blames me for Dorne's death. He blames me for what happened to Merielle. He hated my father for helping me get away. He wants me to suffer the way he's suffered all these years. Killing my father and mother would accomplish that.

"Give me another suspect," Ethan demanded of his friends. "Tell me who else has a motive to attack me and my family."

Ethan's two friends remained silent.

At last Frank said, "You need to find Chester. He could tell you who asked him to put the poison in the milk. That way you'd know for sure."

Ethan took off his hat, shoved his fingers through his hair in agitation, and pulled his hat back down. "I can't help thinking he won't go far. Not on his own, anyway."

Frank grinned. "I wonder who Horace will find to milk his cows now. Do you think he'll do it himself?"

The three men looked at each other and broke out laughing at the thought of Horace Felber sitting on a milkstool with his hands on a pair of udders. Their common dislike of the man ran long and deep. Horace hadn't been the kind of shopkeeper who offered free licorice to penniless eight- and nine-year-old kids. The three inseparable friends had each taken a turn distracting Horace while the others stole candy from the jars on the counter. Their sugary loot was relished all the more for the fact it had been taken from beneath Horace Felber's nose.

Boyd sobered first, recalling the day when they had finally been discovered in the act. Horace had caught Boyd red-handed with his fingers in the jar of licorice. Boyd would never forget the humiliation of being seized by the ear and yanked all the way across the street to the sheriff's office. He was thrown into a cell with Cyrus McFee, the town drunk.

The cell stank of vomit and urine, and Boyd gagged trying to breathe. Even worse was the knowledge of what his father would do when he came to get him out. Boyd had known he was going to get a licking. The anticipation of that beating was making his stomach roll.

What he hadn't expected was that his father would just leave him there. He spent three days in that cell, the second two alone, before Clete Stuckey showed up to claim him. Boyd had felt relief when he first saw his father's face. It lasted no longer than the first blow of his drunken father's fist on his back. He had fled the jail—and his father—as fast as his legs could carry him.

Boyd had learned later that when he didn't get out of jail the first day, Ethan had begged his father to do something to help. Alex Hawk had gone hunting Clete. It had taken a day to find him and a day to sober him up enough to sit on a horse. Clete hadn't thanked either Alex or Ethan for the favor. Boyd had done it himself. Boyd had had no use for his father after that. He had resolutely and thoroughly killed what little love he'd had for him.

He hadn't mourned when Clete Stuckey had fallen off his horse drunk one rainy winter night and died of exposure. Despite the fact that by then Boyd was comfortably well off, he had allowed his father to be buried in an unmarked pauper's grave. He had given back to his father exactly what he had gotten from him—nothing.

Boyd jerked reflexively when Ethan put an arm around his shoulder. He forced himself to relax. They had no way of knowing that the wounds of the past still had the power to hurt him. He hid his bitterness, his anger, and his regret in a charming smile.

"Come on," he said to his friends, throwing his free arm around Frank's shoulder. "Let's go see the sheriff."

Frank excused himself before they got to the main street of town. "Considering Trahern's my boss, I think maybe I'd better leave you two here. Remember to watch out for Calloway," he said to Ethan in parting.

"Who's Calloway?" Boyd asked once Frank was gone.

"The gunfighter Trahern has hired to put me six feet under."

"Calloway. Sounds familiar." Boyd repeated the name several times to himself, then snapped his fingers as he recollected where he had heard it before. "I remember now. Calloway's a bounty hunter. Goes after outlaws with a price on their heads, men wanted dead or alive. Rumor is, Calloway brings them back dead. All done legal, of course."

"Of course." Ethan frowned as he considered what Boyd had revealed. "I'm not wanted by the law anymore. I wonder what Trahern told Calloway about me when he hired him on. Especially if Calloway likes his killing to be legal."

"You can bet he made it look like the fact you're not a wanted man is just a technicality," Boyd said. "And I'm sure he put the price high enough for Calloway to ignore the small print."

"Still, it might be worth having a talk with Calloway sometime."

Boyd grinned and shook his head. "You never cease to amaze me, Ethan. What makes you think that bounty hunter is going to let you get two words out of your mouth before he shoots you?"

"You've been living on the right side of the law too long, Boyd. There is such a thing as honor among thieves."

Boyd grinned his charming grin. "I'll take your word for it."

They stepped out of an alley onto Main Street a few doors down from the jail. And saw Jefferson Trahern leaving the sheriff's office.

Ethan froze. Here was the man who had murdered his father. Poisoned his mother. Put him in prison for seven long, nightmarish years. Here was the man who wanted his sister orphaned. Who wanted him dead.

"Trahern!" he shouted. "I'm going to kill you!"

The whole of Main Street stood frozen in tableau as Ethan made his threat.

Ethan had reached the middle of the street by the time Boyd caught up to him. Boyd grabbed Ethan around the chest from behind and pinned his arms so he couldn't reach his gun. "Have you lost your wits, Ethan?" he hissed in his friend's ear. "Do you want to end up swinging from a rope for murder?"

"Let me go, Boyd. I'm going to kill him."

Trahern had opened the jailhouse door and called inside to the sheriff. Careless immediately appeared on the boardwalk beside him. It was clear the sheriff didn't want any part of what was happening, but Trahern gave him a shove and he headed toward Ethan.

"Now, Ethan," Careless said, shoving his gunbelt down under his belly where it was more comfortable. "What's all this about?"

"Trahern killed my father. He poisoned my mother. He deserves to die."

"What are you ranting about?" Trahern demanded from where he stood on the boardwalk. "I did no such thing."

"No sense lying," Ethan said. "We found the arsenic you used to do the job."

"You're insane! stark raving crazy!"

The townsfolk listened with big ears. No one had ever challenged Trahern. Not until now.

"It's your turn to watch your back, Trahern," Ethan shouted across to Trahern. "You won't know when the bullet's coming, or where it'll happen. But if it's the last thing I do, I'm going to kill you."

Trahern didn't dignify Ethan's final threat with a response. He simply called to Careless, "Sheriff, arrest that man."

Careless felt like a worm in a bed of ants. If he wasn't careful, he'd get eaten alive. "Hell, Mr. Trahern. What'm I goin' to arrest him for? Ain't no law 'gainst talkin' like a jackass."

"Ethan Hawk just threatened to kill me," Trahern said, exasperated with the lack of response from the sheriff.

"Well, he ain't committed no crime till he does!" Careless snapped back.

The flush shot up Trahern's neck and left his cheeks ruddy with rage. "Do *something*, Careless, or you'll find yourself looking for a new job."

Careless swore up one side and down the other. He turned to Ethan and said, "Go on home 'fore I arrest you for loiterin'."

When Ethan began to back away, Boyd released him.

"I'm going," Ethan said. "But don't forget what I said. Soon, Trahern. Someday soon."

Ethan untangled the reins of his horse from the post in front of the saloon where he was tied, mounted, and rode out of town, leaving several nervous people behind him.

One man knew what had to be done now and set his plans in motion.

✳13✳

Ever since Patch had kissed Ethan in the barn, he had kept his distance. She wasn't sure what it was that made him stay away. She had the sneaking suspicion that Ethan thought he had to treat the lady she had become with kid gloves, and that his leather ones weren't a good enough substitute.

Patch wrinkled her nose in disgust. She had gone to a lot of trouble to become a lady because that was what she thought Ethan wanted her to be. But it seemed there wasn't much use for a lady on a ranch like the Double Diamond. More often than not, the work was backbreaking, grueling. It couldn't be done in a corset. Velvet and satin had no place on the prairie. Cotton and wool absorbed sweat better and could be cleaned easier.

Because being a lady hadn't seemed as important on the ranch, Patch had slipped back into a few old habits. A *garn* here and a *durn it* there hadn't seemed so bad. Sometimes the occasion demanded it. Like when she had found that hawk with a wing broken, flapping around in the chicken house, and Ethan had wanted to kill it.

"Durn it, Ethan! This bird wouldn't be caught dead chasing chickens if he could fly!" she had shouted.

"Well, he can't fly! I've got enough things to do on this ranch without running a refuge for chicken-stealing hawks!"

"I can fix its wing!" she had protested. "I know I can."

"Then what? Once you tame an animal like that, it won't want to fly free again."

"Garn! Who said I plan to tame it? I just want to help it get well! Then it's free to go whatever way it wants."

"What if it doesn't want to leave you? Then you'll be stuck with it!" he yelled.

"So I'll be stuck with it!" she shouted back. "I happen to *love* the poor, dumb animals that cross my path—and I don't feel *stuck* when they love me back!"

She had thought he was going to explode, he was so mad. He bit out, "Suit yourself!" and marched off in high dudgeon.

She had named the hawk Penny, because his feathers had a coppery sheen like a new Indian head penny. She kept him tied by one foot to a perch in the kitchen, and he had learned to take raw meat from her gloved hand. She had seen him eyeing the kittens and moved their basket to safety in the bedroom she shared with Leah. The raccoon, Bandit, knew enough to keep himself out of harm's way.

Leah had been fascinated by the hawk, and Patch had let the girl take over his feeding as she had with Dearie. In this particular respect, the love of wild animals, the two of them were in perfect accord. So when Leah found a rabbit caught in one of the rat traps Ethan had set around the barn, she brought it directly to Patch.

Patch took one look at Leah's white face and asked, "What's wrong?"

"His foot is cut nearly in two."

Patch hadn't been able to save the rabbit's left front paw. She had done some quick surgery and stopped the bleeding, and the rabbit seemed to be healing fine.

Ethan laughed when he heard Leah had named her new pet Lucky. "What's lucky about losing a foot? Especially a *rabbit's* foot."

"Don't you see?" Leah said as she cuddled the small brown rabbit close to her chest. "If I hadn't found him when I did, some coyote or hawk or snake might have come along and eaten him. I rescued him, instead. Wasn't that lucky?"

Ethan had protested that between Patch and Leah his home would soon be overrun by animals. In fact, since that night the menagerie had grown by a horned toad and a jar that contained a leafy stem upon which a caterpillar had spun itself into a chrysalis.

The kitchen door grated open, and Ethan leaned in to say, "Patch? Are you ready to go?"

"I'll be with you in a minute, Ethan."

She had begged Ethan to show her the cave he and Boyd and Frank had used as a secret hideout, and he was finally taking her there today. She had talked Grandpa Corwin into coming to the house to keep Leah and Nell—who was feeling better every day—company while they were gone.

Patch put down her pen and blew on the letter she was writing to her parents, to make sure it was dry before she folded it. She would get Grandpa Corwin to take it to the post office when he went back to town today. She stood and stretched out the kinks from sitting so long at the kitchen table writing.

Ethan was staring at her strangely, so she asked, "Is anything wrong?"

"Those are the pants you're wearing?"

Patch turned in a circle for him. "What do you think?"

He swallowed hard. "You look . . . fine. Hurry up. I'll wait for you at the barn."

Patch looked down and tried to figure out what it was Ethan didn't like about the way she was dressed. He was the one who had insisted she wear pants. She had put on the jeans she had bought in town her first day in Oakville. While they were a little snug in the hips, she couldn't see anything wrong with them. She certainly wasn't about to change now.

Once they were on the trail, Patch could barely contain her excitement. "I've been wanting to see this cave ever since Frank first mentioned it."

"Why?"

"I guess because I've pictured the three of you there in my mind, and I wanted to see the real thing."

"Don't get your hopes up. It's not much to look at."

"Are you sure you don't mind taking the time to do this with me?"

Actually, Ethan had a dozen other things that should have claimed his attention. But at breakfast, when Patch had asked, he hadn't been able to say no. She had looked so beautiful, her eyes radiant, freckles scattered across her freshly washed face, that the thought of spending the morning with her had been too much to resist. He had agreed that, once his chores were done, he would show her the cave.

Ethan didn't regret his decision. But he could see he had underestimated the temptation he would face, alone with her like this, especially with her dressed in those pants.

He didn't want to talk about what was uppermost in both of their minds, so he remained silent. To his surprise, Patch was content to ride beside him, enjoying the peace and quiet.

When he pointed out the cave to her at last, she reined her horse to a stop and shaded her eyes so she could see it better. Their secret hideout was located along the bank of the Nueces, shaded by hackberry and elm. The cave opening was hidden by mesquite bushes and guarded by a patch of catclaw cactus.

Patch urged her horse into a lope and jumped down from the saddle when she arrived at the cave opening, ready to explore. Ethan quickly followed her, caught up in her unrestrained enthusiasm.

"So this is the infamous secret cave. It's bigger than I expected it to be. I'll bet I could stand up in there." Patch stuck her upper body in the narrow opening and peered down inside. "It seems to go a long way back." She leaned in and shouted, "Helloooo!" Patch laughed when her voice echoed back to her.

Ethan was too busy looking at Patch's rear end in those damned tight-fitting pants to pay much attention to the cave. Why on earth had he agreed to bring her here? He should never have insisted she wear pants. It had been a distinct shock to see her long legs and shapely hips when what he had expected was the same shabby, formless trousers she had worn as a child. The snug Levi's were a forceful reminder that Patch Kendrick was a grown woman.

What was worse, Ethan knew they were completely alone, and that they were unlikely to be disturbed. The ideas he was having about Patch were enough to get him hung.

"Can we go inside the cave?" she asked.

"If you like."

"Which is better, to go in headfirst or feetfirst?"

"Let me go in first," Ethan said with a rueful grin. He wouldn't be able to stand the sight of Patch wriggling her way inside. "We used to keep a lantern in there and some matches in a tin box. I'll see if I can get you some light so you don't break your neck."

Patch was enchanted with the interior of the cave. Though the morning was sunny and hot, the cave was cool. It was bone dry inside, but the rock walls and floor were polished smooth as though water had once run through it. "How did you ever find this place?"

"I didn't. Boyd found it and shared it with me and Frank." Ethan lit the lantern and set it on a natural stone shelf.

Patch sat on a low, flat-topped rock that made a perfect chair. "You three must have had some wonderful times here."

Ethan forked himself down over a wooden crate that had been left in the cave. Between them lay a darkened circle ringed with stones that had obviously been a fireplace. "We used to meet here and talk and plan and dream."

"About what?"

"Girls, mostly."

"Did you have a special girl back then?"

Ethan shook his head. "Boyd was the ladies' man."

"I can believe it, as charming as he is now."

Ethan picked up a polished stone and smoothed it between his fingers. "We used to plan how we were going to own all the land around here. How we'd have so many cattle that at roundup time our longhorns would stretch as far as the eye could see.

"It's strange how our fortunes have changed. Of the three of us, Boyd had the least back then. Now he's a successful businessman with a ranch of his own. Frank is foreman of the largest spread in these parts. While I . . ."

"You have the Double Diamond," Patch said.

Ethan snorted. "What's left of it. Most of the cattle have been rustled, the buildings all need repair, and the house is falling down around us. I'm flat broke, and I can't borrow money from the bank."

"Maybe Boyd would loan you some money."

"Sure he would! If I asked. But I'm not going to. All I've got left is my pride, dammit!"

Ethan threw the stone he was holding with all the force of the frustration he felt. It ricocheted off the stone wall and headed back toward Patch. "Look out!"

Ethan moved at the same time he yelled, grabbing Patch and tumbling her out of harm's way. They ended up on the floor of the cave in a tangled heap of arms and legs.

Patch was lying under Ethan, her single braid coming undone. She smiled up at him. "Seems like we've done this before."

Both of them were reminded vividly of the first day they had met in the Oakville Hotel, when Ethan had admired her, before he had known who she was. Ethan took his weight on his elbows, and his body slipped between her thighs. There was less cloth between them this time, only his jeans and hers.

Patch could feel the shape of him, the contours that made him male to her female. She felt his arousal, saw the quick flare of need in his eyes.

"Make love to me, Ethan," she said. "Show me what it means to be a woman."

Ethan tenderly brushed a stray hair back from her face. "Patch, you don't know what you're asking. Nothing in my life is settled. In fact, things are worse than ever. There's a hired gun dogging my footsteps—"

She put her fingertips on his lips to shush him. "I don't want to think about tomorrow. I want to live for today."

Ethan turned his head away to avoid the appeal in her liquid eyes.

"You don't want me?"

His head snapped back around. Feral eyes found hers. "Woman, I'm on fire for you! But I like and respect your father too much to—"

"What about liking and respecting me? What about what I want?"

"You're too young—"

Patch shoved Ethan off her and scrambled to her feet. "If I hear again how *young* I am, I think I'll scream."

"But you *are* young!"

Patch screamed.

Ethan caught her and put a hand over her mouth. "That's enough, brat! I get your point!"

When the echo ended, Patch pulled his hand down so she could speak. "I'm old enough to know my own mind, Ethan. I'm old enough to know what I want and go after it. And I want a life with you."

"When you grow up, Patch, you find out that you don't always get what you want," Ethan said bitterly.

Patch bit her lip on further argument. There was time still to wear him down. He wanted her. It was only circumstances that were keeping them apart. She had to work harder, investigate further, faster. In the secrets of the past lay the hope for her future with Ethan.

"I'm supposed to meet Merielle this afternoon. We're going on a picnic together. Can you join us?"

"I don't think that's a good idea."

"Why not?"

A muscle jerked in Ethan's cheek. "You know why not. Besides, I've got work to do."

"Then I guess I'll invite Boyd to come along. He's good company."

Patch had been hoping for a jealous reaction from Ethan. She was unprepared for the one she got. Lickety-split he had her pressed up against the stone wall of the cave. He pinned her there with his hips and tangled his fingers in her hair.

"Don't play games with me, Patch. If you choose Boyd, I won't stand in your way. He's a good man. But don't play us off against each other. He won't like it. Neither will I."

"So noble of you to stand aside for your friend," Patch said with a sneer. "Now get out of my way. I want to leave."

Ethan found the thought of Patch with Boyd unbearable. He wanted to claim her as his own. So he kissed her. And knew right away he had made a mistake, because Patch responded. She always responded. With her heart. With her soul. He took and took with his mouth and gave back what he had no right to give. Somehow he pulled away. He wasn't going to let her goad him into doing something he would be sorry for later.

He was having trouble drawing breath.

So was she. Her mouth was slightly open, her eyes dilated, her body quivering with need.

"It isn't going to work, Patch. I'm letting you go."

It was harder than he had thought it was going to be. He was aware of how silky her hair was as his hands slid free. He felt her shudder as he levered himself away from her. Her chin was trembling, and he wanted to pull her back into his arms and hold her tight and be her bulwark against the world.

"Damn you, Patch," he muttered. "You don't fight fair."

Patch didn't speak again as she shimmied her way out of the cave. Ethan got tired of watching her fanny wriggle like a worm on a hook. He gave her a shove that sent her out through the opening before he ended up taking the bait like some stupid fish.

Patch leaned down and called, "Are you coming, Ethan?"

"I think I'll stay in here for a while."

"Suit yourself!"

He could tell she was angry. And frustrated. So was he.

With any luck she would think of *him* when she spent the afternoon with Boyd Stuckey.

"Ethan! Come quick!"

Ethan scrambled out of the cave the instant he heard Patch's cry for help, his heart in his throat, his adrenaline pumping. "What's wrong? Are you all right?"

Once outside the cave he looked where she pointed and saw what had caused her distress. "A fox? You scared the pants off me for a *fox*?"

"A kit—a *baby* fox," Patch said, her chin stuck defiantly in the air. "He's stuck in this patch of cactus." She was on her knees beside the mouth of the cave. Her fingertips and the backs of her hands were covered with cactus stickers she had apparently collected while trying to rescue the fox from where it was trapped in the thorny maze.

"How do you suppose it got in there?" Patch asked.

"I don't know. I can't believe you tried getting him out of there without wearing gloves. Give me your hands."

"I need to—"

"Give me your hands!" Ethan snarled.

Patch extended her hands.

He took them in his and turned them over. "Dammit, Patch! Look what you've done to yourself. You're a bloody mess. We'd better get these hands taken care of, and fast."

When he tried to draw her to her feet, she wouldn't rise.

"Ethan, please, will you help me get the kit free? It's going to starve if we don't do something."

He didn't know whether to be irritated by her stubbornness or enchanted by the look of appeal on her face. He settled for a quick, hard kiss.

"What was that for?"

"Because . . ."

I love you.

He was appalled at the words that leapt to his mind. At least he knew better than to speak them.

"Because you're going to need something else to think about besides your hands when I start pulling out those cactus needles."

"The kit—"

"After I free the kit, of course."

He took her by the shoulders and moved her bodily aside, then pulled on his leather gloves and reached down through the thorny cactus to retrieve the baby fox.

The kit snapped at him, and he jerked back his hand. A bead of red welled through the rawhide.

"Feisty little son of a gun," Ethan murmured.

"Be gentle," Patch admonished.

"I hope you're talking to the fox," Ethan said. "He's the one with the rotten temper."

Patch grinned. "That goes for both of you."

The instant Ethan freed the fox, it took off like a pack of hounds was chasing it.

"Happy now?" Ethan asked.

"Happy." Patch looked down at her hands. "But I think it's time we took care of my hands—and yours."

They walked down to the riverbank and made themselves comfortable while Ethan painstakingly picked the stickers out of Patch's fingertips and the backs of her hands.

They spent the next half hour soaking their wounded hands in the cool river water. Patch took off her shoes and soaked her feet too. She laughed at him when he told her he'd keep his boots on. She looked adorable. Lovable. Kissable. It was all he could do to keep his hands off her.

With the thoughts he was having about Patch, Ethan thought his time would have been better spent soaking his head.

He was jealous, he realized, of his best friend.

"Are you going to invite Boyd on that picnic?" he asked.

She flashed a wary look at him. "Yes."

Ethan's jaw tightened, but he refused to let her provoke him to anger again. He rose abruptly. "We'd better get moving, then, if you're going to have time to get ready."

Ethan tensed as he felt Patch's fingertips on his arm.

"Are you sure you can't come, too?"

He purposely avoided looking at her, afraid he would succumb to the entreaty he was sure to find in her eyes. He didn't want to spend the afternoon in her company, watching her be charmed by Boyd Stuckey. Because he was liable to end up punching his best friend in the nose.

"I've got work to do," he said in a harsh voice.

He saw her flinch. He was aware of the moment she removed her hand from his arm and drew away from him.

"All right, Ethan," she said. "I understand."

He watched her walk away from him, her back stiffened by that iron rod, reminding him of who and what she was—and why he had no right to claim her for his own.

He held himself rigid to keep from running after her, to keep from pulling her into his arms and holding her close, to keep from laying her down on the cool grass and loving her as he longed to do.

"Damn, damn, damn," he muttered.

It was time to find the man responsible for Merielle's rape. Therein lay his only hope for a future with the shamelessly saucy lady who was slowly but surely claiming his heart.

———————

Trahern turned a jaundiced eye on the gunfighter sitting across from him in his parlor. "Why isn't Ethan Hawk dead yet?"

"I like to get to know a man before I make my move," Calloway said.

"You've had a week. How long does it take?" Trahern demanded irritably.

Calloway focused wintry gray eyes on the man who had hired him. "I've had my doubts about this job from the day I got here. Your telegram said Ethan Hawk was wanted by the law, but there's no poster on him that I can find."

Trahern flushed guiltily.

"I'll make up my own mind when and where—and whether—I'll handle this job. If you don't like the way I do business, find yourself another man." Calloway stood to leave.

"No need to be hasty," Trahern said, rising to block the door. "You can understand my concern. After all, the man threatened my life."

"Seems to me he had some provocation."

The narrow smile on Calloway's face chilled Trahern to the bone. He sputtered a denial. "It's not the same thing at all. The man raped my daughter!"

"So you said." Calloway started for the door.

Trahern stood to block his way. "So? Are you going to do the job or not?"

Calloway waited for Trahern to move aside and let him pass. Trahern debated the wisdom of staying where he was. He took a step to the left. "Where can I contact you?"

"You can't." Calloway left the parlor, then turned back to Trahern from the central hallway. "You'll hear from me."

Calloway reached the front door at almost the same time as Merielle reached the foot of the stairs.

"Hello," she said. "You must be a friend of Father's."

Calloway tipped his hat. "An acquaintance only, ma'am."

Merielle didn't notice the distinction, but Trahern did. He marveled that his daughter seemed unafraid of the intimidating gunfighter.

Merielle saw only kindness in the face that looked down at her. The tenderness in the gunman's gray eyes for the child-woman would have amazed her father and appalled Calloway, had he realized it was visible.

"Excuse me," he said to Merielle. "I have business that needs tending."

When Merielle shut the door behind the gunfighter, Trahern joined his daughter. "You're looking very pretty. What's the occasion?" he asked.

"Have you forgotten? I'm going on a picnic this afternoon with my new friend, Patch."

"I had forgotten. Where are you planning to have this picnic?"

"Somewhere along the river, where it's shady and cool."

Trahern looked at his precious child and debated the wisdom of letting her go off alone with that Kendrick woman. He knew it was unreasonable to deny her the pleasure of going, simply because he would worry about her while she was gone. He decided the best solution was to send someone along to keep an eye on her. "What would you think about taking Frank along on this picnic?"

Merielle smiled brightly. "Why, what a wonderful idea, Father! I'll go ask him now."

When Patch arrived in a buggy with Boyd at her side and a picnic basket under her feet, she found Merielle waiting on the front steps with Frank beside her.

Merielle looked like a flower in springtime. She was wearing a yellow gingham dress, with short, puffy sleeves trimmed in eyelet lace. A wide-brimmed straw hat banded with matching yellow gingham was tied with a large bow at her chin.

In contrast, Patch looked more like the cool moss that draped the live oaks. Not that she wasn't dressed well, just more sedately. She wore a pleated white cotton blouse and a moss green skirt of sturdy bombazine, something she knew would be comfortable and durable for an afternoon spent sitting on the ground. Seeing how lovely Merielle looked, Patch wished she had been less practical.

"Frank's going with us," Merielle said. "I hope that's all right with you."

"And I invited Boyd," Patch replied. "I hope that's all right with you."

Merielle glanced quickly at Boyd and then back at Patch. "I guess it's okay."

Frank helped Merielle up into the buggy he had harnessed for the two of them. "Follow us," he said. "Merielle has a spot all picked out."

Patch laughed when she realized Frank had driven straight to the cave. "I was just here this morning with Ethan," she confessed to Boyd. "I can't say I'm sorry to be back. It's a wonderful place."

They chose a shady spot under an elm and began unloading the picnic supplies from the buggy, including a jug of cold lemonade. Patch had brought a quilt, which they spread on the ground to make it harder for the ants to get to the food.

Patch noticed that Merielle shied away from Boyd when he came in her direction and clutched Frank's arm.

"Shall we eat now, or later?" Frank asked.

"Can we go for a walk along the river first?" Merielle asked.

"Why don't you and Frank go for a walk, while Boyd and I finishing setting out the food?" Patch saw the grateful look on Frank's face. She had seen how he watched Merielle from afar with his heart in his eyes. It couldn't hurt to give them some time alone together. That would also give her the opportunity to get to know Ethan's best friend better. It was important that she make it clear to Boyd that she wasn't interested in being anything but his friend. Hopefully, she could spend time with Merielle after lunch while the men went down to the river to fish.

"Enjoy yourselves," Patch said. "Come back when you get hungry."

Merielle was already chattering to Frank as he led her away. "Do you think it would be all right if I took off my shoes and stockings and walked barefoot along the river?"

"I don't know, Merielle—"

"It would be so much fun, Frank. Do you remember how we used to spend hours sitting on the bank, letting the fish nibble at our toes?"

Frank stared hard at Merielle. "You remember that?" he asked sharply.

She smiled up at him, apparently unaware that her recollection of the past had any special significance. "Of course I do. I remember lots of things."

"Like what?"

"First you have to promise to take off your boots and socks and join me," she teased.

"All right. I promise," Frank said with a grin that made his eyes crinkle at the corners.

"I love the way you look when you smile," Merielle said.

Frank didn't know what to say. He wasn't used to compliments from Merielle, especially not the kind that a woman gave to a man. It made him uncomfortable, and he had to struggle to keep the smile on his face. Somehow, for her sake, he succeeded.

They had reached the riverbank, where Merielle plopped down on a rotting log and pulled her skirt up to her knees so she could get to the laces on her shoes.

"Let me help you." Frank went down on one knee and took her tiny foot in his hand. He felt her resist and looked up to reassure her that he wasn't going to hurt her. There was a stunned look on her face, and he wondered what she was thinking.

"Merielle?"

"Frank?" Merielle stared at the handsome man who knelt at her feet. She couldn't remember a time when Frank hadn't been near. Yet, it was as though she were seeing him for the first time. It was confusing because she expected him to look younger. This face was more mature, weathered by age and sun, and there was a shadow of a beard where before there had been none. His hair was thick and dark, and somehow she knew how it would feel under her hands.

Merielle slipped Frank's hat off without asking for permission and set it on the log beside her. She traced the line of his jaw and felt him swallow. She tried to make the person before her match the image in her mind.

"You're so much older," she murmured.

Frank felt his heart leap with hope. "It's been a long time since I've seen you, Merielle."

She looked down into his eyes. "Where have you been, Frank?"

"Right here," he whispered through a throat swollen with joy. "Waiting for you to come back to me."

Merielle laughed. "That's silly. I haven't gone anywhere. Hurry up, Frank, and unlace my shoes. I want to go play in the water."

Merielle was gone again and the child was back. Frank concentrated on unlacing her shoes, and watched her rip off her stockings with a childlike lack of modesty that only endeared her to him.

"Hurry up, Frank," she urged. "Take off your boots and socks and come play with me."

Frank forced himself back into the role of protective older brother. He would be for her what she needed him to be. Once Frank was barefoot he took her hand, and they ran down toward the water. At the very edge, Merielle stopped abruptly.

"Do you think it's cold?"

"Like ice," he said.

She grinned. "Good!" She leaned over and splashed a handful of water right in his face. Then she ran.

Frank caught her up in his arms and swung her around in a dizzying circle.

She laughed like a child, but she felt like a woman in his arms. He stopped and stared down at her, his heart pounding.

She looked up at him, and her eyes clouded. Her fingers threaded into his hair, and she pulled his head down toward her mouth.

"Frank, where are you?" Boyd called. "We're ready to eat."

Frank let Merielle's legs slide down the front of him until she was standing on her own. They never took their eyes off each other. Their bodies were pressed close together. He kept waiting for her to change back, to become the childlike Merielle. When she didn't, he kissed her, like a starving man who has found the sustenance that will keep him alive.

And she kissed him back. Without fear. With enthusiasm. With delight.

He broke the kiss and hugged her tight against him, hardly able to believe the miracle in his arms. "Merielle. After all these years. Finally. Merielle."

"Frank, my head hurts," she said. "It hurts so bad."

He felt her go limp. She would have fallen if he hadn't caught her. "Merielle? Merielle!"

She was unconscious.

"Boyd! Patch! Somebody! Help!" He fell to his knees with Merielle in his arms. "Somebody please help."

✤ 14 ✤

PATCH AND BOYD CAME on the run. It was immediately apparent that Merielle had fainted. It was not so apparent why.

Patch looked anxiously from Frank to Merielle and back again. She had stopped suspecting Frank of rape. He had seemed too attentive, too much in love with Merielle. But the situation raised her doubts again.

"What happened?" Patch asked as she dropped to the ground beside Frank.

Frank never took his eyes off Merielle. "I don't know. She said her head hurt, and then she fainted."

Boyd went down on one knee and reached across to check Merielle's pulse at her throat. "Her pulse is strong."

"Do you know what caused this to happen?" Patch asked Frank.

"She was remembering."

Patch could barely contain her excitement. *"Remembering?"*

"You mean she got her memory back?" Boyd demanded in a taut voice.

Frank winced under the force of Boyd's grip on his shoulder. "Not exactly. It was more like she seemed to be *here,* you know, not stuck in the past."

"Has this happened before?" Boyd asked.

"Not the same thing, but something similar," Frank replied. "A week or so ago she remembered a time in the far past when the two of us were together."

"I can't believe this is happening," Patch said. "I mean, I prayed for it, and I hoped for it, but . . . It's like a miracle!"

Frank nodded. "It is a miracle."

Merielle's eyelids fluttered and a moan issued from her throat. When she opened her eyes, they were clouded with confusion. She looked around at the trees and the river and the three people staring anxiously down at her. Her brow furrowed in thought. "Where am I? How did I get here?"

"Don't you remember?" Frank asked in a gentle voice. "We came to the river for a picnic."

Merielle's eyes sought out Patch. "Yes. I came with my friend, Patch." Her glance slid past Boyd and back to Frank. "We went for a walk by the river. I wanted to take my shoes and stockings off and play in the water."

Frank took one of her bare feet in his hands. "So you did."

She placed her palm on Frank's cheek. "I remember splashing your face."

He smiled. "So you did."

"Then . . ." She looked up at Frank. "Then . . . then . . . Why can't I remember any more, Frank?"

Frank tucked her head under his chin and held her close. He met Patch's somber face and Boyd's sympathetic gaze. "It's all right, Merielle. It doesn't matter."

Patch put a comforting hand on Merielle's shoulder. She felt like howling with disappointment. To get so close! And then to have the doors shut again. But if it had happened once, it might happen again. Patch couldn't help feeling optimistic.

However, from the wan aspect of Merielle's face, remembering had taken its toll on her. "Maybe we should postpone our picnic to another time," Patch suggested.

"Oh, no!" Merielle said. "I feel fine! Please, let's stay."

Patch looked to Frank to see what he thought. When he nodded she said, "All right. We'll stay. But let's go eat. I'm starving!"

After they ate, Frank settled on the blanket with a lapful of daisies that Merielle began weaving into a chain, while Patch and Boyd took a walk.

Patch had been itching to discuss Merielle's situation all through lunch but felt constrained to be silent in the young woman's presence. As soon as they were out of earshot, Patch turned to Boyd and said, "Do you know how much it will mean to Ethan if Merielle regains her memory?"

"You're assuming, of course, that Ethan didn't rape Merielle," Boyd said flatly.

"Of course he didn't! You're his best friend. You of all people should know he couldn't possibly—"

Boyd held up both hands in surrender. "You win. I'm convinced Ethan is innocent." He reached out and put his hands over hers, which were perched in balled fists on her hips. "Can we talk now about something nearer and dearer to my heart?"

Patch was still bristling from Boyd's accusation of Ethan, and his ready capitulation hadn't done much to assuage her wrath. "Like what?"

He gently pried her hands loose and opened them so her fingertips rested in his. "You."

Patch wasn't sure how to respond. She hesitated an instant too long, and Boyd's fingers closed over hers. He turned her hands over and lifted them one at a time to kiss her palms.

"Boyd, I . . ." Patch had promised herself that if Boyd tried to kiss her again she would slap him. But she had expected him to seek out her lips, not her hands.

While she was deciding what to do, his fingertips found and caressed the calluses she had developed the past couple of weeks at Ethan's ranch. "You should have servants waiting on you, Patricia, instead of working like a mule for Ethan Hawk."

Patch's chin lifted a notch. "I happen to like working," she said in a cool voice. "It gives me a sense of satisfaction to earn my keep." Patch resisted the urge to pull her hands free. She didn't want to get in a tug-of-war with Boyd that she couldn't win.

"You're beautiful when you're angry, Patricia," Boyd said as he surveyed her flashing eyes.

"If you know I'm upset by what you're doing, why don't you stop?"

"I'm waiting for some clear sign that you don't appreciate my attentions."

Patch snatched one hand free and slapped his face. "Is that what you had in mind?"

Boyd worked his jaw to ease the soreness and laid a hand against his reddening cheek. "That'll do."

Patch shook her head in disbelief. "Are you pixilated, possessed, or what?"

Boyd grinned. He waited a heartbeat before he said, "I just wanted to see how far you'd let me go." His smile invited her to forgive him. "Shall we continue walking? Or do you want to go back?"

Patch knew he was a rogue, but given the choice, and now that things were crystal clear between them, she decided to enjoy the beauty of the day. "Let's walk."

Boyd offered his arm, but Patch declined it. "I think it'll be safer if I keep you at a distance."

He reached down and tore off a stem of grass. He chewed on the sweet tip as they continued strolling the riverbank.

In a little while Patch said, "Can I ask you a question?"

"Shoot."

"Sheriff Lachlan told me the only reason Ethan wasn't hanged for killing Dorne Trahern was because you spoke up for him. With Trahern being so rich and all, why did they listen to you? Are you really that influential in town?"

"Over the years I've made a loan here and there to certain people. I run several thousand head of cattle on my ranch, so a lot of cowboys work for me. My wagons haul freight to wherever it's going when it leaves town. I own the cotton gin and press. If you count assets, I'm probably worth as much as Trahern. But he has more land."

"How did you get so rich?"

"Nosy, aren't you?"

Patch shrugged. "Just curious. You have to admit it boggles the mind that anyone could rise so far, so fast."

"I had an aunt who left me money—"

"You told me that. It must have been a huge inheritance."

"It was enough to get me started. It gave me the bankroll I needed to make some investments. After that, whenever I saw an opportunity, I took advantage of it."

He stopped walking, and Patch turned back to see why. He was looking at her intently. She marveled again at how striking a figure he made, with his hair blowing in the wind and his intriguing features demanding attention. But she was totally unprepared for what he said next.

"I'd be willing to share it all with you, Patricia. Will you marry me?"

Patch gaped. She realized how unladylike a pose it was and shut her mouth. She stared at Boyd in bewilderment. "I don't think I heard you right. Did you just propose marriage to me?"

Boyd grinned. "I did."

Patch turned her back on him and began striding toward the spot where they had left Frank and Merielle. Boyd caught her arm and swung her around.

"You haven't given me an answer."

"A question that stupid doesn't deserve an answer."

"Didn't seem stupid to me. You're a lady. You deserve to live like one. I can provide everything you'd ever want. Between my golden eyes and your golden hair we'd make beautiful children together."

"Why not just mold them out of the real thing? It sounds like you're rich enough to do it!" Patch exclaimed sarcastically. She increased her pace.

Boyd kept step with her. "Maybe I've jumped my fences a little early. But I wanted you to know how I feel about you."

"Really? I didn't hear one word about love or caring during that entire ridiculous proposal."

"A man doesn't wear his feelings on his sleeve."

"I don't want to talk about this anymore," Patch said.

"Ethan can't give you—"

Patch stopped abruptly. Her finger poked Boyd in the chest as her temper flared. "Don't you *dare* compare yourself to Ethan Hawk!"

"Ignoring facts won't change them," Boyd retorted.

"How can you say something like that and call yourself Ethan's friend?"

Patch watched Boyd struggle to contain his temper. She had a fair idea how angry he was. She could hear him grinding his teeth.

"As you pointed out yourself," he said through tight jaws, "I stood up for Ethan when nobody else would. I offered to buy his ranch when it looked like his mother would lose it. I've spent the past week hunting night and day for Chester Felber. And as far as you're concerned, Ethan knows I plan to marry you!"

The blood drained from Patch's face so quickly that she thought she might faint. But two fainting ladies in one day was really one too many. She closed her eyes until the dizziness passed. When she opened them again, she said, "I think I'd like to go home now."

Boyd put a tentative hand on her shoulder. "Are you all right? You look ready to fall over."

She shrugged out from under his touch. "Probably too much sun. I should have worn a hat."

Back at the picnic site, Patch practically pulled the quilt from under Frank and Merielle. She packed all the leftovers into the straw picnic basket in record time. Her parting from Merielle was as warm as she could make it, considering her state of distraction, and they agreed to get together again soon.

The last thing Patch wanted to do was ride back to Ethan's ranch alone with Boyd, but there wasn't any other choice. Frank had to take Merielle home. She climbed into the buggy without waiting for Boyd's assistance and sat with the iron rod down her spine waiting for him to join her.

During the ride home Boyd asked, "How much longer do you think you'll be staying at Ethan's ranch?"

"As long as I'm needed."

Patch refused to be cajoled, teased, or goaded into further conversation. The two people in the buggy were equally agitated by the time they arrived back at the Double Diamond.

Ethan took one look at Patch's sun-warmed, rosy face as the buggy came to a stop in front of the house and felt his body flood with jealous possessiveness. Patch, *his* Patch, was seated in easy familiarity next to his best friend, her thigh practically resting against Boyd's. Adrenaline flowed. His senses came alive, and he could see and hear and feel everything as though it were magnified under a glass.

He saw the way Patch jerked as her elbow bumped against Boyd when she raised a hand to wave a greeting. Heard the rustle of fabric as Patch's skirt brushed against Boyd's trousers when she reached for the picnic basket under the seat. Felt the charged atmosphere between them when Boyd took Patch's hand to help her down from the buggy.

He knew without being told that Boyd had made advances to Patch. There was an unmistakable tension between them that reeked of intimacy. Had Boyd tried to kiss Patch? Had she let him? Did Boyd know how Patch tasted, how she felt cradled in his arms? His muscles flexed and tightened. Rage banded his chest, making it difficult to breathe.

Before today, if anyone had asked him how he felt about Patch Kendrick, Ethan would have replied that he felt affection and a certain responsibility for her, feelings rooted in the past when a twenty-five-year-old man had admired the spunk and fire of a twelve-year-old hoyden in britches. He had come to realize that all the things he had cherished in the child, the daring and the gumption, the mettle and nerve and spirit, were embodied in the woman she had become. And he wanted that woman for his own.

"Hello, Boyd. Have a nice time?" Ethan's words were laced with menace that Boyd was quick to discern.

"Certainly did. Spent the afternoon with a beautiful lady. Even got her to listen to my proposal of marriage."

Ethan's eyes narrowed. "What did she say?"

"I told him it was ridiculous," Patch snapped, annoyed that the two men were talking to each other as though she weren't even there. She turned to Boyd and said, "Thank you for driving this afternoon."

Before she knew what he was going to do, Boyd took her hand again and turned it palm up. She managed to jerk her hand away, but not before he had kissed it. "Good-bye, Boyd," she said pointedly.

Patch felt Ethan come up behind her. If she could have seen the deadly look in his eyes, she would have known why Boyd didn't persist in his attentions to her.

Boyd tightened the cinch on his horse, which he had left tied to the rail in front of the house, mounted, and waved a wordless good-bye with his hat. When he was gone from sight, Patch turned and ran square into Ethan's chest. His hands clamped down on her shoulders.

"Why didn't you say yes to Boyd's proposal?" Ethan demanded. "He can offer you everything I can't."

"I don't happen to love Boyd," Patch retorted.

"Did he kiss you?"

"That's none of your business."

"Did he?"

"If you care so much, you should have come along."

"Did he?"

"What does it matter to you?"

Provoked beyond rational thought, Ethan responded as primitive man had for ages when possession of his mate was threatened. He picked Patch up, threw her over his shoulder, and retired to the closest dark cave to stake his claim in the most demonstrative way possible. Of course, a cave not being particularly handy, Ethan made do with the barn.

Once inside, Ethan dumped Patch off his shoulder and turned to barricade the doors. She had barely gotten her balance when he picked her up again. He headed for a stall at the rear of the barn that was filled with clean straw.

"Ethan, stop! I'm sorry! I shouldn't have provoked you! What are you going to do?"

"Something I should have done a long time ago."

"You're not going to spank me! You wouldn't dare!" But he had once. When she was twelve, she had snuck into his cabin and played with his gun. It had gone off accidentally, shattering a window. Ethan had come on the run—or as close to a run as Ethan ever got—and caught her trying to wrap the gun back up in the blanket in which it had been hidden.

She had felt sheer bliss when he hugged her tight in relief that she wasn't hurt. The next minute, however, he had taken her over his knee. She couldn't sit down for an hour. Worse, she had been so humiliated at being treated like a child that she hadn't been able to face him for a week.

Ethan threw Patch down off his shoulder, and she landed hard on the straw. While she stared at him, with the wind knocked out of her, he began unbuttoning his shirt. He pulled the tails out of his Levi's, yanked his shirt down his arms, and tossed it behind him. She saw two scars where he had been struck by bullets, one on his shoulder and one near his ribs.

"Take off your clothes," he said.

"I most certainly will not!"

"Then I'll take them off for you." Ethan dropped to his knees and reached for the buttons on her blouse.

Patch protected them as best she could, but Ethan wouldn't be denied. He got impatient and tore her blouse off. "You're out of your mind!" she cried.

"I wouldn't doubt it. You've been driving me crazy ever since you crossed the threshold of the Oakville Hotel."

Patch had wanted Ethan to make love to her for so long she didn't know when it hadn't been a part of her dreams. But not like this. Not in a frenzy. Not in anger. Not the first time, anyway.

"Do you love me, Ethan?"

He had her skirt off and was working on her petticoat. "What kind of question is that?"

Patch bucked under him and kicked her legs to hinder him as much as she could. "Just answer it!"

"How could any man not love you?"

It wasn't exactly the answer she wanted, but it wasn't a denial, either.

Ethan got the tapes undone and pulled her petticoat down over her legs, leaving her in chemise, corset, and pantalets. He rolled her over and began unlacing the corset.

"I don't know why the hell you wear this thing," he muttered. "With your figure, you don't need it." He yanked the corset up over her head.

"A lady—"

"I don't make love to ladies, only to women." His green eyes glittered with need. "Are you my woman, Patch?"

There it was. The need for her and her alone. The claim of belonging. She hadn't known she was waiting to hear the words of commitment until they were spoken. They signaled her surrender to the man she loved—not with the infatuation of a child, but with her heart and soul, as a woman loves the man she is destined to be with forever.

"I'm yours, Ethan. I always have been—always will be—yours."

He pulled the delicate pink bow that laced her chemise, spreading the cotton wide with his fingers so her breasts sprang free in his hands.

"Good Lord, Patch, you're so beautiful!"

The frenzy was gone from his eyes and his hands. In its place was reverence. For a moment Patch feared he might stop. Then she saw the possessive light in his eyes and felt the solid shoulders under her hands.

Patch wasn't afraid, exactly. Molly Gallagher had been an exceptional stepmother, in that she had explained the pleasures to be found in the sexual act. But it was one thing to understand how things were supposed to happen. It was quite another to actually experience the feel of a man's hand against her flesh.

The medal hanging on a piece of rawhide around Ethan's neck felt cool against her skin. She took it in her hand and read the inscription. *For Valor.* "This is a medal for heroism! Is it yours?"

Ethan took the medal out of her hands. "No."

"Then why do you wear it?"

"For luck." Ethan slung the medal around so it lay on his back and concentrated on kissing his way down Patch's body.

She soon forgot entirely about the medal. Being loved this way was like nothing she could have imagined. Her skin felt taut, and her body arched reflexively toward Ethan. When his lips caressed her, when his mouth sought the tip of her breast, she moaned. It was as though a drawstring pulled up tight inside her belly.

Ethan's whole being was focused on bringing pleasure to the woman in his arms. He felt her hands circle his neck and twine in his hair. His mouth tasted her—breast, shoulder, throat, the shell of her ear, temple, cheek—and finally found her mouth, which was open and eager for him.

He thrust his tongue inside, mimicking the action of bodies joined. She tasted of cinnamon and ginger. He knew she must have eaten some of the gingersnaps she had made that morning for the picnic. His hands roamed, uncovering more of her and touching virgin flesh.

Patch writhed in his embrace, loving the feel of his strong, callused hands, wanting more, but not certain what that *more* was. Her hands roamed his back, feeling muscle and tendon and bone. Then she sought out the scars on his chest, marveling that he had survived so long, against such odds. She let her fingers slip down into his Levi's and felt him jerk when she touched the crease where his buttocks began.

She froze. "Is it all right to touch you, Ethan?"

He swallowed hard. "Do you want to?"

"I do." Her voice was husky and sounded nothing like her own.

"All right. What do you want to touch?" He sat up, and Patch rose to face him.

She reached out a hand and touched his nipple, which immediately tightened into a hard bud. "It happens to you, too," she said in wonder. Her hands tangled in the black curls on his chest that arrowed downward. When she reached for the top button on his jeans, he covered her hand with his.

"Have you ever seen a naked man?" he asked.

Patch blushed rosily. "No. But I'd like to."

Ethan stood and reached down a hand to Patch. "Let's do this together."

Patch stood slowly, aware that her breasts were bare and that she wore only a pair of pantalets. Ethan pulled her into his arms, and she couldn't believe how right it felt. His flesh was warm and the hair on his chest abraded her breasts, sensitizing her flesh. She felt Ethan's hands sliding into the back of her pantalets and tensed as he slid them down over her buttocks. When she stepped out of them, she stood there in her shoes and gartered knee-length stockings, naked except for the remnants of her chemise.

Ethan reached up and pulled the last of the pins out of her hair so it flowed like golden silk down her back and over her shoulders.

"Your turn," he said.

"Take off your boots and socks," she said.

Ethan balanced on one foot, then the other, as he complied with her command. "Now what?"

"Come here."

Ethan took a barefooted step closer, wincing as the straw prickled under his feet. He sucked in his stomach reflexively when Patch reached again for the buttons on his jeans. He held his breath while she tugged one free and reached for the next. His jeans hung on his hipbones for a moment before she shoved them down.

He noticed she was looking into his eyes, rather than down at what she had exposed. He watched her swallow hard before she said, "Take them off."

He pushed his Levi's and long johns down and stepped out of them, kicking them out of his way. "All right, Patch. You can look now."

He saw the uncertainty in her eyes before she glanced down. She took her time looking. The longer she looked, the harder he got. He felt himself flushing with embarrassment, but there wasn't a damn thing he could do about it.

"Can I touch it?" she whispered.

"If you like," he croaked.

But it was the scar on his leg she touched, not that other part of him.

"It's ugly," Ethan said.

Patch shook her head. "No part of you is unpleasing to me." Then her hand traced its way upward to the part of him that made it very clear how he felt about her.

Soft, Patch thought. *Smooth and warm. But hard too.* She circled him with her hand and heard a wrenching groan. She released him immediately, but his hand caught her wrist and brought her hand back to cup him.

"Don't stop touching me. It feels good."

"When you groaned like that, I thought I'd done something wrong," she explained.

"It was good. Great," he amended. "Would you like me to touch you, too?"

Patch nodded shyly. She had her eyes lowered, so she saw his hand moving toward her. It took all the courage she had to wait for him to touch her *there*. His hand slid down her belly and through the dark curls at the apex of her thighs. He slowly pressed inward with a finger. She thought her knees would buckle then and there. She caught herself by grabbing his shoulders.

"Okay?" he asked.

She nodded jerkily.

"More?"

"Yes, please."

Ethan grinned. "You have lovely manners, young lady."

Patch laughed. "Why, thank you, kind sir."

Ethan made love to Patch with his hands, watching her face constantly to gauge her reactions. Her eyes were lambent, heavy-lidded, her mouth open, panting for breath, her skin flushed with pleasure.

"Ethan, I can't stand any more," she said at last.

Abruptly he let her go. She swayed and almost fell. He caught her and said, "Can you manage on your own for a minute?"

She felt the silly grin on her face. "I'll try."

He arranged the remnants of their clothing over the scratchy hay to make a more comfortable bed. Sunlight streamed in golden bars through the wooden slats of the barn. The air was warm and their bodies glistened with sweat. The outside world seemed far away, only cattle lowing in the distance and a horse munching hay in the corral beyond the wall.

They might have been alone on a desert isle. There was only each other, and this moment in time. Warm eyes. Shy smiles. Taut bodies. Muscles that flexed and tendons that bunched. Hardness. Softness. A single thrust. One sharp cry of pain, caught by another's kiss. Tenderness. Sighs of pleasure. Moans of wonder and delight. Groans of ecstasy. At last, heaven. And finally, panting breaths and sighs of repletion.

Patch snuggled close, her head nestled in Ethan's shoulder, her body aligned with his. She didn't want to leave this place, ever. She wanted to remember every sensation, even the pain, because it had been the first moment they were truly joined. She had given Ethan a special part of herself and taken part of him in return. She knew there were certain times of the month when a woman was more likely to conceive, and hoped this day was one of them.

Ethan held Patch tight against him, circling her slender body so he could feel the weight of her breast on his arm. He didn't want to leave this place, ever. He wanted to remember every sound, every sensation, because he knew it was going to be the last time he enjoyed them. He had been wrong to take Patch like this, without benefit of marriage. A lady—and Patch was one—deserved more. He hoped to hell he hadn't gotten her pregnant.

"Ethan? What are you thinking?"

"This was a mistake, Patch."

Patch was in such a state of euphoria that even Ethan's flat tone of voice didn't penetrate at first. Then the gist of what he had said sank in. "We're not the first couple to anticipate the wedding night."

"There isn't going to be any wedding night."

Patch pulled herself free of Ethan's hold and sat up. "I don't understand."

Ethan rose, pulled his long johns out of the pile of clothing under them, and began putting them on. Patch followed his lead, grabbing her pantalets and turning her back to him.

"I had no business making love to you," Ethan said. "I might be dead tomorrow. Or spend the rest of my life walking this town with a cloud of suspicion over my head. What I did this afternoon was selfish and stupid, and I'm sorry for it."

Patch whirled on him wearing pantalets and her half-laced chemise. "Where does that leave me? I gave myself to you because I love you. You knew that, Ethan. How can you just walk away like nothing happened?"

"It's because I love you that I'm walking away!" he snarled. "Don't you see? What kind of life could we have together?"

"A perfectly wonderful life. If one of us wasn't so intent on being a bean-headed jackass!"

"I refuse to argue with you, Patch." Ethan yanked on his pants and buttoned them up, then sat down to pull on his socks and boots. He was shoving his arms in his shirt before he looked at Patch again.

She held her bloodstained petticoat in her hand. Her eyes brimmed with tears. She closed them to shut him out, and a tear spilled onto her cheek. It slid slowly down her face until she caught it with her tongue.

"Patch?"

"I'm all right, Ethan," she said in a quiet voice. "I'm a big girl now. I can take care of myself." She found the opening on the petticoat and slipped it on. Her skirt followed over her head. She folded the corset into a tiny square and set it aside. With shaky hands she buttoned the remaining buttons on her blouse, then tucked the torn ends into her skirt. She straightened the wrinkles as best she could, but her clothing looked like it had spent a night in bed with her, which, in a sense, it had.

"I'll be leaving for Montana tomorrow," she said.

Ethan stared at her with horrified eyes. "When did you make this decision?"

"It's obvious there's no reason for me to stay any longer. I came here to find you, to hold you to the promise you made seven years ago—"

"Eight."

"—eight years ago. You've just made it plain that you're never going to marry me. I might as well leave now and save myself the heartache of hanging around where I'm not wanted."

"Who says you're not wanted?" he retorted harshly.

Patch's eyes opened wide in feigned surprise. "Why, you did. Or was I mistaken in what I just heard?"

Ethan flushed. "*Wanting* you and *deserving* you are two completely different things. If I weren't accused of rape, if I weren't a hunted man, things would be different."

"Oh. Well, then, perhaps I will stay a little longer. There were definite signs today that Merielle may be able to remember something soon."

Ethan eyed Patch through narrowed eyes. He had the sneaking feeling he had just been manipulated by a master fisherman. She had wiggled the worm and he had taken the bait and she had reeled him right in.

"What's all this about Merielle regaining her memory?" he asked. "When did this happen?"

Patch's eyes lit with enthusiasm. "This afternoon on the picnic. Frank said Merielle was looking at him as though she really saw him. He also said that a week or so ago she remembered a time when they had been together in the past. Doesn't that sound encouraging?"

"Maybe. If Frank isn't reading more into what Merielle says and does than is actually there."

"Don't be a pessimist," Patch chided as she finger-combed her hair. "Merielle *will* remember. Just you wait and see."

Patch was completely dressed, but when she looked down at herself, she groaned in dismay. "Your mother and sister will take one look at me and know exactly what happened here."

Ethan grinned. "You look fetching to me."

Patch arched a brow. "You really want me to walk into the house looking like this?"

Ethan eyed her speculatively. Her hair hung in tangles over her shoulders, laced with pieces of hay. Her brow and chin held a glowing sheen of perspiration and pink patches where his whiskers had abraded her skin. Her lips were swollen from his kisses. Her blouse was ripped, her skirt was dirty, and she was holding a scrunched-up corset in her hand. "Maybe it would be better if I go first and make sure the coast is clear."

Ethan and Patch snuck out of the barn together and raced for the kitchen door.

"You wait here, and I'll go check Leah's bedroom. If it's empty, I'll open the window and you come around and climb in."

"A lady doesn't climb through—"

Ethan eyed Patch. "I don't see any lady. Just a well-loved woman."

"Oh, well, in that case, I'll be waiting under the window." Patch turned and marched around the side of the house. She ducked under Nell's window and met Ethan at the window to Leah's room. When he opened it, she reached up her hands and he pulled her inside.

"Hurry up and change," he whispered. "Ma heard me come in and she asked where you were."

"Tell her I'll be there in a minute," Patch whispered back. "Tell her—"

"Tell me what?"

Patch and Ethan stared thunderstruck at the elderly woman in the doorway.

Patch cleared her throat. "Hello, Nell. I'll be with you as soon as I change."

Ethan's heart was thumping so hard in his chest he thought it was going to burst. He had no idea how his mother would react to this situation. The last thing he wanted to do was upset her when she was just beginning to recuperate. For some reason he felt like a small boy again, caught in an indiscretion. His mother had never laid a hand on him in all the years he was growing up. All it took was one disapproving look from her gray eyes, like the one he was receiving now, for him to feel remorse and pledge to reform.

It felt strange to receive her censure now as an adult, after all the missing years of growing up without it. But she was still his mother, and he still wanted her love and approval. Amazing how effective her method was.

She waited until he was seated across from her at the kitchen table with a cup of coffee in front of each of them before she spoke.

"Patch is a lovely woman."

"Yes, she is."

"Are you in love with her?"

"I care for her," he hedged.

"I see."

He waited for further questions, but they didn't come. "Aren't you going to ask me whether I intend to marry her?"

She sipped her coffee, making a slurping sound because it was still too hot to swallow. "All right. Are you going to marry her?"

Ethan smiled grimly. "In a simpler world, I would marry her and bless every day I had with her. But my life hasn't been simple for more years than I can count. I want you to understand why I can't marry her. Not now. Not yet."

Ethan waited for his mother's blessing, her sanction of his relationship with a young woman living in her house. He wanted her to say it was all right for him to make love to Patch Kendrick even though he couldn't—or wouldn't—marry her. It was asking a lot.

"You're my son and I love you. I also love Patch like a daughter. I don't want either of you hurt. Be wise, Ethan. Let your head rule your heart. At least for now."

"Are you telling me to leave her alone? I don't think I can."

"Then make an honest woman of her."

"I can't do that, either."

"Whatever the risks—"

"What if Trahern goes after her? He might, you know, if I married her. What if she's in the wrong place when that gunfighter wants a showdown? I can't take that chance, Ma!"

"All right, Ethan. You have to do what you think is best." She reached out a hand and smoothed his hair back from where it had fallen over his brow.

He took her hand and held it against his cheek. "I love you, Ma. And I miss Pa."

"I know, Ethan. I miss him, too."

Patch had heard most of the discussion from where she stood just outside the kitchen door. She hadn't meant to eavesdrop, but once she was there, she didn't want to interrupt, and she was afraid she would be discovered if she tried to back up over the creaking floorboards.

Patch could understand Ethan's reasons for not marrying her. They were mostly the same ones he had given her the day she arrived in Oakville. But she knew something now that she hadn't known then.

Ethan cared for her.

That made all the difference. She could wait. It was only a short step from caring to love. Something was bound to happen soon to tip the balance in her favor.

❊15❊

CHESTER FELBER HAD BEEN sighted in Three Rivers. The word came to Ethan through Frank, who had gotten it from one of the Tumbling T cowhands who visited his mother in Three Rivers every Sunday for dinner.

"Are you going after him?" Frank asked.

"Damn right I am!" Ethan said.

"Maybe you should send for the sheriff."

"I have the feeling Chester would have an unfortunate accident on his way back to Oakville if I sent Careless after him. No, this is something I have to do myself."

"Just be careful," Frank urged. "Chester isn't very smart, and he's liable to panic when he realizes you've found him."

Ethan didn't tell Patch where he was going. Chester didn't have any answers that affected their relationship. The only thing Chester could tell him was who had wanted his parents poisoned. Ethan already knew what Chester would say. He just wanted to hear it from Chester's lips.

Three Rivers had gotten its name from the fact it was situated on the fork of the Nueces, Atascosa, and Frio rivers. Ethan rode into town from the south and tied his horse up in front of the boardinghouse on the main street. According to the cowhand from the Tumbling T, Chester Felber had been spotted having supper there.

There were no boardwalks in Three Rivers. Frankly, Ethan thought, there wasn't much of a town, either. Just the boardinghouse, a saloon, the stage depot, an eatery, and a general store, along with a few mud-chinked wooden houses. It was a place for passing through, not a place to stay.

The boardinghouse parlor was empty except for a very old lady sitting in a rocker, staring out the front window. She didn't acknowledge Ethan's presence, so he ignored her and headed toward the din-

ing room and kitchen, hoping to find some sign of Chester. He was
thwarted there, too. From the kitchen window Ethan could see a
woman out back hanging sheets on a line. He figured she must be the
owner. Would she be likely to cooperate?

Ethan decided to do some further checking on his own before he
let it be known why he had come to town. He found the registration
book on a desk in the parlor and, after a quick glance at the old lady
in the rocker, began thumbing through it. Sure enough, Chester Felber
was registered in Room 4. Ethan did a quick inventory downstairs and
found Rooms 1, 2, and 3. He looked up the stairs. Likely Room 4 was
up there. And maybe Chester Felber.

He checked his gun and headed up the stairs on tiptoe, not wanting to alert his quarry. He paused when the stairs creaked loudly, but
when there was no sound from upstairs, continued his climb.

Room 4 was at the top of the stairs. Ethan checked the knob to
see if the door was locked. It wasn't. He held his gun in one hand and
shoved the door open with the other.

The room was empty.

Ethan felt a flood of disappointment. Had Chester somehow been
alerted and fled? He turned and ran back down the stairs. To his surprise the lady in the rocker turned and asked, "Who's it you're lookin'
for?"

"Chester Felber."

"Poor boy fretted somethin' fierce stayin' in that room day and
night. He's down to the livery, helpin' Rufus Finney."

Ethan tipped his hat. "Thanks, ma'am."

"You ain't gonna shoot that boy, are you, Mister? Chester don't
have a mean bone in his body."

Ethan didn't know what to say. "I won't kill him unless he gives
me no other choice." He left the boardinghouse before the old lady
could say more.

Ethan tried to remember what Chester Felber had looked like
when they were boys. He had always been bigger than everyone else,
his neck thick, his chest broad, his legs like tree trunks. His hands and
feet had been too big even for his big body, making him awkward and
ungainly. His hair was brown like tobacco, his nose had a slight hook
in it, his chin had a deep cleft, and his eyes—Ethan couldn't remember
his eyes, because he had never much looked Chester Felber in the face.

Nobody wanted to be Chester's friend, because he was slow-witted and clumsy. He was too dumb even to recognize when he wasn't wanted, because he stood around on the fringes of whatever game the other boys were playing, waiting for his turn—which never came. Ethan was ashamed to remember the incident that finally drove Chester away once and for all.

A bunch of boys from town had been playing baseball. Boyd was pitching, Ethan was catching, and Frank was playing in the outfield. Chester was standing in the outfield not too far from Frank, as though he were fielding balls as well. The batter hit a high pop fly ball that went over Frank's head, close to where Chester was standing.

Chester had watched the ball land and headed in that direction at a lumbering run. Even though Frank had farther to go, he beat Chester to the ball because Chester tripped over his own feet and fell. While Chester was facedown on the ground, Frank threw the ball back to third base and the runner was tagged out. The third baseman then threw the ball back to Boyd, who concealed it in his glove.

Ethan wondered later what would have happened if they had continued play immediately, so Chester would have known the ball had been recovered. It didn't happen that way. Chester had rumbled to his feet and shouted, "I'll get it! I'll get it!" and started toward where the ball had landed.

Of course, when he got there, the ball wasn't to be found. The boys had sniggered behind their hands and snorted their ridicule and finally laughed out loud at Chester's confusion. Finally Boyd had shouted, "We can't play anymore until you find that ball, Chester. You let us know when we can come back."

Then Boyd and Frank and Ethan and every other boy on both teams had left the field, giggling like girls, chortling through their fingers at how that stupid idiot Chester would probably spend the next hour hunting for a ball that wasn't there.

It was almost midnight that night when Ethan was awakened from sleep by someone pounding on the front door of his home. He ran to see who it was along with his father and mother. Horace Felber stood there, his eyes red-rimmed, his face haggard.

"Have you seen Chester?" he asked. "Lilian and I have searched everywhere. No one's seen him." He had looked at Ethan, his eyes pleading, "Do you know where he might have gone?"

Ethan didn't like Horace, but he was alarmed that Chester wasn't home. He couldn't believe that some other boy closer to town hadn't told about the trick they had played. He must have looked guilty because his mother said, "If you know anything about this, Ethan, speak up."

The whole sordid story spilled out. How the boys had fooled Chester and sent him off on a wild-goose chase after a ball that wasn't there.

"Where was this?" Horace asked.

"We were playing in the pasture behind the Silver Buckle after school today," Ethan said.

Ethan's father had insisted on going with Horace and had brought Ethan along to show them the exact spot where Chester had begun his search for the missing ball.

Amazingly, Chester wasn't ten feet from the spot where the boys had left him that afternoon. He had apparently become convinced that the ball must be lost in a patch of thorny mesquite nearby. He was covered with bloody scratches when they found him. And he was crying, blubbering like a baby.

Ethan was embarrassed that such a large person could act like such a tomfool. It wasn't until Chester spoke that he felt ashamed, as well.

"I'm sorry I lost the ball, Ethan. I looked and looked. But I couldn't find it. Now nobody can play ball 'cause of me. I'm sorry. So sorry. Don't tell them I couldn't find it. Please don't tell. Please."

Horace Felber had pulled his distraught son into his arms and held him tight. It looked funny because Chester was so much bigger than Horace. Somehow Ethan didn't feel like laughing. He felt his nose pinch and his eyes sting.

His father's hand tightened on his shoulder—in rebuke, in reprimand. He was afraid of what his father might say to him, but his continued silence was worse than any scolding. At last he said, "Come on, son, let's go home."

Chester hadn't come to school after that, and he stopped hanging around the other boys when they played games. Most everybody was grateful that he wasn't bothering them anymore. Ethan felt guilty about his part in driving Chester away. He made slight amends by keeping Chester's secret. He never told the other boys about finding Chester late that night, still hunting for the ball.

Ethan wondered if Chester had the ability to remember back that far. The day and night were still vivid in his mind, giving him more sympathy for Chester than he wanted to feel at the moment. He knew how easy it was to manipulate the slow-witted man. Could Chester really be held responsible for what he had done?

Ethan was surprised at how easy it was to find Chester when he knew where to look. The big man was wielding a pitchfork, cleaning out the stalls of the stage livery.

"Hello, Chester."

Whatever Ethan had been expecting, it wasn't the smile of genuine pleasure on Chester's face at the sight of him.

"I know you," he said. "Your name is Ethan. You were in prison. Did you come to see me? I had to go away from Oakville, because . . ." Chester's lips pursed, and he scratched his chin. "Ma said I did something bad. I don't know what it was. She didn't tell me that."

Ethan wondered just how much the big man would be able to tell him if he couldn't even recognize the difference between right and wrong. Ethan would just as soon do his questioning without the pitchfork in Chester's hand. "Can you stop for a little while and talk to me?"

"Mr. Finley said I could get a drink if I got thirsty." Chester grinned. "I'm thirsty now."

"Let's go to that eatery across the street."

"All right, Ethan. Whatever you say."

Ethan was having trouble working up any desire for revenge against Chester Felber. How could he blame a gullible lack-wit for his father's death or his mother's illness? There had to be intent in order for there to be guilt. He could find nothing in Chester's behavior that presented him as a monster capable of murder.

Furthermore, Ethan couldn't see that locking Chester up would resolve anything. Chester would have to be watched more closely if he was left free, but Ethan felt certain Mr. and Mrs. Felber would be willing to do that. All Ethan wanted from Chester, he realized, was the name of the person who *could* be held accountable.

Once they were sitting across from each other in the Three Rivers Café, Ethan pulled out the bag of arsenic Boyd had found in the barn and set it on the table between them.

"Do you know what this is?" Ethan asked.

"Hey! That's mine!"

Ethan didn't try wrestling the bag away from Chester. He simply said, "I found it in your father's barn. Do you know what's in the bag, Chester?"

Chester nodded. "It's medicine. I put it in the milk to make your ma get better."

Ethan felt his stomach roll. What devious mind had come up with that ruse? "Who gave you the medicine, Chester?"

Chester frowned and hugged the bag close to his chest. "It's a secret. I'm not supposed to tell."

Ethan tried pleading, but Chester remained surprisingly firm. He tried threats and Chester clammed up completely. Finally, in desperation he said, "If your mother said it was all right, would you tell me then?"

"If Ma said I could, I guess it would be all right."

Ethan wasn't sure what Mrs. Felber would do when he showed up with Chester, but at least she would be capable of listening to reason. Especially since he was more interested in prosecuting the real guilty party than Chester Felber.

"Let's go get your things so we can ride back to Oakville," Ethan said.

Chester shook his head. "Ma said I can't go home until she comes for me."

Ethan ground his teeth in frustration. It took a great deal of persuasion to convince Chester that his mother wouldn't mind if he came back to Oakville with Ethan. "Otherwise," Ethan explained, "there's no way you can ask whether it's okay to tell me who gave you the bag of medicine."

"Oh. Yeah," Chester said at last. "Okay. I'll go."

Ethan gave whoever had explained the use of the poison to Chester great marks for patience. It wasn't easy dealing with the simple man. At last they were on their way.

"Do you think my cows missed me?" Chester asked.

"I'm sure they did,' Ethan replied.

"I missed them, too. They like me, you know."

They were halfway to Oakville when two shots rang out.

As far as Patch was concerned, the investigation of Merielle's rape was moving much too slowly. But when she had broached the subject to

Ethan early this morning, he had told her his work on the ranch had to take precedence over clearing his name.

"It's been seventeen years," he'd said. "The investigation can wait a few more days for my attention. My cattle can't."

Patch disagreed. So right after Ethan rode off to round up his cattle for branding, she harnessed up the buggy and headed for town to interrogate Careless Lachlan.

She dressed like a lady because she thought that might entitle her to more consideration when she started asking pointed questions. She considered taking a gun with her in deference to the danger Ethan had suggested lay waiting for her in town, but she wouldn't have known how to fire it. Patch would have to trust to her wits—and her fists. She had considerable experience using both.

Patch visited Careless at lunchtime because she knew the sheriff ate at his desk.

"Don't bother getting up," she said as she closed the jail door behind her.

Careless bobbed up and sat back down, his fork still in his hand. "Afternoon, Miz Kendrick. What can I do for you?"

Patch emptied a ladderback chair of a stack of newspapers by shoving them onto the floor. She ignored the sheriff's grunt of dismay and set the empty chair beside his desk.

"Make yourself comfortable," Careless said sourly.

"Thank you, Sheriff Lachlan. I will. Now, where shall we start?"

"Mind if we start *after* I finish my lunch?"

"Feel free to continue. I just have a few questions."

"Don't know nothin'," Careless said through a mouthful of sweet potato pie.

"You don't even know what I'm going to ask!"

"Word's all over town you're hopin' to clear Ethan of that rape. I'm tellin' you, I don't know nothin'."

"Did Trahern order you not to talk to me?" Patch asked.

"Trahern don't own me," Careless said.

"Then why won't you tell me what you know?"

"Because I—"

"—don't know nothin'," Patch finished. "What if I say I don't believe you. You must have asked some questions, at least found out the details of—"

"I did go look at the place where it happened the next day."

Patch inched forward to the edge of her chair.

"And?"

"Lotta footprints there. More footprints than there shoulda been."

"What does that mean?"

"Means maybe somebody else was there 'sides Ethan and the girl."

Patch knew for sure that Frank had been there, but she wasn't going to mention that to Careless.

"Who do you think it was?" she asked.

"Couldn't say for sure. Big man, I think."

"A big man? Like a *grown* man? Ethan was just a boy then! How could you not speak up about something that important?"

Careless put down his fork. "Listen, Miz Kendrick. When Jefferson Trahern tells me Ethan Hawk raped his girl, I ain't gonna contradict him."

"But that's your job! You're the sheriff! You owe your allegiance to the people who depend on you to be the law, not any one man."

Careless wasn't going to sit still while some strapped-down, starched-up lady gave him what-for. He jumped up, snatched the checked napkin from under his chin, and said, "Now lookee here, little lady. What gives you the right—"

Patch was out of her chair and nose to nose with the sheriff in two seconds flat. "Are you the sheriff, or aren't you? That's what I want to know!"

Careless let out a string of cuss words that would sizzle bacon. Nobody—except Trahern—had ever thrown in his face the fact that he had let himself be bought. It didn't sit well on his stomach. Or maybe he had eaten too much sweet potato pie. "You've got a lot of nerve, lady," he said to Patch. "Who says what I saw would've made any difference? Ethan was guilty, all right."

"Thanks to you, we may never know the truth," Patch accused. "And an innocent man has been robbed of a normal life! Think about *that* the next time you decide to abdicate your responsibility to this town."

"I ain't aba—abik—dicktated—I ain't done nothing wrong!"

The door slammed open, and Gilley stood there with his eyes bugged wide. "Ethan Hawk just rode into town. He brought Chester Felber in with him. Chester's been shot!"

"Is he dead?" Careless asked.

"Naw. But he's hurt bad. Doc Carter's looking at him now."

Careless pulled his pants up under his belly, rearranged his gunbelt on his leg, and marched toward the door. He stopped before a stunned Patch long enough to say, "You wanted a sheriff. Well, now you got one."

Patch hurried after the sheriff.

"Make way! Make way!" Careless forced his way through the crowd that surrounded Ethan.

The moment Careless reached Ethan's side he said, "You're under arrest."

Ethan's lip curled sarcastically. "Aren't you going to ask me what happened?"

Careless caught sight of Patch's arched brow and scowled. "All right. What happened?"

Ethan started to reach beneath his leather vest, and Careless pulled his gun. "Hold it right there."

Ethan held both hands up. "There's a pouch in my shirt pocket."

"Gilley, you reach in there and see if he's telling the truth," Careless said.

Gilley did as he was told. "Here it is."

"Look inside," Ethan said. "You'll find a white powder. Arsenic."

Gilley looked. "It's a white powder, all right. Don't know about it being arsenic."

"I had it checked by a chemist in San Antonio," Ethan said.

"So what does this have to do with Chester gettin' shot?" Careless asked.

"I went looking for Chester because I found out he was putting arsenic in the milk Gilley delivered to my mother and the whiskey he delivered to my father—whiskey that poisoned him to death."

The crowd gave a collective gasp as they became aware for the first time that Alex Hawk had been murdered.

"Ethan did ask me about poisoned milk," Gilley confirmed for the crowd.

"And he asked me where I got my whiskey," Slim volunteered.

"Chester found out that I suspected him and ran off," Ethan said. "I got word that he was in Three Rivers, and that's where I found him. We were riding back to Oakville when we were ambushed. Someone— whoever gave Chester the poison—didn't want him telling any tales."

"You tryin' to tell me you didn't shoot Chester?"

"You're damn right I am!" Ethan said heatedly. "Why would I want him dead? He's the only one who knows for sure who wanted my parents dead."

"Maybe Chester told you, and then you shot him," Careless suggested.

"If I knew who the culprit was, I would have delivered you his corpse," Ethan said in a deadly voice.

"Who—" Careless cut himself off. The answer to his question was obvious. Ethan Hawk meant to kill the man who had poisoned his father. That didn't mean he hadn't also taken advantage of the opportunity to shoot Chester.

"Yeah, well, how do I know you're not lyin'?" Careless demanded of Ethan.

"You'll just have to take my word for it—unless and until Chester comes to and can tell you himself."

Careless pulled on his chin hairs. He sneaked a peek at Patch and looked back at Ethan. "Guess you wouldn't've brung him in alive if you'd'a been the one who shot him. You got any ideas who *did* shoot him?"

"You'll be the first to know," Ethan said grimly.

Mrs. Felber had been visiting a friend at the other end of town, so it had taken a few minutes for word of Chester's fate to reach her. Then her shrieking wails could be heard as she made her way through the crowd.

"Chester! Oh, my God! Chester! What happened to my son?"

"He's with Doc Carter right now, Miz Felber," the sheriff informed her.

Her ululating cries sent chills down Patch's spine as several ladies ushered her to the doctor's office.

Then Horace Felber arrived. He looked right at Ethan and demanded, "What happened?"

"I was bringing Chester back to Oakville. Someone shot at us from cover, and he was hit."

"Why?"

"I thought maybe you could tell me something about that." Ethan watched the blood drain from Horace Felber's face. *He knew! He knew about the poison!* "I think we need to talk."

Horace shook his head vigorously. "No! I can't help you. I don't know anything. Not a thing. Nothing." Horace fled.

For a man who knew nothing, Horace Felber had protested too long and too loudly. Ethan felt a surge of excitement. When he first realized Chester had been shot, he had felt as though he would be forever thwarted in his search for the truth. He had reached the bottom of a sinkhole with no hope of climbing out.

Even though Chester was still alive, Ethan had his doubts whether the big, simple man would survive. Now he suddenly felt hope again. Horace might not know everything. But he knew something.

Ethan had been so wrapped up in his confrontation with Careless and his excitement over confronting Horace that he hadn't focused on the crowd. But as he started after Horace, he found himself facing Patch.

"What are you doing in town? I told you it's too damned dangerous—"

Patch's fingertip poked him before he could evade it. "Look who's talking! You were supposed to be rounding up cattle. What on earth possessed you to go after Chester Felber on your own? You could have been killed! You could have been shot! You could have—"

Ethan grabbed Patch by the hand and dragged her away from the avidly watching crowd. "Let's finish this discussion without an audience."

He headed into the lobby of the Oakville Hotel, but that wasn't empty, either. He grabbed a key from the shelf behind the unattended desk and headed up the stairs, seeking a place where he could be alone with Patch, where he could vent the fury and frustration he had suffered when Chester was shot.

Patch realized she could either walk on her own two feet or get dragged. Walking seemed more dignified.

When they were in the hotel room alone with the door locked behind them, Patch opened her mouth to continue her tirade and found it covered by Ethan's.

Anger gave way to passion. Without Patch knowing quite how it happened, the two of them landed on the four-poster bed. She wasn't sure who undressed whom, only that they had removed the necessary clothing in less time than it took for the sounds of the crowd to die down in the street.

Patch clutched Ethan close and sighed as with a single thrust he joined their bodies. Her fingernails made crescents in his shoulders as he moved inside her. His hand slipped between them, and she gasped as her body responded with a speed and intensity she wouldn't have believed possible.

It wasn't lovemaking, exactly. It was an affirmation of their need for each other, a quick, spontaneous release of the anger and fear and dread they had both recently experienced.

When it was over, they lay half-dressed on the bed and let the breeze from the open window cool their musky bodies.

"Do you think we'll ever find out the truth about who poisoned your father without Chester's help?" Patch asked.

Ethan sighed. "I don't know, Patch. I just don't know."

Patch rolled over with her back to Ethan. "I'll never be able to hold up my head in front of these people again," she said. "They'll know exactly what we were doing up here."

"No, they won't," Ethan said. "You'll leave here looking about as warm as an icicle, with your hair in that tight little bun and your nose tilted up in the air, and they'll know a lady like you wouldn't let an outlaw like me within forty feet of her drawers."

Patch laughed. The laugh was cut short when Ethan's hand roamed across her belly and into the still-damp curls below. "Again?"

He answered by slipping a finger inside her. He edged her onto her back, and his mouth found hers, his tongue tasting the edges of her lips before slipping between them. He ran his tongue along the inside of her upper lip, then sucked on her lower lip and teased it with his teeth.

Patch learned quickly how to please Ethan, where to touch, where she could taste to wrench groans of pleasure from him. She loved the feel of his skin, the textures of his body, the strength and the softness of him.

Their second joining was slower, and Patch surrendered like a willow in the wind. She was arched off the bed with need before Ethan finally released her from the throes of passion. Afterward, Patch was embarrassed at the noises she had made, at the scratch marks she had left on Ethan's shoulders and buttocks. When she tried to apologize, Ethan laughed.

"You're in worse shape than I am," he said.

"What do you mean?"

"You may want to knot that bow on your shirt-waist a little higher when you leave," he said.

"Why?"

"To hide the marks I left on your neck."

Patch ran to the mirror over the dry sink and looked at her neck. "Goodness." She turned and smiled coyly at him. "How would you like one of these?"

Ethan grabbed his long johns and started yanking them on. "No thanks, young lady. Your reputation will be in tatters if I turn up with a love bruise after having spent half the afternoon up here with you."

Patch looked out the window at the setting sun. "Good Lord! Look what time it is!" She scrambled around, tugging on clothes as quickly as she could, but was slowed down by Ethan's insistence that she look as perfectly dressed and coifed as she had when they entered the room. Fortunately, Patch had a comb and some extra hairpins in her reticule. Ethan had lost her other pins somewhere in the bedding.

"Remember," Ethan cautioned. "Cold as ice. You go down those stairs with that satin skirt swishing like a high wind in tall grass. Won't anybody dare say a word to you."

Patch did as Ethan said. There were no smirks, no smiles, no snickering. She kept her chin up and exited the hotel with a smug smile, thinking, *No one suspects a thing!*

Behind her, at the top of the stairs, Ethan eyed every manjack in the lobby, daring any one of them to look cross-eyed at Patch, making it plain that any man who insulted his woman was flirting with death.

When Ethan reached the lobby, he looked out the plate glass window, expecting to see Patch.

She wasn't there.

He hurried outside onto the boardwalk and looked up and down both sides of the street.

Patch had disappeared.

❊16❊

PATCH HAD REALIZED THAT if she didn't go immediately and offer her sympathy to Mr. and Mrs. Felber that the opportunity wouldn't likely arise again anytime soon. She was afraid Ethan might try to stop her, so she took advantage of the fact he planned to remain awhile longer than she had in the hotel to make her escape.

She hurried down the street and into the Oakville Mercantile, hoping she would find the Felbers, or at least someone who could tell her where they lived. The store was empty. Patch waited a few moments after the bell over the door jangled to see if someone would come. No one did.

Patch headed for the muffled sounds she heard beyond the blanket that separated the front of the store from the back. She found Mrs. Felber sitting on a small barrel of salted pork, her face hidden in her hands. Patch sat down on a nearby barrel and put her arm around the sobbing woman. "I'm so sorry," she said. "I know Ethan—"

Mrs. Felber's head jerked up at the mention of Ethan's name. Tears drenched her face, and she wiped her dripping nose with the hem of her apron. "What are you doing here?"

"I came to say how sorry I am—"

"I'm glad it's almost over!" Mrs. Felber said fiercely. "I'm glad my son will soon be laid to rest. I've been waiting seventeen years for the other shoe to drop. Now that it has, I'm *glad*!"

"I'm sure you don't mean that."

"Are you?" Mrs. Felber focused desolate eyes on Patch. "Now I don't have to keep that *damnable* secret anymore. Seventeen long years I kept quiet. But no more! There's no reason everyone shouldn't know all about it once Chester is dead."

"Know all about what?"

Mrs. Felber's lip curled derisively. "Ask Ethan's good friend, Boyd Stuckey. He could tell you."

Patch was getting more concerned by the minute. All this talk of "seventeen years ago." Could Mrs. Felber possibly know something about Merielle's rape? The big woman's face had flushed an alarming red. "Please, Mrs. Felber, don't keep me in suspense. Do you know something about what really happened to Merielle Trahern seventeen years ago?"

Patch heard a sound behind her and looked up to find Ethan framed by the blankets in the doorway.

"Come in, Ethan," Mrs. Felber said. "You'll want to hear this, too."

Patch and Ethan exchanged uneasy glances. Mrs. Felber was obviously agitated, her eyes wild-looking, her voice harsh and guttural.

Ethan came and stood at Patch's side, his hand on her shoulder. "You have something to say, Mrs. Felber?"

Lilian Felber gave a shuddering sigh. "Horace wanted to put Chester in an orphans' home when he found out he was slow-witted. Did you know that? But I loved my boy too much to send him away. I think Horace learned to love him, too. Otherwise, he would never have done what he did."

She remained silent for so long that Ethan asked, "What did Horace do, Mrs. Felber?"

"He saved his son from the law. He paid and paid and paid again to keep the truth hidden. For seventeen years he paid."

"Paid what?"

"Blackmail."

"Someone blackmailed Horace? Was it Careless? Did the sheriff know who did it all along?" Patch asked.

"What? No, not Careless. Boyd Stuckey."

"You're lying!" Ethan said. "Boyd wouldn't need to blackmail anybody. Why are you accusing him?"

"Because it's true. Where do you think he got the money to buy that ranch of his?"

"His aunt left him money," Ethan retorted.

Mrs. Felber laughed. It was a jarring sound. "Meet Boyd's aunt Lilian," she said, spreading her arms wide. "Because all the money Boyd ever got came from Horace and me."

"Why was Boyd blackmailing you? What did he know that you wanted kept secret?" Patch asked.

"Boyd was there."

"Where?"

"Boyd was there with Merielle and Chester when Horace found them. Boyd said Chester had raped Merielle. He hated Horace, and he gloated about how Chester was going to hang for what he had done. Horace took one look at the fingernail scratches on Chester's face and knew there wasn't a court in the world that wouldn't convict his son. So he offered Boyd money to keep his mouth shut."

"And Boyd took it?" Ethan said in a raw voice.

Mrs. Felber nodded. "Over the years, he kept coming back for more. And more. We paid. And paid.

"Now Chester is dying. We won't have to lie anymore. We won't have to pay Boyd any more to keep our awful secret."

Mrs. Felber raised her eyes to Ethan and then lowered them again. "I'm sorry you had to be the one who took the blame. But you could take care of yourself. My Chester, they would have hanged him like a dog. I'm sure he didn't meant it to happen. I'm sure it must have been an accident. He isn't right in the head, you know."

Ethan left the storeroom and walked into the empty store. He crossed behind the counter and fingered the glass candy jars. Licorice. Cherry balls. Cinnamon candy. Boyd had liked the licorice best.

Ethan's stomach rolled and acid bit his throat. His best friend had taken money and hidden the truth. Ethan had spent ten years of his life running from the law, had spent seven hellish years in prison, because Boyd had cared more about money than he had cared about his best friend.

Ethan picked up the jar of licorice and hurled it against the wall.

The shattering glass brought Patch to the opening between the two rooms. "Ethan? Are you all right?"

"Sure. I'm fine," he muttered bitterly.

Patch closed the distance between them, but Ethan moved away from her to the other end of the counter.

"Do you know what Mrs. Felber's confession means?" Patch asked.

"It means my best friend betrayed me!" Ethan snarled.

"It means you're free!" Patch retorted. "Jefferson Trahern has no reason to want you dead anymore. He'll call off his gunfighter." Patch hesitated and said, "We can be married."

Ethan turned on her like a cornered wolf. "Free? My father was murdered. My inheritance has been destroyed. I've lost years I can never get back. My best friend is a Judas. If you can call that free, I'm *free*."

Ethan turned agonized eyes on Patch. "How could he do it? How could Boyd watch my life being destroyed and do nothing to stop it? All those years. Maybe at first I could understand him taking the money. He always hated being poor. But later, when he had so much, couldn't he have said something then?

"I want to kill him. I want to strangle him with my bare hands. I want to empty a gun into him and watch him die. All those years, Patch, I never had anyone except Trahern to blame for what happened to me. At least he had an excuse. What excuse is there for what Boyd did to me? *I trusted him!*"

Ethan flung himself toward the door.

"Ethan! Where are you going?" Patch cried.

"I don't know."

"You're coming back home, aren't you?"

"I don't know."

The bell jangled for several moments after Ethan slammed the door behind him. Patch realized suddenly that Ethan might actually go after Boyd. Maybe even kill him. Then it would start all over again. Ethan would run, and the law would chase after him. And she would end up living miserably ever after.

When Ethan rode out of Oakville, he wasn't aware of heading in any particular direction. His thoughts had turned inward. It was hard to imagine a life where he didn't have to be constantly looking over his shoulder. It was hard to believe he could marry Patch and settle down and raise a houseful of kids with her. But knowing who had raped Merielle Trahern didn't resolve all the questions in his life that needed answers.

He believed, because he had no evidence to the contrary, that Jefferson Trahern had murdered his father and poisoned his mother. Unfortunately, he had no proof of Trahern's perfidy. The one man who could have told him the truth was clinging to life by a thread.

So what should he do now? If Trahern called off his dogs, could Ethan in good conscience leave his father's death unavenged? Simply retreating from the field of battle would end the armed conflict between himself and Trahern. But would he ever know a moment's peace while his father's murderer ran free?

Without evidence, he couldn't accuse Trahern. But how the hell was he going to prove that Trahern had given the poison to Chester, if Chester died? There had to be some clue he had missed, something that would point a finger at Trahern. He would just have to go back and find it.

Ethan reined his horse to a stop. And realized he could see the gate to Boyd Stuckey's ranch on the horizon.

Ethan wasn't ready to confront Boyd just yet. He was still too angry. And confused. How had he so misjudged his friend? How had Boyd been able to sit at Ethan's dinner table, drink with him, smile at him, knowing all the while that he had betrayed him?

"Howdy."

Ripped abruptly from his thoughts, Ethan found himself confronting death in the form of the bounty hunter Jefferson Trahern had hired to kill him. Calloway's eyes were cold, merciless. But his gun was still in his holster.

Ethan felt a flash of hope. At least he had a chance to outdraw the other man. "I wondered why you were taking so long to come after me. Now I see you were just waiting to catch me with my pants down—figuratively speaking, of course."

Calloway shrugged. "Don't like to shoot a man in the back. Ambush isn't my style. Figure it's more sporting to give the other fellow a fair chance."

Which meant he must be damned fast with a gun. Forget trying to outdraw him.

Ethan wanted to laugh. Talk about bad timing. He felt confident that once Trahern knew Chester had been the rapist, he would call off Calloway. Unfortunately, Ethan was in the awkward position of trying to convince the gunfighter that it was no longer necessary to complete his job.

"What would you say if I told you I'm innocent of what Trahern has accused me of doing?"

"You'd be amazed how many guilty men say that."

"But I really am innocent. The man I brought into town draped over his saddle today is the actual culprit."

"Awful damned convenient to let another man take the blame, wouldn't you say?"

Ethan snorted in disgust. "Then shoot me and get it over with."

Calloway kneed his horse and closed the distance between them. Ethan thought of Patch. What would happen to her if he was killed? Would she go back to Montana? Would she end up with Boyd? That thought made his neck hairs stand on end. He would be damned before he would allow that to happen. Maybe the chance he was about to take would get him killed, but he was probably going to die anyway.

Ethan saw his opening and took it. He spurred his horse, and as it lunged forward, he launched himself at the gunfighter. The force of his body knocked Calloway off his horse, and they tumbled to the ground. The horses shied away as the two men rolled beneath them. Calloway got off one shot as they fell, but it went wild. They struggled to see who would end up with possession of his Colt.

Ethan grabbed Calloway's wrist and banged it against a rock. The gunman released the .45, but before either man could recover it, they were rolling in the opposite direction. Ethan tried to get to his own gun, but the instant he freed it from its holster, Calloway knocked it away. Fingers gouged. Fists landed vicious punches to face and belly.

At last they stood across from each other, staggering and bloody, waiting to catch their breath before they went at it again. Ethan was leaning forward with his palms braced on his thighs when the sun caught the swaying medallion he wore on a thong around his neck.

"Where'd you get that medal?" Calloway asked.

Ethan tucked the medal back inside his shirt. "It's just a worthless piece of tin."

"Where'd you get it?" Calloway demanded.

"Man gave it to me."

"What man?"

"Ran into him late one night. Never got his name. Never even saw his face, it was so damn dark. He was gone before first light."

"Hell," Calloway said. He walked away from Ethan, picked up his gun from the ground, holstered it, and headed for the shade of a mesquite.

Ethan picked up his own gun, wiped it clean of dust with his bandanna, and put it back in his holster. He followed Calloway into the shade.

"Mind telling me what's going on?"

"I gave you that medal."

"That was *you* I saved?"

Calloway grinned. "Afraid so. Nice to know I can finally return a ten-year-old favor. I'll tell Trahern he has to get another man for the job."

"I always wondered who you were, what happened to you," Ethan said, leaning against the mesquite and putting one booted foot against the trunk. "With that posse chasing you, it wasn't too hard to guess you were on the wrong side of the law. At the time, so was I."

"Wasn't a posse," Calloway said. "It was personal. I was much obliged to you for hiding me, for taking care of my wounds, for feeding me and giving me your horse. Not many men would have done that." Calloway dabbed with his bandanna at the blood dripping from his lip.

"That horse of yours was a pretty good cayuse once he got some rest and a little green grass in him," Ethan said.

"I'm surprised to see you're still wearing that medal. I wondered if you'd hang on to it."

"It's my good luck charm," Ethan said. "After all, the way I figure it, you had to be a pretty damned lucky man to outrun that bunch."

Both men laughed. Calloway stuck out his hand. Ethan shook it.

"So long, friend," Calloway said.

"You'd do to ride the river with."

Calloway mounted up first and headed for the Tumbling T. Ethan stood in the shade of the mesquite for a while longer, trying to decide what he should do next. He might as well give Calloway a chance to deliver his news to Trahern before he made his own peace overtures. Maybe he would go see Boyd after all and ask for some answers.

Ethan mounted up and turned his horse toward Boyd Stuckey's ranch.

Patch arrived at the front door of Boyd's ranch house half expecting to find him already dead. Ethan had left town a half hour earlier, and knowing his state of mind, Patch had been certain he would seek Boyd out and demand an explanation. When Boyd answered the door with a huge smile on his face, Patch knew he was unaware that his treachery had been discovered.

She wasn't about to enlighten him. There was no telling what he would do if he knew Ethan was looking for him with murder on his mind.

Patch hadn't formed any notions of what Boyd's ranch would be like, but she was nevertheless surprised. It wasn't ostentatious, as she might have expected from someone who had been very poor and become very rich. The house was the typical wood frame, single-story dogtrot Texas home, with a central hallway leading to rooms on either side of it.

The inside was tastefully if not richly decorated. Patch might have been more amazed by how neat and clean it was, except almost the first thing Boyd did was introduce a shy, sloe-eyed Mexican girl as his housekeeper. Patch had never seen a housekeeper quite so young or lovely in a bachelor household. But since the house was immaculate and smelled strongly of the beeswax used to shine the hardwood floors to a polished sheen, she kept her speculation to herself.

"Come on into the parlor," Boyd said. "To what do I owe the pleasure of this visit? Theresa, bring us something cool to drink. Is lemonade all right?" he asked Patch.

Patch ignored the first question and answered. "Lemonade will be fine."

"Welcome to my home," Boyd said. "Please sit down and make yourself comfortable."

Boyd had arranged a brass-studded leather couch and chairs in the parlor around a stone fireplace, with a Navajo rug on the floor. A rolltop desk and swivel chair faced the front window, which looked out over a vista of rolling prairie that stopped with a line of pecan and willow trees that grew along the river. A longhorn skull, with impressive horns at least six feet across, hung over the oak mantel.

There were no photographs of family on the mantel, no knickknacks placed here and there to reveal the character of the man who lived here, or to preserve the memories of a past life. Perhaps the absence of those things spoke more loudly than their presence would have.

As Patch looked around, she realized this was what Boyd had bought with his ill-gotten gains. A home. The home he had never had as a boy. She wanted to feel sorry for him. He had been given a choice between honesty and fulfilling a lifelong dream. He had chosen the dream. Morally, it was the wrong choice. Boyd had bought seventeen years of the kind of life he could never have hoped to lead. But at what price?

"Do you ever feel guilty?" Patch blurted.

"What?" Boyd had settled on one of the two leather chairs that faced each other in front of the fireplace. He stared in confusion at Patch in the chair opposite him. "Guilty about what?"

"About making your own dreams come true at Ethan's expense."

"If you're referring to my offer to buy the Double Diamond before Ethan got out of prison, I spoke to Mrs. Hawk because I was afraid otherwise she would end up with nothing."

Patch bit her lip, realizing that Boyd had misinterpreted her question, knowing she shouldn't say any more. This whole situation was a powder keg, and she didn't want to be anywhere near when it blew up. She changed the subject. Sort of. "Chester Felber was shot today."

Boyd's eyes widened. "I didn't know. That's too bad. Now Ethan will have a devil of a time finding whoever gave Chester that arsenic. Too bad Chester's secrets died with him."

"He isn't dead." Patch bit her lip again.

Boyd sat forward in his chair. "Has Chester said anything about where he got the poison?"

"No. He's in a coma. But Doc Carter thinks there's a good chance he'll live."

She watched for some reaction from Boyd to that news, but all she got for her trouble was a noncommittal "You don't say."

Patch's nerves forced her to her feet. She walked over to the mantel, as though she were examining the longhorn skull in greater detail. In fact, she marveled at the size and sharpness of the steer's horns. It was hard to believe cowboys faced down these animals daily with no more than a horse and a rope.

She turned around to face Boyd. "When she thought her son was dying, Mrs. Felber admitted that Chester was the one who raped Merielle."

Boyd jumped to his feet. "Good God!" He paced back and forth across the room, his hands thrust through his hair.

Patch stood frozen where she was. She waited for Boyd to realize that she must also know that he had been blackmailing Mrs. Felber. To her surprise, Boyd didn't come to that conclusion at all. Instead he turned to her and said, "Has anybody thought to let Trahern know about this? The chances are good that if he knew Chester was the guilty party, he'd call off that gunfighter he has chasing Ethan."

Patch stared, stunned that the first words out of Boyd's mouth appeared to be concern for Ethan. This, from the man who had betrayed Ethan over and over for seventeen years? It didn't make sense. However, she could see the wisdom of Boyd's suggestion.

"I'll go with you," she said.

"No, it would be better if I go alone. I can get there faster on horseback than if we both go in your buggy. In matters like this, every second counts.

"You go on back to the Double Diamond and make sure Ethan keeps his head down until we know for sure what Trahern plans to do with this new information."

For an instant, Patch considered confronting Boyd with her knowledge of his blackmail scheme against the Felbers. But she couldn't see that any purpose would be served except to make him defensive. Better to let well enough alone, at least for the present.

Boyd urged Patch to stay and finish her lemonade, but she was anxious to find Ethan and recount Boyd's reaction to the news that Chester was guilty of Merielle's rape. Maybe Ethan could find more sense in it than she could. She hadn't gone a mile toward home in the buggy when she met Ethan coming toward her on horseback.

"What are you doing out here?" he demanded.

"I went to see Boyd."

"Are you crazy? Or just plain stupid!"

"I was scared out of my wits for you!" she retorted. "I thought you might have gone after Boyd. I take it from the fact you're here that I was entirely wrong."

A slight flush stained Ethan's cheekbones. "I thought I might talk to him."

"You just missed him," Patch said. "He's on his way to the Tumbling T."

"Then there's no sense in my going any farther. I have to admit I wouldn't mind a little more time to think about all this before I have to confront him. And I've got cattle that need to be rounded up for branding."

Ethan tied his horse to the back of the buggy and joined Patch on the seat. He took the reins from her and set the horse in motion.

"I suppose Boyd has some more 'business' with Trahern." Ethan couldn't keep the bitterness from his voice.

"That's not why he's going there today. As soon as I mentioned that Mrs. Felber had admitted that Chester was the guilty party in Merielle's rape, he asked whether anyone had informed Trahern. I didn't know. He's on his way there now to see whether Trahern will use this information to call off that gunfighter he hired to hunt you down."

Ethan shook his head. "I've already had a showdown with Calloway."

Patch's stomach did a flip-flop. "What happened? Did you kill him?"

"Bloodthirsty, aren't you?"

Patch glared at him. "Well, you're not dead, so I figured he must be."

"It turns out Calloway and I had crossed paths ten years ago. I saved his life then. He decided to return the favor."

"You're kidding! Why didn't he recognize you in town?"

"I never saw his face or learned his name the night I saved his life, and he never saw mine. We were just two strangers who met one dark night. If it hadn't been for Calloway recognizing the medal he gave me that night, things might have ended up a lot less happily than they have."

"That sounds like something I might read in a novel."

Ethan grinned. "It was damned coincidental, all right. When Calloway left me, he was headed for Trahern's place to resign."

"Then Boyd's trip will be wasted." Patch paused and said, "Do you find it as strange as I do that Boyd's first concern seemed to be for your safety?"

Ethan scowled. "Why not? It isn't going to cost him anything to help me out this time."

"Maybe he regrets what he did. Maybe he saw this as a way to make some amends," Patch speculated.

"It's too late for that," Ethan said. "Years too late."

"Do you think you can ever forgive him?"

Ethan stared off into the distance. "I don't know. I've never trusted anyone the way I trusted Boyd. I ran into him after I left the line shack where Dora fixed me up. He was on his way home with his pa. Clete was dead drunk, so Boyd and I were able to talk without being bothered.

"He promised to watch after my family for me," Ethan said in a hoarse voice. "He told me not to worry, that he wouldn't let my parents get lonely. He would be their son until I came home."

Ethan swallowed over the thickness in his throat. "All that time, he knew who was really guilty. When we hugged each other good-bye, there were tears in his eyes. . . . I thought they were for me."

A band tightened around Patch's chest, making it hard to breathe. *Monstrous.* There was no other word for Boyd's actions. Patch became convinced that, considering the past, it was likely Boyd's race to Trahern's ranch had nothing to do with helping Ethan.

But if not, why had Boyd been in such a hurry to go there?

✺17✺

JEFFERSON TRAHERN FISTED HIS hand around the fifty-dollar gold certificates Calloway had shoved into his palm. Nothing he could say had swayed the bounty hunter. Calloway had quit. Trahern felt a rage born of frustration. Once again, his efforts to kill Ethan Hawk had been thwarted.

"Father?"

Trahern turned away from the front window to face his daughter. Seeing her every day over the past seventeen years had fanned the flames of his ire, so the fire had never died. Being angry was the only way he could survive the agony of watching his child grow up, but never grow older. "What is it Merielle?"

"Did your friend leave?"

"Yes, he's gone."

"Is he coming back?"

"No. He wasn't somebody you should know, Merielle."

"I liked him."

Trahern didn't argue with his daughter. He had learned from experience that he always lost. She saw only the good. The bad had ceased to exist for her since that awful night. She had been the soul of amiability—until the last couple of weeks.

Lately, she had been unusually contrary. And she had headaches all the time. He worried that something might be wrong, that she might be getting ill. But he avoided seeking out a doctor because that would be giving his fears substance.

"There's someone coming, Father. Maybe your friend decided to come back after all."

Trahern wasn't expecting anyone. The ranch was virtually abandoned. Frank had taken every cowhand who could fork a horse out to round up and brand the spring calves. Maria had gone along with her husband to manage the chuck wagon.

426

Trahern leaned over to look past the draped curtain in the parlor to the front yard. Sure enough, a rider was approaching. It wasn't Calloway; it was Boyd Stuckey. Trahern headed to the front door to greet his visitor. "Stay here, Merielle."

Over the years, Trahern had spent a great deal of his fortune on private detectives and bounty hunters to track Ethan Hawk down, on lawyers and judges to convict him, and most recently, on gunfighters to shoot him down. He had sold off his assets one at a time to finance his campaign against the man who had murdered his son and raped his daughter.

He didn't like or trust Stuckey, but over the years he had found it advantageous to do business with him. He wondered what had brought Boyd to the Tumbling T in such a hurry.

Trahern opened the front door before Boyd knocked. "What are you doing here? I thought we'd finished our business together."

"I have some news that might be of interest to you . . . and Merielle."

Trahern might not have invited Boyd inside, except anything that concerned Merielle had special significance. He hadn't missed the fact that Boyd's horse had been ridden hard and was lathered with sweat. "Come on in."

Trahern knew Merielle was in the parlor, but it was the most logical place to take Boyd. As he stepped over the threshold he said, "Merielle, Boyd has—"

He didn't get any more out before his daughter gasped. "You!" She stared at Boyd across the width of the parlor, her eyes wide. Then she shut her eyes tight and put a hand to her head. "Father?"

Trahern stood frozen with fear for his daughter. "Merielle? Are you all right?"

"My head hurts, Father."

"I have some news that might make her feel better," Boyd said as he stepped farther into the room. "Chester Felber was shot today."

Merielle's eyes opened wide in fright. "Chester?"

Trahern stood at the apex of a tense triangle that also included his daughter and Boyd. "I think you'd better leave now. You're upsetting my daughter."

"You'll want to hear what I have to say," Boyd countered.

"Then get it said and get out!"

"Chester Felber is the man who raped Merielle!"

"What?" Trahern stood stunned, his jaw agape.

Boyd took advantage of Trahern's inaction to approach Merielle, circling like a wolf that knows its prey is crippled and helpless. He stopped behind her, his mouth close to her ear. His voice was no more than a whisper, certainly not loud enough for Trahern to hear. "It was Chester, wasn't it, Merielle? You remember, don't you, how it was? You screamed and screamed. Chester hit you again and again to stop those horrible screams. It was Chester who raped you."

Merielle shook her head no.

"Leave her alone!" Trahern snapped.

But Boyd's sudden appearance, his command to remember, had already sent Merielle's thoughts spinning backward in time. She tried to shut everything out, but the memories kept flooding in, until there was no holding them back.

And she remembered.

She had come home right after school and told her father she was going to her room to rest before the party. Then she had climbed down the tree outside her window and started for the cave where she was supposed to meet Frank. They sky had been so blue! The wind was blowing in the grass so it almost sang. She had never felt so happy!

She had been nearly to the cave when she saw Boyd coming toward her.

"I came to wish you a happy birthday, since I wasn't invited to the party," Boyd said.

"Thanks, Boyd."

"You going to meet Frank?"

She smiled shyly. "He has a present for me."

"I've got one, too," Boyd said.

Since he didn't have anything in his hands she asked, "Where is it?"

He pointed to his lips. "Right here."

Merielle laughed. "Right where?"

"Here."

He grabbed her before she realized what he was going to do and kissed her right on the mouth.

She wiped her mouth with the back of her hand in disgust. "Boyd Stuckey, you snake! You skulking stinkworm! How dare you kiss me!"

She was so busy being outraged that she didn't notice the expression slowly changing on Boyd's face. When she finally looked at him again, she was frightened at what she saw. His features were contorted, and his face had turned red.

"So I'm not good enough for you, huh! Frank, the dirt farmer's son, is good enough. But not Boyd, the drunk's kid. Hoity-toity, high and mighty Merielle Trahern! You're no better than a whore in the saloon, spreading your legs for Frank whenever he asks."

"Stop it, Boyd!" She held her hands to her ears, appalled that Boyd could say such awful things to her face. "I won't listen!"

He grabbed her hands to pull them from her ears. "You'll listen to me, Merielle Trahern. I'm as good as Frank Meade. Better. I'm smarter, and I'm going to be somebody someday, just you watch and see. Frank will never be anything."

"You're not even good enough to lick Frank's boots," Merielle retorted.

Boyd shoved her, a little push to shut her up, but she lost her balance and fell. That made her even madder, because she had on the skirt she planned to wear to her party, and now it was dirty. She shouted, "You're *nothing* compared to Frank, Boyd! Just a nasty old—"

He straddled her and held her hands down on either side of her head, taunting her that there was enough of him to hold her down. She kicked and bucked under him, but he was too strong for her. She wasn't sure when she realized that his hands had suddenly tightened on her wrists. He switched both wrists to one hand and began rubbing his body against hers as she bucked against him.

"Stop it, Boyd!" she screamed.

He hit her in the mouth with his fist. While she was still stunned, he pulled her skirt up and ripped her drawers off. She twisted under him, terrified, frantic. "Nobody will want to be your friend anymore when I tell them about this. Just you wait until I tell Frank and Ethan—"

She felt a sharp, tearing pain, excruciating pain.

She screamed. A long, loud wail of horror and indignation, of pain and fear.

Finally, the pain stopped. She felt something dripping down her thigh. She was afraid to touch herself to find out what it was.

"You say a word about this to anyone, and I'll kill you," Boyd whispered in her ear. "Hell, you say a word about this, and I'll kill Frank! Before I do, I'll tell him that you liked it, that you asked me to do it to you!"

Suddenly her hands were free. She lashed out and felt her nails strike flesh. She curved her fingers into claws and dug deep. When she looked, it wasn't Boyd's face before her, it was Chester's.

She was confused. She wanted to apologize to Chester. But when she tried to speak, no words would come out.

She could see everything that was happening around her, but she couldn't seem to form the words she wanted to say. She watched Horace Felber's arrival, paralyzed by fear. What if Boyd did what he had threatened? Frank would hate her if he thought she had wanted Boyd to put himself inside her. But if she accused Boyd of rape, he would kill her! He would kill Frank!

She tried to tell Horace Felber that she didn't know who had hurt her. Her mouth moved, but the sound was stuck in her throat.

She didn't understand why they left her all alone. She tried to stand, but her knees kept buckling. Dusk fell. And Frank came. She was terrified again. She tried to tell him she hadn't wanted Boyd to do it.

He pleaded with her to speak to him. Her eyes were open, but she saw everything through a mist of what she realized must be tears. She answered him, but he acted like she hadn't. Finally, she realized that the words were only sounding in her head. Frank couldn't hear them. She closed her eyes to shut out the pleading, terrified look in his.

She heard Ethan come and try to send Frank away. In her head she heard the words form, begging Frank to stay. Then Dorne was there. She could hear him shouting at Frank. She didn't want her brother to see her like this and squeezed her eyes closed as though to hide her shame in darkness.

She began trembling violently when Dorne attacked Frank, and jerked when she heard shots fired. She chanced a look from beneath lowered lashes and saw Dorne lying on the ground beside her with blood spurting from his leg. She closed her eyes again, shutting out the horror. Shutting out everything.

Much later, she heard her father's voice, but she couldn't face him. It was too horrible. It was too awful. She could never tell him what had happened.

That was the last thing she remembered. How long ago had that been? Traces of the past few weeks flashed before her eyes.

"You're a beautiful young woman."

"Ethan Hawk is an old friend of yours."

"Do you remember kissing me, Merielle?"

"I won't let Father keep us apart, Frank!"

Merielle opened her eyes and looked around her. She was in the parlor of her home. Her father—God, he was so old! She put her hands to her face and felt the changes in her features. She looked down at her body. Her breasts had grown! And she had hips! *I'm all grown up!*

"Chester did it," Boyd repeated like a litany. "Don't you remember? Chester did it!"

"No!" Merielle put her hands to her ears to stop Boyd's voice. "Stop! Stop!"

"Leave her alone," Trahern barked again. "Get out, Boyd. I think you've said enough."

"It wasn't Chester!" Merielle cried. She turned to face Boyd, then backed away toward her father. She pointed her finger at Boyd. "It was you, Boyd! *You raped me!*"

Both men were stunned at her outburst.

"She's talking crazy," Boyd bluffed.

"Don't believe him, Father." Merielle turned to face her father. She looked up into his searching eyes. "I remember everything. Boyd raped me. Chester came along and tried to stop him."

"Boyd wasn't there when we found you, Ethan was."

Merielle grabbed a fistful of her father's shirt. "Ethan came later! He didn't do it, Father. It was Boyd!"

Trahern was still having trouble accepting the idea that Merielle had her memory back. It was horrifying to think he had sent the wrong man to prison and welcomed a viper into his home. Trahern lunged for the rifle that was mounted over the mantel, but he didn't get two steps before Boyd shot him in the back.

"Father!" Merielle raced to where her father had fallen on the carpeted floor. He was bleeding from a terrible wound between his shoulder blades. "You've killed him!" she cried.

"Good riddance!" Boyd said. "Now I'm going to take care of you!"

When Boyd aimed the gun at her, Merielle did the only thing she could think of to save herself.

"Have you seen my friend, Patch? We went on a picnic and it was lots of fun. I want her to come play with me again."

Boyd grinned. "Crazy as a coot again, huh?" He walked over and knelt beside her, looking into her eyes.

Merielle didn't move. *Look hard, Boyd. See what I want you to see.* "What happened to Father?" she whimpered.

"Ethan shot your father. Remember that. *Ethan* shot your father."

"Ethan shot my father," Merielle repeated obediently. *I know exactly who killed my father. And you're going to hang for it!*

"Good girl. I'll be leaving you now, Merielle. I've got to get to the sheriff with the tragic news. Ethan Hawk just made good on his threat to kill Jefferson Trahern. He's finally gone too far. A lynch party ought to go after him. Yeah. That sounds good. A lynch party."

You fiend! "Can I come to the party?" Merielle said.

Boyd laughed. "Not this one." He stopped at the door and turned back to her. His eyes narrowed until his face looked cruel. "By the way, Merielle, next time you start remembering the wrong thing, I *will* kill you. Remember that."

Merielle remained frozen where she was until she heard Boyd's horse gallop away. She looked down at the blood pooling around her father and knew there was nothing she could do to help him. If she hurried, there might still be time to save Ethan Hawk.

She wanted to fly to Frank. She needed to feel his arms around her. She needed to know whether he still wanted her after everything that had happened. But she had no idea where he was. He could be anywhere on Tumbling T range. If she stopped to search for Frank, Ethan might end up getting hanged.

Merielle raced upstairs and put on a split riding skirt and boots. As she saddled a horse for herself in the barn, Merielle tried to think what would be best to do. It probably wasn't a good idea to go to the sheriff by herself. Boyd would convince everyone she was deranged. But there was someone who would believe her. Someone who would listen to what she had to say and warn Ethan.

Merielle left the Tumbling T and rode straight for Patch Kendrick at the Double Diamond.

Boyd knew he had to move fast. He was lucky the hands were all gone on the roundup. Apparently, no one had heard the shot that killed Trahern. He wasn't sure he had done the right thing leaving Merielle alive, but it was easier to accuse Ethan of murder if Trahern was the only victim. He felt certain that he could intervene in time if Merielle did begin to regain her memory, and that he could get her committed to some asylum where she would never be heard from again.

He was running on adrenaline. How the hell had it come to this? Killing Trahern had never been part of his plan. But if he didn't want to lose everything he had gained over the past seventeen years, he had to cover his tracks, and fast. That meant accusing Ethan of the crime and making sure he died before anyone had time to investigate Trahern's death. Luckily, no one was likely to believe Ethan's protestations of innocence.

A lynch party would solve Boyd's problem nicely.

Before he incited a riot, he had a little business that needed taking care of. He rode down the back alleys into town and dismounted behind the Oakville Mercantile. He looked around to make sure he wasn't being observed before he stepped inside. The change in light blinded him momentarily, but he could feel the room was empty. He stood where he was and inhaled deeply.

He had always liked the way the storeroom smelled. Vinegar. That was pickles. Leather. That was a new saddle. Wool. That was bolts of fabric. Wood. That was new-made barrels and casks and crates filled with everything and anything. This room smelled of all the things he had craved as a child and never had. He had liked coming here to get his money from Horace Felber. He had insisted on it.

"What are you doing here?"

He realized Mrs. Felber must have heard him come in. "I need to speak with you. And with Horace."

"Horace isn't here. You can talk to me."

"I know you've already told some people what Chester did. I just came to make sure you don't flap your jaws about other things."

"Like what a poor excuse for a human being you are?" Mrs. Felber taunted.

Boyd would have hit her if he had been closer. Fortunately, several barrels blocked his way, and by the time he could get past them, he had regained his temper.

"It might interest you to know Jefferson Trahern is dead."

"Why should that make any difference to me?"

"Because I'm the big man in Oak County now. Everything Jefferson Trahern controlled will fall to me. For instance, I'll own the sheriff."

Mrs. Felber gasped.

"I see you're beginning to get the picture. In case it isn't crystal clear yet, if you or Horace say one word to Careless Lachlan about blackmail, I'll have Horace arrested as an accomplice to the rape of Merielle Trahern. And I'll make sure he goes to prison for a long, long time."

Mrs. Felber remained mute. It was already too late to comply with Boyd's demand for silence. Horace was with Sheriff Lachlan right now, spilling the beans. Whatever happened now would happen. She would never let herself be blackmailed by this man again. "You've said your piece, now get out. And don't ever come back."

Boyd smirked. "I'll be back next month for my money. Just like always. Nothing's changed."

Mrs. Felber's mouth tightened grimly. "Get out."

Boyd backed his way out of the room. He didn't like the look in Mrs. Felber's eyes. But she would keep her mouth shut and pay. Frightened people always did.

Boyd used the alleys to take himself back to the edge of town. Then he spurred his horse and raced down Main Street at a gallop, shouting and waving his hat to draw attention to himself. He slid his horse to a stop on its haunches in front of the Silver Buckle and came out of the saddle on the run. He shoved the batwing doors so hard they swung back and forth behind him.

"Where's the sheriff?" he shouted. "Ethan Hawk just killed Jefferson Trahern!"

If anyone had been thinking, they would have realized that the best place to look for Careless, especially at noontime, was the jail. Boyd wasn't really interested in getting Careless involved until he had done a little rabble-rousing. Men with a few drinks in them didn't always think clearly.

"You all heard Ethan Hawk say he was going to kill Trahern," Boyd said. "It looks like that's exactly what he did!"

"Murder's a hanging offense," someone shouted.

"Probably just send him to jail again," Boyd said.

"Not if I have anything to say about it," another man said. "Man kills someone deserves to pay at the end of a rope."

Another man agreed. And another.

"He'll probably get away before the sheriff can arrest him," Boyd said.

"The hell you say! Let's go get him, boys!" someone yelled.

"He oughtta hang!" yelled another.

Boyd followed the drunken mob out through the batwing doors. He couldn't have formed a lynch party faster or better if they had been following a script. The drunken men hadn't even thought to ask him how he knew Ethan had done it.

The first glitch came when Careless caught up to the crowd. The men from the saloon were already mounting their horses.

"Where're all you fellas goin'?" Careless asked.

"Gonna find Ethan Hawk and hang 'im!" someone shouted.

"He deserves a trial first," Careless said, alarmed when he saw someone working a rope into a hangman's noose.

"We'll give him a trial," one man said. "*Then* we'll hang 'im!" The crowd laughed.

"You can't just lynch a man," Careless protested.

"Watch us!"

"You comin' or stayin'?" someone called to the sheriff.

Careless realized the only way he could control the crowd was to join it. "I'm comin'," he grumbled. "Give me a minute to saddle my horse."

"Take mine," one of the men standing in front of the saloon said. "My wife'd have ten fits if I went along, but she don't have to know I sent my horse to a lynchin'." He laughed and slapped his knee.

Careless took the reins and mounted.

One man kicked his horse into a gallop, and eight more followed quickly after him. Careless was left in the rear with Boyd.

He stared at the young man riding beside him with new eyes. He had just had a very informative session with Horace Felber. Amazing how Boyd Stuckey had fooled them all. Everybody thought he was a fine, upstanding citizen, even if he was Ethan Hawk's best friend. When word got out what he had done, how he had double-crossed a friend for money, there wasn't a man, cowboy or drunk, who would give him the time of day.

Unfortunately, there was no proof of Horace's accusations. It was just Horace's word against Boyd's. With Trahern dead, Boyd was the richest man in the county. And he had made a lot of friends over the years. If Careless tried to arrest Boyd, Boyd just might get him fired. It would be a damn shame to keep his job all these years and lose it now that Trahern was no longer around to be a burr under his saddle.

Careless spurred his horse closer so he could talk to Boyd without shouting. "I just had a talk with Horace Felber," he said to Boyd.

Boyd immediately slowed his horse to put more distance between the two of them and the rest of the lynch party. "Whatever he told you is a lie, Careless. And if you know what's good for you, you'll forget you ever heard it."

"But Horace—"

"Horace will keep his mouth shut. Or I'll shut it for him."

"Those are pretty big words . . ." Careless shuddered under the look in Boyd's yellow eyes.

"I'm the big man in Oak County now, Careless. If you want to keep your job, you'll do as I say."

Boyd didn't wait to see whether Careless was willing. He just spurred his horse and headed for the front of the mob.

"Grits and galoshes!" Careless swore. "There goes my job again!"

Maybe not. If he could just manage to arrest Boyd when Boyd wasn't expecting it, he could put him in jail. Let Boyd try to talk his way out once the word was on the street about exactly how Boyd had gotten the stake that made him into a rich man. Boyd would be lucky if the town didn't lynch *him*! With Trahern dead and Boyd taken care of, there would be no one to tell Careless what he could and couldn't do. For the first time in twenty years, he wouldn't have to answer to anybody. Except the people of Oakville.

"I'm the law," he muttered. "I am the law." He would take care of Boyd when the time came. First he had to get control of this situation. "When we find Ethan, I'll bring him in for trial," he said aloud.

Careless took another look at the men riding pell-mell toward the Double Diamond and shook his head. "Grits and galoshes."

Could one man—even if he was the sheriff—stop a lynch mob on the prowl?

❊18❊

Patch couldn't understand a word Merielle said. The woman was completely hysterical. She grabbed Merielle's hand and pulled her toward the ranch house. "Come inside with me, Merielle. You need a cool drink. I promise you we'll talk."

"You have to listen to me, Patch," she begged as they stepped onto the porch. "Boyd is going to hang Ethan."

That made no sense at all to Patch. "Just calm down, Merielle."

"I *won't* calm down!" She stomped her foot like a six-year-old having a tantrum. "Listen to me! *I'm not crazy!*"

Nell heard the commotion and came running to the front door along with Leah.

Leah's eyes widened in fright when she spied the red-faced, shouting woman on the porch. "What's wrong with her?"

"Leah, would you get a cold drink from the kitchen?" Patch asked as she ushered Merielle across the threshold and on into the parlor. "Nell, please come here and sit on the sofa on the other side of Merielle."

Patch got Merielle settled between herself and Nell. Each of them had an arm around Merielle trying to calm her down. Tears began streaming down Merielle's perfect face.

"Please listen to me," Merielle begged. "Ethan's life is in danger."

That got their attention. Leah had returned with a glass of lemonade and stood listening raptly.

"What's all this about Ethan being in danger?" Patch asked.

"That's what I've been trying to tell you," Merielle said. "Boyd shot my father, and he's going to blame Ethan. When he left my house, he was on his way to town to form a lynch party. He wants Ethan hanged before anyone can start asking questions."

Patch stared at Merielle. The Merielle she had first met wouldn't have understood the danger involved in such a situation, or even acknowledged it. Something was very different about this woman from the Merielle she had known. "You've got your memory back!"

"Enough to know it was Boyd who raped me!"

"But Chester—"

"Chester tried to stop him! When my father heard the truth, he reached for a gun to kill Boyd, and Boyd shot him in the back."

Patch shivered. "Oh, my God! My God! We have to find Ethan and warn him."

"Isn't he here?" Merielle asked.

"When he found out that Chester had—oh, Lord, but it wasn't Chester! I can't wrap my mind around the fact it was Boyd. Mrs. Felber told us Chester had raped you. Ethan thought you might be needing Frank, so he went hunting for him. He was going to send Frank to you."

"Frank? You know where Frank is?" Merielle asked.

"I know where Ethan went looking for him."

Nell was quicker than Patch to realize the real ramifications of what Merielle had said. Boyd was truly evil. He would stop at nothing to get what he wanted. If he couldn't manage to hang Ethan, he might shoot Ethan in the back, as he had Jefferson Trahern.

"We've got to get word to Ethan *now*," Nell said. "He won't realize he's in danger from Boyd."

"I'll go on horseback," Patch said, rising from the sofa. "That'll be the fastest way to reach him."

Merielle jumped up after her. "I'll go with you."

Patch tried sitting Merielle back down, but the girl wasn't yielding. "If you just wait here, I'll send Frank back to you."

"You can't leave me here!" Merielle cried hysterically. "Don't you understand? Boyd is coming here with the lynch party! If he finds me here, he'll know I'm not crazy anymore. And he'll kill me!"

"We can hide you," Nell said.

"No! No! I'm scared! Please, Patch, take me with you!"

Patch hugged Merielle tight and met Nell's eyes over her shoulder. "Maybe it's for the best if I take her with me. There's no telling how far Boyd will go. He might search the house. If he found her . . ."

Nell rose and patted Merielle on the back. "All right, both of you go. But hurry! Leah and I will stall Boyd here as long as we can."

Patch took time enough to strip off her day dress and put on one of Ethan's shirts, Levi's, and boots for the hard ride ahead. Then she and Merielle headed for the barn for fresh horses, slamming the door behind them.

Nell opened her arms and a frightened Leah stepped into them.

"Will Ethan be all right, Ma?"

"We'll do everything we can, Leah, to protect him. He's managed to survive worse danger for a lot of years. He's always careful."

"But he won't be expecting Boyd to try and kill him."

"We'll just have to pray, Leah, that Patch and Merielle get to Ethan first."

Leah started to cry. "I didn't know I was going to love Ethan so much, Ma, but I do. I don't want him to die."

Nell tightened her arms around her daughter. "Shh. Shh. God willing, you and your brother will have many long years to tease each other to death."

Leah laughed and wiped her nose with her sleeve. "Aw, Ma."

Then Leah's head whipped up at the rumbling sound of galloping horses. "They're coming!" She raced to the front window and looked out. "They're here!"

Nell crossed to the window to look for herself. "You stay inside, Leah. I'll handle this."

Nell was frightened, but she had lived in the West long enough to know that the fact she was a woman gave her a certain immunity to harm. Women were so scarce that those who braved the loneliness and the danger of the West were revered and protected. These men might hang her son without a qualm, but they would hunt down and kill anyone who dared to lay a finger on her.

She patted her hair once and straightened her apron before stepping out onto the front porch. "What can I do for you gentlemen this afternoon?"

"We're lookin' for Ethan," one of the men said. "Send him on out."

"Ethan isn't here."

"Hidin' behind his mother's skirts, more likely," someone muttered from the crowd.

"I'm telling you the truth," Nell said in a calm voice. "Can I offer you gentlemen something cold to drink?"

Boyd could see that Nell's courtesy made the crowd uncomfortable. If he didn't do something fast, she would have them all inside drinking lemonade, instead of hunting Ethan down.

"We're going to have to look in the house for Ethan," Boyd said. "And in the barn."

"Of course," Nell said. "But just a few of you in the house, please." The longer they spent searching the house, the more time it gave Patch and Merielle to find Ethan and Frank.

Boyd picked a few of the rowdier men to search the house, those without wives and family, who would be less finicky about looking under furniture. He joined them. The rest he sent to the barn and area surrounding the house. Boyd was surprised when Careless insisted on staying with him.

"If you find Ethan, I wanta be there to see what he has to say for hisself," Careless insisted.

That was exactly what Boyd *didn't* want, but nothing he said could budge the sheriff. "All right," he said at last. "Come on. Let's get this over with."

The presence of the sheriff lent credibility to the search, but Boyd wasn't really surprised when they didn't find Ethan. However, he suspected that Nell Hawk knew where her son was. If Careless hadn't been along, he would have used force to get the information from her. He wasn't quite sure what to do now.

Shouts and gunshots from outside brought all those in the house to the porch on the run.

"Did you find him?" Boyd shouted.

The man they dragged out of the chicken coop wasn't Ethan Hawk.

"Corwin!" Nell cried. "What are you doing here?"

The mob dragged the old man up onto the porch where Boyd was waiting with Careless.

"I wanted to surprise you," Corwin said sheepishly. "I decided to build that roost you've been wanting for your hens."

"Swears he don't have the least idea where Ethan Hawk is," said one of the two cowboys who was holding Corwin hostage.

"You better tell us what you know, old man," Boyd said.

"I wouldn't tell you the time of day," Corwin retorted. "You're what you've always been, Boyd Stuckey. Nothing."

Boyd drew his pistol and cracked the old man on the head with the butt of it. Corwin sagged like a bag of grain in the arms of the men holding him. They let go and he fell to the ground.

"Corwin!" Nell dropped to the ground beside the old man, and put the hem of her apron to his temple to stanch the flow of blood. She looked up at Boyd and found that he was staring back at her defiantly with those golden yellow eyes of his.

"Does it make you feel important to pistol-whip a defenseless man?" she said.

"You'll be next if I don't get some information quick," Boyd threatened.

The crowd suddenly hushed.

The next thing Boyd knew, Leah had jumped on his back and was strangling him. He reached up and tumbled her over his shoulder.

"Hey! Leave the kid alone," Careless warned.

"She attacked me first," Boyd retorted. He grabbed both of Leah's hands in one of his and held her at arm's length, so she couldn't kick him. But then he couldn't reach her mouth to shut her up.

"You two-legged coyote!" she ranted. "You back-shooting coward."

Boyd flushed at the names she was calling him. He started to raise his hand to her when Careless warned, "The girl ain't guilty of nothin'. Leave her alone."

The crowd that had been hushed began to make ugly noises at Boyd's rough treatment of the girl.

Boyd realized he would be the one at the end of a rope if he didn't let go of the brat. When he released her hands, she backed off, but only far enough to give her room to kick him hard in the shin before running to the protection of her mother's arms.

He rubbed his leg but didn't dare lash out at her as he wished. His face ruddy with rage, Boyd demanded, "Tell us where to find Ethan."

"I don't know where Ethan is," Nell answered.

"You must have some idea what he planned to do today," Boyd insisted.

"No, I don't."

The cowboys shifted restlessly. None of them had bargained for this kind of confrontation when they left the saloon.

"Hey!" one of them said. "Leave the lady be!"

"We'll find Hawk some other time," another shouted.

That was exactly what Boyd did *not* want. The time to strike was now, before Ethan had a chance to establish an alibi or profess his innocence. He raised his gun to strike at the old man again, and Nell cried, "No! I'll tell you! Don't hit him again!"

"Where is he?" Boyd demanded.

Nell knew she had bought the two women as much time as she could. Surely they had enough of a head start to find Ethan and warn him. "Ethan went to find Frank at the Tumbling T roundup."

"If you're lying," he said, "I'll be back."

"I'm sorry for you, Boyd," Nell said. "I can't imagine what any of us ever did to make you hate us so."

Boyd leaned close to Nell and spoke in a guttural voice that was barely loud enough for her to hear. "It's nothing personal. I'm just doing what I have to do to survive."

When Boyd turned around, he discovered that the lynch mob, which had been so hot for revenge in town, was now colder than a dead snake. Boyd had work to do if he was going to whip them into a frenzy again.

Careless didn't help matters. "Maybe it would be a good idea if you and me go after Ethan and bring him back to town."

"These men have as much right as anybody to witness a hanging," Boyd said. "You don't want to rob them of all the fun, do you?"

The drunkest of the bunch yelled, "I ain't seen a hangin' for nigh on to two years. Don't aim to miss this one!"

Reminded of how long it was between adventures of this sort, the mob mounted up, revived and refreshed by its gory purpose.

Careless didn't try any longer to stop the crowd. He rode off at a gallop after them. He hadn't realized how ruthless Boyd Stuckey was. Maybe he had better rethink his plan to thwart the richest, meanest bastard in Oak County.

Patch and Merielle were in a race with time. They had to reach the spot where the Tumbling T cowhands were dipping, branding, and castrating calves before Boyd's lynch mob caught up to them.

Patch's greatest fear was that Merielle might slow her down. After an hour on the trail, Patch conceded she had vastly underrated Merielle's grit and gumption. The young woman had dried her tears, squared her shoulders, and ridden as hard as a horse thief with a prize stallion under him and the law on his tail.

Their horses were blown by the time they spotted a crowd of

cowboys squatting down around a branding fire. "Ethan!" Patch shouted. "Ethan!"

Merielle joined in with a different verse. "Frank!" she shouted. "Frank!"

Only one cowboy came out of the bunch around the fire.

Frank started running toward them. Merielle came flying off her horse straight into Frank's open arms. He hugged her so tight she could barely catch her breath.

"If you don't loosen up a little, she's going to faint," Patch pointed out.

Frank let go a little, but kept his arms around Merielle. "What's happened? What are you two doing here?"

"Where's Ethan?" Patch asked.

"Haven't seen him. Why? What's wrong?"

"Boyd shot and killed Father," Merielle said. "He's blaming Ethan, and he's hunting him with a lynch mob."

"Why would Boyd shoot Trahern? Why is he after Ethan?" Frank's confusion was easy to understand, and the answers he was getting weren't doing much to clear things up.

"Boyd shot Father because Father was going to shoot him."

"Why was Trahern going to shoot Boyd?" Frank demanded in exasperation.

Merielle couldn't just blurt it out. Not in front of Frank. She turned to Patch.

Patch was more concerned about Ethan than about making explanations to Frank. "Ethan told me he was coming here to meet with you. So where is he?"

"For the second time, I haven't seen him," Frank said. "Why was he coming here?"

"We heard that Chester Felber was the one who—"

"It wasn't Chester," Merielle contradicted. "Boyd raped me!" Merielle realized what she had said and turned to Frank. "It was Boyd, Frank. I didn't want to do it! He forced me!"

Frank's face bleached white. He grasped Merielle's shoulders so hard she winced. "You remember? Everything?"

Merielle bit her lip and nodded.

"You're sure it was Boyd?"

"I'm not likely to forget a thing like that!" Merielle snapped back. The three of them looked at each other and laughed nervously. It wasn't funny. But it was.

"What I don't understand," Frank said, "is why the lynch party is after Ethan, when Boyd is the guilty party."

"Boyd plans to tell everyone in town that Ethan made good on his threat to kill my father," Merielle said.

"Meanwhile," Patch added, "the Felbers are under the impression that *Chester* committed the rape. Boyd has been blackmailing them all these years to keep silent."

Frank met Merielle's dark eyes. "I thought you said Boyd—"

Merielle lowered her eyes to avoid Frank's gaze. "He did."

Frank took off his hat and rubbed his head with his knuckles. "I'm confused."

Patch explained. "Horace found Chester and Boyd together with Merielle the day she—" She cut herself off and began again, avoiding actual mention of the word *rape*. "Merielle had scratched Chester's face while he was trying to rescue her. But Boyd told Horace that Chester was the guilty one. It wasn't until Merielle got her memory back that she confronted Boyd with the truth."

"Which was when Trahern tried to shoot him, and he shot Trahern," Frank concluded.

"Right!" both women said together.

"If Boyd knows you recognized him as the . . . one who hurt you, why did he let you go?" Frank asked Merielle.

"Because I made him think I'd lost my memory again."

Frank's face was grim. "I'd like to get my hands on him. And it looks like I might get a chance real soon," he said, pointing to a bunch of riders approaching in a hurry.

"That can't be the lynch mob already," Patch said. "It's too soon!"

"It takes a crowd to raise that much dust. I don't have that many cowhands working out here."

Both Frank and Patch thought of Merielle at the same time. When they looked at her, she was standing frozen with her wide eyes focused on the riders jostling for position at the head of the pack.

"He'll kill me," she whispered. She turned to Frank. "And he'll kill you, too!"

"He's not going to kill anybody," Patch said.

"He'll know I remember. He'll know—"

"He'll know what we tell him," Patch said. "You keep quiet and let me do the talking."

Patch had barely finished speaking when Boyd separated himself from the crowd and rode toward them.

"Who's that with you, Boyd?" Patch asked.

"The sheriff and a posse," Boyd said. "We're hunting Ethan."

"What for?"

Boyd eyed Merielle sideways. "Didn't Merielle tell you?"

"She came to my place crying, very distressed," Patch said. "She was so hysterical, I couldn't understand a word she said. I brought her here hoping that Frank could calm her down. As you can see, she's all right now. Do you have any idea what might have upset her?"

Patch held her breath, waiting to see if she had assuaged Boyd's suspicion. From the corner of her eye she watched Frank's arm tighten around Merielle. His hand slipped down toward his gun. A muscle jumped in his jaw. She hoped Frank wouldn't take the law into his own hands. There was altogether too much of that going on in Oakville.

Patch felt the tension palpably increase while she waited for Boyd to assess the situation.

At last Boyd said, "Merielle probably witnessed her father's murder."

"Jefferson Trahern is dead?" Patch let her mouth fall open in surprise.

"Apparently Ethan made good on his promise to shoot him."

"Did someone see Ethan do it?" Patch knew as soon as she saw Boyd's lips flatten that she was only making trouble for herself by asking pointed questions that Boyd would be forced to answer with lies.

"As a matter of fact," Boyd said. "I saw him. Do you know where we can find him?"

"I can't imagine he would be anywhere within a hundred miles of here," Patch said. "Especially if he knows you can identify him as Trahern's killer."

Boyd snorted in disgust at how he had trapped himself.

"By the way," Patch said, "how did Ethan escape in the first place? I mean, if you saw him murder Trahern, why did you let him get away?"

Boyd was clearly flummoxed by Patch's question. "Ethan just shot and ran. There wasn't time to react."

Patch could have kicked herself for forcing Boyd into a corner. He was clearly suspicious again.

Boyd had been leery of approaching the branding fire when he realized Patch and Merielle were there with Frank. When he first rode up, the look in Frank's eyes was deadly. He felt certain Merielle had somehow recovered her memory and exposed him. But no sooner had he identified the danger in Frank's eyes than it was gone, replaced by a bland friendliness.

He had been put off guard at first by Patch's smooth explanation of Merielle's appearance. Then she had started asking those pointed questions.

She knows.

Boyd glanced at Merielle from the corner of his eye. She was staring straight at him, and there was no confusion in her dark eyes, just fear and loathing. Her second loss of memory had been a fraud.

The bitch told them everything!

His eyes narrowed in calculation. It appeared, from the tension in Frank and from Patricia's verbal attack, that they believed Merielle's accusations against him. He would have to send Careless and the lynch mob back to town. His pursuit of Ethan would have to be postponed while he took care of more pressing business.

Patricia and Merielle and Frank all had to die.

❋19❋

ETHAN KNEW HE WOULD never be free to settle down with Patch until he had made his peace with Jefferson Trahern. Since all the Tumbling T hands were gone on the roundup, there would never be a better time to beard the lion in his den. Trahern's big bay gelding stood saddled and waiting in front of the house. Chances were good Trahern was still inside.

Ethan rode right up, tied his horse on the rail beside the bay, and knocked on the door. When no one answered, he looked around him uneasily. Maybe he was walking into some kind of trap. A narrow-eyed search revealed nothing unusual. In fact, the place looked deserted.

Ethan felt the hair prickle on the back of his neck. He took the few steps to the front window, cupped his hand against the glass, and looked inside. A second later he had let himself in and was running for the parlor.

"Anybody home?" he shouted. "Anybody here?"

He knelt beside Trahern's inert body. The big man lay on his stomach, his arms outstretched. He had been shot in the back at fairly close range. Blood stained his suit jacket and the carpet beneath him. Ethan checked for a pulse and was amazed when he found one.

"Son of a bitch."

Ethan faced a choice he would rather not make. Should he try to save the man who had murdered his father? Or let him die? He stood and paced the length of the parlor once. He turned and paced back again. When he reached the parlor door, he walked through it.

Trahern groaned.

Ethan stopped just beyond the doorway. His chin dropped to his chest. He couldn't leave the man to die. He had to do what he could to save Merielle's father—if not for Trahern's sake, then for his own. He had no idea who had shot Trahern, but he had a pretty good idea who was going to get blamed for it. He had been a loudmouthed idiot, threatening Trahern in front of the whole damn town. They would be after him again, and this time he might very well hang. Ethan had no choice. He had to help the man who had murdered his father.

Ethan searched quickly for a downstairs bedroom where he could take the wounded man and tend to him. He found it at the back of the house. It was obviously a guest room. He pulled the quilt off and yanked the sheets down. Then he hurried back to the parlor—long step, halting step—turned Trahern over, and lifted him enough to circle his arms around Trahern's chest from behind. He dragged the heavy man across the parlor and down the hall to the bedroom.

Getting Trahern onto the bed wasn't easy, but Ethan finally managed it. He pulled off Trahern's coat and shirt, so he could bandage the bullet wound and stop the bleeding. The bullet had entered Trahern's back high enough to miss the heart and lungs and far enough to the left to avoid the windpipe. But if Ethan didn't do something quickly, Trahern was going to bleed to death.

The hole where the bullet had gone in wasn't too big. Ethan managed to plug it with cloth he tore from a pillowcase. However, the hole in Trahern's upper chest, where the bullet had come out, was substantially larger. Ethan used pressure to stop the bleeding, and then tied on a tight bandage with more strips of the pillowcase.

When Ethan tightened the knot, Trahern grunted. And his eyes opened.

When he saw Ethan, Trahern tried to rise, but he had lost too much blood. He fell back and clutched his chest. "What the hell are you doing here, Hawk?" he rasped.

"Trying to save your life," Ethan muttered. "Lie down and be still."

Trahern grasped weakly at Ethan's arm. "Merielle . . . Where's Merielle?"

"How the hell would I know? There wasn't a soul around when I got here."

"Maybe she got away. She must have . . . or he would have killed her, too." Trahern clutched Ethan's shirt. "You have . . . to find her!" he gasped.

Ethan freed his shirt and took a step back so Trahern couldn't reach him. "What the hell went on here? Who shot you? Is Merielle in some kind of danger?"

"Please . . . You have to go look for her!" Trahern's voice was a bare whisper as he struggled to make Ethan understand his desperation, his fear for his daughter's safety. "You can't make her pay for what I did to you. I know now how wrong I was. Oh, God, I'm so sorry!"

"What the hell happened here?" Ethan demanded.

"I didn't know," Trahern said. "How could I know?"

"Stop talking in riddles," Ethan said irritably. "What is it you didn't know?"

"That Boyd . . . raped Merielle."

Ethan froze. He met Trahern's eyes and saw the shame, the regret. His blood curdled. *Not Chester. Boyd?* "Who said he did it?"

"Merielle. She remembered everything." Trahern took a labored breath. "When she pointed a finger at Boyd, I reached for a gun to kill him, and he shot me in the back." Trahern tried to raise an arm to cover his eyes, but the pain forced him to abandon the effort. "Once Boyd shot me, Merielle was left to fend for herself with that rotten bastard." Tears appeared in the old man's eyes. "I'll never forgive myself . . . if anything happened to her."

Ethan sank down onto the mattress at the far end of the bed. He leaned his head against the foot post. "So it was all for nothing. All that running. All those years in jail. The murder of my father. The loss of—"

"Your father wasn't murdered. He got sick and died."

Ethan rose like an avenging angel and towered over Trahern. His face contorted with rage. "Are you trying to tell me you didn't give Chester Felber the arsenic he put in the whiskey that was delivered to my father."

"*Arsenic!* I sure as hell did *not*!" Trahern blustered. "I never did a thing to hurt your family. My argument wasn't with them. It was with you."

"You didn't rustle my father's cattle, or pay someone to do it?"

Trahern shook his head. "I did not."

Ethan was perplexed. He had blamed every bad thing in his life on Jefferson Trahern. He had just assumed Trahern was guilty. But if not Trahern, then who?

Who had raped Merielle Trahern? Who had blackmailed the Felbers? Who had misdirected Ethan at the mercantile so Lilian Felber could warn Chester and allow him to escape? Who had found the arsenic in the barn? Who had gotten rich over the years on Judas silver?

Boyd Stuckey.

But why would Boyd want to kill Alex Hawk? And why poison Ethan's mother? How much of the calamity he and his family had suffered could actually be laid at Boyd's doorstep? Ethan wanted answers—answers he could get only from Boyd himself.

Ethan walked away from Trahern to the oval mirror that was set over a dry sink that separated two paneled wardrobes. When he got there, he couldn't look at his reflection. He was afraid of what he would see. Horror. Disgust. Hatred. Loathing. Malice. Dark, malevolent emotions that were new to him. Feelings that rose when he thought of the man who had been his best friend.

He poured some water from the pitcher into the bowl at the dry sink, washed Trahern's blood from his hands, and dried them on a shaving towel.

"Are you okay?" Trahern asked.

Ethan barked a laugh. "That sounds odd coming from you."

"I suppose it does."

Ethan threw the shaving towel onto the dry sink and turned to face Trahern. "Dorne's death was an accident," he blurted. "I never meant to kill him. He pulled his gun, and we fought and the gun accidentally went off."

Trahern sighed. "I suppose, ultimately, Boyd Stuckey has to answer for Dorne, too." He eyed Ethan. "I wonder which of us Boyd has made a bigger fool of."

"He was my best friend," Ethan said bitterly. "I suppose that makes me the bigger idiot. I thought I knew him, but I never did. I don't. What I can't understand is *why?*"

"I can offer at least one reason," Trahern said. In brief, breathless phrases he explained, "It's still not definite, but there's a good chance the railroad's coming to Oakville. Their proposed route cuts right across your father's land. It'll make your property worth a fortune."

"So money was at the root of all his evil?"

"A great deal of it, anyway," Trahern said.

"Are you all right here by yourself for a while?"

"I suppose I can manage if you bring me that rifle over the mantel. You heading anyplace in particular?"

"As long as you're alive, it's safe for me to go to the sheriff," Ethan said.

"Would you keep an eye out for Merielle?" Trahern's eyes were bleak. "I'm hoping and praying she got away. Because if she didn't . . ."

"If anything's happened to her, Boyd will pay," Ethan said. "He'll pay for everything."

Ethan watched from concealment as a crowd of men led by the sheriff rode down Main Street on tired, sweaty horses. He wasn't sure who they had been chasing, but he could make a good guess. Deciding discretion was the better part of valor, he kept to the alleys and let himself in through the back door of the old rock jail.

Careless froze in his chair when he felt the bore of a gun in his back. "Who's there?"

"It's me," Ethan said.

"Been out lookin' for you," Careless said. "Heard you killed Jefferson Trahern."

"Put your hands where I can see them, Careless," Ethan said.

Careless slowly raised his hands in the air and swiveled his chair around to face Ethan. "You gonna kill me, too, Ethan?"

"Nope. Just want a little information."

"Sure."

"Have you seen Boyd today?"

"He's the one told us how you killed Trahern."

"Trahern isn't dead, just wounded. He was shot in the back by Boyd Stuckey."

"Aw, hell." Careless laced his hands together on top of his balding head. "You want me to arrest Stuckey?"

"Not before I have a chance to talk to him."

"I'm sorry 'bout what happened to that old man and your sister."

Ethan's heart skipped a beat. "When did you see Leah?"

"We went huntin' you at the Double Diamond. Boyd started askin' questions, but your ma wasn't givin' him any answers. Then that old man, Corwin Marshall, turned up in the chicken coop. He wouldn't talk, either. Boyd got a little rough, I guess."

"You guess?" Ethan interrupted curtly. "Where does Leah come into this story."

"Well, Boyd was threatenin' your ma, and Leah come outta nowhere and jumped on Boyd's back and started scratchin' him like a she-cat. Can't blame a man for defendin' hisself."

Ethan stiffened. His eyes narrowed dangerously. "Boyd hurt Leah?"

Careless realized suddenly that he was looking death in the face. He swallowed hard. "He let her go 'fore it come to that."

Ethan was on his way out the back door when he stopped abruptly and said, "Have you seen Merielle Trahern today?"

"Yeah. She was with Frank, both her and Miz Kendrick, when the lynch—uh, when the posse got to the Tumblin' T brandin' fire. That's where Miz Hawk told Boyd we'd find you. Course, we didn't. Boyd sent us all back here and stayed to visit with 'em."

Ethan was gone before Careless could finish his sentence. From what Trahern had said, Merielle was in mortal danger. He was already spurring his horse before he acknowledged his fears for Patch. If Merielle had told Patch about Boyd—and why wouldn't she?—Patch's life was in just as much peril. Ethan's chest squeezed tight, and he fought to draw breath.

All the questions in his mind concerning how he felt about Patch Kendrick were answered in the moment Ethan realized he might lose her forever. Life without her was unthinkable. He wanted a chance to explore all the different facets of her personality—the lady and the hoyden. He wanted the chance to love her in all the ways he never had.

Ethan knew that fear made a man too careful. He needed every advantage he could find if he was to win against a villain as ruthless as the one he chased. He swallowed back his terror for Patch as he raced toward a showdown with Boyd Stuckey.

———————

Patch was searching desperately in her mind for a way to disarm and capture Boyd without someone getting shot. She could see it wouldn't take much provocation for Frank to draw his gun, but the danger to herself and Merielle constrained Frank from acting. The two women were bound to get caught in the crossfire if there was a gunfight.

"I'm going to head on back to town," Boyd said. "Why don't I take these two ladies off your hands so you can get back to work?"

Patch watched Frank's gray eyes darken like storm clouds. Before he could speak and ruin everything, she said, "Frank's going to take Merielle home. But I'd be grateful for the escort."

"It's no trouble to take both women," Boyd assured Frank.

Frank tightened the protective arm he had around Merielle. "I'll take care of Merielle."

Again, Patch was afraid Frank would say too much and provoke the gunfight she was trying so desperately to avoid. She took the few steps that separated her from Boyd and linked her arm through his. *Just let him try to get the gun out of his holster now!* she thought.

Boyd realized that he had lost whatever chance he might have had of going off alone with both women. At least he had Patricia. He could take care of Frank and Merielle while they were on their way home.

Patch watched Frank open his mouth to object to her going off alone and hurriedly said, "Don't worry about me." The rest of what she had to say, she spoke with her eyes as she met Frank's worried gaze. *Find Ethan fast! Come and get me, but be careful!*

Patch looked over her shoulder once as she rode away with Boyd. Frank and Merielle were already headed for their horses.

Boyd remained broodingly silent until they were well away from the Tumbling T campfire. Then he said, "Ethan won't get to you in time."

Patch jerked her head around to stare at Boyd. "What did you say?"

Boyd's lip curled up. It was his charming smile, but with a cruel twist. "I said Ethan won't be in time to save you."

"Save me from what?"

"Don't play stupid with me," Boyd said curtly. "I think you understand very well what's going on here."

"Why don't you spell it out for me? Just so there's no misunderstanding."

Boyd chose actions, rather than words, to make his point. Before she realized what he had in mind, Boyd shoved her out of the saddle. She hit the ground hard and was still trying to catch her breath when he arrived beside her with a short piece of rawhide, which he used to tie her hands in front of her. Then he yanked her to her feet.

When she tried kicking him, he swept a boot under the leg she was standing on, and she found herself flat on the ground again. He grabbed her by her hair, which had fallen free, and pulled her painfully to her feet.

"Try that again, and you'll wish you hadn't," he said in a nasty voice.

"Ethan will kill you!"

"Not before I have a chance to enjoy your charms." Boyd looked her up and down with lust in his eyes. He dug his hands into her buttocks hard enough to bruise her. "I like you in pants, Patricia. I can see what I'm getting."

Patch ignored him.

He roughly fondled her breast through her blouse and grinned as he pinched her nipple.

Patch spat in his face.

Boyd slapped her hard. "Don't play high and mighty with me! I'd be willing to bet Ethan's been between your legs. You're no lady, that's for sure!"

"You're not even human!" Patch retorted.

Boyd barely restrained himself from hitting her again. He wiped the spittle from his face with his sleeve. "Don't make me angry, Patricia. I've discovered I have a bad temper. Sometimes it gets out of control and bad things happen."

"Like Merielle's rape!" Patch accused.

"Like Merielle's rape," Boyd confirmed.

Patch shivered. When Boyd was done with her, he would kill her and bury her where no one would ever find her. This was a time when she needed to use her wits instead of her fists. Especially since her fists happened to be tied up at the moment.

"All right, Boyd," she said. "I'll do whatever you want, just don't kill me."

Boyd smirked. "I might be tempted to keep you around for a while if you're a lot nicer to me."

"Oh, I will be," Patch assured him.

"How about a little test."

"What kind of test?" Patch asked warily.

"Give me one of those kisses you've been guarding so carefully."

Patch swallowed back the gag that rose at the thought of kissing Boyd Stuckey. *Better a kiss than a bullet.* Given that choice, Patch figured she could suffer through it.

"All right," she said. "Untie my hands first." She held them out in front of her.

"Sure. Why not? I like a little spit and fire in a woman."

Patch watched while Boyd untied her. Her hands were still numb as his mouth lowered toward her. Her body tensed, and her spine went rigid. She kept her mouth firmly shut.

Boyd wasn't having that. He grabbed her cheeks with his hand, forced her mouth open, and thrust his tongue inside.

The skills Patch had learned fighting boys as a hoyden of twelve stood her in good stead now. She bit him at the same time as her clawed fingers scratched at his face and her knee came up hard between his legs. While Boyd was bent over bleating like a new-sheared sheep, Patch ran for her horse. The animal had been ground-tied, which meant the reins had been left trailing so the horse could graze, but wouldn't go far.

Unfortunately, one of the dragging reins had caught between two rocks, and refused to come free. Her desperate tugs only seemed to lodge it more firmly. At last, she yanked it clear.

But it all took too much time. She managed to get a foot in the stirrup, reached for the horn, and lifted her other leg halfway over the horse before she was hauled back out of the saddle.

Boyd's temper had obviously gone a degree past hot. He was still bent over from the pain of her attack, and he was out for revenge.

"As long as I'm bent over, you might as well join me," he snarled. He hit her in the stomach with his fist as hard as he could.

Patch fell to her knees and curled into a ball. He didn't try to pick her up to hit her again, he just kicked her.

"That's enough, Boyd."

Boyd cursed the fact that Patch was so doubled over with pain that she couldn't stand on her own. She would be more of a liability to him as dead weight than useful as a shield. He turned to face Ethan with nothing more separating them than twenty feet of Texas grass.

Ethan had his Colt in his hand. It was aimed at Boyd's heart.

"Hello, Ethan. You're a little early. I'm not finished with her yet."

"You're finished, Boyd. I'd say you've done quite enough damage for one lifetime. Get rid of your gun. Do it nice and slow. I won't need much provocation to shoot you like the rabid dog you are."

Boyd slowly pulled his gun out of the holster.

"Throw it as far as you can," Ethan instructed.

Boyd hesitated an instant, as though he was deciding whether to take a chance on using his gun.

"Don't try it," Ethan said. "You'd be dead before you hit the ground."

The gun went flying in a shiny arc as sunshine reflected off blue metal. It soared high but didn't go far, maybe fifteen feet, and slid to rest under a mesquite bush. Boyd noted where it landed.

"Patch, are you all right?" Ethan asked.

"I'm not going to be dancing a jig anytime soon," she gasped.

Ethan smiled briefly. "Move away from Boyd," he instructed.

Patch crawled painfully away from Boyd a few feet, toward where his gun had landed, until she was out of the line of fire.

Boyd lifted a hand and Ethan said, "I wouldn't move a hair, if I were you."

"We're best friends, Ethan. Surely you're not going to kill me over one slightly used woman."

Ethan bit back a retort. If he had learned one thing in all the years he had been on the run, it was that the man who stayed in control of his emotions was the man who survived. "It isn't just Patch you have to account for, Boyd."

Ethan paused and waited for Boyd to start confessing his sins and pleading for mercy. He should have known better. Boyd hadn't survived all these years by worrying about the wrongs he had done. Ethan looked right at Boyd and said, "Trahern is alive."

Ethan marveled at how little Boyd's expression changed. His mouth flattened slightly and his eyes narrowed, but otherwise he didn't move a muscle.

"You know, then," Boyd said.

"About the rape, yes. About how you blackmailed the Felbers, too."

That surprised a raised brow out of Boyd. "You know about that?"

"Mrs. Felber confessed everything, including the fact Chester was responsible for raping Merielle. Only that turned out not to be the truth. Trahern told me how Merielle remembered everything. You raped her, Boyd. *Why?*"

Boyd glanced at the gun, fifteen feet away, then focused his gaze on Ethan. "It just happened."

"Why accuse Chester?"

"I hated Horace Felber. It was a way to make him suffer."

"And the blackmail?"

"He offered me the money before I asked for it."

"You could have turned him down."

Boyd's lips curled downward. "Could I? He offered me what amounted to a fortune. More money than I could make in ten years of riding herd. All I had to do was keep my mouth shut. You know what my life was like. I saw a chance for something better."

"What about me?"

"How could I know you would be accused?" Boyd said. "I was damn sorry about that, Ethan."

"Not sorry enough to take the blame yourself!"

"You have to understand, Ethan. With that money from Horace, I had a chance for a new life," Boyd explained. "I could have everything you had."

"Including my parents!" Ethan snarled. "When I think how I asked you to take care of them—I get sick to my stomach, Boyd. Were you a good son? As good as I was?"

"Better," Boyd said sharply. "I appreciated them more, because I knew what it was like to do without."

"Then why did you poison them?"

Boyd cocked his head sideways. "How did you know I did that?"

"I didn't. Until now."

Boyd shook his head in disgust at how he had been tricked.

"Why?"

Boyd tried to look at Ethan, but found his stare too intense for comfort. His gaze dropped to his feet. He kicked at a tuft of grass with his boot. When he spoke, his voice was barely audible. "Your father caught me rustling cattle. He was going to turn me over to the law."

Ethan frowned. "But Pa didn't die right away. It took a while for the poison to kill him. So why weren't you arrested?"

"Oh, I promised I'd pay him back the money I got for the cattle and that I wouldn't do it again, and he gave me a second chance."

"Then why did you have to kill him?" Ethan asked in an agonized voice.

Boyd looked up at Ethan, his eyes pleading for understanding. "I found out the railroad was coming through Double Diamond land. I knew he wouldn't sell to me. Besides," he said with a shrug, "there was always the chance he would change his mind."

"Dear God." Ethan's heart pounded in his chest. His ears buzzed. His eyes glazed, and he blinked to clear them. His gunhand wavered, and he tightened his grip, forcing himself to keep his finger away from the trigger.

"And my mother?" he said in a hoarse voice. "What good thing did she do for you that you figured she ought to die?"

"I wanted the Double Diamond," Boyd said bluntly. "I always have. I figured if she were dead, you'd have no reason to stay in Oakville, and you'd sell the ranch to me." He shrugged. "I guess I miscalculated the dose."

"Too damn bad for you," Ethan said bitterly. "What about Chester? Did you shoot him, or have him shot?"

"One less person to tell tales if I did the job myself."

"I don't understand you, Boyd. What makes a person like you tick?"

"You only had to walk a mile in my shoes," Boyd retorted. "All my life I had nothing! I *was* nothing! Just poor white trash, son of a drunken sot, with nothing but the shirt on my back to call my own. Nobody gave a damn what happened to me!"

"*I* cared! You weren't nothing to me!" Ethan cried. "You were my *friend*, the brother I never had. *I loved you!*"

Boyd smiled sadly. "I never knew."

Ethan stood stunned. "How could you not?"

"Maybe I did," Boyd conceded. "I guess it just wasn't enough to fill up the hole inside me."

"Did all that blood money make you feel like *something?*" Ethan demanded.

"It gave me power," Boyd said. "It made people listen to me. It bought me respect and respectability. I'm someone, something, in Oakville."

"*Were* something," Ethan corrected. "Things will change a bit once the truth is known."

Boyd smiled grimly. "I'll be *nothing* again? I don't think I could stand that, Ethan. I'd rather die."

"That can be arranged."

"If you're going to shoot me, get it over with."

"A bullet in the heart is too quick and easy a death for you, Boyd." Ethan holstered his gun and began unbuckling his gunbelt. "I figure it's time we settled things between us once and for all."

Boyd was smiling as he took off his Stetson and hooked it on his saddle horn. "A fair fight?"

"You don't know the meaning of the word *fair*," Ethan said. "Just a fight. To the finish." On the last word, Ethan dropped his gunbelt on the ground and walked—long step, halting step—toward Boyd.

When Ethan was only a few steps away from him, Boyd ran for the mesquite bush where his gun had landed. He had the advantage because Ethan was prevented by his awkward gait from getting back to his gunbelt before Boyd would get to his gun.

But Boyd hadn't reckoned on Patch, who stuck her foot out and tripped him.

Or on Ethan, who knew his limitations, and launched himself at Boyd rather than trying to reach his gun.

The two men landed in a heap and rolled several times before they came to a breathtaking stop.

That was when Patch realized Boyd had a knife.

❊20❊

"ETHAN, LOOK OUT! HE'S got a knife!"

Patch's warning came barely in time for Ethan to keep Boyd from cutting his throat, and the two men went rolling over and over in the dust. The underhanded attack made Ethan furious. It was further proof that the man who had been his best friend was every bit as deceitful and treacherous as his actions in the past had proved him to be.

"You fight dirty, Boyd," Ethan said through gritted teeth as he struggled to keep the knife from his throat.

"You didn't ask for a fair fight," Boyd replied through equally clenched jaws.

It was a contest between two men who, physically, were evenly matched. But even though Boyd was a bad man, he had spent his life in a much more civilized world than the one Ethan had inhabited. Outlaws and derelicts, killers and thieves had taught Ethan a few tricks that Boyd had never learned.

Ethan delivered a quick punch to the throat that, if it had been harder, would have killed Boyd. As it was, Boyd dropped the knife and grabbed his throat, trying to catch his breath through his bruised windpipe. Ethan recovered the knife and held the tip of it under Boyd's ear.

"I ought to slit your throat."

"Go ahead," Boyd taunted. "Murder me. And live with it the rest of your life."

Ethan smiled wolfishly. "When did you get so good at manipulating people?"

"It's a talent I've always had," Boyd said. "You were just too gullible to see it."

"Unfortunately, you're right about how I'd feel later if I killed a defenseless man. Even if you do deserve to die." Ethan stood and left Boyd on the ground still holding his throat. He threw the knife so the point landed in the bark of a mesquite, then gave Boyd his full attention. "On the other hand, I wouldn't feel a damn bit guilty about beating the hell out of you before I turn you over to the sheriff."

Boyd struggled to his feet. "You going to let me catch my wind first?"

"This isn't a fair fight," Ethan reminded him.

"All right, Ethan. Whatever you—" Boyd lunged before he finished his sentence, his shoulder driving into Ethan's solar plexus and knocking the air out of him as both men landed hard back in the dust.

Patch watched the combatants with bated breath, terrified for Ethan until she witnessed several of the lethal maneuvers he used on Boyd. The viciousness of the fight amazed and appalled her. The two men were engaged in a knock-down, drag-out brawl, with no holds barred.

Blood flowed from a cut over Ethan's left eye, blinding him on that side. His cheekbone and chin suffered bruising blows. His knuckles were rubbed raw from punching Boyd, who was in even worse shape. Boyd's lips were puffy, his right eye was swollen almost closed, and his nose was broken and dripping blood. He was half bent over to protect the ribs Ethan persistently and effectively attacked.

The two men circled, each trying to keep his prey in sight with his one good eye. Every once in a while one or the other got in a blow, but just as often they swung and missed.

Ethan kept punching at Boyd's stomach and ribs, trying to wear him down. His head was ringing from the jabs Boyd had managed to deliver. Ethan leapt back to avoid Boyd's boot aimed at his crotch and grinned raggedly. "Missed," he taunted.

Boyd replied with an uppercut to the jaw that left Ethan reeling. He responded with another blow to the belly that doubled Boyd over. To his surprise, Boyd fell to his knees. Ethan staggered back a step. "Get up, Boyd."

"Can't fight anymore, Ethan," Boyd gasped. "Need a rest."

"Get up, Boyd."

All three of them heard the sound of galloping horses at the same time.

Patch joined Ethan as they sought out the figures in the distance, wondering whether help was on the way, or whether they were in for more trouble.

Boyd didn't hesitate. He saw his chance and took it, crawling stealthily toward where his gun lay in the dust, careful not to draw either Ethan's or Patch's attention.

Keeping Patch close beside him, Ethan headed for the spot where he had left his gunbelt on the ground. He had just reached it when Boyd called his name.

"Ethan."

Ethan's reflexes were so finely honed that he reacted to the glint of sunlight off steel without thinking. He shoved Patch out of the line of fire and snatched his Colt from his holster in one smooth, swinging arc of his arm. He fired as soon as he had a target.

Boyd grunted when the bullet struck him. He fired back, but his aim was thrown off, and his bullet sailed harmlessly wide.

"Drop the gun," Ethan said.

Boyd shook his head. "You're going to have to kill me, Ethan. I'd rather not hang, if it's all the same to you. As my best friend, just do me this one last favor."

Boyd aimed his gun at Ethan, and Ethan fired.

The force of the shot toppled Boyd backward. His legs crumpled under him and he came to rest with his arms flung wide and one leg bent under him.

"Damn you, Boyd!" Ethan swore. "You son of a bitch. I didn't want to kill you!"

Patch arrived at Ethan's side just as Frank and Merielle brought their horses to a sliding stop in front of them.

"Are you all right?" Frank called to Ethan as he came off his horse.

"We're fine," Ethan said. Then, in a flat voice, "Boyd is dead."

Frank helped Merielle down, then slipped his arm possessively around her waist and walked the short distance to Patch and Ethan. "Don't waste your pity on him," Frank said. "He deserved to die."

"I'm glad he's dead," Merielle said in a hushed voice. She glanced at Boyd's blood-soaked body and hid her face against Frank's chest. Her whole body trembled.

Frank rocked her in his arms. "It's all over, Merielle. You're safe now, with me."

Merielle looked up at Frank. There was nothing childlike about the glow of love in her eyes.

Frank swallowed so his Adam's apple bobbed up and down.

"Once upon a time, when we were kids, I proposed to you. Do you still want to marry me?"

"Oh yes, Frank!" Merielle said. "I love you. I always have."

Frank met Ethan's eyes over Merielle's head and said, "Then we'll be married. And no one and nothing will stop us."

"My father can't stop us now," Merielle said sadly. "He's dead."

"No, he's not," Ethan corrected.

Merielle whirled to face Ethan. "Father's not dead? But I saw Boyd shoot him. At least, I thought I did. I . . ." Merielle put a hand to her head. It was clear she was afraid her memory had tricked her again.

"Your father was shot, all right," Ethan explained. "But Boyd's bullet missed his vital organs. I got the bleeding stopped, and I doubt it'll be long before he's back on his feet."

"Oh, thank goodness! Not thank goodness my father was shot," Merielle amended quickly, realizing how she had sounded. "But it's a relief to know I wasn't wrong about what I recollected," she explained. "Things are kind of mixed up in my head right now. I'm not sure what I remember from the past and what I remember from the present."

"Give it a little time," Patch said encouragingly. "Things will straighten out."

"With Frank's help, I know I'll be all right," Merielle said.

The way she looked up at Frank, with such love and trust in her eyes, made Patch believe Merielle Trahern would be just fine. What made Patch even more envious was the look in Frank's eyes. What she wouldn't give to see such open admiration, such adoration, aimed at her by Ethan!

"I'll send the sheriff back to pick up Boyd's body if you want to take Patch home," Frank volunteered.

"Thanks, I'd appreciate that," Ethan said.

"You'd better wipe the worst of that blood off your face," Patch warned. "Or you'll frighten your mother and Leah."

While Ethan dabbed gingerly at the cut over his eye with his bandanna, Patch retrieved their horses. Ethan took advantage of the opportunity to speak privately for a moment with Frank. Then he walked over to where Boyd lay. He knelt down and straightened out Boyd's leg, then crossed Boyd's arms over his bloody chest. Finally, he closed Boyd's golden eyes for the last time. The odyssey that had begun with Merielle's rape seventeen years ago was over at last.

A month ago, before Patch Kendrick had shown up in Oakville, Ethan had been resigned to his fate. He had been playing the rotten cards he'd been dealt and had even considered throwing in the hand. Patch had forced him to ask for new cards, and he had come up a winner. Now that he didn't have the past hanging over his head, he was free to make choices that had never been his to make. The most important of those involved Patch.

"Ready to go?" Patch asked.

She had already mounted her horse. Ethan took the reins Patch handed him and vaulted into the saddle without touching the stirrups. "Let's go home."

Patch had a thousand questions she wanted to ask Ethan, but she held her tongue, waiting for him to speak. There was just one question she wanted him to ask her.

"Will you marry me, Patch?"

She waited, but no proposal was forthcoming.

Ethan remained silent. His troubled gaze had turned inward, and his expression was brooding. He didn't look like a man who was contemplating a proposal of marriage. At least, not one he was happy about making.

Patch's heart was in her throat. She had latched on to the rape accusation against Ethan as the main reason he hadn't wanted to marry her. But she hadn't forgotten the other reason he hadn't jumped at the chance to make her his wife.

"I don't love you, Patch."

Not once in the month since she had been in Texas had Ethan said he loved her. Not even when he made love to her. She had just loved him so much, and for so long, that she couldn't conceive of him not loving her back. If she had to face that possibility, she would. But it would be devastating to walk away from the man who was the other half of her being.

What if he doesn't ask me to marry him? What if he doesn't love me?

Patch opened her mouth to ask Ethan what he was thinking and snapped it shut again. She could wait. If it was bad news, she didn't want to hear it. If it was good news, the wait would be worthwhile.

Leah was sitting on the porch steps with the Winchester across her knees, guarding the house much as she had been the first day Patch had met her.

Leah stood as they tied up the horses at the rail. Ethan never took his eyes off his sister as he walked—long step, halting step—over to her. Standing on the ground level, his eyes were even with Leah's, who stood on the top step. He took his sister's chin in his hand to look at her. Patch joined Ethan, but she had to look up slightly at Leah.

"Are you all right?" Ethan asked.

Leah nodded shyly. "Sure. It was you I was worried about."

"I'm just fine." Ethan affectionately tousled Leah's blond hair, as he had done with Patch when she was the same age, as he had done to his sister only once before.

This time Leah reacted more naturally, as Patch had, by shoving his hand away. She ducked back out of his reach. "Hey! Cut it out, Ethan."

Ethan grinned. "Big brothers gotta tease little sisters."

Leah grinned back. "Then you won't mind me telling you that your face looks like you chased a turpentined cat through a bob-wire fence."

Ethan reached for Leah's braid to yank it.

"Let go, you toad!" She turned and raced for the door, shouting, "Ma, Ethan's bein' mean to me!"

"Ma! Don't listen to her! She was callin' me names!"

Patch laughed and grabbed Ethan to keep him from running after Leah. For the first time, the brother and sister were acting like ordinary siblings—fighting like cats and dogs, and driving their mother crazy with it.

Ethan slipped an arm around Patch's waist. "Let's go on inside." The smile faded from his face. "I might as well get this sad, sordid story told."

Ethan and Patch trailed Leah to Nell's room, where Ethan was shocked to find Patch's grandfather propped up reading a book in Nell's bed, while she sat in the rocker beside him knitting.

"This looks cozy," Ethan said.

Nell heard the acid undertone in Ethan's voice and rose. "I'm so glad to see you're home safe!" She embraced her son, who remained stiff. Nell stepped back and saw Ethan was bristling at the sight of Corwin in his father's bed. For Ethan, his father's death had happened only two months ago. For Nell it had been two years. She refused to defend what she had done, but she offered her son an explanation.

"I couldn't very well send Corwin off to town in the condition he was in. He might have a concussion, and he needs to be looked after."

Corwin was equally sensitive to Ethan's stiff posture. "I'm sorry to impose," he said. "But Nell insisted." He paused and, when Ethan didn't bend, said, "Now that you're here, maybe you can talk some sense into her. I ought to be getting on home."

Patch stepped into the breach. "Of course you're not going anywhere, Grandpa Corwin." She crossed to the head of the bed and unnecessarily fluffed the pillows behind him. "Tell him he's welcome to stay, Ethan. Your mother could certainly use the company. And if anything happened to Grandpa Corwin, I'd feel responsible."

She raised innocent blue eyes to Ethan, whose lips curled in a rueful smile. His gaze slid from Patch to Corwin to his mother. The tension visibly eased in his shoulders. It was hard to let go of the memories of his parents in this room. But his mother deserved whatever happiness she could find.

Ethan nodded to the old man. "You should stay, Corwin. Rest easy and get well."

"Thank you, Ethan," Patch said.

Ethan saw the worry in his mother's eyes and gave her a quick hug. "Don't wear yourself out playing nurse," he cautioned. "You just got out of the sickbed yourself."

"I won't," she promised.

"When are you going to tell us what happened with Boyd?" Leah interjected impatiently.

"As soon as everybody gets settled down somewhere," Ethan said.

Nell sat back down in the rocker, Patch curled herself up near her grandfather's side, Leah sat cross-legged on the bed, and Ethan sat down at the foot of the bed and leaned his back against the footpost. He recounted everything he knew about Boyd Stuckey's nefarious activities, from the time he had raped Merielle to the moment when he had forced Ethan to shoot him down.

There was a stark, shocked silence in the room when Ethan was done.

"That poor, poor boy," Nell said.

"He made a lot of bad choices," Corwin agreed.

"Don't waste your sympathy on Boyd Stuckey," Ethan countered in a harsh voice. "He was a bastard, and he deserved to die."

"I liked him," Patch said.

Ethan scowled.

"I liked him when I met him," she amended. "He was so charming—"

"Maybe I should have stepped aside sooner," Ethan said.

"That's not fair!" Patch said. "I couldn't help liking him. He was charming."

"And I suppose I'm not?" Ethan snarled.

"Not when you're growling at me like a grizzly!"

"If you don't like the company around here, you can always leave," Ethan said in a dangerous voice.

"Maybe I will! Maybe I'll just pack my bags and head for Montana!"

"Children, children," Nell said. "Why don't you take your argument outside, so Corwin can get some rest?"

"That's a damned fine idea." Ethan grabbed Patch's wrist and dragged her through the bedroom door.

When Leah started to follow, Nell said, "I need some help with Corwin, Leah."

"Aw, Ma. I miss all the good stuff."

Nell straightened Leah's braids over her shoulders. "You'll have lots of chances to watch them fight. Right now we need to give them a little privacy so they can make up."

"Is Ethan gonna marry Patch?"

Nell smiled. "If Ethan isn't already sure what his feelings are for Patch, I think he's about to find them out."

Patch was dreading the coming confrontation. It looked like Ethan was looking for any excuse to send her back to Montana. She was going to shrivel up and die. But not before she gave Ethan a piece of her mind. He had to see that they belonged together! He had to see that they were two halves of a whole!

To Patch's surprise, Ethan didn't seek out another room of the house for privacy. He dragged her right out the front door, hoisted her into his saddle, and slipped onto the horse behind her. His arm tightened around her waist as he spurred his gelding into a steady lope.

"Where are we going?" Patch asked.

"You'll find out when we get there."

Patch soon realized where Ethan was taking her. "The cave! But what if Frank—"

"I told Frank to stay away this afternoon," Ethan said.

Patch tightened her grasp on Ethan's arm where it circled her. "You spoke to Frank about bringing me here? When was that?"

"Earlier today. Before we headed for home."

Patch felt her heart beat faster in anticipation. She was afraid to hope too hard because she didn't want to be disappointed. When they got to the cave, Ethan slid down off the rump of his horse, then came around and put his hands on Patch's waist to help her down.

"I didn't have a girlfriend before I had to run away," Ethan said. "If I had, I would have brought her here. Boyd stole that experience from me. I want a chance to get it back."

Ethan led the way into the cave and insisted Patch wait until he had the lantern lit before she shinnied inside. She had never felt as uncomfortable with Ethan as she did now, when they were alone with so much left unsaid between them.

She sat down on the chairlike rock and pressed her hands flat between her knees.

"Patch?"

When Ethan called her name, she realized he had gone down on one knee beside her. He slowly pried her hands from between her knees and took them in his.

His eyes were focused on her hands, and she felt her whole body tingle as his callused fingertips abraded her soft palms. She stared at their joined hands, fascinated by the way he could elicit so much feeling with such a simple touch.

"Patch?"

When Ethan spoke, he tightened his grip. Patch looked up to find that he was staring intently at her. She searched his eyes for some sign of what he was feeling. The knowledge of Ethan's love started as a spark somewhere deep inside her and spread its warmth outward, resulting in a smile of utter delight.

"Yes, Ethan?"

Ethan cleared his throat. "I don't know quite how to say this. It's hard to imagine myself married to the same three-year-old brat who left wet patches on my shirt when I was fifteen."

Patch laughed nervously.

"Or the twelve-year-old girl with budding breasts and a hankering to fight, who wanted so badly to be a lady for me, but couldn't say two words without a *garn* or a *durn* slipping out."

Patch grimaced.

"But I'd be a damn fool if I didn't jump at the chance to marry the elegant lady . . ." Ethan put Patch's palm to his cheek.

". . . the sexy woman . . ." He rubbed her hand across his bruised jaw and down to his lips, where he kissed it with his lips parted. He let his tongue slide along the most sensitive part of her hand until he felt her shiver.

". . . the feisty hellion . . ." He pulled Patch onto her feet and into his arms, holding her buttocks pressed tight against his arousal.

". . . who moved in at the Double Diamond and turned my life rightside up again."

"Ethan, I . . ."

He kissed her open-mouthed, a gentle, questing foray, that asked for her love and offered his. He broke the kiss and caught her hair up in both hands. His voice grated with emotion when he said, "I love you, Patch."

Tears of joy welled in Patch's eyes. "I love you, too, Ethan."

"Will you marry me? Will you have my children?"

"Yes, Ethan."

He brushed her tears away with the pads of his thumbs. "I remember your pa used to say that these freckles of yours tasted like brown sugar. I think I'd like to find out for myself."

"Now, Ethan . . ."

Ethan kissed a freckle on her cheek, then licked his lips. "Yep. Definitely sweet."

Patch giggled.

"Let me try a couple more." He kissed one more freckle on her cheek and two on her nose. "Seth was right. They're absolutely delicious." He began kissing Patch all over her face, everywhere he could find a freckle.

Soon she was laughing, fighting him off—not too hard—and loving every breathless minute of it. When the giggles died down she said, "Do you remember when it was that Pa used to do this?"

"When?"

"Right before he tucked me into bed," Patch said with a naughty grin.

"Is that so?"

Patch nodded.

Ethan put an arm around Patch's shoulders and under her knees, sweeping her off her feet. "I think maybe this is one tradition we should keep in the family."

Patch laughed and slipped an arm around Ethan's neck to hang on. "Ethan, there's no bed in this cave."

Ethan looked around. "It seems you're right about that. We'll just have to make do with what we have."

Patch took one look at the stone floor of the cave and said, "I get to be on top."

Ethan laughed. "Somehow, Patch, I can't conceive of you ending up anywhere else."

AUTHOR'S NOTE

For purposes of my novel, I have put the town of Three Rivers on the map thirty-seven years before it was actually established. Three Rivers was founded in 1913 and was originally known as Hamiltonburg. The U.S. Post Office renamed the town Three Rivers because of its location near the fork of the Nueces, Atascosa, and Frio rivers.

Supposedly, the old rock jail in Oakville was surrounded by three large oaks, one of which was actually used for hangings. The Oakville Post Office, which has always been and continues to be in the Oakville Mercantile, dates back to 1854.